Praise for

THE NEWS
FROM THE END OF
THE WORLD

"In *The News from the End of the World*, Emily Jeanne Miller deftly shows how lifetimes can be contained in four days, how memories inhabit a place, and how returning home means always confronting oneself. The characters in this novel consistently surprised me; they find grace in quiet moments, forgiveness when least expected. And it's all so beautifully written that by the end I felt as if I had lived in this town my whole life, and could walk its haunted streets."

—Peter Rock, author of *My Abandonment*

"Told in the diverse voices of several characters, one cannot help but empathize with the differing situations while getting to the crux of each one's concern . . . Contemplation runs deep, making this a thought-provoking read." —*New York Journal of Books*

"Emily Jeanne Miller's *The News from the End of the World* recalls Tolstoy's line that 'every unhappy family is unhappy in its own way,' an idea less tragic than simply true; shared pain is what solders us. This is a book about the soldering of one family, about the love between brothers and sisters and fathers and daughters, all written in heartbreaking, true, and gorgeous prose." —Lea Carpenter, author of *Eleven Days*

"Immersive . . . The unique landscape of Cape Cod in the off-season sets the stage for Miller's poignant, fast-paced family drama. Told in alternating points of view, this gripping novel gets to the heart of familial trust, independence, and the struggle to overcome the past in order to forge a happier future." —*Publishers Weekly*

"Emily Jeanne Miller is a master storyteller. In her brilliant *The News from the End of the World*, she summons a way of seeing reminiscent of Virginia Woolf: the male characters are as vivid as the female, and as their stories unfold, you cannot look away. This moving and deeply satisfying novel weaves several stories over a New England weekend, without one false note. I will be thinking about the Lake family for a long time."

—Robert Bausch, author of *Far as the Eye Can See* and
A Hole in the Earth

"Miller has created a quirky, relatable family. It is impossible to finish this book until everyone's issues are resolved, while hoping in the meantime that the resolutions will be positive."   —*Library Journal*

THE NEWS
FROM THE END OF
THE WORLD

ALSO BY EMILY JEANNE MILLER

Brand New Human Being

THE NEWS
FROM THE END OF
THE WORLD

Emily Jeanne Miller

Mariner Books
Houghton Mifflin Harcourt
Boston   New York

First Mariner Books edition 2018
Reading Group Guide copyright © 2018 by Houghton Mifflin Harcourt
Publishing Company
Copyright © 2017 by Emily Jeanne Miller

For information about permission to reproduce selections from this book, write to
trade.permissions@hmhco.com or to Permissions, Houghton Mifflin Harcourt
Publishing Company, 3 Park Avenue, 19th Floor, New York, New York 10016.

hmhco.com

Library of Congress Cataloging-in-Publication Data
Names: Miller, Emily Jeanne, author.
Title: The news from the end of the world / Emily Jeanne Miller.
Description: Boston : Houghton Mifflin Harcourt, 2017.
Identifiers: LCCN 2016034707 (print) | LCCN 2016041145 (ebook) |
ISBN 9780547734415 (hardcover) | ISBN 9780547734514 (ebook)
ISBN 9781328745460 (pbk.)
Subjects: LCSH: Families—New England—Fiction. | Domestic fiction. |
BISAC: FICTION / Family Life. | FICTION / Literary.
Classification: LCC PS3613.I5356 N49 2017 (print) | LCC PS3613.I5356 (ebook) |
DDC 813/.6—dc23
LC record available at https://lccn.loc.gov/2016034707

Book design by Greta D. Sibley

Printed in the United States of America
DOC 10 9 8 7 6 5 4 3 2 1

For Andrew

Turning our backs on the outward world, we thus looked through the knot-hole into the Humane house, into the very bowels of mercy; and for bread we found a stone.

—Henry David Thoreau, *Cape Cod*

SUNDAY

1

IN VANCE'S DREAM, nothing is the matter. He's home with Celeste, it's sunset, and the sky through the west-facing windows of their living room glows pink. Celeste, fresh from her post-run shower, sits on his lap, straddling him. She looks sleek and lovely, with flushed cheeks and her wet hair combed straight back, and there's music playing—her music, sitars, singing bowls, bells. She's holding a glass of wine and teasing him with it, tipping it toward his lips and, just before he can taste it, taking it away.

And then she's doing other things, odd things—kneading his cheeks roughly, tapping her fingernails against his teeth—and when he asks her to stop, the dream changes: darkness descends, Celeste dissipates. He tries standing up but he can't, there's a great weight on him, something heavy holding him down.

When he opens his eyes it's dark, and it takes a few moments for him to remember where he is—that he's not at home, not with Celeste. He's in his brother's attic, sweating under an itchy army blanket that smells of mothballs, of the past. Only the heaviness he felt in the dream is real. As his eyes adjust he sees that the thing holding him down is a person: his niece, Helen, is sitting on his chest.

He tries to sit up again and fails.

"Well, well," he manages, "the face that launched a thousand ships." He's been saying this to her for years, since she was a baby. Because she always smiles when he does, he assumes it pleases her, though she's never once asked what it means.

"You're not dead," she says.

"Are you disappointed?"

She wrinkles her nose. "It smells in here," she says, lisping the s.

"Eau de Old Man, I'm afraid."

"You're not old. You're the same age as my dad."

"Precisely. Do you mind?" he says. With the hand that isn't pinned by her knee, he reaches for the lamp, a porcelain shepherdess that, years ago, lit the room he used to share with Craig. Long since missing both sheep and crook, she now stands atop the cardboard computer box that's serving as Vance's nightstand, casting anemic, gold-colored light.

Lying down again, he closes his eyes, massaging one of his temples with the fingers of his free hand. He's still exhausted from the ride up, which, thanks to a couple of wrecks, one north of Wilmington and a second just before Fall River, took thirteen hours. The second one involved another motorcycle; the rider had been taken away by the time Vance passed on his, but he saw the bike, a Ducati Monster, lying on its side on the grass.

Bouncing on his chest, Helen says, "Look, you're a horse. You're Taffy. Taffy's short for Taffeta." She squeezes his ribs with her knees. "That means trot. Trot, horsey."

Naked under the blanket and still half hard from the dream, he feels more than a little obscene. Plus it's stuffy in the attic to begin with, and her weight on him makes it difficult to breathe. "No offense," he says, "but you're like a ton of bricks. Would you be terribly offended if I asked you to move?"

She grins, apropos of he doesn't know what, displaying a plank of pink gums instead of teeth. "They measured us at school," she says, shifting off him and arranging herself on the air mattress, still so close her knees butt up against his hip. "I'm in the nineteenth percentile. That means nineteen of the kids in my class are smaller than me."

"How about that," he says, instead of correcting her, and sits up slowly, mindful of the steeply sloped ceiling hovering only inches above his head. Scanning the floor for his clothes, he asks Helen if she knows what time it is. Before she can answer, they hear a voice from downstairs: Craig.

"I'm in the bedroom," he shouts. "Christ, Gina. I'm right here."

"Don't fucking yell at me," shouts Gina, Craig's wife. "I hate it when you yell before noon."

Vance waits, but they seem to be done; he has no idea what they're yelling about and has zero interest in finding out. He looks at Helen. She appears unfazed by the exchange. She's looking down, scratching at the inside of her wrist, her hair hiding half her face. She's had it cut since he last saw her, he notes, into a blunt, chin-length bob like her mom's.

His head hurts. What he'd like to do is smoke some weed, take the edge off. He asks her if she would mind getting his phone off the steamer trunk, where the night before he laid out some of his things, and she pops up and pads across the room, giving him the opportunity to retrieve his shorts from the floor and, while her back is turned, pull them on.

"What's this?" she asks, holding up his pipe, which is rainbow-colored, swirled glass—a gift from Miriam, whom he was with before Celeste.

"A paperweight," he says.

"It's not very heavy."

"I don't have a lot of papers to hold down. My phone?"

She sets the pipe down, unplugs the phone, and delivers it to him on the bed. He thinks she might go then—he hopes—but before he's even turned the phone on, she sits back down and starts talking, telling him about a video game, something to do with a farm. "There are golden eggs, and rotten eggs, and foxes," she explains, "and a farmer with a pitchfork, and his wife wants the eggs for a cake."

He nods vaguely, waiting for the screen to light up. When it does, he learns that (1) it's barely seven A.M., which means he slept just under five hours, and (2) Celeste hasn't called. Considering the things she said, he shouldn't be surprised, but he is. In the past when they've fought, she's always called. But this time feels different, he has to admit. He can still see her, in her robe and Bean boots, standing under the portico, watching dry-eyed as he fastened his helmet, as he strapped his duffel behind him on the seat.

Helen is still talking, now about horses, again, and he interrupts her monologue to ask if she can please turn on the light. She nods eagerly, stands up again, and goes to the center of the room, where underneath a naked bulb a bright orange fishing bobber hangs from a silver ball chain. She tugs on the bobber and hard light fills the room. She's wearing a one-piece pink pajama, he sees now, and she's still talking—now about a ballet recital being put on by her class. Sitting in his dad's old Harvard rocker and drawing up her knees, she says the theme is spring and that she's been practicing her routine. Starting to get up, she says, "Want to see?"

"Not just now," he says, and gathers the rest of his clothes from the floor, dressing under her unwavering gaze. She's always been an intense little person, but the way she's watching him this morning, it's kind of freaking him out. It doesn't help that with the new haircut, she looks like an exact miniature of Gina.

"Your parents must be wondering where you are," he says. "How about you go downstairs and I'll catch up?"

She ignores the suggestion, watching him button his jeans, then pull his T-shirt on over his head. He can smell the past couple of days on it: his own stale scent, plus the lavender detergent Celeste uses, plus the McDonald's he ate in Havre de Grace. And underneath all of those, something else: Celeste's perfume. He breathes in deeply, closing his eyes, thinking about her skin.

"Vance. Look. *Vance*," Helen is saying. Reluctantly he opens his eyes. She's gripping the rocking chair's burnished wood armrests and pitching her weight wildly back and forth. He watches, silently willing her to go. Then he could smoke, which would help. Smoke and then jerk off, purge the specter of Celeste from his thoughts.

Planting one pajamaed foot on the floor, Helen brings the rocker to an abrupt halt. "Your name rhymes with *pants*. And *ants*."

He clears his throat, attempting to focus. "You're studying poetry in school?" He tries to remember what grade she's in. "I know a thing or two about poetry, you know."

"And *France*," she says. Abandoning the rocker, she comes back over to the air mattress, sits, and nudges him with her knee. When she says "It's your turn," he's aware of drops of spittle leaving her lips and landing on his, and he makes an effort not to grimace.

"For what?"

"To rhyme."

"Right. Gotcha. *Glance*."

She nods her approval and opens her mouth; at the same moment, they hear footsteps on the floor below—Craig or Gina, he hopes, coming to take their daughter off his hands.

"It's not here," Craig shouts. "I told you it wasn't."

"Well, it didn't just disappear," Gina shouts back.

"Come and look for yourself if you don't believe me. It's not fucking *here*."

Vance looks at Helen. She's stuck the tip of her finger through a hole in the army blanket and is wiggling it around. "*Dance*," she says, nudging him again with her knee.

"All right. *Chance*."

"*Prance*."

"Nice. *Cancer*?" He's thinking of the astrological sign—his and Craig's astrological sign—but Helen's eyes flash.

"That's what Marshmallow had."

"What?"

She nods. "Cancer. It's a germ that gets in your body. Like Grandma Marie."

He takes a moment, absorbing what she said. Marshmallow is his dog, or she was his originally. Now she lives here, with Craig—but Vance was the one who'd found her, four years back. He'd spotted her wandering, collarless and forlorn, by a half-pipe in the skateboarders' park across from his apartment in DC. She was irresistible—fluffy and white, hence the name—and though his building didn't technically allow dogs, he'd taken her in, which wasn't a problem until the humorless Argentine novelist in the flat directly below his began to complain, and Vance didn't have much choice except to bring her up here. It was supposed to be a temporary arrangement, but the kids loved her, and though Craig made a big show of what an inconvenience it was, Vance knew he was smitten too.

He also knows Craig stopped thinking of Marshmallow as his a long time ago. But still, would it have killed him to let Vance know she was sick? On the other hand, Craig hasn't let him know much of anything lately. Whereas usually they check in every few days, once a week at minimum, almost three weeks have passed since they last spoke. They've been trading messages; or, more precisely, Vance has been leaving messages for Craig, and Craig hasn't called him back. Vance knows he's been busy with work—he's competing for the contract to build their old buddy Dov Azulay's new restaurant, for one—and at first Vance attributed his brother's radio silence to that. Now, though, he wonders if it has to do with the dog.

"She got it in her thyroid," Helen is saying. "That's a gland. It's right here." She touches her neck. "It was like she had a Super Ball stuck in her throat."

"Oh, my," Vance says, clearing his own throat and glancing around the room, once again willing his brother or Gina to come upstairs. Where the hell are they, anyway? Why aren't they concerned about the whereabouts of their kid? "I'm sure she'll be okay," he says in what he hopes is a reassuring tone.

She's looking down, scratching intently at her wrist. "She won't be okay," Helen says. "She's dead."

Jesus, he thinks, as something scurries across the roof over their heads. He's trying to come up with an appropriate response when Helen looks up in the direction of the window. It's circular, like a porthole.

"Can you take me to the park?" she asks. "They got new swings."

Not a chance, he thinks. He says, "We'll see."

"That's grownup for 'no.'"

"Says who?"

"Amanda."

He should've guessed: Amanda, Helen's half-sister, is his other niece. "I know it's hard to imagine, but Amanda doesn't know everything," he says.

Helen gets on her knees again and reaches, this time, for his necklace, an antique lion's-claw pendant that Celeste gave him a couple of years ago as a fortieth birthday gift. (He may have been born a Cancer, but he has the heart of a Leo, she said.)

Helen turns the pendant over in her fingers, inspecting it. Her face is so close he can smell her breath, a little fruity, a little sour.

"Speaking of Amanda, have you guys heard anything?" He hopes to sound nonchalant, though inside he feels anything but. Amanda's been away—half a world away, on South America's southernmost tip —since January. Unusually, he's had nothing from her but a couple of letters, the second written just two weeks after she left.

Before Helen can answer, they're interrupted again.

"What crawled up your ass and died?" Craig's voice is closer this time, much closer, almost as if he's in the room.

"Take one guess," Gina snaps back. Her voice sounds closer too, and a little muffled, and Vance realizes that their voices are coming up through the vent.

"I don't know what you want from me," Craig's disembodied voice says.

Glancing around, Vance searches for something he can use to cover the vent, for Helen's sake, but before he can, Gina says, "It's way too early for this. Could you just go?"

"Early for what?"

"Just get *out*."

The bedroom door slams and they hear Craig's footsteps, heavy on the stairs.

"Take the baby," Gina calls after him. "If I don't close my eyes for a few minutes, I'll die."

And then it's quiet. After what feels like ages, Helen whispers, "Have you ever had cantaloupe ice cream? I did. At Janet's. I have an idea," she continues. "Let's stay up here all day. We can play shipwreck. This is our cabin. I'll be the captain and you can be first mate."

"I don't think so," he says, and when she frowns, he adds, "They'll worry," though so far he has little reason to believe this is true.

"Stay here," she instructs, and before he can object, she's jumped up, crossed the room, and disappeared down the stairs. He hears her bare feet slapping the hardwood in the hall below. Her footsteps fade, then pause, then get louder again, and soon she's back in the attic, repositioning herself on the bed.

She holds a deck of cards. "Do you know Go Fish?" she asks, dealing them each a hand. The cards' backs are printed with a photograph, Vance sees: white horses galloping on a wide, flat beach.

"Helen," he says. "H-bomb. It's not a good time to play."

"I take riding lessons, and piano too," she says, again fixing her gaze on the inside of her wrist. "My teacher's name is Mrs. Forrest. Her first name is Laurel, that's a kind of plant. In ancient Rome they made laurel plants into crowns."

"Helen," he says.

"I can make waffles by myself, but I'm not supposed to, because of the iron. I got burned. It's a second-degree burn, the nurse said, because third-degree burns don't hurt. It hurt, but I didn't cry. I never cry. See?" She thrusts her arm toward him palm-up, showing him where a dark crosshatch mars the otherwise milky skin. "Want to feel?"

"That's all right."

She holds her arm closer to his face. "Feel. It's rough."

Taking her wrist in his hand, he runs his thumb over the mark; it is, as promised, rough. He says, "You must be pretty brave."

She looks up at him, confused. From downstairs they hear the front door slam, then the sound of an engine starting up. Abruptly she pulls her hand away.

"I have to find my mom," she says, and jumps up, scattering the cards.

2

∽

CRAIG DOESN'T WANT TO run into anyone, so he drives down to
Eastham, where the chances aren't nil but they're significantly reduced.
Even so, idling outside Dunkin' Donuts, he performs a quick inventory
of the other cars in the lot. He doesn't recognize any, but just to be safe,
he dons his sunglasses (despite the lack of sun) and flips up his sweatshirt's hood. He probably looks like he's getting ready to rob the place,
but he doesn't care. Given his mood, he'd rather be taken for a criminal
than be forced to interact with a client, or worse, a friend.

Inside the store, a girl about Amanda's age stands behind the counter, studying her nails. He thinks she's going to ignore him, but the moment the doorbell jingles she looks up, smiles pleasantly, and says, "Hi."
She wears a white Dunkin' Donuts polo shirt under a black apron, and
her hair is bleached white with a fringe of hot pink on the ends.

"What can I get you this morning?" she asks. Craig recognizes her
accent as Slavic—Bulgarian, or maybe Serbian—right away. They're
all over the Cape. Most come for the summer, on J-1's sponsored by
local businesses, mostly food service, and a handful of them always
manage to stay, which she must have, since it's March. Plenty of people have a problem with it—giving jobs to foreign kids instead of local

11

ones—but not him. He's heard how hard they work—twice as hard as their American counterparts, according to his friend Dov, who hires them for his restaurants. If only they came with construction skills, Craig would gladly do the same.

He asks the girl for a large coffee with Splenda and skim milk, though he probably should be drinking decaf: he can practically hear Gina saying how he's hardly sleeping at all as it is, how it's not healthy to be so tense. She'd be right, of course, but she isn't here, and following that logic, he asks the girl to switch the Splenda to sugar and the skim to half-and-half, and then, while she's snapping the plastic lid onto his cup, he orders some donuts: a cruller for himself, and a manager's special, a Boston cream, a maple-glazed, and an old-fashioned for the kids.

The girl fetches the donuts, humming a tune, something he almost recognizes but not quite, maybe something that's playing on the radio now. He watches her work—her nametag says *Raina*—and while she rings him up he steals glances at her face, which is pretty as far as he can tell, hidden as it is under a thick layer of makeup. She has multiple piercings in her ears, five or six small silver hoops in each one, a tiny crescent moon on the right and a couple of gemstone studs, and high on the left helix, a single silver skull.

Of course, he thinks about Amanda. Starting when she was about eight, she begged him to let her get her ears pierced, and he always said she could when she turned sixteen. On her twelfth birthday, though, Vance took her to the mall and she came back with twin gold studs gleaming in her red, swollen lobes. Vance claimed ignorance, naturally, but if there's one thing Craig has mastered in his forty-two years on earth, it's discerning when his brother is bullshitting him. Plus he isn't blind; he saw the conspiratorial smiles he and Amanda exchanged.

He watches Raina punch the buttons on the cash register. Her fingernails are painted dark purple, almost black. He steals a few more glances at her face. Under the makeup her features are small and delicate, like a child's, and her expression is set, serious: disciplined. The thought comes to him, not for the first time, that instead of sending Amanda away for the semester, he should have made her get a job: given her some responsibility, put her to work. Would things have gone differently if he had? That was Gina's opinion, back in the fall. She thought Chile was a mistake all along. How infuriating, he thinks now, that she was right. Then again, who can say? Hindsight may be twenty-twenty, but the truth is she could've gotten into the very same predicament right here on the Cape.

"Sir? Are you all right?" The girl is speaking to him.

"Sorry," he says. The display on the register says $8.68. He hands her a twenty, she makes change, and he drops a couple of bills into the tip jar, whose handmade label says, COLLEGE FUND, DON'T BE SHY!

In the seat of his truck he tests the coffee, which is scalding hot, so he sets it down in the drink holder to cool off and switches on some music. One of his favorite songs, "The River" (Meadowlands, 1981, according to the display), is just starting, and he turns up the volume, sits back, and lets himself be soothed by the familiar chords. Nineteen eighty-one, he thinks — that was right around the time he became aware of the Boss, *aware* being something of an understatement, he'll admit. Vance accuses him of being obsessed, but he's not ashamed of being a person who knows what he likes.

He turns the volume up and reaches into the paper bag, feeling around for the cruller, which he extracts and starts to eat, watching the clouds out over the ocean gather and grow thick. He wonders if there's a storm coming. Usually he stays on top of the weather forecast, for work, but he hasn't paid much attention to it — or, if he's honest with himself, much else aside from his daughter — in weeks. He looks around. Across the road, in front of the post office, a massive American flag flaps violently in the wind. It's at half-mast. He wonders why. Did something bad happen that he hasn't heard about? On the other hand, these days it seems like bad things are constantly happening; there's such a steady flow of tragedies, he wonders if the post office people ever bother raising it all the way.

Somehow, the cruller is gone. A red Dodge Ram with Connecticut plates pulls into the space next to him, and he watches a couple of guys in work clothes get out. One is smoking a cigarette. Craig would like to bum one, smoke it while he drinks his coffee, or maybe save it for after he's surfed, the time a cigarette tastes best, but Gina would be all over him. She'd smell it on him no matter what he did to cover it up, she always does, and the thought of arguing with her—arguing with her *more*—significantly diminishes the appeal.

His hand drifts into the bag again. He isn't hungry anymore, but he wasn't hungry to begin with, or not in the conventional sense. Ever since the phone woke him up in the middle of the night two weeks ago, he's had an empty space deep in his gut he can't seem to fill, no matter what he puts in his mouth. He pulls out the maple-glazed and makes quick work of it, telling himself he'll stop on the way back and get some more for the kids, and once that plan is in place, he goes ahead and eats the Boston cream.

The manager's special is chocolate cake frosted in white and covered with jimmies, and he eats it joylessly—and guiltily now, thinking not of the kids anymore but of his burgeoning girth. Washing it down with coffee, he assures himself that he'll burn off whatever calories he's consumed, and then some, in the water. Reaching into the bag for one of the paper napkins the Serbian girl tucked inside, he comes up, instead, with the final donut, the old-fashioned, which is his brother's favorite and which reminds him that Vance is, at that very moment, in his house. Most likely he's still sleeping—or so Craig hopes. He looked so ashen when he arrived last night, so *unwell*, Craig actually felt alarmed. He got Vance a beer, which he practically swallowed whole, standing in front of the sink, and he polished off most of another before following Craig up to the attic, where Craig showed him how to inflate the air mattress and dug up a lamp. When he asked Vance if he needed anything else, Vance shook his head. Craig didn't ask what had happened with Celeste, or why he'd come. He was way too exhausted by then to listen to one of Vance's convoluted, meandering accounts —and besides, it's not that hard to guess.

He pushes the last third of the old-fashioned into his mouth. It doesn't taste like much. Then again, the same can be said for almost everything he eats lately; it's like his taste buds have gone numb. As he chews, the cake turns to paste in his mouth. He washes it down with more coffee, despite feeling a little ill himself. Then he crushes the empty bag and tosses it into the back seat, out of sight.

The parking lot at Frenchman's Hollow is more or less empty, a welcome sight even if it doesn't indicate stellar surf. He chooses a spot at the far southern end of the lot, gets out, and walks to the edge of the pavement, where the dunes begin. There he stands with his back to the wind, frowning out at the horizon, stretching his arms over his head.

The wind is from the east, not great for waves. He unzips and pees into some eelgrass, shivering as he finishes; it's a cold morning, but nothing compared to some. During January's surprise deep freeze, for example, Dov persuaded him to come out when it was ten degrees. It was the day his divorce became final—Dov's—and he'd put on the full-court press, proclaiming it Liberation Day, and a glorious morning, which, temperature notwithstanding, it definitely was: waist-high rollers, sunshine, the ocean sparkling like a field of gems. They each caught five or six beauties before Craig shouted to Dov that he couldn't feel his limbs, and they paddled in, blasting the heater in Dov's Wagoneer and passing the flask he'd brought back and forth for twenty minutes before the rime on their wetsuits thawed enough to peel them off.

He zips up his coat and follows the walkway past the boarded-up restrooms and out onto the observation deck, where he leans his elbows on the wood railing and looks down at the waves. They're breaking shoulder-high, he guesses, a little messier than he would have hoped, thanks to the onshore wind, but definitely worth getting wet.

Back at the truck, he removes his board from the bed of the truck and leans it against the driver's side door. It's a nine-foot longboard he bought last June, along with a second, shorter board for Amanda, on the occasion of her seventeenth birthday. It seems almost laughably naïve now, and more than a little pathetic, but his thought was that they'd take up the sport together, a suggestion first made by the counselor at the high school, who'd called in him and Gina after Amanda got caught skipping calculus, last May. Her name was Beth, and in the meeting she informed them—depressingly presciently, as it turned out—that Amanda was on a "dangerous path"; she suggested they find a hobby, ideally something physically demanding, that they could do together. Hence the purchase of the boards.

And at first the plan seemed promising. Amanda was excited to learn to surf, or at least she didn't refuse outright—at first. But then she didn't want the lessons he'd bought for them. (She knew the instructors, it turned out, they'd graduated a couple of years ago, and she'd be way too mortified to take lessons from them, with him, she said.) Finally she agreed to let Dov show them the basics; in addition to being Craig's childhood friend, he was the "cool" dad of her boyfriend at the time, Kevin. So the four of them—Craig, Amanda, Kevin, and Dov—had spent a sparkling late-June morning on the water, a triumph—or so Craig had thought. But that was more than nine months ago. In the meantime, she and Kevin broke up (she wouldn't say why, or really anything about it, at least not to him), whatever interest she may have had in surfing seemed to perish with their union, and her board, which is stenciled with a blue and red geometric pattern, and which cost him $1,186.17, hasn't made it down from the rack on the wall of the garage since.

He opens the back gate, removes the tub of Vaseline he keeps handy, and smears a layer of the stuff over his face, a trick he picked up from one of the surfing blogs he's started reading. Then he strips down and starts the struggle into his wetsuit, a workout in its own right. The suit is a 7 millimeter, as warm as they come; he found it on online, on clearance, and it was a size too small to begin with, and that was when he was thin. He hasn't gotten on a scale lately—he doesn't dare—but no question he's been expanding. He tries not to let it get to him. His weight has always fluctuated, unlike his brother's. Vance eats like a wild animal and never seems to gain an ounce.

If the suit is a pain in the ass to get into, at least the exertion warms him up. Once he's zipped in, with the hood up, in his gloves and boots, his Vaseline-covered face is the only skin left exposed. He glances left, then right, to be sure no one's watching before he sets the keys on the F-150's right rear tire—a risk, but a smaller one, in his estimation, than bringing them onto the beach. Some guys he's met will go as far as leaving their cars running while they're in the water, so they're warm inside when they come out—guys who, he's concluded, have a higher tolerance for risk and/or a greater faith in humanity than Craig does, and also tend to drive crappy cars.

He picks up his board and carries it along the boardwalk, down the long flight of wooden stairs that leads to the beach. A few yards from the water, he pauses to survey his surroundings. In summer the place would be crawling with vacationers, the water filled with novices catching knee-high waves and hooting, flashing victory signs while riding their pink foam rental boards right into each other, and him. Today, though, he has the whole beach to himself, a magnificent thing—and a rarity, even in March. The only other human he sees is a tiny figure in a parka throwing a ball for a dog perhaps a quarter mile up the beach.

Briefly he thinks of Marshmallow. She would've chased a tennis ball until her little heart gave out if he'd let her, the poor thing. Almost three weeks have passed since they put her down—not *they*, he can't help thinking: he. Alone. He won't soon forget that morning, standing by the exam table, holding her still while kind Dr. Elliot slipped the needle into her vein.

He pushes the memory aside, letting his thoughts land instead on the autumn afternoon, years ago, when Vance dropped her off. It was raining, he remembers, and Vance stood on the front steps, holding her against his chest, inside his leather jacket, just her tiny white head pecking out. He claimed to have ridden all the way up from DC that way, with her in his coat. Of course he had a long story about how hardhearted his landlord was, how she'd only be here temporarily (a lie), how well trained she was (another lie), and of course—of *course*—how none of it was his fault.

He sets down his board and stretches his arms over his head again. He doesn't want to think about Marshmallow, or Vance. He doesn't want to think about anything, that's why he's here. He does a couple of twists, touches his toes, and fastens the leash around his ankle before picking up his board and carrying it down to the water. He doesn't believe in easing his way in, that only makes it more painful, and so he marches right into the surf, his mind emptying of thoughts as the icy, churning water permeates his suit. With one hand holding his board steady, he dunks under. While his body heat begins to warm the water between his skin and the neoprene, he lays his belly flat on the board and starts paddling. The waves are even sloppier than they'd looked from above—and bigger—and it seems like the wind is changing, blowing harder now and from the north.

He duck-dives under one breaker and then another, the water frigid on his face despite the Vaseline. Past the breakers, he sits upright and looks back at the beach; the dog walker is gone, and now a couple in matching parkas stands looking out at the waves. He turns around and contemplates the horizon, a soft, indefinite area where gray sky melds into gray sea. He can just make out the outline of a tanker in the distance. Ten or fifteen feet from where he sits, a seal's head breaks the surface, and he watches it swim away. Conventional wisdom says to stay away from seals, they attract sharks, but it seems to him that seals have spent many thousands of years evolving to do just the opposite, not to mention the fact that a shark would much rather eat a seal than him, and only when there are no seals anywhere does he start to feel fear.

He watches the water until he sees a set approaching, and lies down. The first two waves he lets roll under him, but as the third approaches he starts paddling, hard, and when he feels the tug of the water rushing under his board, he stands up. It's a good ride, a little bumpy from the chop, but he stays up, and in the shallows he drops, ass-first, into the foam before getting back on the board and paddling out again. Another set arrives, he catches another wave, and another. He's on his fifth ride, which is shaping up as the best of the day, when he feels the nose of his board go under and the tail lift up, and then he's tumbling forward, falling, waiting for the full weight of the wave to come down on him, which it does; it slams him all the way down to the sand before something whacks him on the temple, and then he's spinning, heels over ass over head, and for what feels like an extraordinarily long number of seconds—he tries counting, but loses track—he is underwater, unable to tell which way is up. He keeps expecting to surface, but every time he lifts his head to take a breath he encounters sand or ocean instead of air. He is under so long, in fact, that an odd calm begins settling over him. He has time to think, and what he thinks of is Gina, whom he promised he'd never surf alone, and the kids, the little ones: will they even remember him? But mostly he thinks of Amanda; she'll probably be overjoyed to hear that he's dead.

Then, just as he's about to give up, his face breaks the surface. There's air. He draws one lungful of it, then another, gulping it greedily down. When he gets his footing in the shallow churning surf he stumbles out of the water, dragging his board, and when he's on dry land he rips off a glove and touches his forehead and his fingers come away red.

Wonderful. Wooziness overtakes him and he falls to his knees, releasing the contents of his stomach onto the sand.

He collapses on his back, spent, blinking at the dull sky. The clouds are thicker now, a single massive unit like a lid pressing down. After some time he feels raindrops on his face. He doesn't get up. The storm isn't coming, he thinks, watching a lone seagull soaring high overhead. The storm is here.

3

THE SECOND FLOOR is quiet, almost eerily so. A little stoned, Vance tiptoes past his brother's closed bedroom door and down to the end of the hall, to the girls' bathroom, where he undresses, dropping his clothes on the floor and running the shower as hot as it will go.

Waiting for the water to heat up, he looks around: beadboard walls, claw-foot tub, old-fashioned black-and-white checkerboard tile floor. It's got to be one of the only spaces in the whole house that hasn't been renovated—though knowing Craig, it's probably only a matter of time. It seems to be his brother's—and Gina's—mission to scrub the old manse of any shred of authenticity, any unique character, any connections to the past.

It's a shame, if you ask Vance—not that anyone has. True, the place was a wreck when Craig bought it, but it's got history. Built in 1833 by a whaling captain (a distant relative of theirs, legend says), the house was for a time one of the most extravagant properties on the Cape, a Federal-style beauty with floors made of teak from the West Indies, Tiffany windows, and an arch at the entry made of crossed whale ribs. It's said to have once harbored, in a secret compartment under the stairs, runaway slaves. (This last bit Craig shares widely, sort of puffing up when he does, as if in addition to the property, credit for any good deeds enacted upon it, throughout history, belongs to him.)

But Craig's never had much use for history, or the past, and Gina fancies herself an architect (she studied it as an undergrad—"at Harvard," she never hesitates to remind whoever's listening), and the first thing they did after settling in (after removing the hundred-year-old oak that impinged on their view) was draft plans to gut the place. Into a Dumpster went the old double-hung windows, the dentil moldings, the dumbwaiter. They even sold off the old whale bones, online. Not even the hand-carved fanlights over the doorways survived. Indeed, all that remains of the original structure now, aside from the exterior walls, is the brick chimney, one of five original fireplaces, and the central staircase, all of which local historic-preservation rules required they leave intact.

Vance steps into the shower, which still isn't very hot—a safety precaution, he supposes, for Helen, whose detritus is everywhere, cluttering every surface: a Barbie in the soap dish, soap crayons on the shampoo rack, plastic stars and flowers suction-cupped to the walls. He kicks a couple of rubber ducks to the side so he can stand.

Under the lukewarm stream, he has the thought that he doesn't deserve this cruel exile. He should be home; he should be with Celeste. She likes to sleep in on Sundays. She sleeps naked, usually on her stomach, and sometimes when he wakes up before her, he'll just stay there in bed, watching the day's first light illuminate her back.

He closes his eyes. When they were first together, she would sometimes join him in the shower. She'd surprise him, appearing ghost-like beside him in the steam, and they'd make love without speaking, his hand pressed between the small of her back and the tiles. His hand drifts south, remembering. Afterward, surrounded by children's things, he feels despicable again. He washes his hair with shampoo that smells like strawberries, scrubs his body with heart-shaped soap that leaves a shimmery, pink residue on his skin.

He's out of the shower, shaving in front of the steamed-up mirror with lilac-scented shaving cream and a dull plastic razor from the medicine chest, when the bathroom door bursts open. He spins around. There in the doorway, not five feet from him, is his niece. Amanda. She looks like she just woke up (her eyes are puffy, and sheet marks stripe her cheeks), in a faded Guns N' Roses T-shirt that grazes the middle of her thighs. But mostly she looks confused—nearly as confused as he feels.

"Oh my God," she says, shielding her eyes and looking away.

"Uh—sweetheart," he stammers, "shit," snatching a towel from the rack behind the door and wrapping it around his waist and catching a glimpse of himself in the mirror; he's still got shaving cream on half his face. "One sec," he says. Finishing the job with a few hurried strokes, he sets the razor down and splashes water on his face. Patting himself dry, he turns to her. "There. Sorry. Now what the heck are you doing here?"

Her cheeks are flushed, whether from embarrassment or the steam he doesn't know. She touches her jaw. "You're, um—you're bleeding."

He faces the mirror again and clears a patch of glass. She's right. A red trickle has made its way halfway down his neck. He tears off a square of toilet paper and dabs at his jaw, looking for the cut.

"Is it bad?" she asks.

"I'll live. You didn't answer my question."

"Sorry for startling you," she says. Her voice sounds strangely thin.

He looks at her. The color in her cheeks has faded, and her eyes look bleary. Is she ill? He feels his heart contract a couple of millimeters. "I'm the one who should apologize. It's your bathroom, after all." After a moment he says, "Are you okay?"

Suddenly she looks miserable. She opens the door and steps out into the hall. "I'm really sorry you cut yourself," she says, and pulls the door closed.

He finds her downstairs in the kitchen, which unlike the girls' bathroom has been completely overhauled since Thanksgiving, when he was last here: gleaming new countertops, new cabinets, the old heartpine floors replaced with wide, cola-colored planks.

"Hey, you," he says from the doorway.

"Hey." She's holding an iPhone and frowning down at it, stabbing her index finger at the screen. She's put on more clothes—a pair of baggy, forest-green wind pants and a steel-gray sweater large enough to be Craig's. The sleeves are pushed up to her elbows, showcasing her thin wrists, which are stacked with bracelets of black rubber and color-ful braided string.

He clears his throat. "I hate to be the bearer of bad news, but this isn't Tierra del Fuego."

She looks at him wide-eyed, affecting surprise. "Oh my God, you're right. Where are the mountains? Where are the trees? Where's that freak from Arkansas who sang about Jesus Christ every night?"

"Ha, ha," he says, going to her and kissing her on the forehead—the same high, broad forehead that he and Craig inherited from their dad. ("The Lake five-head," his father used to say.)

Hugging her, he can feel her shoulder blades and ribs. "You've got-ten skinny down south," he says. "Don't they feed you in the woods?"

"Ouch," she says, and he loosens his grip.

Standing back, he looks her up and down. She has their coloring, too—blue eyes and corn-silk hair—but her bone structure, the deli-cate jaw, the high cheekbones, the aquiline nose, those are Suzanne's. Especially the nose: well proportioned and delicate, it's nothing like the inelegant muffins that mar the countenances of Vance and Craig.

Aside from being skinnier, she looks all right. She looks good—but she always looks good to him. "So you got some time off from your time off, is that the idea?"

"Something like that," she says. He waits, thinking she'll say more, but she returns her attention to the phone. When the coffeemaker beeps, she doesn't react, so he starts opening unfamiliar cupboards and drawers, hunting for mugs.

If she knows where they are—or if she's aware of him looking—she keeps the information to herself, but he finds them eventually in a drawer to the left of the stove, and pulls out two black ones emblazoned with the words *Lake Design Build*, Craig's company, in bright cerulean blue. Filling one for each of them, he says, "The usual, sugar and milk?"

"Just sugar," she says. "Lots, please."

"Roger that," he says, taking three brown-sugar cubes from a gold-rimmed china dish that used to be their grandmother's and dropping them into one of the mugs. A carton of milk sits out on the island. He helps himself to what's left in it and asks if she'd like to sit down.

She still hasn't really looked at him. Without answering, she picks up her mug and holds it with both hands, close to her body, hunching over it as if warming herself, though the room is by no means cold.

"So, what's the news from the end of the world?" he asks. "I haven't heard anything since base camp."

She frowns, as if uncertain what he's talking about. Maybe she's forgotten the letters she wrote. He hasn't: they were ecstatic, gushing, full of descriptions of wildflowers, rushing rivers, snow-capped mountain peaks. He hasn't heard her sound so happy since—well, since he doesn't know when.

"It's not like we had email," she says defensively. "Or phones. It was totally off-grid."

"I was making an observation, not a complaint."

She peers into her mug. "Why didn't Craig say you were coming?" she says. "Where's Celeste?"

It shouldn't, but the question catches him off-guard. He sips his coffee, hoping to appear unruffled while trying to think of what to say. He doesn't want to lie, but he's not prepared to tell her, or any of them, the truth.

"We found some mold in the condo. Turns out the stuff's pretty nasty—toxic—and you know how Celeste is about her health." He smiles but she doesn't smile back. "She's staying in Maryland, anyway, at her folks'." This last part, at least, is true, or it very well could be. Since what happened at the college happened, she's been spending as much time as she can on the Eastern Shore—or in Philadelphia with her sister, or in Charlottesville with her friend Monique. Anyplace will do, it would seem, as long as it's away from him. To change the subject, he says, "Seriously, what are you doing back? Craig didn't say anything."

"Craig's a fucking prick," she says.

If he's a little shocked, he can't say he's completely surprised at the sentiment. He's heard her bash Craig plenty of times—often in less vulgar terms, but the two of them have been butting heads more or less since she learned to talk, maybe even before that. (How telling, Craig always says, that her first word was *no*.)

"Uh-oh. What'd he do now?" Vance asks. As usual, he's more than ready to hear her detail what an uptight, self-righteous hall monitor his brother can be—and, almost certainly, to agree.

But she shakes her head. "Forget it."

Now *this* is surprising. Usually she can't wait to drag Craig's name through the mud. Today, though, she sets down her coffee and says she has some stuff to do upstairs.

"Wait. Never mind Craig. I want to hear about the land of fire." When she doesn't respond, he says, "You know, Tierra del Fuego. Did you go to the woods to live deliberately, like Emerson?"

"That was Thoreau."

He knows that—of course he does, he's the English teacher, for God's sake—but she's making him nervous. Nodding in the direction of the breakfast nook, he says again, "Want to sit?"

"And it wasn't the woods," she continues. "There are no trees there, or much vegetation at all." Her voice rises as she speaks. "It's glaciers, snow and ice. Rocks. You have to be careful because the glaciers are moving all the time, crushing up the rocks. The crushed-up rocks are called moraine, or scree, and they can fall on you, they can crush you. You can die."

"Sounds dangerous," he says, watching her face.

"It was."

"Was?"

"Yes, the past tense of 'is.'" Her voice sounds oddly muted now, like she's in some sort of pain.

"You mean that's it? But it's only March. You're done?"

She lifts her hands, shakes a pretend Magic 8 Ball, and reads its display. "Signs point to yes."

"What happened, honey? Why hasn't your dad—?"

"My dad's a fascist."

Before he can respond, there's a crash above their heads. He hears a faucet opening and closing, and Gina's voice saying something in a harsh tone. A baby begins to cry. The baby: Cameron. Vance had almost forgotten about him.

"Let the games begin," Amanda says. He's not sure, but he thinks there are tears in her eyes.

He has no idea what's happening. He moves closer and puts his hand on her arm. "Sweetheart," he says, "what on earth?" She seems to freeze. "Hey," he says, glancing at the ceiling. "Ask your Magic 8 Ball where I should take you for breakfast. Just the two of us, anywhere you like."

The activity moves to front of the house and down the stairs, and a moment later Helen appears in the doorway, dressed in shades of purple now and holding a plastic horse. "Vance, I can do a flip on the swing, come watch."

"Not now."

"Why not?"

"It's raining, for one."

"I don't care. We have a sandbox with real sand."

"I'm talking with your sister. Could you do me a big favor and give us a minute?" She looks from him to Amanda and back to him. "Please?"

"Can I play Xbox?"

"Knock yourself out," he says, and watches her settle into the sofa in the sunken den, then aim a remote at an enormous TV. When animated animals appear on the screen, he turns his attention back to Amanda. "What do you say?"

"I don't think so."

"What? You're forgoing breakfast? Things must really be bad." He means it lightly but she doesn't smile. She's looking down again, studying her fingernails, which he sees bear a few chipped-away remnants of neon green and have been bitten down to the quick. "Honey, is everything okay?"

Finally she raises her eyes and glares at him. "Everything's fantastic."

He fights the instinct to step back. He's heard her speak this way to Craig plenty of times, but never—not once in the seventeen-plus years she's been alive—to him. Swallowing, he says, "I'm concerned. I'm trying to help."

"Well, you can't." Pressing the heels of her hands into her eyes, she says, "*Fuck*."

He glances into the living room. Softly, so Helen can't hear, he says, "You know, you could ease up on the F-bombs, for your sister's sake."

"Half-sister," she corrects. "And I take zero responsibility for that freak. Besides, Gina has a much fouler mouth than me. Did you hear them this morning? They should just get divorced."

He watches the top of Helen's head. "Could you please keep your voice down?"

"Did you know she banished Marshmallow to the basement— to, like, the *furnace* room—when she was sick? Who does that? The poor dog is on death's door, and she's worried about her precious floors?"

Though Vance finds this news distressing, if not entirely surprising, he says, "Easy, now."

"On the other hand, she *is* married to Craig. He'd probably make Mother Teresa act like a total bitch."

He waits to see if she's finished; for a long moment they stand there, listening to the manic electronic melody emanating from Helen's game. Finally he says, "I've got an idea. Let's start this morning over. Here goes. It's wonderful to see you, honey. Such a pleasant surprise." He steps forward to kiss her on the cheek. "Can I make you some breakfast? How about some eggs?"

Without waiting for her response, he heads for the fridge, humming the opening chords of the song "Amanda," by Boston, his tried-and-true strategy for making her laugh.

"Vance," she says, but he hums louder.

In his exaggerated falsetto, he sings: "I'm gonna take you by the hand and make you understand, Amanda." He holds out his hand, part of the routine. She's supposed to take it, but she doesn't. She isn't smiling, either, but he isn't going to fold this easily. He sings the second verse while peering into the buffalo-sized, stainless-steel tank that's Craig's new refrigerator. The shelves are crammed with kid food: mini-yogurts, string cheese, pouches of juice. No wonder his brother is always in such a shitty mood; he's being starved to death. He spots a carton of eggs, extracts it, and sings, "I'm gonna fry us up some eggs, so good you're gonna beg, Amanda. I'm gonna fry them up for you and your crazy sister too, Amanda."

"You're such a nerd," she says, but when he turns to face her, there it is, an actual smile, and he realizes that she hasn't smiled once all morning, and also that her braces are gone. She looks so pretty, like her regular self again, he can't help smiling too. He sets down the eggs.

"Hey, look, you have teeth," he says. "Congratulations, honey. You look terrific. Like a movie star—who's the one in that surfing movie? She plays the cute maid?"

"I do not," she says, but from the pink that blooms in her cheeks, he can see she's pleased, and it occurs to him that maybe this is the reason she came home—to get the braces off.

He feels his body relax some. It's entirely possible, he hypothesizes, that she came home by choice; maybe not even because of the braces. Maybe she was homesick and is too embarrassed to admit it to him. He says, "Really, you look great, kiddo. Teenage guys of the world, hold on to your hearts."

Her smile evaporates as quickly as it came. Again her eyes fill.

"Oh, Jesus. What did I say?"

"Nothing." She sniffles, swiping at her eyes with back of her hand. "I'm going upstairs."

"Wait," he says. "I mean it, let's get out of here. How does the Main Sail sound?"

"The Main Sail, the Main Sail, the *Main* Sail."

It's Helen. She's standing in the kitchen doorway again, this time holding the jamb with both hands and leaning backwards, swinging from side to side. "Look, Vance, I'm figure skating. The wall is my partner, the floor is the ice."

He catches the look of disdain that crosses Amanda's face as she turns away, draws a glass of water from the sink, and proceeds to the back of the house, to the breakfast nook, where she crosses her arms over her chest and stands in front of the French doors, looking out.

Helen doesn't catch it, or maybe she doesn't care. Abandoning the doorjamb, she comes over to Vance, threads her fingers together behind her back, and butts her head against his hip. "Can we go to the Main Sail, please? They have waffles with chocolate sauce and whipped cream. Please? *Please?*"

Gina appears in the doorway then, the baby on her hip. He looks more substantial than he did in November, with sturdy-looking limbs, electric-blue eyes, and an inch or so of white chick fuzz covering his sizable head.

Vance says, "Good morning."

"Not so far," she says, opening the fridge.

She's no great fan of his, he can tell, and he feels about the same—but she's an unfailingly polite person, and in the decade-plus that he's known Gina, he's always received, at bare minimum, a "Nice to see you" and a perfunctory peck on the cheek. Now, watching her pluck food items from shelves and set them on the counter, he wonders how he possibly managed, over the course of the past twelve hours (during which she hasn't even seen his face), to piss her off.

Closing the fridge, she bends to deposit Cameron on the floor. In sweatpants and a loose-fitting flannel shirt, she looks uncharacteristically disheveled. She pours herself coffee from the pot, reaches for the milk carton, and gives it a shake. "Perfect," she says. "Who finished the milk and didn't put it on the list?"

No one answers. Amanda is still by the French doors, and Helen squats in front of the baby, forcing a rubber lamb chop into his fist.

Vance clears his throat, confesses, and apologizes, and Gina looks at him—for the first time, apparently, because her face changes from irritation to surprise. "Oh God, Vance, it's you. I'm so sorry. Hi." Flushed, she comes around the island to deliver his kiss. She smells like toothpaste and detergent, and her lips leave a cool spot on his cheek.

"He's taking us to the Main Sail," Helen says. "Can we go? Can we, can we, please?"

"May we," Gina says.

"May we? Please?"

"If you don't stop whining this minute, the answer's no."

Helen's face darkens. She spins around and snatches the lamb chop from her little brother, who howls.

Gina pinches the bridge of her nose and closes her eyes. Vance watches the baby's face turn red; he howls some more and flaps his arms but she doesn't pick him up. It seems that she should—that somebody should. Vance notices a spiked blue ball on the floor and nudges it toward the baby with his foot.

"That's the dog's toy," Helen says. She's right beside him now, and she captures one of his hands in both of hers and starts to tug. Hard. "Main Sail, Main Sail, Main Sail," she chants.

"Helen, stop pestering Vance," Gina says. There isn't much conviction in her voice. She starts mashing a banana with a fork.

"But he *said*," Helen says. "Right, Vance?"

"Are you sure you don't mind?" Gina asks, and before Vance can answer either question, she says, "You're a godsend." She adds yogurt to the bowl and stirs in something granular and brown.

He looks over at Amanda—or rather, at her back. "You about ready, A-train?" When she doesn't answer, he looks past her hunched shoulders at the yard, trying to see what she sees: an empty gazebo, bare-branched trees, sodden brown grass.

Again he wonders what she's doing home. He knows her well enough to doubt she's here on her own accord. Probably she screwed up—again. He can't say he's surprised, exactly. Smart as she is, she's never felt particularly compelled to follow the rules. Or, as he prefers to think about it, she's strong-willed. That's what landed her in Chile in the first place: she was smoking pot in the girls' locker room before soccer practice when the coach walked in. There were two others with her, but she was the one holding the joint, and she had to go before the Disciplinary Committee. The school had one of those zero tolerance policies, which meant she was supposed to be expelled. But because she made straight A's and was a soccer star, had already completed her graduation requirements, and had just the week before been accepted at Dartmouth (and because she also happened to be uniformly liked by her teachers, despite everything else), they gave her a choice: expulsion, or spend her senior spring elsewhere, ideally someplace very far from the Cape.

He watches her at the doors. The thing is, he understands. He *gets* it. He knows all too well what it's like, refusing to bow to authority for authority's sake—especially when what you're being asked to conform to is pointless, or worse. But also, he worries. He worries that her nature will make life difficult for her—difficult, like it's been for him.

"A-train?" he says again.

Without turning around, she says, "I think I'll pass."

Gina stops stirring. She looks troubled. "You really should eat something. You'll feel better."

"Thanks for the tip."

She says, "Don't be rude, please." Amanda scoffs, and Gina says, "Please look at me when I'm speaking to you."

She turns and faces them. She looks pale. In a trembling voice she says, "I'm not being rude. You're treating me like I'm seven years old."

"Well, when you speak to me that way, in that tone of voice, you sound like you're seven years old."

"*I'm* seven years old," Helen shouts. "Seven rhymes with heaven. And Kevin."

Amanda turns to her, eyes ablaze. "Do you ever shut up?"

"Do you?"

Gina says, "Stop it now. Both of you."

"Pestilence," says Amanda.

Helen says, "What's a pestilence?"

Amanda says, "A disease. A horrible one that won't go away."

Gina turns away from them. "Fine, tear each other to pieces, what do I care?"

"All right. Ding, ding, ding," Vance says, making a T with his hands. "Come on, A." He's more or less begging now. "It'll be fun. We'll take the Frog. You can drive." The Frog is the green 1984 FJ40 Toyota Land Cruiser that used to belong to their dad. Amanda relishes driving it, or she always has. This morning her expression stays flat.

To sweeten the pot, he says, "We'll ride out to Land's End after, take a look around. What do you say?" Like him, Amanda adores Land's End, the rustic beach camp that's been in their family for almost a hundred years. This morning, though, he's not sure she'll rise even to this bait.

She does rise, sort of. "Whatever. Fine," she says.

He says, "That's what I like to hear."

"Land's End. I want to go to Land's End," Helen whines.

Gina says, "You, my dear, have your riding lesson. How about you go get your bag?"

Helen's arms fly up over her head. "*Woot woot*," she shouts, doing a lap around the island, hands pumping the air. Amanda groans.

Gina ignores them both. "You're my hero, Vance." She smiles at him and pats his arm, passing by, then asks if he'd mind dropping Helen off at Craig's office after they eat, so Craig can take her to her lesson. Before Vance can answer, her phone rings.

"Hi there," Gina says, her voice dropping notably. "Just give me a minute." Holding it against her shoulder, she says, "It's Heather." Heather, her sister, is married to a hotel-chain heir, and they live on a former dairy farm somewhere in Vermont.

"Tell Heather hi," Vance says.

"Will do," Gina says, drifting in the direction of the dining room. "Yes. No. Nothing important," she tells Vermont.

4

∞

WITH A WET CLOTH Gina wipes the baby's face and hands, holding the phone between her shoulder and chin and listening while he talks about Costa Rica, where he's been for the past two weeks with his son. The water was aqua, and warm, and clear as glass, he tells her, and you could hear the waves breaking on the beach through the open doors while you slept.

"I wish you could've been there," he says.

"I'm not sure Kevin would have appreciated that. Not to mention somebody else," she says, as Cam knocks his bowl of yogurt off the counter. She lunges to catch it but misses, and it hits the floor, splattering the dishwasher, the cabinets, and the stools.

Squatting to clean up the mess, she feels pain zap across her lower back. With some effort she stands up and takes a couple of breaths, trying to visualize the muscles relaxing, a technique her sister's massage therapist says helps to control the spasms. While she's standing still, she catches her reflection in the oven door. Even there, in the almost-black glass, she can see how tired she looks. Well, she *is* tired— more tired than she knew a person could be and still be awake, moving through the world, doing things. Occasionally it strikes her as unsafe.

Her back seems to have calmed, and tentatively she takes a step. No pain. With her free hand she massages the spot on her lower spine, near her hip. She can't feel a knot—or her hipbone, for that matter. All she feels is fat, an extra fistful of it where her bone should be, spilling over the waistband of her pants. How did this happen? To *her*. She let it happen, that's how. She scowls at herself in the glass. She's always been the fittest person she knew, even after having Helen. Not that it was easy. It took work, discipline: twice-a-week strength training, calorie counting, unrelenting early-morning runs. But the discipline paid off; she was proud of how she looked, and she wasn't ashamed to admit it.

That's in the past, though. She used to look at women she knew who'd had kids and let themselves go and feel pity for them—pity, and yes, she can admit this now, too—a little disdain. But carrying Cam at thirty-nine changed all that. She's become one of those women whose faces are permanently puffy, who perpetually need a haircut, and who wear yoga pants to social events. Not that it wasn't worth it; she turns away from her reflection and bends to give each of Cam's ample cheeks a kiss.

"You still there?" Dov says.

"Yes," she says, getting a hard pretzel from the cupboard and handing it to the baby, who likes to suck off the salt. "I've kind of got my hands full," she says, surveying the yogurt mess. "Can I call you back?"

"You didn't give me an answer."

"Because I don't have one yet."

There's another silence, but neither of them hangs up. With a sponge she wipes yogurt off the cabinets and then the stools, which she just bought. They're brushed aluminum, and she thinks they give the otherwise traditional kitchen an unexpected industrial edge.

"I'm sorry," he says. "I just—" He sounds so injured, like a little boy. She hates hearing him sound like that.

"Don't be. I want to see you too, I do," she says. Dropping the sponge in the sink, she scoops Cam up under his arms and carries him into the living room, where she arranges him in his Pack 'n Play with a set of colored plastic rings. "And I'm sorry too. It's crazy here, but that's got nothing to do with you." She's about to sit down when she hears the dryer beep, so she heads into the mudroom. "The truth is, talking to you right now is the sanest I've felt in days." She opens the dryer, squats, and begins emptying the hot, sweet-smelling clothes into the hamper by her feet. "Speaking of sanity," she says, "guess who rolled in last night?"

"Give me a hint."

"He looks a lot like someone else in this house." She closes the dryer door and stands up. Back in the living room, she dumps the laundry onto the sofa and starts to fold.

"Really? He usually gives me a heads-up when he's coming home."

"I'm not sure how far in advance this visit was planned," she says, folding a pair of Craig's boxer shorts, blue with white sailboats, a Father's Day gift from a couple of years ago. "I guess he called yesterday afternoon, asking to stay. I was asleep when he got here, but I saw him this morning. That's who I was talking to before."

"So what's the story this time?"

"I don't know, but I could probably guess." She pauses: what a hypocrite she is. "He just went for breakfast with the girls." She folds the last few items, a couple of Craig's undershirts and a pair of Helen's jeans.

"Does he know? I mean about—"

"No," she says, lifting the hamper. "And he won't, if Craig prevails." She starts up the stairs, wishing she hadn't said Craig's name. On the landing halfway up, she stops to catch her breath. "Could we talk about something else? What did you guys eat down there? What were the people like? I want to live vicariously."

Half listening while Dov talks about nesting sea turtles and homemade tortillas and seventy-five-cent beer, she eases Helen's door open with her foot and stands a moment, absorbing the unmade bed, the clothes and toys and books scattered across the floor. Theoretically—and according to the chore chart Gina downloaded from the Internet and printed out—Helen cleans her room every Saturday; in practice, it's probably closer to once a month. They need to be stricter, she thinks for the thousandth time, more consistent. They need to stand behind the rules they make. Otherwise, before they know it they'll have another Amanda on their hands. She shudders at the thought, setting the hamper down and straightening Helen's horse-print sheets.

He's saying something about fried plantains but stops in midsentence. "This can't be interesting to you."

"Believe me, it is. I feel like it's been a decade since I even left the Cape," she says.

There's a pause, then he says, "I don't want to talk about Costa Rica."

"What, then? The weather?" She teases. "Or how about work?" More seriously, she says, "Have you decided yet?" She feels awkward again, steering the conversation back to Craig, but on top of everything else, he's been so anxious about the bid he put in for Dov's new restaurant, and she knows how badly he could use some good news.

"No, and I don't want to talk about that, or anything, on the phone. I want to see you. Just say yes." Dov's Israeli accent—already alluring— sounds thicker now, and there's a gravelly edge to his voice that sends heat creeping up her neck.

She smooths down Helen's quilt and starts putting away her clean clothes. In the mirror on the back of the open closet door she catches another glimpse of herself; this time it isn't fatigue she notices but the color in her face. It's ridiculous, the effect he has on her. She should be ashamed of herself—with a family, with a baby, for God's sake. And she is, a little. But only a little. Not enough to tell him she's a happily married woman and to leave her alone. Not even enough, apparently, to get off the phone.

"I just can't. Not right now," she says, touching her cheek.

"Can't see me, or can't say yes?"

"The latter," she says, though she meant the former. "I haven't figured out the logistics yet."

In a voice close to a whisper, he says, "What are you wearing?"

She laughs, but he doesn't.

He says, "I mean it. Tell me how you look."

She faces the full-length mirror and regards herself: threadbare sheepskin flip-flops, last year's yoga pants, Craig's old, pilled flannel shirt. "You don't want to know, believe me," she says. Turning away, she opens the top drawer of Helen's dresser and starts arranging her socks.

"You have no idea how beautiful you are."

Flushing absurdly, she looks away from her reflection and slides the drawer closed. "Something's wrong with you. You know that, right? You should get professional help," she says, carrying the hamper next door, into Cameron's room.

"I don't want help," he says. "If I'm crazy, so be it. It's because of you."

She laughs again. "I refuse to accept that responsibility," she says, and starts putting Cameron's clothes away. His room is tiny, essentially a glorified closet. In fact it was supposed to be a closet, one of two walk-ins adjoining the master suite; Cam was a surprise, calling for some last-minute adjustments to the renovation plans.

"You should be pleased."

"Should I?" she says, stacking his onesies and putting them and his little socks away. On the wall over the crib hangs his birth announcement—a tasteful, hand-printed card—and as usual, she pauses a moment in front of it, reminding herself what a blessing he is, no matter how tired she feels.

After Helen, she'd wanted another—she'd wanted one very much —but it didn't happen, and after a long time, years, she made peace with the idea of just one child. And then, five years later, surprise. The morning she took the test—two tests, actually—and saw the pink plus signs, she cried. She didn't tell anyone about it for days, not even Heather, not even Craig, who swore he was over the moon when, after nearly a week, she finally got up the gumption to deliver the news. And as the initial shock wore off and the weeks passed, she warmed to the idea too; by the time he arrived, they'd painted the would-be closet powder blue, hung a farm-themed mobile over his crib, and filled an old maple wardrobe with sweet, high-end hand-me-downs from Heather's kids. What she wasn't prepared for—she couldn't have been—was the fatigue: the ceaseless, soul-crushing fatigue that has her feeling half conscious, like a walking corpse, most of the time.

"I kept thinking about it the whole time I was away," he says.

"About what?" she says, though she knows. She closes Cam's wardrobe and carries the rest of the laundry into the bedroom she shares with Craig. Unlike Cameron's, it's enormous, with a cathedral ceiling and exposed wood beams. Like Helen's, the bed—a California king piled high with pillows coordinated with the curtains and rug—is unmade.

Dov is talking about that night now, like she knew he would; he always steers the conversation back there, to that night—the house-warming at Will and Adie Milliken's house. "I can't stop," he says. She's standing in front of the dresser, putting away Craig's underwear. "It's not my fault," he says. "I simply cannot."

She opens the next drawer, which contains Craig's workout clothes. Dov makes a throaty sound. "I should probably get going," she says. But now she's thinking about it too—that night. "I shouldn't keep Meghan waiting," she says, but still she doesn't hang up. When she closes the bottom drawer, her eyes land, rather inconveniently, on a picture in a silver frame.

"I could come by the store," he says.

"No," she says automatically and picks up the photo. It's of her and Craig and their wedding party, taken ten Julys ago, and she holds it close, first examining her own face: she looks happy, genuinely happy, smiling brightly and holding on to Craig's arm. And she *was* happy. Wasn't she? Of course she was. She had everything she wanted: a beautiful summer wedding by the ocean, and she was marrying the man she loved. And she *did* love him, there was no question—she knew she did, or that she could, the very first night they met. That was just over a year before, Memorial Day weekend, and she was on the Cape, staying with friends. They were at a bar in town, Randolph's, when a dark-haired man had approached her. He said his name was Dov—"like the bird," he said—and told her his friend wanted to buy her a drink. "He's a sad man," Dov said, "but I have a feeling you can change that." Dov didn't say *why* Craig was sad—or that he had a petulant seven-year-old daughter at home—and she didn't ask. She turned to look at a corner booth where Dov was pointing, and saw a tall, fair-haired, and undeniably handsome man, Craig, in clean Carhartts and dirty boots, glowering at his friend from beneath the bill of his Red Sox cap.

She told Dov to tell him sure, why not, and one drink became two, then three, and she realized she'd lost track of her friends. She didn't care. They sat in the dark corner booth until after last call, and Craig drove her home in his truck and walked her to the front door, where they stood face-to-face on her friend's stoop. Emboldened perhaps by the late hour, and by the margaritas she'd drunk—she asked why Dov had called him sad. "I'm a widower," he said plainly, and then, "It's been almost a year." Before she could ask anything else, he asked if he could kiss her, and did so, gently, yet with some quiet force. Then he said, "Thank you," and she knew somehow that he was a man she could love —fiercely. And she does love him, still, with all her heart, or at least the overwhelming majority of it; one tipsy interlude—a harmless flirtation —with Dov, who means nothing to her, isn't going to change that.

Her gaze migrates to the other side of the photo, to Dov. He stands between Vance and Marco, a fraternity brother of Craig's—the same triumvirate, she was keenly aware, who'd stood beside Craig nine years earlier, when he'd married Suzanne. They all wear the seersucker suits Gina had chosen so carefully, the white calla lilies on their lapels, and the pink, Cape Cod–patterned ties, and they all look very young, which they were, and pleased—which she doubts they were, at least not Vance—and a little stoned, which, she learned later, they all definitely were.

Her eyes travel down to Amanda, who sits primly on a white, beribboned bench in between Gina's nieces, Bonnie and Anne. The three of them were flower girls, and in smocked white dresses with pink satin sashes, they'd looked perfect. But unlike the other two, who were ecstatic about their roles, Amanda spent the day acting miserable, like some kind of captive. Even here, in the formal photo, she frowns.

"What's this 'no'?" Dov is saying. "I'll bring coffee. A friend bringing coffee. What's wrong with that?"

She sets the frame down. "I don't think so. Meghan will be there, like I said."

"It's no problem. I like Meghan."

She smiles in spite of herself. "You are persistent. I'll give you that."

"Lorna always said she went out with me the first time because she got tired of saying no. I wore her down." She can hear him grinning through the phone, but she feels uneasy: his ex-wife is still her friend. He says, "Please."

She wants to say no again, she does, but the word doesn't come. "Coffee," she says, and finally they hang up.

She wasn't making excuses, she is running late, and there's still Amanda's laundry to put away. She picks up the basket and carries it into the hall, pausing at the top of the stairs to listen for Cameron, who's still down in his Pack 'n Play. She can hear him babbling happily to himself, so she proceeds into Amanda's room, which, in contrast to Helen's, is neat as a pin. Aside from her purple sleeping bag and her apple-green duffel, which sits only partly unpacked on the window seat, it's as if she never came home.

Gina puts her clothes into their drawers. There are only a few items (Amanda's been wearing the same unwashed jeans, or *Wilderness Within* wind pants, and baggy wool sweater almost every day), and when she's finished she sits on the bed, which is made. Since coming home, Amanda has slept on top of the covers, inside her sleeping bag, with the window wide open, every night. Gina hasn't asked why, but she imagines her stepdaughter is doing everything she can to pretend she's still on her trip instead of home—to pretend that what's happening isn't. Denial: it's immature, and moreover, futile, but one doesn't have to look far to see where she learned this particular skill.

She folds the sleeping bag over and lays it at the foot of the bed, then runs her hands over the duvet, which is pink plaid, part of the set she bought Amanda years ago when they first moved in. It was part of a larger gift, decorating the whole room, a surprise executed while Amanda was down in DC visiting Vance. Craig had tried to dissuade Gina, saying Amanda wouldn't appreciate it, but Gina was determined. She'd been married to Craig almost four years by then, but she was still trying to win over her stepdaughter, to prove that, contrary to what Amanda might believe, she'd won the lottery as far as stepmothers went. She knew what she was doing, she assured Craig. (That Amanda *hadn't* been appreciative—she'd never actually thanked her—didn't mean she'd made a mistake.)

Now, despite the time, she lies down on the bed, arranging one of the pink plaid pillows under her perpetually stiff neck. She's so fucking tired. She just needs a minute or two to rest. She closes her eyes and her thoughts drift, again, to Dov. To the Millikens' dark garage. The smell of old motor oil, his hand on her hip. The five minutes, three and a half weeks ago, that she can't manage to forget.

5

THE MAIN SAIL IS LOCATED just off Beach Road, in a shopping plaza called Morningtide, sandwiched between Duane's Market and a Catholic charity's consignment shop whose window displays a poster depicting a 1970s-looking mother cradling a baby under large floating letters that spell out the word *Life*.

Vance pulls the Frog into a space on the far edge of the lot. (Amanda doesn't know why, but he and her father always seem to choose unnecessarily faraway spots.) Sitting shotgun, she avoids looking at the consignment shop, focusing instead on Duane's, where they have bundles of firewood stacked neatly out front.

It's started to drizzle, she notices, watching an old man in a translucent poncho and giant white Reeboks help an even older woman, maybe his mother, out of a van.

Amanda exits the Frog first and walks ahead briskly, her shoulders hunched against the rain. Gina tried to get her to wear a slicker, but she said no, and you'd have thought she'd said she was going to jump out of a plane from the look on Gina's face. Why does everyone have to be all over her every minute? She hates how they watch her, how they monitor her every move.

On a dry square of cement under the restaurant's filthy green-and-white-striped awning, she waits, watching Helen and Vance. In her purple slicker and alligator galoshes, Helen holds on to Vance's hand. Her uncle looks uncomfortable. She doesn't blame him; Helen is annoying and a total spaz, which is why Amanda's a little surprised when Vance pauses in the middle of the asphalt, lifts his hand, and spins her around. Helen grins like a fool, of course, and Amanda feels a stab of antipathy—*she's* the one Vance goofs around with—and looks away, feigning absorption in the fliers by the Main Sail's door: whale watching, ghost tours, a talk at the yacht club about owls.

"Did you put our name in?" Vance asks.

"Ha, ha," she says. It's supposed to be funny; if it were summer, the place would be mobbed, and they'd have added their names to a list and waited amid a throng of impatient vacationers, probably for an hour or more. But today, a cold, sloppy Sunday in March, they walk right in.

"Thank God for God," Vance jokes to the owner's daughter, a heavyset, heavily tattooed woman named Irene, who's been hostess here for as long as Amanda can remember. This joke isn't very funny either (most of Vance's aren't), and Irene doesn't smile, nor does she indicate, beyond the subtlest facial twitch, that she recognizes any of them, despite the fact that they've been patronizing the restaurant for years. This isn't exactly remarkable. ("Good old New England hospitality," Gina would say.)

The room's decor is typical too: lobster traps hang from the ceiling, battered buoys and fishing nets cover the walls. The counter, where she and Vance usually sit (and would today if it weren't for Helen, she thinks, spotting two empty stools at the far end), is built on the hull of a boat—a Boston Whaler, of course. Walking past, she takes a quick inventory of the diners and is relieved to see she doesn't recognize any of them. Ditto for the dining room, a small miracle; the last thing in the world she wants to do is make small talk with someone she's known since she was three.

They follow Irene to one of the smaller tables in back, by the windows, and she wipes crumbs and stickiness off the lacquered wood surface with a wet rag while rattling off the specials: a lobster-cheddar omelet, banana-bread French toast, red flannel hash. Amanda's stomach pitches just hearing the words. She tries to focus on something else. She watches Irene lay down three paper placemats and three sets of silverware rolled tightly inside white paper napkins. She isn't wearing a wedding ring. She has a barbed-wire tattoo circling her ample upper arm and, hanging from a chain around her neck, a silver Celtic knot nearly identical to the gold one on Amanda's pinky ring, which she gives a quick, well-practiced twist. It used to be her mother's. Her father gave it to her when she turned ten, and it's been her good-luck charm ever since. She never takes it off, or she hadn't until recently: at the start of her trip, one of the leaders, Jan, made her seal it in a Ziploc bag and leave it behind, at base camp, locked inside a safe with everyone else's valuables. She knows it's silly, but she can't help wondering whether things would have turned out so terribly if she'd only been allowed to wear her ring.

Helen sits on Vance's left, so Amanda takes the seat on his right, the one facing the window. Resting her chin on her fist, she looks out at the parking lot, where a green-painted Dumpster proclaims CAPE WASTE, NO DUMPING, $500 FINE, and beyond that, into a desolate-looking grove of scrub oak and pitch pine. There, years ago, they'd found the body of a little girl. She'd been taken from New York, Schenectady, and her name was April. Amanda remembers it well, not only because it was horrible and all anyone talked about for months, but because they'd been the same age at the time, seven, and both their names started with A.

"So, what are we thinking, ladies?" Vance says, scanning the placemat, which doubles as a menu.

Before either answers, their waitress approaches the table.

"Amanda? Holy crap," she says.

When Amanda looks up, her heart sinks. It's Sybil Delany, a mousy girl she's gone to school with since pre-K. Or rather, she *was* mousy: formerly meek-looking, with fair, translucent skin and perpetually chapped lips, Sybil has transformed herself over the past year, dying her hair black and wearing exclusively black clothes, black eye makeup, and even black lipstick.

Amanda says, "I didn't know you worked here."

"It's my sister's job. She's in Puerto Vallarta. I'm just filling in over break." She pauses. "Hi, Mr. Lake," she says.

"Mr. Lake's my brother," Vance says.

"Okay," she says, looking a little perplexed.

"He's my uncle," Amanda says.

"Right on," she says. "Aren't you supposed to be in, like, Alaska?"

Eyes on her placemat, Amanda says, "Yes."

"So, are you home for, like, a while?"

"Looks like it," she says, aware of Vance watching her.

"Cool. Hey, Noah Briley is having, like, a gathering tomorrow, some kids from that class who're home. You should come. I mean—" She bites her lip, glancing at Vance.

Amanda says, "Maybe." She looks at Vance, hoping to catch his eye, which she does, and he gets the message, God bless him.

"I think we'd better order up some grub," he says, and Sybil says, "Right on," straightening up and asking what they want to drink. Helen orders pineapple juice, Amanda, a Coke, and Vance, coffee, and Sybil goes away.

"I want chocolate-chip pancakes with chocolate syrup and whipped cream," Helen says. "And bacon and sausage, and maple syrup on the side."

"A-train?" She doesn't answer. "So, the waitress, she's a friend of yours?" He asks, frowning down at the menu.

"Not really," she says.

Helen says, "And I want a cherry on top. Can I get a cherry, Uncle Vance?"

Amanda says, "Gross."

Vance says, "Hey."

"What?"

"She's a kid," he says. "It's her right—no, her duty—to eat all the crap she wants. What do you think they mean by 'Eggs Louise'?"

Sybil returns with their drinks, and this time Amanda keeps her eyes down, pretending to study the menu, though she knows its offerings practically by heart. Vance orders for Helen and for himself, then says, "A?"

Without looking up, she asks for a toasted English muffin, and Sybil starts to go.

"Whoa, whoa," he says. "No Big A?" The Big A is his nickname for the omelet she's been ordering since she was small: three eggs, mushrooms, and extra American cheese. But she's not a kid anymore, a development he seems determined not to notice—nothing's like it used to be, and the mere mention of it causes bile to rise into her throat.

She glances up at Sybil. "Just the English muffin, please."

"Gotcha," Sybil says.

Vance says, "Could you at least add a fruit cup to that?" To Amanda he says, "I refuse to tell your mom that's all you ate."

"I'm not a child," Amanda says, unable to keep the exasperation from her voice. Is he going to start breathing down her neck now, too?

"And she's not her mom," Helen pipes in. She's sawing at the edge of the table with her butter knife, and Vance puts his hand on top of hers to make her stop. He turns to Amanda. "Of course she's not. Sorry, sweetheart."

Amanda says nothing.

Sybil says, "That'll be it?"

Vance nods. When she's gone, he asks Amanda—again—if she's feeling okay.

"Fine," she says, trying to keep her voice steady. Can't he just leave her alone?

"I'm glad," he says. "Because I was starting to feel like I'd done something to upset you."

"I told you, I'm fine. It's got nothing to do with you." She glares at Helen, who's now tapping the butter knife against her glass. "Could you please make that little orangutan stop?"

"If I'm an orangutan, you're an ape," Helen says. "A big ugly ape."

"You should be medicated," Amanda says.

"What's medicated?"

"Hey, cut it out," Vance says. "Both of you, Jesus."

Amanda turns and looks out the window again. A couple of fat seagulls lurk around the Dumpster; one's got something white, maybe old bread, in its beak. She didn't want to come, she thinks, and yet she's here. Why? Nobody listens to her, nobody gives a flying fuck what she wants. It's almost as if she doesn't exist. And how much easier everything would be for everyone, she thinks, if she didn't.

"Come on," Vance is saying. "You're sisters. Do you know how important that is?"

She's begun to feel a little lightheaded. She takes a deep breath, but it doesn't help. "Excuse me," she says, pushing back her chair.

"Where are you going?"

"The bathroom. Is that okay?"

He looks stung, and she regrets that, regrets acting like such a bitch all the time, especially to him, but there are tears in her eyes there's no way she's going to let him see. Turning on the heel of her hiking boot, she weaves her way among the tables to the far side of the dining room and pushes through the swinging saloon doors. The ladies' is at the end of a dark, narrow hallway, demarcated by a lobster with a pink bow on its head (the lobster on the men's wears a Red Sox cap), but a sheet of paper taped to the door informs her it's out of order, and to use the men's, so she tries that door, but of course it's locked. She knocks.

"Occupado," says a gruff voice.

She steps back and leans against the wall as fatigue overtakes her. Resting her head against the wood paneling, she closes her eyes. She feels like she could fall asleep right here, standing up. It's definitely not out of the question, not when these waves hit. No matter how early she goes to bed or how long she sleeps, they come out of nowhere and almost knock her down. It's like being sick, really sick, like having some awful, debilitating disease.

She forces herself up and puts her ear close to the door, but there's nothing to hear. She hates to think what's going on in there. She glances in the direction of the dining room, then rests against the wall again. At least here she's alone. She moves a few feet to her left and, in the hallway's dim light, squints at the hand-painted mural on the wall. It's a childish depiction of the beach on a summer day, and she knows it intimately, every swimsuited sunbather and striped umbrella, the dog catching the Frisbee in midair, the breaching whale, the blue sky, the white clouds, the yellow sun. She knows it not because she's looked at it countless times, though she has, but because she's the one who painted it, back when she was twelve. She won an art contest at school, and painting murals on the walls of businesses around town was the prize. She'd been thrilled—they put her picture in the paper, there was even a spot on the local news. Now the whole thing seems so lame, the mural itself embarrassingly amateurish, not to mention clichéd. She's just glad she signed it with her initials, *AEL*, and not her full name.

From behind the men's room door she hears, finally, the sound of a flush, then of water running. When it stops, the door handle rattles, and a man steps out. It's the man from the parking lot, the one in the white shoes.

"Sorry, the hydraulics don't work the way they used to," he says.

She doesn't know exactly what he means, but she has an idea, and she smiles as politely as possible and looks down at the floor, pressing her back to the wall so he can pass by in the narrow space. But he stays where he is, blocking the door to the bathroom, blinking at her in the low light. "I know you, young lady. You're Craig Lake's girl. I thought I saw your pop out there," he says, dropping his r's in the traditional New England way. "I've been working with him since you were just a little thing. Me and my brother Johnny, we're signed on to wire Dov Azulay's new place, if your old man gets the contract."

"That's my uncle, Vance."

He either doesn't hear her or doesn't care. "Did I hear you went away to school?"

"Sort of," she says, willing him to go.

"You know, I have a granddaughter just about your age. What are you, fifteen?"

"Seventeen."

"Well, pardon me, then. Delilah's not your age at all." He winks at her, then crosses his arms and rocks back on his heels. "Your pop's a good man. Me and Johnny, we don't agree on much, but we agree on that. Not sure I can say the same about Azulay." He winks again. She must look as uninterested as she feels, because after a long pause, he says, "Well, you take care."

Inside the tiny, wood-paneled room she pees and, avoiding looking in the mirror, washes her hands. Closing the toilet seat, she sits down—anything to postpone going back. Being around Vance—around anyone, really, but especially him—is torture. She hates deceiving him. She's never had to before, and it's painful, carrying on this charade. Not that she's considering telling him. That's out of the question; just thinking about it makes her whole body go tense. He wouldn't be angry—that's not what she's afraid of. No, he'd be kind—but he'd be sad, and sorry, and worst of all he'd be so disappointed. He'd never look at her the same way again. And who could blame him? She can hardly bear to look at herself.

Still seated, she takes her phone out of her pocket and checks the screen, but there's nothing from him. Christian. Silently scolding herself for thinking—hoping—there might be, she puts the phone back.

It's extremely unlikely he's going to get in touch, she reminds herself. He's six thousand miles away, for starters, and he's got his whole life—his *real* life, as he said. Plus, as far as she knows, he doesn't even have her number—she didn't give it to him. That was on purpose. The last thing she wanted was to be back home, wondering whether or not he'd call.

Which of course, now, she is. He *has* to be thinking about her, at least once in a while, doesn't he? Because it was real, what happened between them. She knows it was. She isn't some stupid teenager, blinded by a crush. She's been in love before, she knows what love feels like, or she knows enough. Besides, he felt it too, she knows he did, he was right there with her. She could see it on his face, hear it in his voice. *God*, he'd whispered in her ear late one night when they'd managed to sneak away from the cluster of tents, *when I'm with you I feel so fucking alive.*

She stands up and, for a moment, faces herself. As is often the case lately, looking at her face fills her with contempt. She glares, and the dumb blue eyes glare back. She takes in her stupid, pointy nose, her huge forehead. (The "Lake five-head," Vance likes to say. "Do you know what a five-head is?" he'd ask when she was a kid. She'd shake her head no, and he'd show her five fingers, then bop her forehead with his palm.) Before the trip—before everything—she felt fine toward her face, even occasionally benevolent. Now, though, she hates it, every aspect, every idiotic feature, including her newly straight teeth. Especially those: she doesn't deserve them. Her eyes sting. She just wants to not be her anymore, to not be Amanda Lake, if only for a few minutes.

There's a knock on the door. "Just a minute," she says, wiping her nose with the back of her hand. She splashes her face with cold water, blots it dry with a rough paper towel.

Back at the table, the food's arrived. She sits in front of a plate with a split, dry English muffin and a white ceramic cup of cut fruit from a can. Across from her, Helen's already wrist-deep in a gargantuan pile of pancakes smothered in chocolate sauce and whipped cream—revolting—and on Vance's plate, two fried eggs and some limp-looking bacon float in a pool of orange-tinted grease. She pierces a pear cube with the tines of her fork.

Nobody says anything for what feels like a long time. At some point she looks up and the man from the bathroom is steering his elderly mother past their table by the elbow. She's afraid he's going to stop and start talking again but, touching the brim of his baseball cap, all he says is "Bon appétit."

"Who was that?" Vance asks once he's gone.

"Some electrician, I guess? He thought you were Craig. I think he might be senile. You two don't even look alike anymore, Craig's so fat."

"That's not nice."

"Sometimes the truth isn't."

"All right," Vance says, reaching for a wicker basket of butters and jams, which he sets beside her plate. "Your muffin must be cold."

She says it's fine.

"You have to eat something."

"Says who?"

He raises an eyebrow but doesn't say more.

She stands up. "I think I'm going to walk home."

Vance looks surprised. "Pardon?"

"You have to take Helen to Dad's office, and I could use the exercise."

He says, "But it's pouring out."

"I don't care. I've been totally cooped up in the house. Thanks for breakfast."

"Just hold on a minute, okay? You haven't even touched your food," he says, scanning the room a little frantically for Sybil.

"I'm touching my food. Look," Helen says. And she is; she's dragging a strip of bacon through the liquefied whipped cream on her plate, then holding it up to her face. "Look, it's a mustache. I'm Yosemite Sam."

"You're a pig is what you are," Amanda says, and starts to go.

Vance frowns, motioning again for her to sit. "Please, honey. You don't even have a coat. You'll freeze."

"I just spent two and a half months on a glacier, hello."

"Everything all right over here?"

Sybil.

"Everything's great," Vance says.

"Are we still working, or should I clear?"

Vance says they're finished, they'll take the check.

"Don't forget about the party," Sybil says to Amanda before she goes.

Amanda starts to walk away but Vance catches her sleeve. He fishes the car keys out of his jeans pocket and hands them to her. "We'll be ready in two minutes, okay? Just wait in the Frog."

She takes the keys. They're on an orange nylon lanyard advertising a motorboat brand. She can feel Vance's eyes on her back as she crosses the dining room. She throws her shoulder against the heavy wooden door, pushes, and steps into the rain.

Her sweater is soaked, her pants too, but she doesn't care; she feels as good as she has in weeks, partly because she's by herself and mostly because she's free. She wasn't lying about being cooped up. Ever since she got home, Craig's been treating her like a prisoner: she isn't allowed to drive or see friends, and he's always casting not-so-clandestine looks over her shoulder at her computer screen and her phone. It's almost comical. Like, what is he worried is going to happen at this point?

She walks briskly through the downpour. She wants to get as far away from the Main Sail as possible before Vance realizes she's gone, and besides, it feels good to move her legs, to get her heart pumping. She follows Beach Road east, toward the ocean, passing by a strip of boarded-up storefronts—Dino's Pizza, the Seaside Scoop, Brandy's

Beach Grill—past Hancock Pond, where she learned to swim (and where Craig and Vance did also, so she's heard countless times), and finally past one of the marinas, its parking lot packed with bright white shrink-wrapped boats. (Her father doesn't keep his boats there. It's his policy never to pay a third party to perform a service he believes he can do as well or better himself, so he keeps his boats—a Whaler, a Sunfish, and a twenty-five-foot day-sailer he hasn't taken out in years—under green tarps in the gravel lot behind the offices of Lake Design Build.)

After the marina, the sidewalk ends, so she switches to the shoulder, which is narrow and consequently not very safe, especially with the rain. The traffic this morning is minimal, though, compared to summer, when between the lead-footed vacationers and the landscaping trucks, you basically take your life in your hands going for a jog.

She's walked half a mile or so when she feels her phone buzz in the back pocket of her jeans. Like it does every time, her heart flutters: could it be him? She ducks under the awning of a vacation rentals office, takes the phone out, and checks the screen. No, it could not. It's a number she doesn't recognize, though the area code is local, 508. She swallows her disappointment, like every other time, and touches Decline.

For a few minutes she just stands there, numb, watching the rain run off the awning and looking vaguely into the cemetery across the street.

Eventually she looks back up the road, in the direction of the restaurant. They'll have paid by now, and they're probably outside. Vance will have found the keys, and he's probably pissed—or he should be, though it's possible, even likely, that he's not. He never actually gets angry with her, is the truth, never raises his voice or really reprimands her, even when she deserves it. Yet another example of how different he is from her dad.

Before leaving the shelter of the awning, she takes her earbuds out of her back pocket, plugs them into the phone, and puts on "San Diego Serenade" by Tom Waits. It's one of the songs Christian played for her that first day in the tent. Unlike her and the rest of the students, he, as a leader-in-training, was allowed to bring his phone into the field —ostensibly for safety reasons—but he wasn't supposed to use it, was supposed to be saving his battery for emergencies. But Lucas and Nan, the co-leaders, had a portable charger, he told her, and besides, this *was* an emergency—"a music emergency," he said, grinning and fitting one of his earbuds into her ear. He was obsessed with Tom Waits, he told her; he couldn't believe she'd never listened to him before, and he played song after song for her, watching her face, charting her reaction to each one. Christian had dark brown eyes and freckles and shaggy, dark brown hair; she'd thought he was handsome when she'd first met him, at the base camp—all the girls on the trip had—but that first day in the tent made her realize his looks were nothing compared to how kind and compassionate and brilliant he was.

Stop it, she thinks now. She needs to stop *thinking* about him, all it does is make her depressed. He lives a million miles away, on a different *continent*, for Christ's sake, and besides, it's been almost two weeks and he hasn't emailed, hasn't texted, hasn't called. He doesn't care about her, that's clear enough. She shakes her iPhone to change the song. The Pogues come on, their rendition of "The Wild Rover," which is better; it reminds her of summers when she was small, of being out at the camp, when her mom was still alive; of Vance and her dad and mom all singing together (almost impossible to imagine these days—Craig and Vance actually doing anything together besides arguing—but it's true). They'd be gathered around a driftwood bonfire, the four of them and whatever woman Vance was dating at the time, Amanda nestled securely between her parents or the brothers. They'd sing "Blackbird" and "Bridge over Troubled Water" and "500 Miles," plus a slew of old Irish songs, "Whiskey in the Jar," "Fields of Athenry," and her favorite, "Black Velvet Band," her parents singing, Vance playing guitar. Her mom had a high, clear voice that perfectly complemented her dad's, which is lower and a little husky—or so she imagines it still is. She hasn't heard him sing in years.

She looks up the road. The Frog will be approaching soon. She checks once more for oncoming traffic before jogging across the road and up the hill, through the cemetery's open gates.

It's a huge cemetery, and old, one of the oldest on the Cape, which means one of the oldest in the country—some of the graves go back more than three hundred years. Even so, plenty of the names are ones she recognizes—Luther, Dennis, Aubry, Crowley, May. They belong to families who still live here today, kids from her school. (Her former school? She's still supposed to get her diploma from there, or that was the plan. She has no idea what will happen now.)

A wide paved road leads up the hill to the cemetery, then splinters into six or seven narrower paths. The one she selects veers off to the left, and she follows it steeply upward, toward the knoll, the highest point in town. At first she feels good, climbing; her legs feel strong and so do her lungs, and as it tends to when she's exerting herself physically, her mind feels blissfully clear. But halfway up, just like that, she's winded. She has to stop and lean her hands on her thighs to catch her breath, and as soon as she does, thoughts rush into her head; it all comes flooding back. *Fuck,* she thinks.

Sitting on a wet stone bench, she looks around. She's in one of the oldest sections, and most of the stones have been worn smooth. Some are cracked or have fallen over, and almost all of them are spotted with apricot-colored lichen and black-green moss. She squats in front of a miniature stone. According to the inscription, Infant Crocker was born on May 9, 1726, and lived all of eleven days.

She stands up, but instead of returning to the path, she climbs, slowly, to the top of the knoll and then veers east, left, to the edge of the woods, where patches of old snow linger amid bare brambles now, but where in summer wild raspberries grow. She knows this because Kevin showed them to her—the raspberry bushes—calling them his secret stash. That was when he first brought her up here: it was the summer after her sophomore year, she was sixteen, and they'd just started going out. She wasn't allowed to date yet, so she'd told her father she was sailing with Hadley Marcus's family, and when she got home she'd had to make up a second set of lies to explain the dark stains on her fingertips and under her nails.

She follows the brambles over the crest of the knoll, thinking now about Kevin. She heard, thirdhand, that he was on a surfing trip in Costa Rica with his dad, and she imagines him suntanned and lean, charming the surfer chicks. She wonders if he ever thinks about her—about them—anymore. Surely not as often as she does about him. That was one of the things that was so amazing about being so far away, in a completely new place: nothing reminded her of him. Now that she's back, though, everything does—places they went, things they did. It sucks, and it isn't fair. He gets to be away at college and wherever else (Costa Rica), around new people, seeing new places, doing new things, and she's stuck here. What makes it even worse is that, in a way, all of this, everything that's happening to her, is his fault—maybe indirectly, but if he hadn't dumped her, if she hadn't been such a wreck last fall, she wouldn't have gotten in trouble, she wouldn't have gone to Chile, and she wouldn't be in the shit-ball situation she's in now. She'd be a second-semester senior, getting ready to go to Dartmouth and basically goofing off, enjoying life, like her friends.

She's maybe fifty yards down the other side of the knoll, and she stops. Here the gravestones are newer, with clear inscriptions and still-sharp edges, their faces polished and free of moss. Some are decorated with American flags or Christmas wreaths or plastic flower bouquets, and she recognizes more of the names: Willard, Bryant, Goodson, Hugh. It's just about the highest point in the cemetery, and on a clear day, if you stand on a stone bench dedicated to someone named Arthur Meade, you can see the ocean. Kevin showed her this, too. She climbs up and looks east, but today there's nothing to see but clouds. Climbing down, she finds herself hoping he and Dov had shitty weather, or no waves, or at least he got stung by a jellyfish. It's petty, but she can't help it; she wants him to hurt.

The rain is still falling steadily and the wind's picked up; she's shivering a little, but she isn't thinking of going home. She keeps moving, the soaked sod springy under the soles of her boots. By the time she reaches her destination, at the top of a second, smaller rise, her fingers have gone numb, but she doesn't mind. Truth is, she welcomes the discomfort, the pain. She deserves it—and secretly she hopes she gets sick, really sick, like with pneumonia. Maybe that would be enough to bring this disaster to an end.

She sits on a marble bench in front of her mother's stone and crosses her legs under her. The stone displays her full name, Suzanne Lacey Carrollton Lake, *Beloved Mother, Daughter, Sister, Wife,* and 1973–2005. It was a freak accident, what happened. She was scuba-diving in Belize with Craig, she swam to the surface too fast, and air bubbles got into her brain. She went into a coma, which she stayed in for almost two months, and then she died. Amanda was down in DC when it happened, staying with Vance while her parents traveled, and though it was ten years ago, more than half her life, she clearly remembers the sound of the phone ringing in the middle of the night, and the shell-shocked look on Vance's face when he sat on the edge of her bed.

She'd come up here with the vague notion of talking to her mom (which she sometimes does, when a certain mood strikes), asking her what she should do, but today she finds herself tongue-tied. Staring at the cold, gray face of the stone, she wonders, as she has so many times before, if her mother is watching over her from somewhere. She hopes so, because if she isn't, if her mother is nothing but fading memories and crumbling bones, then Amanda really is all alone.

Except she's not alone, not exactly. Without wanting to, she starts thinking about the thing inside her. *The Thing*—that's how she thinks of it, when she does. Once, late one night right after she got home, she made the mistake of visiting a website, one of the myriad that apparently exist, sites that purport to offer helpful information but really are just selling stuff. It was appalling, anyway, not just the blatant commercialism—the indefatigable banners and pop-up ads hawking everything from monogrammed diaper bags to breast pumps to video monitors to stretch-mark cream—but the tone. This particular site, the one she made the mistake of visiting, called The Thing "your baby" incessantly; it displayed pictures of tiny, pink, thumb-sucking gnome things that couldn't possibly be anatomically correct; it compared the size, week to week, to food—always something benign and jaunty, generally fruit: *Your baby* (it just wouldn't quit with that word) *is the size of a blueberry!* Or, *a walnut!* Or, *a small fig!* And later, an avocado, a grapefruit, a cantaloupe, and on and on. Never a maggot or a millipede or a cockroach or a mouse, all of which were much closer, biologically speaking, to what The Thing actually is. But no, she'd thought then, that isn't right either: it's a leech, a bloodsucker; a blind, deaf, parasitic worm that wouldn't survive six seconds outside its host. Like giardia. What if she'd gotten giardia on the trip? She'd go to the doctor, who would prescribe some medicine to eliminate it, The End.

Water permeates the seat of her pants; she can feel the stone slab on which she sits right through them, freezing cold against the backs of her thighs and her ass. She stands up and takes out her phone again. Nothing from him—and there isn't going to be anything, she tells herself once more. *He isn't going to come to your rescue. No one is. You're on your own.* This isn't necessarily bad news, she tells herself. Indeed, viewed in that light, it's liberating. It means she's the master of her own fate. It means she can—she must—*act.*

She stops the song that's been playing—"Hallelujah" by Leonard Cohen, another one of Christian's picks—and moves the audio file to the trash. Then she listens to the voice message from the local number that called before. It's Sybil. She says she's been freaking out, worried she blew it by mentioning the party in front of Vance. Noah will murder her, she says, if Vance narcs them out. She sounds like she's about to cry. Amanda thinks, *Get a life.* She's about to delete the message when she changes her mind.

With the tip of her frozen index finger she punches out a text in reply: *I'll definitely be there tomw, woo-hoo!* she writes. *And ps. I promise, you don't need to worry about Vance.*

6

❦

"FOR SHIT'S SAKE," Vance says. He's standing outside the Main Sail, holding the lanyard in one hand and shielding his eyes from the rain with the other, turning east, then west, then north, then south.

Helen says, "April showers bring May flowers. What do May flowers bring?"

"Get in," he says, holding the Frog's door open for her and waiting while she climbs into the back. He tells himself not to be angry with Helen for taking so goddamn long in the bathroom; it's not her fault Amanda is gone—it's his. How could he have been so stupid? He gets into the driver's seat and tells Helen to buckle up. Glancing in the rearview mirror, he sees she's fastening the strap of her riding helmet under her chin. "I mean your seatbelt," he says. "I hope that's not an expression of your confidence in my driving."

He turns the key in the ignition. The engine sparks and turns over but doesn't catch. He tries again but it doesn't even turn over, and he decides to give it a few seconds to rest. While he waits, he wonders whether Amanda sabotaged the engine somehow, but he knows the true culprit is Craig. He's supposed to be taking care of the Frog—getting it regular tune-ups, multipoint inspections, changing the oil; at a bare minimum he's supposed to be driving it around town once a week to keep the battery charged.

"If you get in a car crash and you have to pee, your bladder explodes and you die," Helen says.

"Let me guess, Amanda told you that?" He turns the key again. This time the engine revs.

He pulls out of the parking lot onto Main Street, looking east and west but seeing no sign of her. The wind has picked up and the rain is really coming down now, sliding down the windshield in sheets, and he sets the wipers to the highest speed. She must be soaking wet. He wishes he'd at least had the chance to give her his coat.

He heads west, toward Craig's office, figuring once he divests himself of Helen he can embark on a serious search. He imagines he'll find her on Herring Run or maybe on Maple, halfway between the Main Sail and the house. She'll climb in and he'll take her to the Gull, or maybe Francie's, for hot chocolate with two squirts of almond syrup, and she'll talk to him, tell him whatever it is she's done. He'll tell her it's okay and offer her some insight, maybe a story or two about what a fuck-up he was when he was young, and by the time they're finished the cocoa, she'll be the niece he knows.

The windshield is fogging up. He reaches for the defroster and turns the knob, but nothing happens. He flips it back and forth a few times, then leaves it on high and holds his hand over the register: no air is coming out. Silently cursing Craig, he tugs his sleeve down over his hand and clears a patch of glass. How many weeks has it been sitting, he wonders, idle and damp in Craig's cold garage? You can't let a vehicle, especially a vintage one like the Frog, just sit. It's not like Craig doesn't know. Vance wonders if he's started it even once since the fall, but he knows it's likely he hasn't. He doesn't give a shit about its welfare — a discouraging development in its own right, but also a symptom, Vance knows, of a far more troubling disease: that Craig's basically lost interest in — he's forsaken — the camp, Land's End. When they'd talked about it at Thanksgiving, Craig had actually suggested they tear it down. "It's a liability, nothing more, at this point" were his exact words. Vance couldn't believe what he was hearing. Tear down Land's End? If there were a place on earth that stood for their youth, and for their fraternal bond, the very best of it, it would be there—where they'd spent some of their happiest child-hood days, where they'd been boys together, where they'd learned to gut fish and build fires and chart the stars. Where they'd brought their friends, and their girlfriends—where they first got drunk, and smoked weed, and did plenty of other new, exciting things. (Vance lost his virginity there, and he's pretty sure Craig did too.) That af-ternoon, in the interest of decorum, Vance had bitten his tongue. But it confounded him then, and does still: how can this hard-hearted, unsentimental, impenetrable being possibly be made of the exact same stuff he is, cell for cell?

He tries the stereo next, and is relieved when music begins to play —Springsteen, of course—the opening chords of "Human Touch." Craig listens almost exclusively to Bruce Springsteen, it's been that way for as long as Vance can remember, at least since they were nine or ten. It's a little extreme, comparable to eating only white food or wear-ing only blue clothes, but that's Craig, all or nothing, and Vance has had a lot of time to get used to it, and he doesn't have a problem with the Boss per se. This particular morning, though, he isn't in the mood to listen to Craig's music, and he turns the stereo off.

Scanning the sidewalks for Amanda, he follows Main Street through town, which, save for the various church parking lots, is more or less deserted at this hour, this time of year. At the intersection of Routes 139 and 6, he makes a right, then a left, pulling into the driveway of number 63, a yellow-painted Victorian on a quarter-acre, which serves as the official headquarters of Craig's company, Lake Design Build, LLC.

He leans over the passenger seat and opens the door for Helen, who climbs out, shoulders her purple backpack, follows the brick path up to the black-painted door, and rings the bell. While she waits, Vance looks around.

Since he was last here, back in the fall, the office—much like Craig's house—has gotten a thorough overhaul: new paint everywhere, some high-end landscaping, and a spanking-new sign out front bearing the same logo as his coffee mugs: a bright blue wave cresting over the words *Lake Design Build, Bringing You Home Since 1998.* Vance shifts in his seat. For someone who complains about money as much as his brother does, he certainly appears to be flush.

He lets his gaze drift across the road, to the Old Jailer's Pub and Jayne's Sloppy Seconds and Two Healing Hands: nothing new here. His eyes migrate to the water; it's leaden gray today, mottled with white chop. Even so, and despite the deluge, a couple of hardy souls in waders—a man and a woman, if he had to guess—stand thigh-deep in the saltwater, dragging rakes through the muck. Their dad used to clam. When they were kids, Vance and Craig would follow him down to the marsh and watch while he filled a wire bucket. They'd tussle over who got to haul it over the dunes, back to the camp, where Frank would steam the clams in a pot with garlic and linguica sausage and a can of Narragansett beer.

A gust of wind throws rain against the windshield, and his thoughts return to the present. To Amanda. She's got to be frozen solid by now. He hates the idea of her out there, wandering around. He looks up at the porch. What the hell is taking Craig so long?

He rolls down his window and shouts, "Did you ring the bell?" Helen nods. "Is it working?" She nods. "Well, ring it again." For Christ's sake, he thinks, picking up his phone and dialing his brother. It goes straight to voicemail. He's turned it off, the bastard. "Hey, we're out in front, open up," he says. To Helen, he shouts, "Can you see in?"

She shields her eyes and peers through the glass, then turns and faces him. "It's just dark," she shouts back.

He peers behind the house, into the gravel lot where Craig parks, but there's no sign of his truck. He calls out to Helen again, asking if she knows how to get to the stables where her riding lessons are. She nods, and he tells her to get in.

She guides him back into the center of town. The church parking lot has emptied, and a small crowd is assembled on the grass in front of the Odd Fellows Hall, where a rummage sale is under way, people in rain gear parsing miscellany under a dripping white tent.

"That's where my recital is," Helen says. "It's Wednesday night. Will you come?"

"We'll see," he says (how right Amanda was, after all, that it's grownup for "no"), continuing through town toward the bay. He keeps his eyes peeled for Amanda, though he can't imagine a scenario in which she'd be way the hell over here. Even so, when they cross over the highway and he spots a woman walking on the shoulder, he slows down. But it isn't Amanda, he sees as they approach; it's one of the women from the Jesus commune, or so he assumes, based on the full, ankle-length skirt she wears under her coat.

"Are we close?" he asks Helen, who says, "How does a pig go to the hospital?" Before he can answer, she says, "In a *ham*bulance. Get it?"

They're close to Seal Harbor now; it's low tide, and he can see the expanse of sand flats through the trees. He knows this area well—extremely well. It's where his high school girlfriend, Dylan, used to live.

He glances at his watch: a few minutes after ten. "What time's your lesson?" he asks. In the mirror he sees Helen's cheeks are puffed out and her face is red. He asks if she's okay.

She nods vigorously and points off to the right, at an old graveyard. When they've passed by, she exhales.

He says, "I asked what time your lesson was. Gina didn't say."

She's looking out the window, and she only shrugs. He doesn't ask again. If she wants to keep quiet for the rest of the ride, he's not about to object.

They're very close to Dylan's old house, and despite the decades that have passed since he saw her last, he feels a little surge, like the ghost of all the anticipation he used to feel. They go by the Captain Crowley Inn, which is supposed to be haunted by the ghosts of murdered prostitutes. After the cranberry bog, they pass a cedar-shingled saltbox with a magenta door, bunting in the windows, and a banner welcoming home someone named Alexander. At the very next house, Helen says, "Here."

"It can't be," Vance says, turning in his seat. "Are you sure?"

She is.

His skin prickles under his collar and his fingers feel damp on the wheel as he guides the Frog onto the driveway that was once oyster shells but has since—sometime in those intervening decades—been paved. Cutting the engine, he says, "Are you getting out?"

She does, gathering her things. Watching her approach the house, he tells himself how silly he's being, getting so worked up. Ten different families have probably lived here since the van Dornes did.

And that's when he notices the sign in front: "Salt Meadow Stables and Vet." So it has been sold, after all. Twenty—no, twenty-three—years have passed. And why is he so agitated, anyway? Twenty-three years is nearly a quarter of a century, more than a quarter of a life, more than half of his. What happened twenty-three years ago may as well not have happened at all.

On the concrete stoop, Helen rings the bell. He watches. It all seems a little surreal: how many times did he stand there, on that very stoop, ringing that very bell? (Or, more often than not, he'd forgo the bell. Most nights he avoided the front door altogether, leaning his bike against the dilapidated old barn and tossing handfuls of oyster shell shards at Dylan's window until a light came on. She'd lift the sash, smiling, raising a finger to her lips, and climb out, a thick wool sweater over her nightgown if it was cold.)

But that was ages ago, he reminds himself. He and Dylan haven't been in touch for eons—since August 6, 1989, to be exact—and while he regrets that (and pretty much every single thing about how things ended between them), he learned a long time ago that thinking about it—about her—only causes him pain, and in the interest of self-preservation, he's done his best to keep her out of his thoughts.

On occasion, though, he does wonder. He can't help it; she'll appear in his dreams, she'll ambush him, and her presence will be so vivid, it takes several minutes, upon waking, to convince himself that the visitation wasn't real. Then, once he does, he'll feel heartbroken all over again, aching for her in a visceral way, like he's wrapped in a cloak of shame and melancholy that lingers, sometimes, for days.

There's really no reason, he always reminds himself, to be so morose. Somewhere along the line he heard she'd moved to Arizona, or maybe it was New Mexico, some desert place, married a physician, or maybe it was a physicist, and had kids. In other words, she's done just fine. Hell, by most people's measures, it sounds like she's done a whole lot better than him.

Helen is about to ring the bell again when a figure appears behind the storm door. As the figure—a woman's, tall and a little top-heavy, with dyed, ruby-red hair—takes shape, Vance's mouth goes dry. He knows that figure; it's Carolyn van Dorne. It's Dylan's mom. He can't believe she's still here. Is it even possible? In his head he does the math: she'd be close to seventy by now. He squints through the windshield. Maybe it's the fogged glass, but aside from a few extra pounds around the middle, she looks exactly the same as she did then—it's uncanny. She wears a lime-green tracksuit and stands with a hand resting on Helen's shoulder, telling her something, and Helen turns and looks at Vance, who rolls the window halfway down and sticks his hand out to wave, hoping she'll assume he's Craig, which apparently she does. Even so, his hand trembles as he pulls it back in. His insides feel liquefied. He watches Carolyn van Dorne close the storm door. For some reason, Helen's coming back.

"Did you forget something?" he says, doing his best to feign composure.

"Riding's canceled. The ring's too muddy."

He glances at the house. "She's just deciding now?"

"She said she left a message."

He looks at Helen; she's getting drenched. "I'm sure she did. You better get in," he says, and when she's settled again in the back, he turns the key in the ignition. But this time nothing happens—nothing at all. Not a groan, not a spark. He tries again, in vain.

Helen says, "What's wrong?"

Vance says, "You can ask your goddamn dad."

Mrs. van Dorne is watching them from behind the storm door, he can tell. He says a silent prayer and turns the key once more.

"Motherfucker," he says, when nothing happens. Behind the glass, Mrs. van Dorne pulls on a pair of muck boots and a yellow slicker and steps onto the stoop, where she flips up the hood and shouts something Vance can't hear. He rolls down the window and says, "What was that?" but she's already heading down the path.

She's perhaps twenty feet away when she says, "Hello, Craig. I said, it looks like you need a jump."

She's coming closer, and he can feel his face reddening as he says, "I'm sorry to startle you, Mrs. van Dorne, but I'm not Craig."

She stops abruptly just a few feet from the Frog. Something resembling a smile plays for a moment on her lips, then disappears. Removing the hood of her raincoat, she says, "And I'm sorry to startle *you*, but I'm not Mrs. van Dorne."

7

❧

THE CUT ON CRAIG'S FOREHEAD is a couple of inches long and very neat, as if the skin simply parted on impact with the board. In the bathroom at Lake Design Build, sometime after eleven, he splashes water on it to flush away any leftover sand, which is hard to see because of the blood, which is still flowing. When it's as clean as it's going to get, he leans closer to the mirror and dabs at the cut with a peroxide-soaked cotton pad and watches it foam. It stings like hell, but he deserves that, it's an idiot tax, he thinks, gritting his teeth and holding on to the side of the sink.

Once the foam subsides, he gets a couple of the butterfly bandages from the office first-aid kit and does his best to close the wound. Best-case scenario, he's going to have a scar. He just hopes he doesn't wind up with an infection. He read recently about a local kid who scraped his toe on a rock in his yard and ended up in the hospital with anti-biotic-resistant staph. That's all he needs. The way things are going, though, it's probably about what he should expect.

He leans in again and gently pats the dressing. Blood is soaking through the bandage's pad. He could probably use a few stitches. He considers going to the hospital, but it's twenty-eight miles away, and all they'll do, realistically, is make him wait forever, then charge him a fortune for a couple of bandages and some thread. Plus they'll probably insist he submit to a battery of expensive, unnecessary tests.

He steps away from the mirror. He could drive himself over to the fire station, which is only a mile, and let one of the EMTs stitch him up. But does he really want to explain to them what happened? Take all the shit they're practically duty-bound to give him? Worse, one of the guys will undoubtedly ask him how things are going—how Amanda's doing, in particular (they know her from the previous summer, when she was a youth volunteer)—and he'll have to lie, which he dislikes even more than unnecessary tests.

In the first-aid kit, which sits open on the toilet tank, he finds the gauze pads, folds one into a thick square, and tapes it tightly over the Band-Aid, which seems to do the trick, at least for the time being. In the galley kitchen he puts the kit back under the sink, washes his hands, and, though he isn't hungry, opens the refrigerator. The pickings, as usual, are slim: Diet Coke, a carton from the Lucky Panda, a few key-lime-flavored Yoplaits. No beer. It's not noon yet, but he could use one. In the freezer he finds a couple of cold packs, one of which he applies to his head, and some vodka that, according to the label, tastes like birthday cake. He's not that hard-up. He closes the freezer and goes back to the fridge for the Lucky Panda carton, which contains noodles in a viscous brown sauce with shreds of what he guesses is pork. He lifts it to his nose and sniffs. It doesn't smell great, but he feels hungry suddenly, or at least he feels a strong compulsion to eat. He considers nuking it, but instead gets a fork from the dish rack and carries the carton into his office, where he sits behind his desk and digs in.

The noodles are soggy and taste like salt and not much else, but he eats them, all of them, and when he's finished he goes back into the kitchen for a Diet Coke, which he drinks in a few gulps, standing in front of the stove.

Back at his desk, he turns on his computer, opens his calendar, and tries to focus on the week ahead. Since Amanda came home, he's been falling behind, neglecting things, which is no way to run a business— it's sure as hell not how he built LDB up from scratch. He double-clicks on tomorrow, Monday: he's supposed to be in Boston, meeting with his old friend and fraternity brother Marco. It nearly slipped his mind—that's how distracted he's been. Marco's hiring Craig to build his family a house on Nantucket; it's a big job and, knowing Marco and Maureen, likely to get bigger, a veritable godsend considering the state LDB's finances are in.

He opens up a file called, absurdly, "McElroy Paint Schedule" with a password only he knows, and for a long moment stares at the numbers—with which he's already depressingly familiar—on the screen. To say he's been "falling behind" is, indeed, a gross understatement. What he is, is in a hole, a deep one—$259,000 deep, plus interest, to be exact. That's how much the renovation cost, 150 percent more than they'd planned. He'd like to say he doesn't know where it all went, but he can't. With more than a little shame, he thinks of the vaulted ceilings, the wide-plank floors, the commercial-grade appliances, the Italian marble countertops, the hand-painted ceramic tiles—silly things, things they couldn't afford, things they certainly didn't need, and yet, by some deeply flawed decision-making, things they decided they couldn't—or shouldn't—live without. He's seen it happen before, so many times, to other people: watched seemingly reasonable clients sashay down the very same pernicious path. But he, of all people, should have known. He's responsible, he's circumspect, and most important, he's in the business. Somehow, though, here he is.

He looks once more at the spreadsheet before closing the file and returning to his calendar. The meeting with Marco, that's what he needs to focus on—Marco's house. Between that and Dov's restaurant, he'll at least have a chance. He thinks about Marco. He hasn't seen his friend for a while, and he's looking forward to it—and honestly, to getting away. He's reserved a hotel room in the North End, and once they get business out of the way, he'll take Marco out for drinks. He might even tell him what's going on at home. He hasn't told anyone—not Dov, in whom he'd usually confide, and surely not Vance. Gina insists it's not healthy keeping things so bottled up, and she's probably right, but he just can't do it. Dov's too bitter—he's been such a wild card since his divorce from Lorna, Craig doubts he would understand. (Plus there's the issue of Kevin; Amanda would hate Craig twice as much, if that's possible, if Kevin found out.) And Vance, well—Vance is Vance.

The last thing Craig needs is his brother taking Amanda's side, which he almost certainly would.

Marco's different, though; he'll get it. Craig can practically see the two of them, sipping expensive scotch in some dark, swanky bar Marco frequents, Craig unburdening himself while Marco listens carefully, nodding his head. Unlike Gina—and Amanda—he'll understand the awful position Craig's in. And he'll have Craig's back. He's a family man, too, and a brother, after all—a Sig Alph—which, as they used to say in college, means more than blood.

He picks up the earth ball that resides on his desk, sits back, and swivels around to face the street. He can see the cove from his chair, just glimpses in the summer, but now, with all the branches bare, he can see all the way out to the break. He squeezes the ball—which is composed of rubbery foam and supposed to reduce his stress—once, then again, harder, watching whitecaps on the water rise and disappear.

After a few minutes or so, his phone buzzes: Gina. She'll want something from him, something to do with the kids. He lets it go. A badge pops up, telling him she left a message, but he doesn't listen to it. He hasn't listened to the one Vance left earlier either. The only person in the world he wants to hear from at this moment is Amanda, and she's probably the least likely person to call. She won't even look him in the face these days unless it's to say something cruel.

He swivels back around, opens the bottom right drawer of his desk, and pulls out the small framed photo he keeps in there, not hidden exactly, but he doesn't feel entirely comfortable putting it on display. It's of Amanda and Suzanne, taken years ago. They're out at the camp, at the little crescent-shaped sandy beach on the marsh—the baby beach, they always called it—wading in water that hits Amanda's hips, Suzanne's shins. Amanda couldn't have been more than two or three—she's brown and naked and holding her mother's hand. And Suzanne: in a crocheted bikini and one of the floppy, wide-brimmed hats she always wore, she looks so glamorous, and so young. He misses her so much, suddenly, it's like he's been punched in the chest. He misses her more than he has in a long time, maybe years, which makes him feel guilty. Shouldn't he miss her just as much when things are going well?

He brings the photo closer to his face, so close the images cease to be images, and he studies the thousands of tiny, diffuse dots that make them up. This is what Suzanne is now, it occurs to him, a diffuse collection of dots.

She'd surely object. She was religious, a devoted Catholic who believed wholeheartedly in the Father and the Son, in the Virgin, in the Resurrection, in Heaven and Hell, and that death is a beginning, not an end. And though it's not how he was raised, he tried, especially in the beginning, right after she died, to believe *something*—to have some modicum of faith. If literal Heaven was a stretch, then at least in the notion that her soul, or whatever you wanted to call it, carried on. That she was somewhere peaceful, in other words, watching over them, looking down. How desperately he wanted to believe that back then, and how guilty he felt that he never quite did. (Ultimately it was meeting Gina—and not faith—that helped him move through the grief.) But this morning he finds himself hoping Suzanne was wrong about all of it—that gone is just gone—because he can't bear the thought of her knowing, in any capacity, what a terrible job he's done.

Closing his eyes, he squeezes the ball again and thinks back to before, to so long ago, when she was here on earth, when she was flesh and bone. Back in high school, when they first knew each other, she had long blond hair, like Amanda's, and the same dark blue eyes and long fawn legs. But she wasn't like Amanda; she radiated something—gentleness, goodness, or maybe just peace. They didn't date then, he admired her from afar like everybody else. It wasn't until the summer after they graduated that he got up the courage to ask her out. She said yes, and he took her to the Wellfleet Drive-In, then to a bonfire on the beach. That first night, he knew he was finished. He'll never forget standing across from her, watching the firelight dance on her face.

Jesus, how he misses her: so powerfully it's like a force of nature, gravity or an ocean current, something immense and invisible pulling him down.

Sitting up, though, he tells himself to cut it out. He has no right, he reminds himself, to miss her, to mourn, to feel sorry for himself because she's not here. It's his fault she's not, after all. They can tell him he's wrong, everyone can—they can say "accidents happen" until they run out of air, but he knows the truth, and they all do too.

He's still holding the ball. He raises it to his temple and presses it, hard, against the cut. It hurts, but not nearly enough, so he presses harder, but it's never going to hurt enough, it can't. He opens his eyes and puts it, along with the photograph, back in the drawer.

8

THE STORE, Cottage, occupies the ground floor of an 1830s carriage house, which is tucked between the post office and an upscale new wine shop on Main Street. With its cedar shingles, cerulean-blue trim, and egg-yolk-yellow door, the vibe it conveys—Gina hopes—is equal parts stylish and quaint.

Inside, the scales tip toward quaint, or they did, with the ancient woodstove in the corner, the slightly sloped pine floors, the original leaded glass windowpanes, and the smell of must and old wood smoke that lingers no matter what remedies Gina employs.

"God, it's intense today," she says, stepping inside and wrinkling her nose, setting Cameron's car seat down beside the jewelry case. "Is it getting worse, or is it me?"

Two-plus years ago, when she took over the lease, she scrubbed the place top to bottom, strung up lavender-scented sachets, painted the stove bubblegum pink, and put bright, modern colors on the walls—goldenrod, peach, aqua, teal—a palette that draws frequent compliments from customers, a few of whom have asked if she'll help select the colors for their homes.

Which is, in truth, the store's raison d'être. On the advice of a college friend turned executive coach, Gina persuaded Craig to back her, explaining that the store might not generate much income itself, but she only needed to snag a few private clients for her reputation as a designer to take hold. Her design business would grow, eventually eclipsing the retail, and ultimately they'd let the store peter out. She had no interest in retail, after all. She'd studied architecture as an undergrad and was still considering the grad program at MIT when she met Craig. But then she was moving to the Cape, then she was getting married—things she wanted, very much, too—and then there was Helen, and without Gina exactly deciding against it, the grad school window had closed. But that didn't mean she couldn't use her skills. She wanted to work—she *needed* to work, she told Craig, who was skeptical—then again, he's always skeptical, it's who he is, and he didn't say no, and the fall Helen started kindergarten, Cottage opened its doors.

And then, just ten days later, Gina learned she was pregnant with Cam, and things haven't gone according to plan. She's had a handful of design clients (mostly small jobs, none of which led to anything else), and to her great chagrin it's not her design business but the store, which sells quirky women's clothing and eclectic jewelry, plus wildly overpriced organic home goods and toys, that's taken off.

"It's the wet weather," Meghan says now. "It's like it pulls the past out of the walls. Do you want me to run to Duane's for some of those things you plug in?" She's standing in front of the register, looking way too chic for a Sunday, or really for any day on the Cape, in tall boots and a bamboo-print silk dress. She's got one hand resting on a canted hip, and she looks preternaturally fresh, which, while irritating, seems to be the case every morning, regardless of how little sleep she's gotten or what she's consumed.

"I hate breathing those chemicals," Gina says, "especially when all they do is mask the scent. Is the dehumidifier running?"

Meghan nods. "For an hour or so. Since I got in," she says, and Gina wonders if she's trying to drive home the point that she arrived before her, yet again. She comes out from behind the counter and squats in front of Cameron. "Hi there, handsome," she says, offering him her index finger, which he grabs, grinning gummily. "He gets cuter every day. I swear, I could just eat him up. What would you think of that, mister, getting eaten up?" Meghan's dress is one of theirs, Gina notices, and she's accessorized it with a wide, woven belt, which they also sell. If she makes Gina feel frumpy, at least she's a good advertisement for the store. She stands up. "I made coffee, if you want. It should still be hot."

Gina wonders whether this is another thinly veiled dig, then admonishes herself for being so petty: she should appreciate Meghan more. (She always seems to be telling herself this.) A junior at RISD, Meghan's taken the year off to be home with her sick mom—so not only is she overqualified to work here, she's strapped for cash, and largely without a social life, and thus available pretty much whenever Gina asks. And perhaps most relevant, she adores Cam. She told Gina during their interview about being an only child—how lonely she was growing up, how she loves babies, and how she plans, someday, to have a whole houseful of kids, and Gina can't say she didn't consider this, how hiring her would kill two birds with one stone, when she offered her the job.

"Would you watch him a second? I'll be right back," she says, removing her raincoat and carrying it into the back office, which they share. Quickly she scans the desk. She closes the store for a couple of weeks in March every year, to get the books in order and prepare for the upcoming season; the plan is to start on the taxes this morning, and she sees that Meghan has organized everything meticulously, separating orders from invoices, then separating each by month, then clearly labeling each stack, none of which Gina even considered instructing her to do.

She sets her purse down, hangs her coat on the back of the door, and takes a moment to check her reflection in the seashell-framed mirror over the desk. As usual, she's disappointed: her skin looks dull, her hair's a mess, and though she went to the considerable effort of washing her face with soap and changing out of her yoga pants, she still looks like she just rolled out of bed.

In front of the mirror, she tucks in her dryer-faded black top and smooths down her jeans. She looks so drab. The only touch of adornment anywhere on her person is the pair of 14-karat gold earrings that dangle from her ears, tiny gold birdcages with tinier gold birds inside.

They're antiques, and exquisite—worth real money, according to Heather, though Gina wouldn't sell them in a million years. They're one of the only things she has of her mom's, and she hardly ever takes them off. In her mind they've taken on a talismanic quality; it's a little loony, maybe, but when she's nervous or lonely or scared—the times she misses her mom most—she finds herself fingering them, asking whatever power resides within them for strength or protection or luck. Frowning at her reflection, she touches one, then the other, wishing she'd taken the six seconds it would have required to put on some blush.

Meghan's forest-green, fringed purse sits on the chair in the corner, and Gina is wondering whether there's a compact handy when she spots a gray hair sticking straight up from the crown of her head—*gray* being a euphemism, as it's really bright white. Wiry and short and oddly translucent, it's nothing like the rest of her hair, which has always been dark and sleek (the sole aspect of her appearance that, since Cameron, doesn't make her cringe). Leaning closer to the mirror, she pinches it between finger and thumb. She can almost hear her mother telling her not to pull it out, that it will come back with two friends, but she plucks it out anyway, inspects it up close, and frowns.

Which draws her scrutiny to her face again—the dark blotches, the sagginess around her jaw, the proliferating lines. When did this middle-aged woman's face become hers? She wonders how it looks to strangers—or, she can't help thinking, to him. Dov. He's constantly saying she's beautiful, but words come easily to him, she knows this—which makes it that much more pathetic, how greedily she eats them up. But *beautiful*—it's not a word she's heard often. *Pretty,* or *put-together,* or even *striking* once in a while, but she's never been the beautiful one. That was always her mother, who supposedly won the Pan Am flight attendants' beauty contest three years running, or her sister (Heather's the spitting image of Rosemarie, everyone says). And now of course it's Amanda. Ever since her stepdaughter was a little girl, people have been gushing over how gorgeous she is; it's no exaggeration to say that every person who comes in contact with her, or just sees a photo of her, feels compelled to comment. Not that they're wrong; Amanda is, inarguably, an extraordinarily attractive girl. Even now, in her baggy boys' clothes and with her unwashed hair, Amanda could easily grace the cover of any fashion magazine on the shelf. It's just how it is. Apparently it's Gina's destiny to live in close proximity to someone who makes her look plain.

She steps away from the mirror. She's had the thought—and not a kind one—that if Craig has his way, Amanda's looks will take a major hit, because no one, not even a stunning seventeen-year-old, comes through pregnancy completely unscathed. Thinking of Amanda, she takes her phone out of her purse. Rachel, her doctor friend, was supposed to call yesterday but didn't, and Gina hopes it's not a bad sign. Dov hasn't called again either, and neither has Craig. She tucks the phone away.

Sitting at the desk, she starts looking over Meghan's stacks, but it's hard to concentrate, and her thoughts wander—first, to Rachel. It's not too late to call her off—to call the whole plan off—but she can't do that. She won't. Amanda needs help, and Gina, of all people, seems to be the only one willing to give it. The fact that Craig might never forgive her—might well decide he doesn't want to be married to her anymore—is something she simply can't afford to think about. If she does, she'll lose her nerve for sure.

So instead she thinks of Dov. Silly Dov, calling her beautiful, making her blush. She should have put him off unequivocally, but she didn't. Why? Is she really so desperate, so starved for attention? Maybe so. She wonders whether he'll really show up. Like before, part of her hopes he does, and another part hopes she never sees or hears from him again.

That's unlikely, though. He's Craig's closest friend—or more accurately, his oldest: Dov, Craig, and Vance. Dov's family moved to the Cape from Israel, so the story goes, when he was eleven, into the house next door to the Lakes'. Dov's birthday, they discovered, was just four days after the twins', so they celebrated together that year and those that followed. They were a trio, the three of them, carpooling to and from school together, playing sports together, eating and sleeping at each other's houses, sharing clothes, money, music, cars. To hear Craig tell it, they were practically joined, three ways, at the hip.

But that was a long time ago—decades, she reminds herself—and history notwithstanding, Craig and Dov aren't particularly close anymore, at least not in any way she would call close. The truth is Craig isn't close to anyone, except maybe her, or so she's always assumed—though recently, with everything going on, that assumption is one she's begun, unhappily, to doubt. He won't talk to her about Amanda—he just *can't*, he says—and he's basically shut her, along with everyone else, out. He's suffering, blaming himself, she knows he is, and there's nothing she wants more than to help, but the harder she tries, the more violently he pushes her away.

She loves him, no question she does. But he doesn't always make it easy to be his wife. The irony is that at first his reserve—how self-sufficient he seemed—was one of the qualities that attracted her to him. He struck her as so strong, so self-contained. He didn't need to be coddled or taken care of like the men she'd been with before. But after a while—maybe when she was carrying Helen—she began to find herself feeling lonely and wishing that he needed her more. And God knows he's never said she's beautiful. "You look nice" is generally the most she'll get. When she's raised it, he says that giving compliments wasn't something he and Vance learned to do, growing up with just their dad. "Blame our Puritan roots," he jokes, but the truth is that even Vance has a way about him, a certain charm or attentiveness, that Craig lacks.

Not Dov, though; if she's starving, then he feeds her. This is the problem. When he calls her beautiful, she's sure she can feel the endorphins or oxytocin or whatever chemical it is exploding into her bloodstream. In nine and a half years with Craig, even back when they were first together, she's not sure she ever experienced that.

She looks in the mirror again, touches her neck. Her thoughts return, yet again, to that night—to the party at the Millikens'. Will and Adie are former clients of Craig's—he built them their house up in Winslow—but they're from Michigan originally, and she didn't expect to know anyone that night. But there he was—Dov—standing by the picture window, alone, when they came in.

"Small world," she said, and he said, "Small peninsula. You're looking luminous this evening," and kissed her cheek. She'd known him, through Craig, for a decade, and had liked him well enough (even if she'd told Craig more than once that his ego was way too big), but he'd been treating her differently—kissing her cheeks, using words like *luminous*—ever since his divorce. He was grateful for how they'd helped out with Kevin, she knew, and that's what she chalked his new attentiveness up to at first, gratitude. But all night at the party he was watching her. She could feel it, the weight of his gaze. And the thing was, it felt good. Really good. He never seemed to be more than a few steps away, smiling at her a little wickedly every time she looked up. She worried Craig would notice, but he'd disappeared; he was courting potential clients, most likely, maybe smoking cigars out by the fire pit, or else playing video games with the kids down in the rec room.

"Come here, I want to show you something," he whispered in her ear at some point, and without taking the time to think better of it, she let herself be led around a corner, through a door, and into the garage, where he put two fingers under her chin and kissed her with his eyes closed. She could smell alcohol on his breath, and garlic from the sausages they'd eaten. "Yes?" he said, and she nodded, feeling outside herself. That was really the only way to explain it—the way she felt when she was with him—as if she were a marionette and someone else, some greater power, was operating the strings. She didn't stop him when he kissed her again, or when he moved his hand from her shoulder down her back and pulled her hips toward his.

She looks up: is that the sound of a car pulling up out front? He couldn't be here this early, could he? She hurries over to Meghan's bag and finds a miniature plastic brush, which she runs through her hair. There's also a tube of lip gloss, and she dabs some on her mouth and cheeks.

When she goes outside, though, there's no car after all, and she feels simultaneously disappointed and relieved.

"I hope you don't mind," Meghan says. She's taken Cameron out of his parka and is holding him on her hip. "I couldn't resist these fat little legs. Just look at them."

Gina says, "He's all yours," and moves through the home furnishings and into the back section, where they display the women's clothes, which she buys from companies that treat their workers fairly, use as few chemicals as possible, and whose supply chains are sweatshop-free.

She shifts a few items between racks before moving into the toy section, where everything is wood or paper or cloth. It's amazing, she's discovered, the amount some people will pay for a toy they've been promised is petrochemical-free. Not that she blames them: they're just terrified—for themselves, for their kids, for the world they're passing on—and if spending eighty-seven dollars on a baby blanket made in Brooklyn of silk from worms fed on organic mulberry-leaf shoots makes them feel better, even temporarily, she's not going to complain.

She moves through the kids' section, then through jewelry, and finally to home goods, which puts her in front of the window display, which is new, and which she somehow didn't notice coming in.

This—decorating the window—is one of the responsibilities Meghan has taken on. It was her idea: in the same interview during which she spoke about her love for babies, she told Gina that she believed she'd been put on the earth to make beautiful things. "Creating something that didn't exist before, you know?" she said, and Gina nodded, but she didn't know, not really. A dirty little secret she's always carried—or maybe it's not so little—is that despite decades of referring to herself as a "creative" person, and years of working in a "creative" field, she's never actually created an original thing (her children, and the two scarves she's recently knitted, notwithstanding) in her life. As a little girl, she preferred coloring books where the images already existed and your job was to color inside the lines. And the shameful truth is that all she's ever done—her work as a student, then as a designer, and now running the store—is gather together things that already exist. A monkey could do it, she sometimes laments, or a properly programmed machine.

But Meghan is different—that other kind of person. An artist through and through. Her first day, she showed up with a cardboard box full of leaves she'd cut from swaths of autumn-colored, vintage cloth, and that weekend she made a tree trunk from driftwood she found on the beach and turned the window into a tableau—a piece of art, really —that people drove from all over town to see. After that she made a fairy-tale snowscape using old wedding veils she'd been collecting from curiosity shops; that made the local paper's front page. Now, for the past week or two, she's been arriving early and staying late, even coming in on Mondays and Tuesdays, when the store's closed and Gina isn't there. She works upstairs, in the bedroom of the carriage house, a space Gina was using for storage but where Meghan installed an old Singer sewing machine, the kind with a foot pedal, and a large craft table, which she's covered with her assorted supplies. Gina doesn't venture up there often—she doesn't keep tabs. Now, though, standing before the window, she can see how Meghan's been spending her time.

She's covered the floor with shimmery, emerald-green cloth—the grass—and she's dotted the driftwood tree's formerly bare branches with tiny, yellow-green buds. With eelgrass she's woven six or seven exquisite Easter baskets, each of which she's filled with brightly colored, papier-mâché eggs. Among the baskets, too, various papier-mâché animals roam: white and brown rabbits, yellow chicks, a lamb.

"My goodness," Gina says, feeling suddenly depressed.

Meghan joins her at the window, still holding Cam, who stares at the display, transfixed. "What do you think?" she asks, bouncing him gently on her hip. "I might redo the rabbits. They look a little evil. Something about the eyes."

"I wouldn't change a thing," Gina says. Maybe it's what the window represents—the creative energy Meghan has, or maybe all the energy she has in general, while Gina can barely drag herself out of bed, or maybe it's simply Meghan herself, how earnest she is about everything, how without guile, how full of hope. Whatever the reason, there are times, like now, when Gina finds herself hesitating, withholding the commendation she knows Meghan so clearly desires—and deserves. She wishes she weren't so stingy. Meghan's still basically a child, she reminds herself, and her mom is ill. "It's terrific, really," she says, at the same moment the store's phone begins to ring.

Meghan goes to answer it, so Gina's alone by the window when a wood-paneled Wagoneer with two surfboards strapped to the roof pulls up in front. Dov. He glides into the parking space behind hers, right on the street, and brings the boxy old Jeep to a whining halt. He really has no fear, does he? But she already knows. One of the first things she learned about him was that he spent the four years after high school— years she spent stressing over whether to pledge Kappa Kappa Gamma or Pi Phi, and whether to minor in art history or French—in the Israel

Defense Forces. He's fearless, yes, and he's shameless, and quite possibly, since his divorce, a little unhinged.

She moves closer to the door. Through the clouds reflected in his windshield she can see his black Ray-Ban Wayfarers and his broad grin, and just like that, her mood soars. She grins back. He takes a hand off the steering wheel to wave. She doesn't dare turn around to see if Meghan's watching.

He gets out. He's wearing a sweatshirt and tan work pants and a striped knit hat, from which a few of his ample, dark curls escape. Before coming in he pauses to stretch his arms over his head, and his sweatshirt lifts up, exposing a swath of toned, suntanned belly above his pants. She wonders if he's doing this on purpose, showing off. He closes the door and goes around to the passenger side, where he takes a cardboard coffee carrier off the seat. Only once she's opened the door for him and he's standing in front of her does she notice the carrier holds three cups.

Inside, he says, "I was just in the neighborhood," loudly enough for Meghan to hear. "I thought I'd swing by. I come bearing mochas. Meghan?"

Meghan has the phone to her ear, and she raises her index finger, nods, and mouths the words "Thanks, Mr. Azulay." She's still holding Cameron, who keeps reaching for the phone in her hand.

"Come on, I've told you before, it's Dov." He hands Gina a cup.

"You're trouble," Gina whispers, lifting the cup in a mock toast and taking a sip.

Before he can respond, Meghan joins them, accepting the cup Dov hands her. "How's your mom doing?" he asks—something Gina realizes she hasn't done for days, maybe weeks.

"Okay, thanks. Some days are better than others," she says. Cameron's playing with a gold cross that hangs from a chain around her neck, tugging on it, clutching it in his fist. When he moves it toward his mouth, she laughs and says, "No, baby. That's not food," and covers his fist in hers. "So, what's Kevin up to?" (Gina always forgets that she and Kevin overlapped at Mid-Cape High—that Meghan's just a few years older than Amanda—an easy thing to forget, since she acts at least a decade more mature.)

"Right now he's probably sleeping one off," he says. "He's got a few more days of break."

"So he's home?"

Dov nods. "And I think he's a little lonely. You should give him a call." She smiles, and he says, "That kid can't say I never did anything for him," and winks. *Winks*. Gina's heart contracts. Not only does she feel a flash of indignation on behalf of Amanda, whom she happens to know Kevin dumped, quite unceremoniously, back in the fall, but he's flirting with her—with *Meghan*. It's absurd—and humiliating, not just for her, for him. The three of them stand there awkwardly, no one speaking, until finally Meghan says, "Gina, I'll be upstairs. When you want to take a look at the forms, just shout."

"Wait," Gina says quickly. "Dov was just leaving."

He says, "Oh?"

"We've got work to do," she says. He's trying to catch her eye, but she won't give him the satisfaction.

Looking a little baffled, he says, "Well."

Meghan's still standing beside Gina, and they both watch him climb into his Jeep.

As he pulls onto the street, Meghan says, "Didn't Amanda used to date him? Kevin, I mean."

Gina nods, watching his taillights disappear around the bend. Meghan seems to be waiting for her to say more on the subject, but she doesn't feel like it. "I'll take the baby," she says, holding out her hands. Cameron turns away, though, burying his face in Meghan's neck.

"Sweet boy," Meghan says. "I don't mind watching him a while longer."

Gina says, "I said I'll take him. Here," and she lifts him out of Meghan's arms. He's still holding on to the pendant, and when Gina pries it, a little roughly, from his fist, he wails.

9

⸎

"WHAT EXACTLY GOES ON IN YOUR HEAD?" is the first thing Vance hears, entering the house. He can't imagine what they're arguing about now. Helen hurries into the kitchen, but he takes his time in the mudroom, hanging up his coat, removing his boots.

"No, really, in all seriousness," his brother shouts. "I'd like to know."

In his socks, Vance follows the voice through the kitchen and into the living room, which he notices for the first time has been painted blood red.

Here's Craig, sitting in an oversized leather armchair, one leg crossed over the other, ankle on knee, a Coors Light in his hand, the left side of his forehead hidden behind gauze and medical tape.

"What happened to you?" Vance asks, but Craig doesn't answer; he's glaring at him. Gina's there too, on an enormous leather sofa that matches the chair. She has her glasses on and her feet are tucked up under her, and she doesn't greet him. "He was surfing," she says. "Alone. In forty-degree water. Does that sound wise to you?" She's frowning down at her hands, which hold two long needles. In her lap is a neat loop of pumpkin-colored yarn.

"Hello, I asked you a question," Craig says, and Vance stands there a moment, blinking, until it dawns on him that his brother wasn't yelling at Gina, he was yelling at him.

Craig shakes his head. "Do you have a single brain cell left, or all they all fried?"

"Babe," Gina says.

"What? It's the truth." To Vance, he says, "Where the hell have you been? It's almost one. Gina was getting ready to call the police." Gina shakes her head but says nothing.

"We were—" Helen begins, but Vance cuts her off.

"We were stranded over at Seal Harbor. The Frog's battery died. I thought you were going to keep it charged." He waits for a response but none comes. "We had to get a jump—from Dylan van Dorne. I thought she was her mother at first. It was mortifying. Would it have killed you to give me a heads-up?"

It's not clear whether Craig registers any of what Vance says. "What the hell were you thinking," he says, "just disappearing like that? When you're responsible for children, you don't just go dark."

Vance looks at his brother. There's not much point in arguing when he gets like this. Helen climbs onto the couch beside Gina and reaches for the yarn.

"Careful," Gina tells her. "Remember how long it took us to wind?"

Apparently Craig isn't finished. "Did it even occur to you to let someone know you were alive?" he asks. "To pick up the phone?"

Vance waits a beat before turning to face his brother. "Of course it did. I tried you, but you didn't answer. I tried here, too. I left you a voicemail." He looks at Gina for affirmation but she keeps her eyes down. "What are you so riled up about, anyway? She's fine. Everything's fine."

Craig stands up. He's wearing a brown wool sweater that zips at the neck and clean, pressed-looking jeans. "Where is she?"

Vance looks at Helen, then back at Craig. "Who?"

"Amanda, who the hell do you think?" Craig sets down his Coors Light. "Is she moping in the garage?"

Vance looks at Craig's socks, which are gray-and-green argyle, and then at his face again. He clears his throat. "She's not—she isn't with me. Us."

"What the hell are you talking about?"

"She wanted some exercise. She said she was going to walk home."

"And you let her?"

"Sure—no—I mean, I told her to wait in the Frog, and when we came out she was gone. I looked for her, but she wasn't anywhere, so I figured—"

"Fuck," Craig says.

Vance says, "What's the big deal? She knows the way. I don't understand."

Craig says, "Well, there's one thing we can agree on."

"She's grounded, Vance," Gina says wearily. Her needles are still and she's got her eyes on Craig.

Vance says, "How the hell was I supposed to know that?" Neither answers. Their eyes are locked together. "What did she do?" Vance asks, but he may as well be asking the yarn in Gina's lap.

"Babe, it's *okay*, it is," Gina says, but Craig shakes his head. Then he's out of the chair and in motion, heading into the kitchen, then the mudroom, where there's a loud thump. "God *damn* it," Craig yells. "Where the hell's my coat?"

Gina pushes the knitting off her lap and leans back, letting her head rest on the back of the couch. Eyes closed, she shouts, "Would you please calm down?"

Vance is still standing on the threshold between the living room and kitchen. He says, "Gina? Could you tell me what's going on?"

"It's not your fault" is all she says. Raising her voice again, she says, "You're acting like a crazy person, you know."

"Uncle Vance," Helen says. She's left the couch and moved over to the piano bench. "I can play 'Für Elise.' Want to hear?"

Gina turns to her and hisses, "Don't you dare. The baby. *Craig*," she calls again.

"What's he doing?" Vance asks.

"Going after her would be my guess."

"He knows where she is?"

"No, but that won't stop him from driving around town like a lunatic."

"What will he do when—if—he finds her?"

"Make a big scene, you know, drag her back to the cave by her hair."

Vance leaves the two of them there and goes into the mudroom, where Craig is sitting on the bench, looking bereft. One of his feet is half in, half out of a hiking boot, and coats of varied colors and sizes litter the tiles.

From the doorway, Vance asks his brother, in a calm voice, what's wrong. "It's not like she's in danger. What gives?"

Craig looks up and blinks at Vance a couple of times but doesn't answer. He pushes his foot the rest of the way into the boot, yanks at the laces, and ties a knot. Then he stands up, lifting a brown canvas jacket from the floor and putting it on. When he tries to exit the mudroom, though, Vance blocks his way. "It's my fault she's out there," he says. "I'll go look."

"No, thanks. Could you please move?"

Vance stays put. "Like I said, I didn't know she was grounded. Shit, I didn't know she was in the Northern Hemisphere until a few hours ago."

"I asked you once. I'm not going to ask you again," Craig says. His hands are balled into fists.

"Would you please just tell me what happened? Was there an accident? Did someone get hurt?"

"Babe," Gina's voice says. Vance turns around. She's standing in the kitchen, by the sink. "Maybe we should explain."

"Gina, Jesus, stay out of this, okay?"

"No. I can't. How many times do I have to say that before you hear?"

Craig glares at her over Vance's shoulder. His face is fuchsia and his blue eyes blaze. He steps even closer to Vance. "Are you going to move, or do I need to make you?"

Vance hasn't seen his brother this upset in years. Holding up his hands, he says, "You need to get a grip," and takes a step back.

"I second that," Gina says.

"I'm hungry," Helen says. She's in the kitchen now too, standing by the oven, fiddling with one of the dials.

"There are crackers in the cupboard, but don't have more than a few. I'm about to get the baby, then I'll make lunch," Gina says, and leaves. Vance hears her clogs in the hallway, then on the stairs.

Back in the mudroom, Craig is sitting again, only now he's got his face in his hands.

Vance considers going and sitting beside him, but the truth is he's a little afraid. He says, "Craig?"

Something touches his wrist, and he turns. Helen stands behind him, holding out a tan, waxed-paper sleeve.

"Want a Ritz?" she says, spewing crumbs.

He shakes his head and turns back to Craig, who's gotten up and is gingerly putting on a Red Sox cap. "Excuse me," Craig says, and Vance turns to let him pass.

Vance follows him through the kitchen and into the front hall. "I meant what I said," he says. "I want to go."

Craig ignores him, fishing his car keys out of a woven seagrass bowl, and Vance sees him catch his reflection in the gilt-framed mirror on the wall. Straightening the bill of his cap, he sniffs.

In spite of everything, Vance feels a stab of tenderness for his brother. "Come on, at least let me keep you company."

Craig faces him. "In case I wasn't clear before, or you're too burnt-out to understand, I'll be as direct as I can. This doesn't concern you. It's none of your business. So please, do us all a favor and butt out." He doesn't wait for Vance to respond. He's reaching for the doorknob when the door swings open and Amanda steps in, in a rush of cold air.

She stands a moment, taking the two of them in, her gaze traveling from Craig to Vance and back to Craig. Her eyes are bright and her cheeks have a healthy flush to them. Unlike this morning, she looks robust, Vance notes—or at least not like she's about to faint.

She plucks a set of earbuds out of her ears one by one and says, "The welcome committee, how nice."

"What the hell do you think you're doing?" Craig says.

"Taking off my boots," she says, dropping to one knee.

"Don't start that smartass shit," Craig says. "You're grounded, in case you forgot."

Vance says, "Whoa, easy. She's here now," but neither brother nor niece seems to hear.

"That's right, I forgot, I'm on lockdown."

"Cut the attitude, I mean it."

"Or what?" Her voice is so hard, so full of contempt, Vance feels queasy. He's never heard her speak this way—not to Craig, not to anyone. He looks at his brother: his face is red again, and on his neck a green vein throbs. He opens his mouth to say something, but she beats him to it.

Raising her palms, she says, "Look, I give up, okay? I shouldn't have ditched Vance, I should have come right home, I should have called. I'm a horrible person, you hate me, I've disappointed you in a thousand ways." Her pitch rises steadily, until Vance thinks she might cry. "Ground me for the rest of my life, okay? I don't even care."

"Sweetheart, no," Craig says in a thick voice. But before he can say more, she's halfway up the stairs, taking them two at a time. They both hear her bedroom door slam.

Craig is holding on to the newel post. "We have a rule against slamming doors in this house, you know," he yells.

Helen, who has materialized beside the radiator, says, "What about the rule 'no yelling,' Daddy?"

"Yeah, Daddy," says Gina, who appears at the top of the stairs with Cameron on her hip. "What about that rule?"

10

PAUL'S PIZZA USED TO BE called Mount Olympus, and the owner, Andreo, had wild white hair and huge teeth, and he always gave Helen free soda refills and licorice-flavored candies wrapped in blue foil. But Andreo's wife got cancer, same as Helen's grandmother and Marshmallow, and she died too, and Andreo sold Mount Olympus and moved to Philadelphia to be with his sons and daughters-in-law, and now Mount Olympus is called Paul's. Helen misses Andreo, who always called her Helenitsa and said how pretty she was. But her mother says change is inevitable, it's part of life, and that the food is of much higher quality now that it's Paul's.

When they arrive, the sky is a twilight pinkish gray, and the Gardiners are waiting for them in the parking lot, the three of them inside their silver minivan, which idles with the lights on. Craig pulls up alongside them, and Gina opens her window to talk to Mrs. Gardiner, who's in the passenger seat, her window already down.

"They're closed," Mrs. Gardiner says. "The sign on the door says they had some kind of flood. Should we go to the Plum?"

Craig says, "Works for us," and her mother stares straight ahead.

The Plum, which is really called the Beach Plum, is on the other side of town, and all the way there neither her mother nor her father speaks. Helen looks over at Cameron. He's in his baby seat, bundled up in a blue one-piece suit, looking out the window, kicking his feet. According to her mother, she's not supposed to say mean things to him, or about him, because he can understand what's going on even though he can't talk. She's not sure she believes this. He seems very stupid most of the time, a big dumb lump, but her mother still acts like he's so fantastic, when all he does is make messes she has to clean up.

Her father turns on the radio, some Bruce Springsteen music, his favorite. The song that's playing is "Hungry Heart," one Helen knows, but her mother says, "My head hurts. Do you mind?" and turns it off.

"Can I get pizza?" Helen asks, more because she wants someone to say something than because she cares.

"Of course you can, my angel," her mother says in a soft, kind voice.

But in the Plum's parking lot her mother squats in front of her, holding on to her arm, and says, "God, you look like a street urchin. How'd I let you out of the house like this? Be still." She licks her thumb and starts rubbing harshly at Helen's cheek.

"Stop, no," Helen says, trying to twist away, but her mother's grip is strong.

"Don't you want to look pretty for Zach?" she says.

"Daddy," she moans. Her father has removed Cameron's car seat and sets it down on the ground.

"Daddy can't save you. No one can," Gina says. After a second pass, she lets go of Helen's arm. "There, all done. Ready? Hold my hand."

Inside the restaurant it's dark, with candles on the tables and pictures of lighthouses on the walls. The bar is much noisier than the dining room, crowded with people watching basketball on TV.

The Gardiners have already been seated in one of the big leather booths at the back, beside the pinball machines. Helen sits between her parents, which puts her directly across from Zach, the Gardiners' son, who is the same age as her and isn't very nice. His brown hair is long and stringy and he's gotten glasses since she saw him last. He says hi to her when his mother instructs him to, and then he takes an iPad out of her purse.

A waitress with two thick, blond braids that hang past her shoulders comes over to their table with a water pitcher, which she almost spills, tripping over Cameron, who's in his seat on the floor by Craig.

"Oh, my goodness, what a little sweetheart," she says. "I almost gave him a bath." She asks if she can get them some drinks. Craig orders a Coors Light, and Gina says, "Wine?" The Gardiners nod.

Mrs. Gardiner pushes a menu across the table and says, "We're easy. You pick."

The waitress turns to Helen and in a silly high voice asks if she'd like some juice.

"Sprite," Helen says, expecting one or both of her parents to object, but neither does. Her mother is studying the menu, and her father is facing the bar, squinting at one of the TVs.

Her mother tells the waitress she's ready and says the name of a wine, and the waitress says, "Excellent choice."

"So, what's new in Lake-land?" Mr. Gardiner says, once she's left.

Craig says, "Nothing," and Gina looks at her nails. Helen looks at her own nails. They still have some polish on them from Natalie Cartwright's birthday party. She'd chosen gold glitter, which she liked until Amanda said it looked like dirt.

Luke Gardiner says to her dad, "You still in the game? I'm hanging on by a thread." Luke works with her father at his company. He's an architect, and he and his family moved to the Cape from California, but he looks more like he came from the olden days, with his thick beard and his too-small, old-fashioned suit.

"Does the winter always feel this eternal?" Mrs. Gardiner asks. "All I can think is, thank God for daylight savings. I was seriously starting to lose it."

"It's true," her husband says. "I was thinking I might have to ship her off to Arizona, to her mother's, until it gets warm."

"Which should tell you how desperate I was," Mrs. Gardiner says, and laughs. She has a flat, pale face, freckles, and a huge halo of orange hair.

"You'll adjust," Gina says. "My first winter here, I complained so much, Craig replaced all our lamps with those full-spectrum ones. Remember, babe?"

Craig doesn't seem to be listening.

"The good news," Gina continues, "is that spring will come. It may not be till June, but it will."

Mrs. Gardiner makes a face. "June? Say you're joking. Please."

The waitress comes back with their drinks, setting Helen's Sprite in front of her and Craig's beer in front of him, and using a corkscrew from her shirt pocket to open the bottle of wine.

"Daddy, can I have some foam?" she asks. Ever since she was a baby, he's been letting her skim the foam off his beer with a spoon.

"No," Gina says, at the same time Craig says, "Sure you can."

Gina narrows her eyes at him but says nothing more, so Helen takes the spoon and dips it into her father's glass. She loves the sour taste and the way the tiny bubbles tickle her tongue. But when she goes back for a second spoonful, Gina says, "No more."

Helen looks at her father, but he doesn't argue, he's sort of staring off into space. She takes the spoon and tries to balance it on her nose, a trick he taught her once, but it slides off and falls on the floor.

"Do you know what you'd like to eat, kids?"

"Pepperoni pizza," Helen shouts.

"Helen, manners. Please," her mother says.

Mrs. Gardiner says, "Pizza works for us."

While Gina orders, Helen pinches her nose like she's going underwater, like the girl in the book her father's reading to her. Her name is Karana, and she lives on an island with her family until some men come on ships and kill her father, and then some more men come and take the rest of her people away. Helen dives under the table. It's not so different from being underwater: it's quiet, and dark, and she's alone. She looks around at everyone's shoes. Her mother wears black boots with silver buckles and Mrs. Gardiner wears purple clogs. Zack wears ugly gray sneakers with Velcro and Mr. Gardiner wears hiking boots, like her dad. She spots her spoon, a small glint of silver on the dark floor by one of Mrs. Gardiner's clogs, and she picks it up but she doesn't surface. She tries to imagine the knees and shins and shoes around her are coral reefs, like where Karana goes to spear fish. There's a giant devilfish she tries to spear, but it's too big and it stings her dog, Rontu, and she has to give up. She turns her attention to her dad's feet, his big familiar brown boots, and she arranges herself so she's sitting on top of them. She waits for his reprimand, his instruction to cut it out, but instead she feels his hand, gentle, on the top of her head, and she relaxes, leaning against his shins. He doesn't take his hand away. If she could, she would stay here, exactly like this, all night.

But of course she can't. "You ready, peanut?" Gina says when the pizzas arrive, and reluctantly Helen surfaces and settles again into her seat. One pizza has pepperoni, her favorite, and the other has black olives and anchovies, which she liked until Amanda said they looked like slugs.

"Careful, people, it's hot," Mr. Gardiner says, laying a slice on her plate. Without heeding his advice, she picks up the slice and takes a bite, and pain explodes on the roof of her mouth. But she doesn't cry. Instead she sucks the ice from her soda until there isn't any more. Then she asks to be excused.

In the ladies' room, she lingers, playing with the automatic faucets and the hand dryer, and then climbing up on the sink and contorting herself in front of the mirror, trying unsuccessfully to see the roof of her mouth.

She doesn't want to go back to the table, and passing by the crowd at the bar, she veers that way instead, pressing her palms together and pretending she's a fish; she's a fish, and the people are the water she's swimming through. She slices her way through, imagining she's chasing something, a smaller fish maybe, or a plankton, which she learned about in school. Or maybe she's the one being chased . . . by a shark. At school, when they were learning about the ocean, Mrs. Forrest explained the difference between *predators* and *prey*. Most animals, including humans, she said, can be both. She turns sharply to the left, then the right. She's imagining a shark closing in on her tail, when she bumps right into a lady, spilling her drink.

"Oh, my," the lady says.

"What the hell?" says the man she's with. He looks to the right and the left, and when he looks down he sees Helen. "What do you think you're doing? Bars aren't for kids."

"I'm a fish," Helen says. There's a lump in her throat.

"You a fish with twelve bucks? That was Grey Goose."

"Lewis," the woman says. She's using a napkin to blot at her purse, which is bright red.

"Lew, Alice, I've got you covered," says another man's voice, and she looks up: it's Dov. He's the owner of the Plum and her father's friend—they've been friends since they were kids. "Grab a seat, cowgirl," he says, nodding at the empty one at the end, and she does as he says, watching him shake some clear liquid and ice together in a large metal cup and pour it into a fancy glass. Then he turns his attention to her. Like always, he says something silly. Tonight it's "Pick your poison, young lady." He's holding the gun that soda comes out of, pointing it at her. "What'll it be? A Sidecar? A Singapore Sling? Or wait, you're more of a purist, aren't you? Shot of whiskey? Gin?"

"Can I have a cherry?" she says.

"That's what I like to see, big smiles. My God, kid, what happened to your teeth?"

He spears three cherries from a plastic tub on a tiny, clear-plastic sword, which he passes over the bar.

She's still smiling when she gets back to the table, but when she says, "Look what Uncle Dov gave me," her mother looks away. "Mama?" she says, and before she knows what's happening, Zach has reached across the table and snatched the sword from her hand.

"Give it back, it's mine," she says, feeling her throat getting tight again.

Zach grins. "You snooze, you lose."

"But my uncle Dov gave it to me. Dad?"

Her father's eyes are locked on the TV.

She looks at the Gardiners, but they're ignoring her too. "Mama," she says, "Zach stole my sword."

"It's just a piece of plastic, hush," her mother says.

Just then the waitress appears with the check, which she sets on the table before piling the empty pizza pans and their dishes onto a tray.

Mr. Gardiner picks up the bill. "Our turn," he says.

"Absolutely not," Gina says.

Reading the total, he frowns. "You guys are cheap dates. I don't know which one of you is the VIP, but they comped our drinks." He reaches into the lapel of his suit jacket and produces a wallet.

"Craig, do something," Gina says.

But Craig doesn't do anything. He's still watching the television, and all he says is "Let him pay if he wants to. It's his fault I put my money on Michigan State."

11

VANCE HASN'T EATEN SINCE the Main Sail, and though he's ravenous, he waits until he's certain Craig and Gina have gone to venture downstairs. On the second floor, he pauses outside Amanda's closed door a moment and listens, hand resting on the knob.

"What do you want?" says her voice from inside.

"It's Vance."

Silence.

He clears his throat. "I wasn't sure whether you'd stayed or not."

"I'm in Gitmo, remember?"

He waits for her to invite him in, but she doesn't. "I was going to rustle up some dinner." He waits again. "Can I bring you a plate?" Another long pause. "A?"

"Whatever."

It isn't yes, but it isn't no either. He decides to press his luck. "Feel like coming down and hanging out while I cook?"

"No," she says.

In the kitchen, he opens and closes cupboards and drawers until he finds a box of pasta and a pot, which he fills with water and sets on the stove. He turns the flame to high and goes into the living room in search of a drink.

On the rare occasion he's not drinking Coors Light, Craig favors high-end single-malt scotch—Balvenie is his brand of choice—distilled, so the story goes, near the Scottish town whence their ancestors hailed. It's expensive stuff, but Craig always keeps a bottle around, and it takes some looking but Vance finds it in the living room, at the back of the cupboard below the wet bar they've recently had installed. He takes it out and sets it on the polished stone countertop. It's true Craig probably wouldn't have offered it—he tends to be stingy with his scotch unless it's a holiday or he's in a rare magnanimous mood—but Craig isn't here, and it's Vance's view that for the hours he spent carting Helen around town today, not to mention the trouble with the Frog, his brother owes him, at the very least, this. He selects a tumbler from a glass shelf over the sink. It's etched with a shield and the Latin word *Veritas*. It's a Harvard glass, which means it could have joined the household with Gina but was probably their dad's. Frank, too, enjoyed his single-malt. Vance pours out an inch or so, then tops it off. (Craig takes a couple of ice cubes, but Vance prefers his neat.)

He carries the drink over to the big leather armchair and sits down, trying a few different positions—legs stretched out, legs crossed at the ankle, legs crossed at the knee—but he can't find one that's comfortable. Whether he feels so awkward because the chair is sized for a giant or because it's so clearly Craig's, he doesn't know, but he gets up and goes over to the window, to the only piece of furniture he recognizes, an upholstered armchair from the house where they grew up. It's roughly half the leather chair's size, the flowered fabric is faded and stained and threadbare in spots along the arms. Even so, this chair is far more comfortable than Craig's.

It's officially evening, the windowpanes have gone black. He drinks and stares at nothing, grateful for the temporary quiet. Obliquely he thinks about his phone, up in the attic: about the fact that Celeste still hasn't called. It doesn't bode well, given that when she's kicked him out in the past, she's always called within a day, if not a few hours. She'd sound confused, even tearful, but in the end she's always asked him to come back. Clearly, this time is different. She'd been so cold, so hard-hearted, telling him to go. She'd already packed his duffel, which was waiting by the door when he got home, and her voice wasn't even shaking when she said, "Let's not make this harder than necessary, okay?"

He sips the scotch, which leaves him feeling warm and, strangely, a little untethered, as if he's floating a few inches above the floor. Which may be apt, he thinks; after all, he is untethered. He has no girlfriend, no job, no home. *Home* — the word sends a chill through him.

This place, this sandy spit of land, isn't his home — and even if it is, or was, there's nothing here for him now. Well, almost nothing — there's Amanda, of course, and the other kids, and Gina and Craig. And an old buddy from the track team who teaches history at the high school and intermittently campaigns for him to come back and coach. But that doesn't add up to much. Not compared to everything else that's here — everything that happened, everything that didn't. All the ghosts. Dylan appears in his mind again — not Dylan from this afternoon, in her slicker and boots, hauling jumper cables, but Dylan from twenty-three years ago: Dylan in his fisherman's sweater, barelegged on the window seat at Land's End. Dylan, young and lovely, telling him that she was sorry, and that she was scared. Dylan, believing him.

He feels frozen in the chair. He hasn't thought about her — about then — in so long; he hasn't let himself. But now, just like that, he's back at BU, in the first semester of his freshman year, when he found it almost impossible to think about anything else. That fall, he made zero friends and earned a 2.2 GPA, which threatened his financial aid. Second semester, he managed to pull his grades up enough to stay, but he never stopped thinking about her: first thing in the morning, drinking dining hall coffee; winding along the Charles with the cross-country team; lying in his twin bed in his overheated dorm room at night. He thought about her when he should have been thinking about Milton and Shelley and Keats, when he was sober and when he was drunk, and on the few occasions he went on dates. He thought about her all that spring and all summer, which he elected to spend on a salmon-fishing boat on the Bering Sea — as far away as he could manage to get from the Cape.

He sits up. His glass is empty, trembling a little in his hand. He leaves it on the windowsill and goes into the kitchen to check the water, which is boiling, so he dumps in the pasta and empties a jar of sauce into a smaller pot. Then he retrieves his glass and goes back to the bar for a refill, half of which he drinks right there.

Feeling a little steadier, he takes the glass to the other side of the living room, looking for distraction on the wall of built-in bookshelves, only a couple of which hold actual books. (His brother doesn't read — he readily admits it, indeed he seems almost proud, saying he doesn't have time. Neither does Gina, though she claims to have been a voracious reader before she had kids.) Instead they display mostly decorative items: a brass barometer and a tide clock, some nautical maps, a whalebone cribbage set, a carved stone bird. One whole shelf is lined with photo albums, another devoted entirely to Craig's extensive collection of Tour de France DVDs.

He wanders over to the window again. Now the moon is up, golden and gibbous behind a thin veil of clouds. In its liquid light he can see the backyard. Everything is bare and cut back: the hydrangeas, the butterfly bush, the rose of Sharon, the thick wisteria vine that in summer all but obscures the back fence. The gazebo's finished, he notes. Craig was working on it over Thanksgiving, spending hours on end out there and, naturally, rejecting Vance's offers of help. He thinks of Amanda, observing the backyard so listlessly earlier in the day, and something sparks inside his head, a connection wanting to be made, a switch asking to be flipped. But the spark doesn't catch — he won't let it. He finishes what's in his glass, then goes to the piano and sits on the bench.

It's a gorgeous instrument, the piano: an antique black Steinway grand that once belonged to their grandparents on their father's side. Gently he opens the fall, slides his fingers over the smooth, yellowed keys, before striking one, middle C. It's profoundly out of tune — which no one's noticed, most likely because no one plays it, not really, and much like with the Frog, Craig doesn't appear to care. Vance isn't surprised. He's long suspected that his — that their — interest in the piano is aesthetic, if not financial. But maybe that's unfair. It does serve another, more utilitarian purpose: the closed lid is covered with photos of the kids.

• • •

Amanda's door is still closed. Not wanting to put down the tray he's carrying, he says, "Room service," and kicks it a couple of times with the toe of his sneaker.

"You can come in," her voice says, but she doesn't open it, so he balances the tray on his knee, rather precariously, and turns the knob.

She sits cross-legged on her bed, wearing a pair of huge, padded headphones and frowning at her laptop's screen. He stands in the doorway, scanning the room for a place to put the tray.

"What is it," she says without looking up.

"Dinner. How does spaghetti sound?" he asks, deciding on her desk. She doesn't respond. She hasn't taken her eyes off the computer.

He sets down the tray and brings her plate, a fork, and a glass of milk over to her, placing the plate carefully on the bed and the glass on her nightstand, by a clock radio in the shape of a soccer ball. She doesn't remove her headphones; she must be in the middle of something—important? Covertly he tries to glimpse the screen, but it's like she can sense his curiosity and angles it away.

He goes back to her desk and sits down to wait, and while he waits he looks around the room. Unlike most of the rest of the house, it hasn't changed in years; it's still every bit as wrong for Amanda as it's always been. Take the bed, a white, four-poster, canopied confection shrouded in a pouf of pink, or the pink plaid duvet, or the wallpaper, which is printed with pink bows. Of course Amanda didn't choose any of it, Gina did. She had the whole room redecorated, top to bottom, as a surprise gift after they moved in, had the work done while Amanda was visiting him, which she did every spring, in DC. Gina had meant well, he supposed, or well enough, but she never asked Amanda, or anyone else, whether she liked the color pink. And the thing was, Amanda hated pink, she always had, and she almost certainly still does. The only features that actually speak to who Amanda truly is, in Vance's opinion, are the stuffed animals on the (pink-upholstered) window seat, the posters on the walls (the Flaming Lips, the Killers, the Cranberries, and a couple of other bands he's never heard of), and, last but in no way least, her bulletin board, the ever-changing art installation hanging over her desk. Vance swivels his seat around to inspect it.

"Was there something else?" she says, and he turns back to face her.

She's taken off the earphones and hooked the headset around her neck. "I mean, did you need something?"

"I thought I'd sit a minute, if you don't mind. We haven't had much of a chance to catch up." After a moment, he adds, "Food look all right?"

Glancing over at the glass of milk on the nightstand, she grimaces. "I'm vegan. Did you forget?"

He nods, keeping his expression flat. She's clearly trying to drive him out. He goes over to the nightstand, picks up the glass, carries it into the hallway, and sets it down at the top of the stairs.

"Did you know we're the only species on earth that drinks another animal's milk?" she says when he returns.

"Someone in pre-K told me it was cow sweat, and I haven't had much of a taste for it since." He smiles, but she doesn't smile back. He sits at the desk again and drinks from his refreshed scotch. "Aren't you going to eat?"

"You didn't have to do this, you know. I'm perfectly capable of feeding myself."

"Is that what passes for 'Thank you' in these parts?"

"Thank you," she says. She's twisting spaghetti around her fork, and he watches as she fits an enormous quantity into her mouth.

Not wanting to make her self-conscious, he turns to face the bulletin board again. It's a crowded and somewhat chaotic collage: photos, bumper stickers, greeting cards, vintage postcards, drawings, quotes, poems, clippings from magazines. Some of it he recognizes, but much is new. One perennial staple, occupying the upper right-hand corner of the board, is a faded photo of Amanda and Suzanne at Land's End, taken by Vance. It was the summer before Suzanne's accident, so Amanda was six, about to turn seven, and she sits between her mother's legs on the camp's wooden steps in bright sunlight, Suzanne brushing her hair. It always breaks his heart a little, the photo—for Amanda mostly, but also for himself; he'd adored Suzanne, and unlike Gina, the feeling was mutual—he never had any reason to doubt that she genuinely wanted him around. She had a quick, sharp wit, a wide smile, and a raucous, hoarse laugh that almost nobody could resist, including Craig—especially Craig. He was so different then: kind and silly, effortlessly generous, more open to the world. But after Suzanne died, all of that, his whole demeanor—even his posture, Vance noticed—changed. It was as if his own broken heart was slowly cauterized, and at this point the wound is sealed up so tightly, nothing can get in or out.

With some effort, he redirects his thoughts and his gaze. Right below hangs Amanda's most recent soccer team photo (the girls kneeling in the front row hold a flag displaying the year). It must have been taken at the start of the season, before her fall from grace. She was the captain, and in the photo she stands in the back, in the center, the tallest in her row. He leans in closer. She looks so hale, so hearty, with her jersey's sleeves pushed up to her shoulders, her face ruddy from exertion or maybe the Indian-summer sun.

He has the urge to ask, again, what she's doing here, but he resists, shifting his attention to something else new, a transcribed poem. "Hey, Yeats, one of my go-tos," he says, leaning in to inspect the text. Whoever's done the transcribing (it's not Amanda, the handwriting isn't hers) is also an artist. Surrounding the text is a drawing of a night sky in black ink. Above a backdrop of mountains, white stars and a thin crescent moon shine from the negative space. At the bottom of the page a tiny ink figure, a man, stands with his arms thrown open, his face turned up to the sky. "*But one man loved the pilgrim soul in you,*" Vance reads aloud. "*And loved the sorrows of your changing face And bending down beside the glowing bars, murmur, a little sadly, how Love fled, and paced upon the mountains overhead, and—*"

"Stop," she says. Looking up, he sees she's put down her fork.

"What's wrong?"

She doesn't answer. She's staring down at her plate. "Nothing."

"And I'm supposed to believe you?" he says.

"Fine. I hate that poem. I thought I took it down. Okay?" She picks up the plate. "I'm finished."

But he isn't about to leave, not like this. He clears his throat. "You still haven't told me about your trip."

She won't look at him.

"Would you like to?"

"Not particularly."

From downstairs he hears the grandfather clock chime. He says,

"You're really starting to freak me out. You don't seem like yourself. You seem—I don't know. A?"

When she looks up, her eyes gleam. "What does that even mean, myself? How do you know what I'm like? Maybe I'm not who you think I am. Has it ever occurred to you that maybe you don't know me at all?"

He swallows. "Come on, honey," he says cautiously. "I've known you longer than—"

A tear slides down her cheek. She wipes it away with the back of her hand.

He gets up, goes over to the bed, and wraps his arms around her—and for a second or two she lets him, she even hugs him back, she hugs him hard—but then she tenses up, pushing him back. "Just go," she says. "Please?"

He starts to protest, but she says, "If you really love me as much as you say you do, if you care about me at all, you'll leave."

Silently he gathers her plate up off the bed and loads it onto the tray. In the doorway, he pauses. "You know I couldn't care less, right, whatever it is you did?"

"You say that, but you have no idea."

"Did you kill someone?"

"No."

"Well, you know what? I'd still love you. I'd be on your side even if you did." She sniffles, wiping her nose with the back of her hand. "The very first time I held you, you know what I thought? I thought, I'd—

"I know. You've told me a hundred times."

"What?"

"You thought, 'I'd lie in front of a train for this kid.'"

"And I still would, you know, if lying in front of a train would do you any good."

She says, "It wouldn't," and puts the headphones over her ears.

Up in his garret, Vance can't sleep. It's hot again, airless, and the scotch he drank was enough to make him woozy but not to knock him out. He tosses and turns, kicking off the old army blanket and, feeling exposed, pulling it back up. Each time he lies still for more than a few seconds, the room pitches, a boat on rough seas, and he has to put a bare foot flat on the floor to make the sensation of motion stop. After what feels like ages, he switches on the shepherdess lamp and gets up. He goes over to the window, unfastens the latch, and cranks it open as far as it will go.

Cold fresh air rushes in. Fishing the Ziploc bag from his Dopp kit, he packs his pipe with a single fat bud, the last of his stash, and as quietly as he can, slides the steamer trunk aside, stands in front of the window, and lights up, putting his face through the porthole and blowing the smoke out into the night.

The pot helps some, but he's still restless. He sits on the trunk and looks around the attic. Old furniture, some of which he recognizes and some of which he doesn't, gathers dust, and carefully labeled, clear-plastic boxes (*Gran's tea service, Craig H.S., kids' ski clothes, Xmas lights*) line the walls.

It's chilly by the window with the air rushing in, and he ventures back over to the air mattress and tentatively lies down. In the lamp-light, he studies the steeply sloped ceiling, the nail points protruding from the beadboard, the tiny sharp shadows they cast on wood. He's just beginning to drift off when he hears them, Gina and Craig, through the vent.

"What kind of imbecile leaves a full glass of milk on the floor?" Craig says. "Something's wrong with him."

Vance moves to the edge of the air mattress, closer to the vent.

"I'm sure it wasn't intentional. You're so tense. Look at you. You need to relax," Gina says.

"You know what I need? For everyone to stop telling me what I need." There's a pause. "You know what the worst part is? I can't help thinking she did it on purpose, to piss me off."

"That's not rational."

"I know, but I keep thinking it anyway. I can't stop."

"Oh, babe. I wish I could help. Do you want a pill?"

Another pause, then Craig says, "Do you think you could—" After another moment, he says, "Jesus, oh Jesus, that's nice. Use your mouth?"

Vance stands up. He doesn't want to hear the rest. He slides a box labeled *A's school books* over the vent and goes back to the window. There's still some bud in the bowl, and he lights it and inhales again, looking out. He can see the ocean, a dark expanse, and many miles away, close to the horizon, three green pinpricks, lights from a ship. And the sky: the clouds from earlier have cleared and the vast black canopy is thick with stars. He thinks of the drawing on Amanda's bulletin board. Surely, judging from her reaction, it has something to do with whatever's going on, but it's hard to connect two such disparate thoughts.

He takes a final hit, holding the smoke in as long as he can, and when he lets it out, he happens to look down into the yard, where he sees a tiny orange light—the smoldering tip of a cigarette.

12

CRAIG IS SUCH A HYPOCRITE, Amanda thinks, hunched against the cold on a bench in the gazebo. It's just too outrageous how he walks around town so pleased with himself, purporting to be this pillar of the community, this upstanding citizen, this family man, when really he's just as full of shit as everyone else— or no, he's worse, much worse, than plenty of people she knows. They may be assholes, but at least they don't pretend. It's the pretending that pisses her off the most.

She takes a long pull off one of his supposedly secret Marlboro Lights. The wind is blowing from the west, and she's got her back to it, hoping it will carry away the smoke. Not that she's so afraid of getting caught, at this point. What can they do to her? They already hate her, and Craig's never going to change his mind. He'll hardly look at her, much less let her speak.

Even so, when she hears something behind her, footsteps on the grass, she spins around. There's a man's shape coming toward her, but she can't see his face because of the floodlights on the back of the house. She can't run, and there's nowhere to hide. Her heart thumps in her chest a couple of times, and then he says, "Honey? A?" and she can breathe again: it's Vance.

"You almost gave me a heart attack," she says.

"You know what will give you a heart attack? Those little fuckers," he says, nodding at the cigarette in her hand.

He climbs the stone steps into the gazebo. He's wearing a black T-shirt that says 9:30 on it, jeans, and no shoes, and his feet are so white against the flagstones they glow. "It's freezing," he says, hugging himself. "Aren't you cold?"

"Don't you have a coat?"

"I didn't want to risk it," he says. He stands there a moment, swaying slightly, and quickly she understands that he's stoned. This isn't exactly shocking. But smoking inside Gina and Craig's house is a bold, and therefore admirable, move. "Okay if I sit?" he asks, and then, "What are you doing out here so late?"

She says, "Dyeing Easter eggs. What do you think?"

He smiles, but then his smile fades. "I didn't know you smoke."

"There's a lot you don't know about me," she says, tapping her cigarette so the ash falls over the railing, onto the grass.

"I meant I didn't know *kids* smoke—I mean cigarettes."

She takes a last drag and flicks the butt into the bushes, then looks down at her hands. She's wearing a pair of fingerless gloves Gina gave her for Christmas. She was supposed to take them on her trip, but when she got to base camp they said she had to leave them behind. ("Cotton kills" was the reason; everything they wore in the field had to be synthetic or wool.) "Kids do all the same shit they've always done," she says, "and they always will. It's stupid for adults to keep wasting their energy trying to make them stop."

"Wise words," he says. He's studying her face, she can feel it, and she looks down, balling her hands into fists and digging them deep in the pockets of her coat. He looks over his shoulder at the house. "Aren't you worried about getting caught?"

"No," she says, fingering the box of Marlboro Lights in her pocket. She already feels buzzed from the first one, and a little queasy, but she pulls another one out. "Want one?"

"God, no. This body is a temple," he says, and then, "That was a joke."

She can feel his eyes on her as she cups her hand around the yellow Bic lighter—also Craig's—inhales, and blows out a thick plume of smoke.

"You look pretty experienced at that," he says. "Did you buy them?"

She shakes her head. "Craig keeps them in the garage. He thinks no one knows but it's totally obvious. You sure you're okay? You're like, shaking."

He nods.

She crosses her legs, wedging the hand that isn't holding the cigarette between her thighs and looking out at the bushes. On the other side of the fence there's a dense thicket where a pack of coyotes is supposed to have a den. There are coyotes and wild dogs all over the Cape. Some people want them "managed," which basically means killed or at least taken somewhere else, but she's glad they're here. Late at night, sometimes, she hears them howl.

"I'm not trying to harass you, honey, that's the last thing I want to do," he says, "but you've always talked to me before, and now you're not, so of course I'm wondering, did I do something wrong? Because if so, if that's what's going on, I might have to throw myself off the Sagamore Bridge."

"That's not what's going on."

"Okay, phew. And?"

"And nothing. You didn't do anything wrong."

"Tell me what's the matter. Please."

Turning her head to the side to exhale, she tries to think of how to put him off. She says, "Only if you go first." He looks confused. "You tell me why you're here. And don't say it's mold."

He doesn't say anything for a while. He's looking out at the bushes, pulling the sleeves of his sweatshirt down over his hands. "There was . . . there was a situation," he says finally. "At school."

"Did you screw another one of your students and Celeste kicked you out?"

She can see the color of his face change, even in the dark. "Jesus, honey. No." He looks down at his feet. "And for the record, she wasn't my student, she was an advisee."

"I stand corrected."

"Anyway, it's nothing like that." Crossing one leg over the other, he clasps his hands together and hooks them over one knee. "I—I said something in my Intro seminar, something I shouldn't have said, and I pissed some people off—you know, the wrong people." He's looking out at the thicket again. She watches the side of his face; she can see his jaw muscle working. In the half-light, and from that angle, he looks exactly like Craig.

"What did you say?"

"It doesn't matter—the exact words—as much as what happened after."

"They fired you?"

"So it seems. I thought Celeste would stick with me, you know, love conquers all, but she didn't. She said something's wrong with me, that I'm missing a chip—those were her words. And yeah, she kicked me out."

He unhooks his hands from his knee and starts cracking his knuckles, one by one. Her dad does that too, when he's nervous. She's always hated the sound.

"Firing you over something you said seems harsh," she says.

"It does. Granted, it was—it wasn't my first brush with the, the powers that be." He sniffs. "At the end of the day, a university's just a bureaucracy, you know? They've got their rules, and their committees, and let me tell you, there's not much room for interpretation—or humor—in a setup like that. Especially when you're on the bottom of the totem pole, like I was, a lowly adjunct. Forget any leverage, any rights." He pauses. "The point is, it was a shitty job in the first place, and mostly I'm glad to be free of it. Of Celeste, too, honestly. She was always after me to change, to be something I'm not. Read this, eat this, don't wear that, don't say that, don't hold that view, pretend my asshole friends are interesting. Like she was trying to mold me, or reshape me into—into fuck knows what."

She looks down at the glowing red ember on the end of her cigarette. She's not sure she believes him; he's not quite meeting her eyes, and his voice sounds a little strange. Then again, maybe it's just that he's high. She wishes she were, too. "You don't seem very glad," she ventures.

"Don't I?" he says, turning to look at the yard. "*For within him Hell he brings, and round about him, nor from Hell one step, no more than from himself can fly by change of place.*"

She suspects he's quoting Milton—he usually is. Drawing both feet up onto the bench, she rests her chin on her knees. "For what it's worth, I never really liked Celeste."

"No?"

She shakes her head. "She was so self-righteous—all the politics, and the yoga, and the health food?"

"Now you tell me," he says, smiling a little ruefully. "If you'd have said something four years ago, you'd have saved me from thousands of wheatgrass shots."

She smiles, too. "Does Dad know?"

"Negative."

"Gina?"

He shakes his head. "Just you." He leans back against the gazebo wall and rubs his hands together. "Tag, you're it."

She hugs her knees close. "First you have to tell me what you said. You have to."

He sighs, looking wistful. "I've never been able to say no to you, not since the day you were born. You know what I thought the first time I held you, right? I thought—"

He really is messed up. "I *know*, We talked about it already," she says.

"Right," he says sheepishly. "So, okay. Basically I have one rule in my classroom," he says. "No phones. Pretty simple, right?" She nods. "Well, they're pretty good about it, pretty respectful, but there's this one kid, Brent, he's just sort of a shit. The kind of kid who rubs you wrong, right off the bat. He's always talking about how he's going to law school, and he's going to be this big sports agent—and you know what, I bet he will. He'll be one of those assholes walking around in a six-thousand-dollar suit with a Bluetooth in his ear." He pauses and looks away for a moment. "Anyway, Brent knows the rules, same as everyone, but every day he's got the damn thing out, checking it, like some wildly important message might come in—like he's more important than everyone else, you know what I mean? A few times it rings during class, and the little fuck-nut, he answers it."

"Wow."

Vance nods. "It's like he's testing me, seeing what I'll do. So one day —*the* day—we're doing *Paradise Lost*, and this girl, her name's Kylie, is reading from Book Five, this terrific, this *spectacular*, passage, and I look over at Brent, and sure as shit he's got the phone out, you know, sort of half under the desk, and he's looking at it, not listening to Kylie or anyone else, and I just lose it. I stop Kylie, and I say, 'Brent, I need you to stop playing with your phone.' He looks up, and I say, 'I'm not going to ask you again.' So he says to me, 'But Professor, I'm not playing with it, I'm just holding it,' and I say, 'Oh, I see. So if I take my dick out of my pants and I don't play with it, I just hold it, that would be okay too?'"

Amanda's eyes get wide. "You said that?" She can't help laughing.

He looks down at his lap. "Needless to say, the administration was less amused." After a moment, he adds, "So there it is. The full story of your poor uncle's fall."

There's a silence. She takes the cigarette pack out again, and though she doesn't want another, she shakes one out and offers it to him. When he refuses, she puts it between her lips. "So, on the trip," she begins, "there was a guy."

"If I had a nickel for every story that started like that."

"I could tell he sort of had a crush on me from the beginning, like even in base camp, and it turned out he was pretty cool, and cute, and a few days into the trip, we kissed, and it happened again." This, at least, is true.

"Okay."

She takes the cigarette, still unlit, from her mouth and looks at it. "Well, that's all. It was against the rules—any romantic contact in the field was—and we got caught, and now I'm here."

"No shit. What happened to him?"

"He went home too." Also not a lie.

"Well, at least you were punished equally."

That couldn't be further from the truth, she thinks.

He leans forward, resting his elbows on his knees. "So that's it? That's the big fucking secret?"

She says, "Pretty much," avoiding his gaze by looking down at her boots.

"Sounds like we both got screwed," he says.

She's grateful for the dark—that he can't see her face, which burns with shame.

He shakes his head. "Why do they always put the biggest prudes in charge?" When she doesn't answer, he says, "I'm sorry that happened to you, honey. I really am."

She swallows again, forcing a smile. "How is it possible that you and Craig have the same DNA, but he's such a dick, and you're—"

"Hey," he cuts in, "you can't just go around calling your dad a dick," but she can see from his face that he's not actually mad. He reaches over and covers her gloved hand with his. "You're a good person," he says. "You got a bum deal."

Before she can respond, a light pops on inside the house.

"Shit," Vance says, and they both watch Craig, in his plaid flannel robe, amble through the kitchen rubbing his face. They watch him take a Coors Light out of the refrigerator and proceed to the back of the house, toward them. In front of the French doors he pauses, shades his eyes with one hand, and peers out.

"Get down," Vance whispers, squatting on the stones.

"We're so fucked," she whispers back.

"Don't worry, he can't see us. Here, give me those." He holds out his hand and she passes him the lit cigarette, the Bic, and what remains of the pack. Her legs ache but they stay there, squatting, holding their breath, listening for the sound of Craig opening the door.

But he doesn't open it, thank the Lord. When Vance stands and looks, he whispers, "It's okay. He went into the living room. He's watching TV."

"Jesus," Amanda says, perching on the bench again. The TV screen is so large she can see clearly what he's watching, a basketball game.

Vance says, "Don't relax just yet. We still have to get you inside."

"I'll wait till he goes up."

"That could be hours. Here's the plan." He says they'll go inside together, through the dark kitchen, and she'll sneak up the stairs while he distracts Craig. "I'll ask him about his bracket, or the game."

"What about his cigarettes? What if he—"

He nods, squinting at the house. "I said, don't worry. If there's one thing in this world I know how to handle, it's Craig."

13

UCLA IS DOMINATING — no surprise, since Craig's money is on Providence. Serves him right for filling out the bracket in the first place, considering the state of his finances.

It's an office tradition, though, and he felt compelled to keep up appearances — to maintain the façade that everything's fine. (If he'd had his way, he'd have skipped the pool altogether, not so much to conserve cash, but to protest the NCAA: the coaches are pimps.) Screw it, he thinks. What's a couple hundred bucks at this point?

He's at the bottom of his beer and contemplating getting up for a second when he hears, from the kitchen, the sound of a door opening.

He pauses the DVR and says, "Who's there?" though he has a pretty good idea.

"It's me," says his brother's voice. "I didn't know anyone was up." From the breakfast nook, he nods at Craig's beer and says, "Don't mind if I do."

"Get two," Craig says, starting the game again. He can hear Vance fumbling around, loudly, in the kitchen — the faucet turning on and off, drawers opening and closing, utensils rattling — and concludes that in addition to being completely inconsiderate, his brother is probably high as a kite.

When Vance appears, he's holding a beer in each hand and has a bag of corn chips tucked under one arm. He's wearing jeans and a T-shirt and no socks or shoes. He descends the stairs into the living room, drops the chips on the coffee table, and hands Craig one of the beers.

Craig can smell the tobacco smoke on him from where he's sitting, a good six feet away. He and Vance used to smoke together, but when Gina came into the picture that changed. She hates the habit, even claims an allergy, and when she got pregnant with Helen she made him swear he would quit, which he did—swear, that is.

"You smell like an ashtray," he says. "Where are your shoes?"

"I couldn't sleep," Vance says. He's standing between Craig and the screen, and when Craig asks him to move, he sits on the sofa and props his bare feet on the coffee table, showing Craig the pink soles.

"The gazebo looks terrific, very professional," he says.

"I am a professional," Craig says. As covertly as he can, he sniffs the air. It's pathetic how good the cigarette smoke smells to him, better than fresh-baked bread. He thinks of the pack he keeps in the garage. It's supposed to be for emergencies, but everything feels like an emergency these days.

Vance is opening the chips—making as much noise as possible, it would seem—and Craig shoots him a look.

"Who's your team?" Vance asks, nodding when Craig tells him, though Craig knows none of it means jack to him. You could put everything Vance knows about basketball—about sports in general—into a thimble and it wouldn't overflow. He's never had any interest in team sports. In high school, while Craig played hockey, soccer, and baseball—varsity in all three—Vance ran cross-country and track.

Providence has the ball. They're moving it around the key, waiting for an opening, when one of the towering UCLA posts steps in and snatches it from the point's hands, candy from a baby. The Bruins lope down the court and set themselves up, but before they even execute a play, one of the guards hits a three-pointer—their seventh for the night, and it's only the first half. The crowd roars. "Fuck," Craig says.

"That wasn't us?" Vance asks.

The ads start—a commercial for something called body spray—and the screen fills with sultry-looking, half-clothed teens. He picks up the remote and presses Fast Forward.

"Does anyone play?" Vance asks, and Craig looks over. He's nodding in the direction of the piano. He's got the bag of chips open on his lap and one hand rooting around inside.

"Helen takes lessons," Craig says. "Once in a while she and Gina will play a duet."

"Not you?"

"Shh," Craig says, turning to the game again.

For a while they're quiet; they watch and drink while Providence falls further behind. When the half ends, Vance says, "Could you turn that down a minute?"

"What for?"

"I just thought—I don't know. We've been playing phone tag for weeks."

Craig feels weary, but he pauses the game. Recrossing his legs, he asks what his brother wants to talk about.

Vance looks a little hesitant. "Well, Marshmallow, for one. She—she died?"

Craig nods.

"That's a shame," Vance says.

He seems to be waiting for Craig to say more, but Craig doesn't have more to say.

"So did she—" Vance pauses. "Did you have to put her down?"

He nods again.

"You mean you were the one who, who went? That must have been hard."

"It wasn't a fun morning, no."

"I'm sorry."

"For what?"

"I don't know—you."

"*You* feeling sorry for *me*—now *that's* sad," Craig says, not a nice thing to say, but he's not feeling very nice, not toward Vance, anyway.

What sort of person drops a dog—a living, breathing being, for Christ's sake—on his brother's doorstep, and for the next four years doesn't lift a finger on its behalf?

Vance clears his throat. If he registers the insult, he decides to let it pass. "Do you want to talk about it?"

Craig looks at his brother. Sure, he could talk. He could tell Vance about the vet's—holding poor Marshmallow, seeing the fear in her eyes, the confusion, feeling her little heart fluttering, feeling it stop. Or about how he couldn't keep himself from crying—blubbering, really, while the pretty young tech, Liz, moved her hand up and down his back. How he'd been embarrassed, and ashamed, but he couldn't stop —and how afterward he drove to the beach and cried some more, cried like he hadn't cried since he was a kid. Even after Suzanne he didn't cry like that. He shrugs and says, "I thought we just did."

Like always, though, Vance seems unsatisfied. They both stare at the still screen, until he says, "Did it occur to you that maybe I'd want to know?"

"I guess not."

For a while Vance doesn't say anything. Then he says, "Same goes for Dylan."

"Dylan van Dorne?"

"You never told me she's back—that she's Helen's riding teacher? I got totally ambushed."

"And that's my fault?"

"A heads-up would have been nice."

"I didn't know she was. Or, I hadn't thought about her being here in terms of you. Why would I? Sure, you went out, but it's been what, twenty-five years?"

"Twenty-three."

"So what's the big deal?"

Vance looks straight ahead. Craig waits, but his brother doesn't say anything else. He picks up the remote.

They watch the game for a while, until Vance leans forward, resting his elbows on his knees.

"You know what I was thinking about today?" he says. "The camp.

And Dad—the clams he used to dig up. Remember his bucket, and the spaghetti he used to make? What was in it besides garlic, sausage, and beer?"

"Beats me."

Vance looks suddenly wistful; probably it's the pot. "We had some good times there, didn't we?"

Craig feels wary, like he's about to be tricked. What does Vance want from him? Probably money, for yet another round of futile repairs at the camp. The place is like a sieve that Craig's dollars flow straight through, but Vance doesn't care about that. He can't see anything outside his own nostalgia, his rose-colored version of the past. Nonetheless, Craig takes a swig of beer and allows himself, just for a moment, to think back: playing war in the dunes, sleeping in musty sleeping bags, Vance trying desperately to keep Craig awake by kicking up the top bunk's slats.

Vance goes on. "I was thinking, we should drive out there and dig up some clams sometime, make Dad's spaghetti for the kids."

Craig smiles in spite of himself. "We'd freeze our balls off."

"I meant when it gets warm, dumbass. They'd love it, you know they would—the kids," Vance says. And then his face gets serious. "You probably don't want to talk about Amanda," he says.

Craig stiffens, sits up in his chair. "Sure don't."

"But I have to get something off my chest or I won't be able to sleep."

"God forbid."

"I think you should go easier on her," he says. "Sure, she screwed up, but she's just a kid, and as they go, she's a pretty special one. And besides, that's what kids do, they screw up. God knows we did."

Craig looks at his brother, really looks at him, for the first time since he came in. His hair sticks up at all angles, his eyes are rimmed in red, and he looks like he shaved drunk. He's got some nerve, doesn't he, to sit here, in Craig's living room, with his feet on Craig's furniture, drinking Craig's beer and telling him how to parent his own child. His head throbs. He touches the bandage on his forehead and looks back at the TV. "I'm not in the mood for this. I came down to watch the game."

Now Vance sits up. "She's my niece, and I care about her a hell of a lot. You know that."

"And *you* know that I already told you—pretty damn politely—to butt out."

Vance looks injured and slumps lower in his seat. "Maybe coming here was a mistake," he says.

Craig keeps his eyes on the TV. "I didn't invite you."

Vance just sits there, and in spite of himself, Craig starts to feel bad. "Jesus, V," he says, "don't look like that."

"Like what?"

"So fucking forlorn. Come on," he says, "I take it back. You're welcome here. You know that."

Vance sits up again.

For a long while they're both quiet. Finally Vance says, "I appreciate it, you know. A lot."

"What?"

"You, letting me stay here. It's"—he pauses, eyes on the screen— "it's very kind."

"I'm not kind, I'm your brother," Craig says. "Now can we please watch the game?"

MONDAY

14

THE DISPLAY SAYS 156, without shoes, which is discouraging, but this scale reads heavier than the one upstairs, so she feels justified in rounding down. Still: standing in front of the mirror next to the tread-mill, she frowns. Her hips belong to someone she doesn't recognize, not to mention her thighs. Even her calves have changed. Before she was pregnant with Cam she weighed 125 and wore a size 6—numbers she'd never truly appreciated, she realizes now, and which seem unlikely if not fantastical, numbers she'd do anything to get back. *Well, not any-thing, apparently*, she thinks, recalling the three slices of pepperoni pizza and two glasses of wine she put away last night.

She's dripping with sweat. She takes the towel off the treadmill's railing, drapes it around her neck, blotting her face, and checks the clock on the wall. She's got less than an hour and a half to eat break-fast, get dressed, get Cameron ready, and meet Meghan—who's agreed to watch him for the day—at the store. She checks her reflection once more. Her shirt is soaked, her hair's wet, and her face is flushed.

She hangs the towel on the railing, picks the baby monitor up off the floor, and heads up the basement stairs in her socks. When she opens the door to the kitchen she's surprised by Vance—it had completely slipped her mind that he's here. He's standing in the breakfast nook, looking out at the yard with his back to her. "Morning," she says, and evidently he's surprised too, because he spins around, sloshing coffee over the rim of the mug in his hand.

"Shit, I'm sorry. I'll get it," he says, setting the mug on the table and coming into the kitchen, where she is.

"I didn't mean to sneak up on you," she says, handing him a towel.

He apologizes again, squatting down and sopping up the spill, and a third time once he's done.

She takes the towel from him and tosses it into the laundry room, onto a pile of dirty clothes. When she turns back around she notices his eyes look red-rimmed and his face, thin—or maybe it's just thin in comparison to Craig's. There's an awkward silence while she pours herself coffee from the carafe. "Can I top you off?" she asks, and he accepts.

"It's so quiet," he says while she pours.

"I know. Isn't it heavenly?"

"I assumed everyone was gone."

"They are, just about," she says. "Helen's at school, Amanda's doing a beach cleanup and spending the night at a friend's, and Craig's in Boston for the night." Automatically she thinks of Dov—his invitation, which she has yet to answer—and, worrying that her face betrays her, looks away.

If he does notice anything, he doesn't let on. He thanks her and takes his coffee back to the window. She wonders, vaguely, what new, and likely sordid, turn of events has driven him here, to their house. It can't be his first choice of refuge. Sure, he visits a couple of times a year, but that's to see the kids—to see Amanda, everyone knows. It's not as if he and Craig delight in each other's company. In fact, as far as she can tell, Craig can barely stand to be in the same room with his brother these days, and from what she's observed, Vance feels much the same. And yet, here he is. There's something between them, some enigmatic, intractable force that continually draws them together—a force that's beyond her ability, and probably beyond anyone's, maybe even theirs, to understand.

She sets down the baby monitor on the counter and fills a glass with water from the tap. Drinking it, she's aware that he's turned back around and is watching her, and she feels suddenly self-conscious in her workout clothes. She opens the refrigerator for milk and surreptitiously adjusts her top, which wasn't engineered to support her breasts in their current capacious state. She wonders what he thinks of her — how she looks to him: does he notice the extra weight? (Craig says *he* doesn't, and that she looks good, which is in some ways more distressing than him telling her the truth.) Not that she cares, particularly, what Vance thinks — he's just Vance — but still, she wishes she'd worn a top that didn't make her feel like a sausage exploding its casing. Until she's down to 135, or 130, maybe, this one is hereby relegated to the drawer.

"What kind of beach cleanup?" he asks.

"Pardon?"

"Amanda."

"Did I say cleanup? It's not quite that. She's volunteering with the Park Service, cordoning off piping plover nests. Setting up signs and fencing, I guess?"

"I thought she was grounded. She said she wasn't allowed to leave the house."

"Silly me, then, I guess I forgot," she says, flashing him a conspiratorial smile before setting her water glass down in the sink. "Not that you would, but if you don't mind, it would probably be best if you didn't mention her going to Craig."

His face is hard to read, but he says, "You don't have anything to worry about on that front."

He looks so lost, she notes, with his rumpled clothes and unkempt hair; she feels a surge of affection for him. "You can't take Craig's behavior personally, you know," she says.

"You mean, like, it's not just me he treats like shit, it's everyone?"

She laughs. "He's very democratic in that way — if only that one." He's smiling back at her, and it occurs to her that it might be one of the most genuinely nice moments they've ever shared.

Quickly, though, his smile fades. "I just feel bad for her," he says. "I mean, I get it, she screwed up. But it strikes me as a bit draconian, sending her home."

Gina pauses a moment, thinking carefully about how to respond. Clearly Amanda's told him something, but judging from what he's just said, it's something short of the truth. Well short of it is her guess. She sips her coffee, stalling. Part of her wants to tell Vance everything. He's way less rigid than Craig; surely he'd be on her side—Amanda's—and it would mean so much for Amanda to have her uncle's, if not her father's, support. But she hesitates: underneath everything, they're still brothers, there's that bond between them, and she simply can't run the risk, no matter how slight, of him sharing her plan with Craig.

As if on cue, her phone buzzes: *Rachel,* she thinks. It's inside her purse, which sits on top of a cluttered section of countertop that's supposed to be used as a desk, and she digs it out, but it's not her doctor friend's name on the screen. It's Dov's. She considers sending it to voicemail, but she knows he'll keep trying until she picks up.

"It's my sister," she tells Vance. "Now's not a great time," she whispers, ducking into the mudroom.

"I'm just calling to say we're all set." He names the restaurant and recites the address. "Twelve noon?"

She's pretty sure she can hear Vance lurking near the door. She whispers, "Okay, yes, fine. But I can't stay long."

"My heart is breaking already."

"You're ridiculous. I've got to go. Heather says hello," she tells Vance when she emerges.

"Is something wrong?" he asks.

"No, not really. Her son's got the flu." What a witch she is, she thinks, involving innocent children—innocent children she loves—in her deceit: surely she'll be punished for this. She glances at her reflection in the oven door and hopes Vance doesn't notice the fresh flush in her face. She opens the refrigerator door again, trying to cool off.

What's most astonishing, maybe, is how quickly it's happened, the transition: one day she's an honest person, a devoted mother and faithful wife, and the next she's arranging clandestine rendezvous and spouting lies.

If only she hadn't gone to the ladies' room last night at the Plum: there he was, behind the bar, looking like he'd been waiting for her, looking downright wolfish, and when she came out, drying her hands on her skirt, he actually was waiting for her, standing in the narrow tiled hall. He caught her arm and pulled her into the phone booth (now phoneless), closed the door, and said he had to see her. "You're fresh air for me" were his words, "and I need to breathe." They'd go to another town, he said, to a little inn he knew of where they make a life-changing pressed pheasant, and where there would be zero chance of running into anyone they knew. The phone booth was old, perhaps original to the building, once an inn itself, and the air inside was stale in an oddly pleasant way, the pine paneling faded to a warm, golden patina with decades of love declarations carved into the wood. She nodded yes. It wasn't right, she won't pretend it is. But that thing happens when she's near him, when he touches her; the good sense that's always been her North Star, her guiding light, dims.

"Gina?"

"Yes." She closes the refrigerator door.

"I asked whether there's anything I can do to help out. I'm so grateful to you guys for letting me stay."

As nonchalantly as she can, she says, "Actually, there is something. I have a client who wants me to decorate her house."

"Okay," Vance says.

She explains that this client is all the way out in Provincetown, but it's good money and something she'd like to do. The lies just tumble, one after the other, from her mouth. "What I'm getting to is, would you mind picking Helen up from school? That way I won't have to race back."

"I'd be happy to."

"Really? Because if it's too much trouble . . ." She's hoping he'll say that actually it is too much trouble, that he'll renege, when her phone buzzes again. She looks at the screen and sees Rachel's name. "Sorry, Heather again. Just a sec," she says, ducking into the mudroom for a second time.

Rachel says, "Is it a good time?"

"Not really," Gina says, resting a sneaker on the bench.

"I'll get right to it, then. Does Wednesday work?"

"Yes. Morning or afternoon?"

"Two P.M., but you have to get there by ten. Should I confirm?"

"Please," she says.

"You sure everything's okay?" Vance asks when she emerges. He's standing by the island now, looking concerned.

"I think so. She tends to panic, but I guess we all do." Her thoughts spin; she'd like to call Amanda, right now, and let her know—she'll be so relieved. But that would be imprudent. Better to wait to the last possible moment, when there's no chance of her telling Craig.

"So, Helen," Vance says.

Gina struggles to refocus. "Right. You're sure you don't mind?"

"I'm sure," he says, regarding her a little curiously.

Thanking him, she forces her face into what she hopes is a normal, gracious smile. "You can take Craig's truck," she says. "Let me get you the keys."

"Do you need to let them know I'm coming?" he asks, following her into the front hall. "I mean, so they don't think I'm some creep?"

She says no and smiles again, genuinely this time. "Don't worry about that. The only creep they'll think you are is Craig."

15

THE PLANE, a Cessna 402C, has nine seats, the pilot explains, which he'll assign to the passengers according to their weight. Standing on the wet tarmac with six other travelers, Craig only half listens, he's heard the spiel plenty of times before, instead staring up at the sky, which this morning is a low blanket of clouds, while the pilot, a kid of twenty at best, looks each of them up and down. He begins by instructing a slim young woman about Amanda's age to sit in the very back. Then he sends a middle-aged couple in matching raincoats to the rear too. Next is a tall man in a leather jacket, then a slight, twentysomething guy with a shaved head, and finally a solid-looking, sixtyish woman holding a tiny, wheat-colored dog against her chest.

Craig is last, which feels intentional. The boy pilot squints at him, then informs him that he'll be sitting up front in the copilot's seat, and while Craig's buckling himself in, the pilot says, "I hope you know how to fly this thing, because I'm wicked hungover."

Craig turns to look at him. He's lean and unseasonably suntanned and wears a Hawaiian shirt, and when he grins, which he's doing now, the tendons in his neck stand up.

"That's a joke," he says. "You ever heard one of those?"

"Once," Craig says, wondering if he's even twenty; he could be nineteen. The only indication that he's officially employed by the airline is a blue lanyard around his neck that says *Island Air*.

Maybe he can sense Craig's discomfort, because he says, "You just sit back and enjoy the view, sir," handing him a headset. Swiveling around in his seat, the pilot reels off a few instructions, then says, "Vamanos." Donning his own headset, he starts the propellers, adjusts some dials and knobs, and they're on their way.

Craig doesn't like sitting up front much. He doesn't care much for flying in general, and with the pilot right there, and all the controls (which look disconcertingly ancient, a melee of lights and switches and dials), it's much harder to tune out the fact that he's on a plane. He tries to cross his legs but there's no room, so he puts his hands in his lap and tries to relax by looking out the window, but all he can think is what it would be like if the plane plummeted into the sea. He would much rather be on the ferry. It's just more civilized, no one asks for your weight, plus there's a snack bar, and sitting by the window staring out at the water always gives him a sense of peace. But this morning the ferry was delayed—rough seas—and his meeting with Marco is at ten, and he wasn't about to ask his friend (and, as soon as he signs the contract in Craig's bag, key client) to wait.

After a smooth enough takeoff, they bank south, drawing a wide circle over the open ocean. When they're over land again, Craig leans his forehead against the Plexiglas window and looks down, hoping to catch a glimpse of the house, but the clouds are thick and swirling and all he can see is clusters of trees, then the solid-looking surface of the water again, and soon he can't even see that, the plane has been entirely subsumed. It's disorienting, with no clear up or down, just white ephemera rushing by on all sides. He glances over at the pilot, who's got a clipboard on his lap now and is filling out a form. Sitting back, Craig wipes his hands, which are damp, on his pants, and closes his eyes, telling himself he might as well take the pilot's advice and enjoy this brief hiatus from his life.

But it's impossible. He hates being up there. Gina contends his aversion to flying is about control—that he can't stand not having any, up in the air—but he thinks it's simpler than that. It's just unnatural, it's *wrong*, to be trapped inside a metal pod, hurtling through the atmosphere miles above the earth. He used to have nightmares about being in a plane that was about to crash. The plane never actually made contact with anything, but the specter of impending disaster was enough to wake him up in a cold sweat. The dreams were the most intense when he was a kid, but they returned, and with a vengeance, in the weeks after Suzanne's death (which was strange, he always thought, because the most terrible thing that could have happened—or so he imagined then—already had). Finally he broke down and got some sleeping pills from his doctor, which helped, and after some months, the nightmares tapered off. Then, around the time he got together with Gina, he stopped dreaming altogether, or at least he simply stopped remembering when he did, which was fine with him.

He must have fallen asleep despite his anxiety, because when he opens his eyes they're out of the clouds, descending, and the sun is out. He looks down and sees Georges Island, with its pentagon-shaped Civil War fort, and north of Logan, the grand, dilapidated Victorians of Revere.

Outside the terminal, he hails a taxi to Charlestown, instructing the driver to let him out a couple of blocks short of Marco's office. He's early, which he doesn't like to be. Never be early, his first boss always said; it looks like you don't have enough to do. He gets out of the cab and stands squinting in the sunshine, orienting himself to the city streets. He's across from a coffee shop and a fancy-looking pet boutique —Charlestown looks more genteel every time he comes—and for no particular reason he thinks of Amanda. Touching his phone, which is holstered on his hip, he feels a compulsion to call her, just to hear her voice, but he doesn't. All her voice will tell him, he knows, is that she despises him.

In an Italian café a few doors down he orders a cappuccino and from the glass case selects a cream-filled cannoli, which he carries on a small white plate to a round marble table by the window, where he sits facing the street. With a fork he pokes at the cannoli. The cream turns out to be lemon, which he didn't anticipate, and overly sweet, but he makes quick work of it anyway. A girl who looks about Amanda's age (must *everyone* look about Amanda's age?) brings him his cappuccino, in whose foam she's drawn a perfect fern leaf. He doesn't know why but tears fill his eyes. He blinks them back. She asks if he wants anything else, and he tells her no thanks, watching her return to her post behind the counter, where she sets about preparing another customer's drink. He wipes his nose on a thin napkin and picks up pastry crumbs with his thumb. When he's finished, he leaves a five-dollar bill on the table, her tip.

Out on the sidewalk, he fishes his sunglasses out of his messenger bag and checks the time. It's one minute after ten. Marco's office is at the end of the block, inside what used to be a candy factory. From the directory on the wall of the marble-lined lobby, Craig learns that Marco's firm, Maroon Capital (named for the school color of their alma mater, Colgate), takes up the top two floors.

He rides the elevator to the seventh floor, gets out, and states his name to a well-groomed young man stationed behind a high wood reception desk. "We're old buddies," he adds. "Marco probably said."

The kid doesn't appear interested. "Mr. Cardoza's on the phone at the moment. You can have a seat," he says.

Craig chooses a chair by a window that looks over the harbor. Five or ten minutes pass before Marco comes out. Seeing Craig, he grins and extends his hand, and they execute their fraternity's secret, folded-down-middle-finger handshake. "Sorry to keep you waiting, brother. You're looking"—he pauses—"robust. What happened to your head?" Craig's hand goes to the bandage. Before he can answer, Marco says, "You should see the other guy, right? Come on back."

Craig follows him to the end of the hall, into the last office on the left. It's a large room with a massive window, also with a view of the water, and a large desk facing two chairs.

"Nice," Craig says.

"We just moved in. Got a hell of a deal on the lease." The phone on his desk makes a bleeping sound and the light blinks. "I've got to take this. Just a sec," he says.

Craig uses the opportunity to look around. On one wall there's a bookshelf holding a set of leather-bound books. On the other hangs a large abstract painting, mostly orange and red. Marco is frowning. He says into the phone, "We're not therapists. Tell him we need the full commitment by Friday, or we close without him." He hangs up, scribbles something on a pad, and turns his attention to Craig. Again he grins. "It's been a while, hasn't it? July Fourth?"

"Two Fourths ago," Craig says.

"Shit. How'd we let so much time pass?"

Craig shrugs. "How's Maureen? The kids?"

"Growing like weeds," Marco says. Leaning forward, he picks up a silver picture frame and hands it to Craig. The photo shows Marco's twins, two suntanned, towheaded boys, life-jacketed and grinning from the prow of Marco's sailboat, the same custom-built J/88 Speedster he took Gina and Craig and Helen out on two summers ago. It was a perfect, clear evening, and they drank Dark and Stormys and watched the fireworks display, listening to the Pops—but it's no great mystery, at least to Craig, why they haven't seen each other since. Marco, emboldened by a few too many tumblers of rum, had gotten going on politics —a not-so-endearing tic he's acquired in the decades since college— starting with a story about calling American Express and being asked if he wanted to continue in Spanish, and how floored he'd been. "It is *American* Express, for Christ's sake, or it was last time I checked," he said, and then worse, a lot worse. Craig, who knew what a standup guy Marco was, also knew to take his booze-fueled invectives with a grain of salt, but Gina didn't. The whole drive back to the Cape, she detailed her disgust. He was an imbecile, she concluded, his children were rude and spoiled, and Maureen was a Stepford wife. How could Craig ever have considered him a friend?

Craig sets the picture down on the desk. "Well, it looks like you're all doing great," he says.

Marco checks his cell phone. "I have an investor coming in at ten-thirty," he says. "The real deal. Raised a truckload for Mitt." He types something into his phone.

Craig glances at the clock on the wall. Ten-thirty? He knew Marco was busy, but that's just a few minutes from now. "Let's get to it, then," he says, trying not to sound offended. "The papers are ready to go." He reaches down and opens his messenger bag. Searching for the folder, he says, "I had Renee draw them up according to the drawings we discussed, the four-bedroom, but we can always extend the scope." He extracts the folder and opens it, taking two copies of the contract off the top and holding them out.

But Marco doesn't take them. He has a strange look on his face. "Listen, about the house. I wanted to talk to you face-to-face," he says.

"Okay," Craig says, pulling the papers back toward his lap.

"You know I respect you too much to pussy around, so I'll just say it plain. We're going with another firm."

Craig doesn't know what he means. "For what?"

"The house."

"What house?"

"Dude, the *house*. We're going with a relative of Maureen's." He pushes back from his desk, crosses his legs, and makes a pyramid with his fingers. "If it were up to me, man, believe me." While Craig's struggles to make sense of what's been said, Marco talks about his wife's cousin, who's apparently a builder. "He's her mom's sister's kid. They were really close when they were young—Maureen and him. Hiring you instead would've caused a major family rift. You know how complicated these things can get, especially when the women are involved."

Craig has no idea what he's supposed to say. He feels like an idiot, and he'd like to punch Marco in the face. But he just sits there, mute. After a long moment, he realizes he's still—foolishly—holding in his hands the papers Marco was supposed to sign. Stuffing them back into his bag, he says, "Why are you telling me this now? Why did you have me come all the way here?"

"I wanted to see you. And shit—like I said, I wanted to explain face-to-face. You're my brother." He looks down at the gold fraternity ring on his right hand, then back at Craig. "I'm sorry, dude. I am. But listen, maybe it's better this way. You know what they say about doing business with friends." His face looks drawn and colorless—Craig can see he's struggling, too.

He realizes he's gripping the chair's armrests with both hands, and he lets go, takes a deep breath, and stands up.

Marco does the same. "You sticking around?" he says. "I was hoping I could buy you a steak after work. It's the least I can do."

"I don't think so," Craig says.

"Next time, then. And let's make sure it's sooner than a year and a half," Marco says, holding out his hand.

Outside, Craig stands on the sidewalk, disoriented, blinking in the bright light. After a long moment he remembers his sunglasses. Putting them on, he starts walking, he doesn't know to where, only that he wants to get the hell out of Charlestown, and that he's not about to go home. He walks to the end of the block and crosses the street, then heads left, toward the water, ducking into a 7-Eleven to buy a pack of cigarettes. In an unlovely pocket park he sits on a wooden bench and smokes. One bench over, a homeless man wrapped in filthy blankets delivers an energetic, nonsensical rant.

This isn't the morning he'd envisioned, not by a long shot. He thinks of all the money he owes the bank, of his extravagant house, of Marco's smug face. Questions ping-pong around in his head: How could his old friend treat him so badly? Was it something he did? And most important, what the hell's he going to do now? Work his ass off, that's what. It'll take three or four regular jobs to make up for Marco's. He can only hope that Dov comes through. He wonders what the hell is taking him so long to decide, anyway. He considers calling him up right now and asking, point-blank, but he doesn't think he can handle more bad news today, and instead he sinks lower on the bench.

The park reeks of urine and the homeless guy is shouting at some birds. Craig finishes the cigarette, which leaves a rancid taste in his mouth, gets up, and offers the man the remainder of the pack.

"No way. You know they soak that shit in formaldehyde?" he says, and Craig throws the pack in the trash.

By the Museum of Science he crosses the bridge, stopping in the middle to look down. The water looks silty and brown, and he thinks about how cold it must be, how foul it must taste. He shivers: the sun's strong but the wind whips at his uncovered head and his face. He continues on, feeling a little frantic, picking up the path along the Esplanade.

When they first moved to Boston, before he and Suzanne were married, they didn't have any money, and they couldn't get enough of each other's company, and one of their favorite things to do on the weekends was walk. One of their favorite walking routes was a giant loop, all the way from Kendall Square to Charlestown, out on one side of the river, back on the other. He remembers how naturally their gaits fit together, how seamlessly she'd take his hand. He can't remember what they talked about for all those hours; probably it was the future, their plans. It wasn't long after they'd arrived that Suzanne found out she was pregnant, so there was plenty to figure out. Jesus, he misses her. What wouldn't he give to have her back here, walking next to him, right now?

He walks and walks, crossing over Storrow Drive and cutting through the hospital complex and past the old Charles Street Jail, which is now a swanky hotel. He's not aimless anymore. He takes Charles Street past the Public Garden, keeps going south to where Charles becomes Tremont, which he follows until he's standing in front of the townhouse whose top-floor apartment he and Suzanne once shared, and turns his face upward, shading his eyes.

The windows are closed, but in his memory they're always open. They moved in in June, and the place had no air conditioning, so they bought beach chairs at Walgreens and sat up on the roof deck most nights that first summer, drinking beer and listening to the Red Sox. It was the first place they lived as a couple, as "adults," though now, thinking back, they seem like children. It's where they lived when Amanda was born—the place they brought her home to. She was so tiny and perfect; as long as he lives, he'll never forget that first morning at the hospital, holding her in his arms. She'd wrapped her tiny fingers around his thumb and squeezed, and he knew right then how special she was, and how strong.

"Daddy's a goner," the nurse had said, and he couldn't protest, he was too choked up.

"Are you all right?" Suzanne had said, and he'd nodded, but looking back it's clear that he wasn't: he knew, or he was about to learn, that having a child was like walking around with a knife in your chest.

"Excuse me," says a voice, and he turns. A girl holding a clipboard and wearing a Greenpeace T-shirt over her coat is standing before him. "Help save the whales?"

"Not today," he says, and walks away, stepping around two pigeons eviscerating an apple on the curb.

He walks to the corner and stops, waiting for the light to change. He's cold: the wind has picked up, and he's wearing only an oxford shirt under his fleece. There are taxis on Tremont and he considers hailing one to take him to Long Wharf, to catch a ferry to Provincetown, but he keeps his hands in his pockets. The light turns green. Before stepping into the street, he turns around one last time and looks up at #5F. He can remember, clear as the sky above him is now, coming home from the real estate office where he worked then and seeing Suzanne's face through the pane. She'd be in the rocking chair, nursing Amanda and waiting for him, and sometimes, by chance, she'd look down and see him. Then she'd smile and press Amanda's little hand against the glass.

A tight feeling fills his chest, an ache. He heads north on Arlington Street to Newbury and keeps going, past places he recognizes and places he doesn't, old parks and new restaurants and all the myriad shops. He's cold and hungry but he doesn't stop. At the Fenway he veers south, and when he finally stops walking it's afternoon and he's at the Isabella Stuart Gardner Museum, standing in front of Sargent's *El Jaleo*, in the very same spot he'd stood nineteen years before, proposing to Suzanne.

It was her favorite painting, her favorite museum, maybe her favorite place on the face of the earth. She'd first brought him here the summer after they graduated, when they'd just begun to date. Her grandmother had brought her here as a girl, she'd told him, and the moment she laid eyes on *El Jaleo*, she knew what she wanted to do with her life, and that was paint. She never got tired of the Gardner. Once in a while she'd bring a stool and a sketchbook, and occasionally she'd point out, for Craig's benefit, the painting's masterful elements: the grand scale, the shadows on the wall, the glints of golden light on the guitars, the folds of the dancer's skirt. But more often she'd just stand here, right here, entranced.

Now he stands under a scalloped stone arch. He's alone in the cloister, and he lets himself imagine for a moment that it's his lunch hour and she's on her way to meet him. He tries to conjure her again—her voice, her scent, her elbow brushing his—but the harder he tries, the more alone he feels.

He looks around. A security guard, a bulky guy about his age, has materialized in the doorway on the left. How long has he been standing there? Does he think Craig's nuts? Craig doesn't care. He steps closer to the painting, and closer again. He has a strong urge to touch the canvas. He lifts his hand.

"Sir," the guard says. "Please step back."

He does. Leaving the cloister, he feels a little panicked, like he's leaving something behind.

He exits the museum. After Mrs. Gardner's dark rooms, the sunlight offends his eyes. He hails a cab, but instead of telling the driver to take him to the wharf, he names the hotel in the North End, the Topaz, where he's reserved a room.

He hands the woman behind the reception desk his credit card. In a stale-smelling room with brown curtains and a view of an alley, he lies atop a brown bedspread, thinking not about Marco anymore, but about Suzanne. What if she hadn't gotten pregnant that summer? Or worse, what if she'd done what he'd suggested, and Amanda was never born? It pains him to remember how he'd insisted on "weighing their options," telling Suzanne they needed to "be smart." Of course she wouldn't hear of anything like that. "This is my *child*, I could never," she said, and she never wavered, and all he can think now is *Thank God*. Because what if she'd listened to him? What would his life be now?

This is what Amanda doesn't understand: what she wants to do would not only insult her mother's memory but, in effect, negate her own existence. More to the point, this is Suzanne's flesh and blood —Suzanne's *grandchild*—she's talking about obliterating. *Terminating.* Just thinking the word sends despair coursing through him. She thinks her life is over, that she's losing something; she doesn't understand that she's not losing anything, that really they're getting a piece of Suzanne back. All he can hope is that someday she does understand, that someday she feels even half the love, and gratitude, for her own child that he feels for her.

His phone buzzes. He gets up and goes to the desk and, seeing Gina's name, switches it off. He decides to run a bath, and while the tub fills he drops his clothes on the floor and stands in front of the mirror, staring at an unfamiliar, unhappy-looking, fat-faced man.

And then, before he can stop himself, he's back there again—at the rinky-dink hospital in Belize City, smelling bleach, standing by the mechanized bed that contained what was left of Suzanne.

He wanted to take her in his arms but he was afraid of hurting her, so he sat in a plastic chair for what felt like ages, watching her unmoving eyelids, holding her hand. After what felt like a year, a doctor came in.

"This is my fault," Craig had blurted before the man even said his name.

He seemed unsurprised, but assured Craig it wasn't; this kind of thing just happens, it's random, he said, and Craig nodded robotically, though not a cell in his body accepted what he said. It was one hundred percent his fault. The trip, an anniversary present, was his idea; he'd bought the tickets; he'd chosen the resort; and of course he'd persuaded her to dive with him. Over her protests (she was claustrophobic, she was afraid of sea life, she preferred the beach) he assured her she'd be fine. And she was fine, for the first three days at least. But on the fourth, their last before going home, she wanted to see the ruins, but he convinced her that they couldn't leave without visiting that divers' mecca, the Great Blue Hole.

The water was clear as glass, and calm, and they dove deeper than they ever had. They were past forty feet when a school of flamboyantly colored parrotfish floated by; he remembers looking over at her, flashing her a high sign, but she didn't return it, pointing her finger at the surface instead. He shook his head. Ignoring him and their guide, Luís, and more important, the protocols they'd practiced so many times, she started kicking to the surface. He tried to follow but she was going too fast, he knew she was, and then—and then. She was maybe fifteen feet above him when she went limp.

Luís made him stop and decompress for two unbearable minutes at twenty-five feet, and another excruciating minute at fifteen. By the time they got her into the boat she was gone, he knew she was. CPR got her breathing, but she never opened her eyes again. Not during the week at the Belize hospital, not when they flew her back to the States. At Brigham and Women's, the doc pulled Craig aside.

He blinked in the bright lights. "You've got some decisions to make."

Craig felt as if all the blood had been drained from his body; he couldn't feel his limbs. He managed to ask the doctor whether he'd ever seen someone in Suzanne's situation make a full recovery, and the doctor said no.

Over the next six weeks they brought in all the best specialists, who tried all the newest therapies, but after nine weeks of failed brain-function tests and flat lines on screens, there was no more pretending anything was going to change.

And no matter what the doctors—or anyone—said, there was no pretending that any of it was anyone's fault but Craig's.

The tub is full. He cuts off the spigot and tests the water with his foot. It's way too hot, practically scalding, but he doesn't care, he wants it that way.

He steps in.

16

AFTER KILLING AN HOUR and a half at Eugene's Beans, nursing a hot chocolate, another hour walking aimlessly around town, and another two at the library, surfing the web and not saving plovers, Amanda waits at the intersection of Eastern and Main for her ride, which turns out to be a Subaru station wagon packed with kids Amanda half knows.

"Party taxi, hop in," Sybil says, smiling through the open window. She's sitting up front on some guy's lap. The back door opens and Amanda squeezes in next to two boys who look familiar and a girl who does not.

It's not a party at all, it turns out, hardly even a gathering, just some kids sitting around playing video games and getting high. She's not in the mood to smoke, and she doesn't give a shit about video games. She's never understood the appeal, plus it's always sort of embarrassing how the boys play and the girls sit there, mute, and watch.

After an hour or so she asks Noah, whose house it is, if she can use the bathroom, and she follows his directions through the kitchen and the dining room. All the rooms are painted white, everything's extremely modern and clean, like you'd see on TV or in one of Gina's design magazines, with strategic recessed lighting, high ceilings, and no clutter anywhere but lots of bizarre modern art. On the dining room wall hangs a huge black-and-white photograph of a naked girl, maybe nine years old, standing in dark water up to her hips.

She keeps going, entering a long hall whose floor is some kind of polished stone or maybe concrete; whatever material it is, it's freezing. Noah made everyone take their shoes off when they came in, and she can feel the cold through her socks.

At the end of the hall she opens the third door on the left, a powder room. There's a modern-looking white toilet and a glass sink, a glass-orb pendant light, and a tall, slim window that looks out over Nantucket Sound.

She doesn't actually have to pee, for once. She washes her hands with fancy-looking liquid soap and looks at herself in the mirror for a moment, then looks away. From the living room, she hears an eruption of laughter. They're all pretty stoned. It's not much fun being the only not-stoned person in the room, but she has no desire to join their ranks. She hasn't smoked since the soccer-practice debacle—not because she learned a valuable lesson or anything like that. The truth is she only ever really liked smoking with Kevin. In groups, or at a party, it makes her feel too self-conscious. That's one ironic twist: of the three of them who got busted, she's the one who smokes the least. She's probably smoked weed five times in her whole life, not counting with Kevin, whereas Lydia and Candace smoke basically every day. Not that she blames them, or anyone. Like the situation she's in now, she may have been unlucky, but there's no one to blame but herself.

She's not eager to rejoin the party, and instead she wanders farther down the hall, to the very end, proceeding into what turns out to be Noah's parents' bedroom, or she guesses it is. Noah's dad runs a hedge fund or something—they're loaded, Sybil said—and now that Noah's away at school his mother spends most of her time in New York and the house sits empty much of the year. This isn't hard to believe. The bed, a low platform covered with a burlap-colored quilt, looks like it's never been slept in, and the nightstands are bare except for matching sky-blue lamps. By an immense pair of sliding doors, Amanda sits in a gray upholstered armchair and looks out at the yard, which is adorned with various sculptures: a giant iron figure-eight, a Roman-looking marble bust, a sort of double-helix thing in neon green, and, closer to the water, an enormous, polished chrome horse.

They've got their own beach, with a long wooden dock on the right and a jetty off to the left, and for a while she watches the Sound slosh and slap against the rocks. It's gotten to be a pretty day out; the sky is clear except for some high clouds, white on top and darker underneath, and close to shore a few brightly colored buoys bob, maybe lobster traps, or maybe moorings for Noah's family's boats. Toward the horizon she can see a couple of fishing trawlers, and she wonders how cold the water is—probably in the forties. Christian once told her that it doesn't matter how strong a swimmer you are when the water's that cold, because it stops your heart. Christian had spent a couple of years in the Chilean navy after high school, which is how he knew.

She wonders what that would feel like, your heart stopping. Probably not anything, maybe just like going to sleep. She's read that that's what freezing to death is like, peaceful more than anything else. Christian told her he went overboard once during a training exercise. He was in the water for a total of four minutes and his heart had slowed so precipitously, he said, he probably wouldn't have made it to five.

He'd told her that, about almost dying, just a couple of days into the trip—maybe three days before she sprained her ankle—the first time they were ever alone. They were sitting on a boulder fifty yards from camp, she remembers, and the sun was beginning to set. She'd always loved this time of day, twilight, best, she told him; it made her feel hopeful for some reason, the lingering, luminous blue light. He listened, interested; she could feel his big brown eyes on her face while she spoke. But he was still in teacher mode then. He told her there were actually three different twilights, and that it was helpful to distinguish between them when you were living outdoors: in civil twilight, he said, you could see terrestrial objects clearly and only the brightest stars; in nautical twilight, there were enough stars out to navigate by; and in astronomical twilight, the light from the stars was more powerful than from any other source.

"Amanda?" she hears—it's Sybil's voice. "You in here?" There's a quick, timid knock on the door, and she steps through. "Howdy," she says. "Everything cool? I've been looking for you."

"I'm fine."

Sybil turns to the sliding doors and looks out. "Isn't this place sick?" Amanda keeps her eyes on the water. "We were getting worried. Wyman thought maybe you smoked too much and fell off the dock. I told him to shut up, but then I got a little paranoid." Amanda doesn't answer. "Want to come hang out? Justin Canova just got here, and the Dwyer twins, and Lily Delk. Noah's making screwdrivers, and the twins brought Jell-O shots."

Amanda's still facing the sliders. The sun's hidden behind a bank of clouds now, and the fishing boats are almost too small to make out.

"Are you sure nothing's wrong?" Sybil says. "You seem kind of . . . I don't know, subdued."

"I'm fine," she says.

"I could totally stay here if you'd rather, like, talk."

Jesus, Amanda thinks, why does everyone want to talk to her? Is she suddenly so fascinating? She wishes Sybil would just go. Because does she think Amanda's actually going to confide in her? They hardly know each other. Sure they've gone to the same school forever, but that doesn't mean anything.

"That's okay. You go ahead," she says. Turning around, she sees the hurt look on Sybil's face. "Really, thanks, but I'm good."

She feels a little guilty watching Sybil leave. But it's not her fault that Sybil's always wanted to be better friends than she has. On the wall by the armchair, she presses a chrome button beside a dark fireplace and blue and orange flames leap up. She opens one of the glass safety doors and holds her hand close to the fire but feels no warmth. Slowly she walks the room's perimeter. On the wall perpendicular to the bed, there's a handle, which she pulls. It's a closet, a large one, but there aren't any clothes. In fact the only signs of human habitation are a pair of well-worn shearling slippers and a collapsed Louis Vuitton suitcase close to the door. She shuts the closet and goes into the master bathroom, which is floor-to-ceiling gray stone, and opens one of the medicine cabinets. There's not much there, either—a man's razor, some Vicks cough suppressant, some hotel bath products, a couple of bottles of prescription pills. She takes one down and reads the label: *Take twice daily or as needed for pain*, it says. She unscrews the cap and looks inside, at ten or fifteen round yellow pills. She could probably sell them (she has no idea to whom, but she could find out), but there's no way a few pills are going to get her anywhere close to the sum she needs. Also, pills? It seems too depraved. She replaces the bottle on the shelf.

Back in the bedroom, she lies on the bed, on top of the duvet. The ceiling, she notices now, is painted blue, a pretty pastel shade, a surprise. She thinks of lying in the tent, looking up at the nylon ceiling, listening to the *pat-pat* of rain on the fly. The tent was gray with yellow trim and a blaze-orange fly (easier to spot from far away or in snow), and it smelled a little dank until it got aired out. She spent three whole days in it after she hurt her ankle. She was depressed at first, knowing the rest of the group would be going off on their various excursions, learning rappelling and doing daylong solos and so forth, but then things turned around: Christian got assigned to stay with her.

At first it was awkward, with him lurking outside, whittling, boiling water, unpacking and repacking his things. But then the rain started, and she told him it was okay if he came in. They played cards, she taught him cribbage, and when that got old they told each other about their lives. He talked about his girlfriend, Malena, and about her disabled eleven-year-old son: how difficult it was, and about her temper, and about how things between them were always on the verge. Malena hadn't wanted him to go on the trip, she said it might be the end of them, he told Amanda, but he went anyway. This was his work, he said. It was what he loved.

And then it was her turn. She found herself telling him things she'd never told another soul, including Kevin—things she'd never said aloud: first about how Kevin had been at Brown for only two weeks before he broke it off—two *weeks*. And even what he said on the phone (the fucking *phone*, how pathetic is that?): he wanted to have a "true college experience," he said, and they were so young, it wasn't fair to either of them to tie each other down. She'd had to press, and press, until at last he confessed that yes, there was someone else: he'd kissed her, this person, and she'd spent the night in his room. After they hung up—she told Christian all of it—how she'd gone down to the kitchen and gotten a paring knife, and back in her room carved a tiny *K* into her arm. Christian didn't look shocked, hearing that, just sad, and she kept talking—about her family: about her father, about Gina, and then finally about her mom: how few things she remembers, how she can't separate what she does remember from home movies and photographs, how bad she feels about that. And the rest, things she thinks about all the time but almost never says: the accident. The phone ringing at three in the morning, Vance's face. The taxi ride to the airport before sunrise, Vance holding her hand on the plane. The hospital. How for ages and ages nobody would tell her what was going on. The tubes in her mother's nose, the gray color of her skin, her chapped lips. The funeral: Vance crying, everyone crying—everyone but her dad. The hymn about eagles that they played. How it was like her dad went somewhere without her and never really came back.

The hours passed. Christian made them maté and pilfered ginger cookies for them from the group's supply. She read to him from her diary, where she'd written down some poems she liked—Robert Frost, Mary Oliver, Yeats—and he played her some of his favorite songs from his iPhone, mostly bands she'd never heard of, one song in particular called "Te Recuerdo Amanda." He translated the lyrics while it played: *I remember you, Amanda, your wide smile, the rain in your hair* . . . Supposedly it had a political message, but it just sounded romantic to her.

Two whole days passed like that—tea, cribbage, confessions, rain on the tent—and then, late in the afternoon of the third day, he kissed her. It felt like the most exciting thing in the world and also like the most normal, like it was supposed to happen. Then he apologized, blushing deep red, and she said she was sorry too, but only because he was sorry, because she wasn't, and he kissed her again.

"Lake," says a voice from the hall. "What gives?" She opens her eyes. She knows the voice: Evan Dwyer, one of the twins. She's known them forever, too. "Get your ass out here," he says. "We're playing Minecraft and we need a ringer on our team."

She sits up.

"I hope you're decent, Lake, because I'm coming in."

The door opens and he steps in. He's a tall kid with a goofy smile and a wild mop of blond hair, which she's pleased to see he didn't feel the need to cut since he went away to college.

"Lake," he says, coming toward her with his arms spread.

"Hey, Muppet," she says, and gets up to give him a hug.

He's a big guy, a rower, and strong, even stronger now than he was in high school, and he hugs her so enthusiastically her feet lift a few inches off the floor. Setting her down, he says, "What's up? Sybil says you're being weird."

"Sybil's weird."

"Fair enough," he says. "Are you going to come play?"

"I'm not really in the mood."

"Huh," he says, glancing around the room. "Aren't you supposed to be gone?"

"Yes." She sits on the bed.

He cocks his head to one side and looks curious but doesn't ask anything else. He sits, too. "How's Kev?"

She looks down at her thumbs. "You didn't hear?" He shakes his head. "You must be the only one."

"You dumped him?"

"Actually, he dumped me."

"For real?"

She nods. "For some dumb slut, apparently." She smiles, but he looks concerned. "It's okay. We're still friends."

He regards her suspiciously. "You sure?"

She nods her head. "I'm just— maybe I'm getting sick."

His face breaks into a grin. "Well, you're in luck, because Doctor Dwyer's here, and he's going to cure what ails you." He stands up and holds out his hand. "Come on." She accepts it—what choice does she have?—and he pulls her up off the bed. She lets him lead her into the hallway, through the kitchen and dining room, and back into the living room, where eight or ten kids, some she recognizes and some she doesn't, sit around holding red Solo cups. Pot smoke hangs in the air and music plays from somewhere, Bob Marley, and one of the *Fast and Furious* movies is showing on the TV, on mute.

In the kitchen, Evan takes a crystal pitcher off the counter, pours some purple liquid into a clean red cup and hands it to her, then fills one for himself. Somehow, they're standing in a circle of kids.

"Skoal," Evan says, raising his cup.

"Prosit," says an unfamiliar kid in a sweatshirt that says *Big Red*.

Ariana, Evan's twin, says, "Slainte."

"Down the hatch," says Noah.

Amanda says, "L'chaim."

"What does that mean?" asks Big Red.

"To life," she says, and they drink.

17

THERE'S A SATELLITE-RADIO STATION devoted exclusively to the music of Bruce Springsteen: this Vance learns on Monday afternoon while he's familiarizing himself with his brother's truck. The song playing when he turns on the engine is "The River," a live version recorded at a concert at Wembley Stadium in 1985, according to the dashboard's digital display. He adjusts the mirrors and searches the various buttons and screens until he figures out how to turn off the heated seat, which feels like it's braising the backs of his thighs. *We'd go down to the river, and into the river we'd dive,* Bruce growls. As Bruce songs go, it's not a bad one, and since there's no way he's going to figure out how to change the station and drive at the same time, he lets it play.

He's not sure where he's headed, only that he needs to be away from Craig's. Even though Craig isn't there, just being in the house sets him on edge; it's like whatever's eating everyone has infiltrated the air. He thinks about swinging by the Plum to see Dov, but Dov doesn't know he's in town, and if he does stop by, he'll have to explain why he's on the Cape, which means either lying or telling the truth.

He takes Beach Road east. He could drive out on the dunes and check on Land's End, but he's supposed to get Helen at two, and between letting the air out of the tires, driving the three miles, making even a cursory inspection of the place, driving back, and reinflating the tires, he'd definitely risk being late.

Beach Road ends—as the name suggests—at the beach, and he parks near Dee's, the clam shack that another guy he grew up with opened and named after his wife. The place more or less prints money during the season, long lines of beachgoers buying lobster rolls for twenty dollars a pop, but this time of year it's boarded up. Same goes for the parking kiosk, the public restrooms, and the Park Service office. Indeed the whole area feels pleasantly desolate; his is one of just three vehicles in the whole football-field-sized lot.

A sand-covered boardwalk takes him past Dee's and onto a wooden staircase that leads down to the beach. Or rather, to the place where the staircase should be but is not—a winter storm must have taken it, again—and he stands on top of the sand cliff and smells the brine in the air and looks out at the water. It's rough today, big ragged waves breaking almost on top of each other and a couple of wide, white rip tides rushing away from shore.

He looks up the beach, then down: two dog walkers, that's all. The wind whips at his face and bare neck. It's a cold day to be out. He flips up the collar of his leather jacket, which isn't insulated but does a good job of blocking the wind, and he wonders where Amanda's plover-protection thing is taking place.

He watches the waves crest and break until he's nearly numb, and then he gets back in Craig's truck, turns up the heat, and heads into town. "Glory Days" is playing, and he finds himself singing along. Maybe it's the song, but something inspires him to detour by their old high school, which is now a regional middle school. He pulls into the parking lot and idles beside a crumbling expanse of blacktop that used to be the basketball courts. He never played, but Craig did. There were pickup games after school, and kids would loiter on the sidelines, killing time and flirting until they had to go to their respective team practices or home.

Being here makes him think of Dylan. He can see her like it was yesterday, sitting on the brick wall, sweeping her long hair out of her face. God only knows how many hours he spent here, pretending to talk to someone, watching her. The fall they got together (her junior year, his senior) she was manager of the men's soccer team. One afternoon he saw her carrying a giant net bag full of soccer balls toward the upper field, and he followed her. When he caught up, he asked if he could help. She said he could open the gate for her, which he did, feeling absurdly gallant, walking beside her all the way to the half-field line, where she set down the bag, turned to him, and said, "What, were you expecting a tip?" and grinned her magical grin.

A sound like a foghorn splits the air, and Vance watches a stream of middle schoolers erupt from the cement-block building and spill out into the yard. It's lunchtime, or maybe recess, and quickly they splinter off into groups. Aside from being smaller, they don't look much different from his own students: the boys in jeans either far too big or too small, and the long-haired girls all dressed the same, their skinny jeans or leggings disappearing into bulky sheepskin boots.

He pulls back onto the road, still thinking about Dylan. He was so awkward yesterday, in his disorientation, maybe even rude. He didn't mean to be, of course, but he felt so blindsided, seeing her after so much time, and so foolish, taking her for her mom—especially once he discovered that she was, indeed, still very lovely, with a new leanness in her face, and new lines around her gray-green eyes, and the same grin she'd always had, perhaps more lovely, in a way, than when she was young.

He decides to buy her a gift, some small token to show her that he really was glad to see her, and to thank her for the jump. Wine, he thinks, and drives to Seahorse Spirits, where he parks out front. Inside, he selects a bottle—French, and about twice as much as he'd usually spend—and carries it to the counter, behind which a guy named Carson Mulcahey, a meathead who played hockey with Craig and graduated a couple of years ahead of them, stands.

"Vance Lake. How the hell are you?" Carson Mulcahey says, extending his hand.

Vance shakes it. He's fairly certain Carson went to Wesleyan, or maybe it was Ohio Wesleyan, on a hockey scholarship, and landed a good—meaning lucrative—job in New York after he graduated. The fact that he's back here, working as a cashier, means something must have gone awry, his fortunes must have reversed, and while Vance knows he should feel sorry for Carson, the truth is it buoys him somewhat, knowing he's not the only one who's hit some bumps in the road.

Carson asks how he's been, and he says, "Getting by. Yourself?" and sets the wine on the wooden counter.

"Where are you living these days?" he asks, punching buttons on the register.

"DC. I teach school." He waits for a response, and when none comes, he adds, "College."

"You don't say. A professor. How about that?"

Vance smiles noncommittally. There's no point in correcting him. Carson asks what subject he teaches, and he tells him.

And with that, the conversation seems to have run its course. By the register there's a wicker basket full of fancy chocolate bars, flavored with things like cayenne pepper and Madagascar vanilla and passionfruit, and because he doesn't know what else to do, he picks one up. Apparently there's a different love poem folded inside each one's wrapper. Also, he sees, they're six dollars apiece. He sets it down.

"You tried those?" Carson asks, consulting a printed price list for the wine. "Mindy's completely addicted. That's my wife."

"I've never had much of a sweet tooth."

"Take it. It's on me."

He doesn't need a handout, he thinks, especially not from this clown, but he accepts it. "So what brings you back?"

"We got tired of the rat race, frankly. We wanted somewhere quieter, for the kids. And then we were here last summer and I happened to hear the Murphys were selling this place and the one in Southwich." Carson says the price of the wine—it's even more expensive than Vance thought—and then, "So I guess you could say it was fate."

This jack-off *owns* the place? "Good for you," he says.

"And likewise. I'm glad to see you and your brother both doing so well." He pauses. "Your brother," he says. "You can't go half a mile without seeing one of his signs."

"He's doing all right," Vance says, handing over his credit card.

"I heard he's building Azulay's new place. *Ka-ching,* am I right? And you? Back here for keeps?"

"God, no," Vance says before thinking better of it. "I mean, it's a great place, but I could never live here. No offense."

"None taken," Mulcahey says, and Vance mutters something about how great it was to see him and goes.

He sets the wine and the candy bar on the passenger seat of the truck and waits for a break in the flow of cars to pull out onto Route 6. When he does, he seems to have misjudged the speed of an oncoming semi, because he has to jam his foot down on the gas pedal to get out of the way. Afterward the wine bottle is on the floor, rolling around, and at a red light he leans over, picks it up, and wedges it between his thighs.

Halfway to Dylan's, he starts to worry. What if she doesn't drink? She sure as hell used to—she was famous for being able to keep up with the boys—but that was a long time ago, she was seventeen, and she could be a teetotaler or a Mormon or in a twelve-step program now, for all he knows.

Flowers—that's what he should have gotten. Flowers or maybe a plant. But he's already by the Captain Crowley Inn, less than a mile from her house, and he doesn't have time to go back. He stashes the wine bottle under the seat and picks up the chocolate bar. *Fig and Madras curry powder*, says the package. It sounds revolting to him, but who knows, maybe she likes that kind of thing.

He pulls into her driveway and stops, but doesn't get out. She's home; the front door is open, and only the storm door protects from the March chill. All of a sudden he's nervous. What is he doing here? His throat feels dry, it's hard to swallow, and all his muscles feel tight. He tugs at his collar, then flips down the visor and looks at himself in the small mirror. He looks okay—not great, but okay. He scrapes a dark speck off his right incisor and runs his fingers through his hair, which he really should get trimmed, and tells himself to get a grip. But still he feels trepidations. The truck's still running; there's no reason he can't just stomp on the gas and drive away. He's got his hand on the gearshift, about to move it out of Park, when from inside a dog starts barking. A moment later, Dylan appears.

She's standing behind the storm door, same as yesterday, one hand on her hip, the other shading her eyes. When she recognizes him she opens the door and comes out. The dog, a chocolate lab, stands on the front stoop, barking. Dylan waves, looking a little perplexed.

It takes him a moment to locate the window control, and by the time he gets it open she's standing next to his door, again. The dog's still barking like crazy, as if it believes Vance poses some sort of threat.

"Easy, killer," he says. "Can you tell it I come in peace?"

"This is Maisie. Sorry. She can be a little protective." She bends to scratch the dog behind its ears, then straightens up. She's wearing a faded denim work shirt with the sleeves rolled up, and her neck is exposed, displaying a triangle of freckled skin and a tiny silver anchor on a chain. "I hope you're on your best behavior, driving that."

"How come?"

"Whatever you do, people will think it was your brother."

"So today would be a good day to kill someone?"

"It would be the perfect crime. No jury in this town's ever going to convict Craig."

"But they would convict me?"

She shrugs, looks off in the direction of the marsh, then back at him. "Did you want to come in?"

She's already started walking away, Maisie at her heels. Snatching the chocolate bar off the passenger seat and slipping it into his jacket pocket, he follows. They're not headed toward the house, but into the meadow, which is half an acre of thick weeds and grass. She's wearing tall boots, but he's not, and after about six steps his sneakers and the hems of his jeans are soaking wet. He's looking down, focusing on where to put his feet, so he doesn't notice the barn until they're right in front of it: a pile of rotting wood and rusty nails when they were kids, it's been completely rebuilt.

"Is this Craig's doing, by chance?"

"As a matter of fact, it is. We were one of Lake Design Build's first jobs. Mom hired him—I was still out west. Since he was just starting out, I guess he gave her a discount." She takes hold of a large iron handle and rolls an enormous aluminum-faced door to the side.

"After you," she says.

Inside the barn it's dark, and it takes his eyes a minute to adjust.

While he stands there blinking, his nose fills with the scents of sweet hay and horseshit.

"Taffeta needs her shot. Usually I do it alone, but I can always use a second pair of hands."

"They're all yours," he says, showing her his palms.

She's already working, taking a black plastic box down from a high shelf and then walking down between the stalls, flipping switches, Maisie in tow. "Hey, babies," she says. "How about some light?" When she reaches the end, she turns, faces him, and says, "Are you coming?" before stepping into a stall.

He hurries down the aisle and joins her in the small space, where the smells are twice as strong and which feels far too confined for the two of them, the dog, and the gigantic brown horse, on whose neck Dylan rests her hands. "Vance meet Taffeta. Taffeta, Vance," she says. "She cut her leg on some barbed wire, poor thing." She moves her hands all the way down the horse's body, to the flank. "How's my good girl doing?" she asks. "How's my very best girl today?"

The horse snorts and stamps its foot, and Vance backs up so he's practically pinned against the wall. He knows that the horse must be friendly, but it's just so *large*; he hasn't spent much time around large animals. He remembers sitting behind Craig on a pony at a carnival, and once, during college, taking a trail ride at a rich girlfriend's parents' estate.

Dylan is watching him. "You look like you're going to be sick," she says.

He peels himself off the wall. "How many of these do you have?" he asks, trying to sound at ease.

"She's the only one that's mine. The rest I board." She steps outside the stall, and when she steps back in she's holding a bridle, which she deftly slips over the horse's head. "It's how I keep the lights on, that and the lessons. Mom started it. I guess you could say it's my inheritance. Isn't it, girl?"

"How is Carolyn?"

She looks at him. "She's—she passed away last May. I assumed you knew."

"No. That's terrible."

"Yes—and no. She had Alzheimer's, so—" She doesn't finish the sentence. She clears her throat. "She needed lots of help, anyway. That's why I came."

"From where?"

"Hm." She's frowning; she's opened the black box and is taking out medical supplies, one at a time: a small glass vial and some sterile paper packages containing a large needle and a syringe. "Could you hold this?" she asks, handing him the needle and setting the box down on the hay-covered floor. He watches her unwrap the syringe, attach it to the mouth of the vial, and draw out some of the clear liquid. "Trade you," she says, twisting the syringe off the vial and handing the vial him. He gives her the needle, which she unwraps and attaches to the syringe. "You ready?" she says.

"What do you want me to do?"

"Hold the reins. Right here, no, a little closer to her mouth. There. You can stand closer, she doesn't bite—or, I should say, she only bites sometimes." She pauses. "Okay, now you just need to distract her."

"How?"

"It doesn't matter. Just take her attention away from the shot."

He stands there, feeling inept. "I'm sorry. I'm not sure what you want me to do."

"Just talk to her. Whisper some sweet nothings in her ear. You've got a few of those in your repertoire, if memory serves."

He's glad she can't see his face behind the horse's head, because he's sure he looks even more uncomfortable than before. He clears his throat. "It's okay, horse," he says in what he hopes is a tender tone. "Everything's going to be okay."

"That's good. I'm sticking her now," she says. "Good girl, easy, just a few seconds more."

He strokes the animal's sleek neck with the back of his hand, and though he feels like an idiot, he says, "It's okay, it is."

"That's it," she says after a few moments. "All done."

"She didn't even flinch."

"I've had lots of practice. And she's a good girl. You're a good girl, aren't you, Taff?" She squats, gathering up the paper wrappers. "She's your niece's favorite," she says.

"Amanda?"

She gives him an impatient look. "Helen," she says, and slips the bridle off Taffeta's head. He follows her out of the stall. She hangs the bridle and a lead on a nail outside the door. At a large ceramic sink she washes her hands, drying them on the thighs of her jeans. Maisie has drifted over to an aluminum water trough and noisily begins to drink.

"Thank you for your help," she says rather formally.

"I didn't do anything."

"It's more of a precaution, in case something goes wrong. Like if she spooked and needed to be restrained."

"I'm not sure how effective I would have been in that situation."

She grins, crosses her arms, and leans back against the sink. There are no windows at this end of the barn, just a single wall sconce, and in the dim light she doesn't look much different than she did two decades ago. "It's nice to see you," she says.

He says, "Likewise."

For a moment neither says anything; maybe she's thinking about the past, too. Then she pushes off the wall. "I should get moving. I have a hundred things to do before my lesson." She narrows her eyes at him, letting her head fall to the side. "What are you doing back, anyway? You never said." She doesn't wait for him to answer. "Mom said she heard you were getting your PhD, but that was ages ago. You're probably a tenured professor by now."

The dog has finished drinking and comes over to where Vance stands, and he leans down to stroke her head, then her ears, which are like velvet. "Not exactly." He can't bear to tell her the truth—that he quit the doctoral program after just one semester. "I have been teaching, though."

"That must be fulfilling."

"It is." He pauses, considering his words carefully. "It was, and then I got—I guess I got a little burnt out."

"Oh?"

"All the paper-grading, and of course the bureaucracy. It's a constant struggle, like I'm twisting these kids' arms to get them to give a shit about literature. It wears you down."

"I can see that, I guess," she says. "You know I always thought you'd do something creative. Like music." She smiles a little mischievously; she means the band he was in back in high school, the Buccaneers. They weren't very good, technically, but what they lacked in skill they made up for with enthusiasm, incorporating wild dance sequences, outrageous costumes, and wacky props into their act. Once in a blue moon, he'd persuade Dylan to come up onstage. Those were their best gigs, hands down. She had a terrific voice—"99 Red Balloons" was her song, and she could really belt it out. She'd have the whole audience up on its feet, shouting along.

He smiles, too. "My light-up drumsticks have been in storage for about fifteen years, but maybe it's time to dust them off. I'm game if you are."

"Yeah, right."

"Come on. It was your idea. Just a few lines."

She shakes her head, but he persists, offering up his best recollection of the opening guitar chords—softly at first, then louder—and then he starts to sing. *You and I in a little toy shop . . .*"

She doesn't look delighted, exactly, but she is blushing—which is every bit as charming now as it was a quarter-century ago, maybe more so. "God," she says, touching her collarbone. "I haven't heard that song in years."

He keeps going, singing the next line.

"You should stop, Vance."

But he doesn't stop. He keeps singing until he gets to the chorus, and she says, "Really, I mean it. Cut it out." She's not smiling anymore, and the flush is gone from her face.

He stops in midline. In the sudden quiet, she looks at the floor. The dog abandons Vance and goes to her, planting her rump by Dylan's feet.

"What's wrong?" Vance asks.

She says, "Nothing," but clearly something's happened. Something's changed.

What an imbecile he is. He wants so badly to back up to a few minutes ago, when she was charmed, when she was laughing with him. "So what about you?" he asks. "You said you were living out west?"

"Did I?" she says.

"Whereabouts?"

She crosses her arms over her chest and glances down at the dog. "I don't mean to be rude, but I have work to do. I'm sure you're busy, too." She bends to stroke the dog's head. "Thanks again for your help," she says. With Maisie at her heels, she walks briskly away.

He follows at a distance, watching her enter the house and close the front door behind her, before climbing back into Craig's truck. He turns the key and the engine growls to life. Now Bruce is singing "Atlantic City," a song Vance likes, but he's not in the mood for Springsteen anymore, or any music, and he punches buttons until it stops. In silence he makes his way back toward town. Only when he's on Main Street, passing by the liquor store, does he remember the chocolate bar.

18

THE ROUTINE OPENS with four *changements*, into four quick *chassés*, then an arabesque, then a high *relevé*, all of which Helen executes flawlessly atop the brick retaining wall in front of her school. After the *relevé* comes a *plié*, then two *grand jetés*, which are like leaps, then a small *glissade*, then a pirouette, then a second arabesque, which is always harder, because her leg is tired, and on the wall she wobbles some but manages to stay upright. After that comes the *pas de chat*, or walking like a cat, which she likes because of the name, and then the *pas de cheval*, which is walking like a horse, which she likes even more. The final move in the sequence is the *pas de bourrée*, which is really three separate moves, and which always trips her up. She's concentrating very hard to get it right when she hears Mrs. Forrest shouting her name.

"Goodness gracious," she says. She's standing below Helen, looking up. "I've asked you to get down from there twice already. Come on."

"But it's my routine," Helen says. "I have to practice. The recital's Wednesday night."

"Well, you can't practice here. It isn't safe."

"I just did a *pas de bourrée*. Want to see?"

Mrs. Forrest frowns. "What I want is for you to get down from there, right now, please. I'm not going to ask you again." She offers Helen her hand.

Helen doesn't take it. She executes a final pirouette turn, arms raised, then a curtsy, like they do in class. After that, she climbs down.

Mrs. Forrest is looking at her watch. "You don't have any idea what might be keeping your mom?"

Helen shakes her head, looking around. She's the only kid left now; all the others have been picked up.

Mrs. Forrest is holding an iPhone in a purple plastic case. "Do you know her number? We'll give her a call."

Helen shakes her head, watching Mrs. Forrest type something into her phone, frowning while she does. Her mother is almost never late to pick her up. The one time she was, it turned out that a tree had fallen across Beach Road and she had to go all the way around. That time was different, though, with most of the other kids waiting too.

"They'll have it in the office." She looks at her watch again. "If Angie's still there."

"I could come to your house," Helen says.

Mrs. Forrest smiles. "I don't think that's a good idea. What would happen if your mom got here and you were gone?"

Helen shrugs. Mrs. Forrest has a cat named Lacy who is all white with orange eyes; she's the most beautiful cat Helen has ever seen. She knows about Lacy because Mrs. Forrest brought her to school one day in a red plastic box called a Cat Caboose after she picked her up from the vet.

"She'd be apoplectic, that's what. I know I would."

"We could just go for a little while."

"It's not going to happen, honey," she says, looking at her watch once more.

"My dog was called Marshmallow, and she died," Helen says. "She had cancer. It was in a gland in her neck. It was like she had a Super Ball stuck in her throat."

"I know, honey. You told the whole class. Remember? Why don't you have a seat on the bench. I need to make a call."

Helen does as Mrs. Forrest asks. The bench is too high for her feet to touch the ground, so she swings her legs back and forth.

"Hi again," she hears Mrs. Forrest say. "Soon, I hope." She takes a few steps away, and Helen can't hear her anymore.

She looks around the yard. It's supposed to be spring soon, but all the trees are still bare and brown and so is the grass, and there are still a few piles of old snow. She looks over at Mrs. Forrest, whose back is to her, and then she gets up and crosses the brown grass. Close to where the woods start there's a low stone wall, and behind that there's a grave-yard. It's old—from hundreds of years ago, when the Pilgrims came —and it's where people who had smallpox got buried when they died. Smallpox is a very bad disease, Mrs. Forrest told the class. It's worse than cancer, she said, because it's contagious, whereas cancer starts for no reason, it's just there inside you, maybe it's even there when you're born (which sounds much worse than smallpox, to Helen).

She kicks a stone in the wall with the toe of her sneaker but it doesn't move, and she turns around. Mrs. Forrest is still talking on the phone, facing away. Helen goes back to the bench, but this time she lies down, resting her head on her backpack and looking up at the sky. There are some high puffy clouds sliding slowly from right to left. Once she flew in a plane that went on top of the clouds. They were so close that if she could have stuck her hand out the window, she could have touched them. They looked so solid, like pillows, and she asked her dad if she could stand on one, and he said no. He explained that clouds are really just water, a zillion tiny droplets of it, and trying to stand on one would be exactly like trying to stand on water: you'd fall right through.

A horn honks and she sits up. Pulling into the school's driveway is her father's white truck, but her father isn't driving it, Vance is. She stands and gathers her backpack, slipping her arms through the straps.

"Okay," Mrs. Forrest says, ushering Helen toward the driveway.

"I'm sorry," Vance says through the window. "I got held up." He's wearing dark sunglasses like her dad's, Helen notices, and a blue Red Sox cap.

Mrs. Forrest says. "We were starting to get concerned."

He gets out of the truck and walks around to the passenger side, where he opens the door for Helen. "I understand. It won't happen again," he says.

Mrs. Forrest looks doubtfully at Vance. Helen stands on the sidewalk, not sure what she's supposed to do.

After a moment, he says, "Hop on in, kiddo."

"I can't."

"Why not?

"I can't sit there."

Vance frowns, then says, "Right. My bad." He opens the back door and she climbs in, squeezing past Cameron's baby seat and settling into her booster. She hates riding in the seat—she feels like a baby—but Massachusetts law says she has to until she's eight years old or fifty-seven inches tall, whichever comes first. Her birthday isn't until January, and she's only forty-six inches, so it's going to be a while.

"See you tomorrow," Mrs. Forrest says before closing the door.

Vance gets in and fastens his seatbelt, then swivels around. "I'm sorry I kept you waiting. I take it she's your teacher?" They watch Mrs. Forrest hold her key fob up to the pad by the school's front door and disappear inside. Helen nods. "She seems nice."

"Why are you picking me up?"

"Your mom had to go see a client. She had work."

"Where's my dad?"

"Boston, so I'm told. How was school?"

She says, "Can we get ice cream?"

"It's forty-nine degrees outside. But if that's what you want." He starts driving, looking both ways before pulling out on the road.

Rather than drive to Cape Cone, he goes to Shaw's, the supermarket, and when she asks why, he says he's cooking dinner tonight, something special, as a thank-you gesture to her and Gina for letting him stay.

"Are you sleeping over tonight?"

He says he is.

"Hooray. And tomorrow night?"

He says, "Chances are," and parks in the southwest corner of the parking lot, by Country Kitchen. As they walk toward the store, she holds out her hand like she always does in parking lots, but he doesn't see—maybe he doesn't know it's the rule—and it's a little thrilling, crossing the whole expanse of blacktop alone, Vance walking several steps ahead.

Inside, he gets a basket and heads to the produce department. By a pyramid of grapefruits he asks Helen if she'd like to provide some input on the meal.

She doesn't want to admit she doesn't know what input is, so she shakes her head.

"Okay, how about this? Do you want spaghetti and meatballs, lasagna, or steak?"

Amanda won't eat steak anymore, she says it's disgusting. She says they inject the cows that meat comes from with chemicals, and they don't have enough room to lie down, and their stalls are full of poo and pee, and when they kill them they drag them around by their feet. She says, "Lasagna."

"Lasagna it is," Vance says. "Do you like mushrooms?" he asks, and she says yes. "Spinach?" She nods, though she doesn't, and nods again for zucchini.

She follows him up and down the aisles. There are many things on the shelves she'd like to ask for, and would if he were her mom or dad, but she feels shy. He's not paying much attention to her. He walks several paces ahead, pausing only at the end of the aisle to glance around for her, as if he's just remembered she's there.

In the checkout line he picks up a package of razors and drops it in the cart, then takes a magazine from the rack and flips through the pages while they wait. She doesn't ask for any of the candy or gum displayed nearby, which takes a lot of self-control, something her mother has told her is important. She decides it would be a good time to practice her routine, and she gets in first position, arranging her heels on the seam between the giant white tiles. She's right in the middle, doing the scale, when her foot makes contact with something solid. She spins around. It's an old man she's kicked, apparently in the shin, and he glares at her. "Watch yourself, little girl, this isn't a playground."

She stands there, frozen.

"Daddy, please," says the woman standing next to him. She's got messy blond hair and wears a plaid scarf around her neck. "I'm sorry, sweetie. He doesn't mean to be such a grump." She looks Helen up and down, then turns to Vance. "How old?" she asks.

After a moment he looks up from the magazine. "Pardon? Oh. Forty-two."

The woman laughs, shaking her head. "I meant your little girl."

"Oh," he says. "She's just my niece."

Helen doesn't know why this hurts her feelings, but it does. And he still hasn't answered the lady's question, so she says, "I'm seven years old," but by then she's facing away, saying something to the old man.

All the way home he doesn't talk, and she wonders if maybe he's angry with her. Her dad doesn't say much either when he's mad. It must be because she was practicing in the store. She wishes she hadn't done that. She should think more before she acts; that's another thing her mother says.

Vance uses the clicker to open the garage and parks the truck inside. Her mother's car isn't there, which is disappointing. Helen asks Vance when she'll be home, and he says he has no idea. He has his hand on the door handle and it looks like he's about to get out of the truck, but he pauses. "Shit," he says. "You wanted ice cream, didn't you? I completely forgot."

She says, "It's okay."

"It's weird to eat ice cream in the winter anyway, isn't it? I'll fix you something."

Inside, she asks him if she can watch TV, and he says, "Fine with me," so she settles into the sofa with the remote while he drops the grocery bags in the kitchen and goes upstairs. An episode of *Judge Judy* is on, and a man and a woman are shouting at each other about repairing a roof. Then there are some commercials. When the show comes back on, the people start shouting again.

"They let you watch that?" Vance's voice asks. She swivels around; he's standing behind the sofa. He looks different now. His sleeves are rolled up and his eyes look sleepy, and he's swapped out his sneakers for sheepskin slippers that look exactly like her dad's. "Better yet, why don't you keep your old uncle company while he cooks?"

Maybe he isn't mad at her, after all. She turns off the TV. In the kitchen she sits on a stool, watching him remove the food he bought from plastic bags: vegetables, tomato sauce, noodles, cheese.

"Want to be my sous chef?" he asks.

She says sure, though she doesn't know what a sous chef is.

Leaving the food, he goes back into the living room, and she watches him pour some of her father's scotch into a glass. He smells it, takes a sip, and starts opening cabinet doors. "I do enjoy some tunes while I cook, don't you?" It doesn't seem like he expects her to answer. "What the hell?" he says, squatting in front of one of the cabinets. "Where did my old stereo go? Don't tell me your father got rid of it." He cranes his neck to look at her, and his expression is a little frightening.

She says, "Dad plays music on the iPad. He has an app."

Vance lets out a long sigh and stands up. "Of course he does," he says, closing the cabinet door. He stands and goes back into the kitchen. "So, this app. I sure as hell don't know how to work it. Do you?"

She shakes her head. She does, actually, but she's not supposed to touch the iPad without an adult present, and she's not entirely sure Vance counts.

He's frowning, eyes darting around the room a little frantically until they come to rest on her mom's work desk in the corner. "Boom," he says, pointing to the clock radio, and he goes to it and presses various buttons until it comes on. Like always, it's tuned to the local public station, WCAI, and at the moment a man is reading the daily fishing report.

"God help us," Vance says, pressing the tuning button. On the first station he comes to, Taylor Swift is singing "Fifteen," a song Helen loves, or used to love, but he says, "Contemporary country music is a crime against humanity," and cuts Taylor off. When he finds a classical station, he stands up and closes his eyes for a moment, then says, "Are you feeling the Rachmaninoff?" Before she can say anything, he says, "Me too."

Apparently a sous chef is someone who watches someone else cook. First Vance slices the mushrooms, then the zucchini, and then he puts the block of frozen spinach in a colander and runs it under the tap. The first task he gives her is to squeeze the water out of the spinach, which she does; it feels slimy, and small green pieces stick to her hands. "Atta girl," he says, watching her. While she squeezes, she wonders where her mother is. She's always home with Helen after school, or else they go to the store, Cottage, together, where Helen sits in the office watching shows or playing games.

When the spinach is as dry as she can get it, she brings the colander to Vance, who hands her a bowl containing ricotta cheese and a raw egg and some green flakes, and tells her to mix it with a fork until it's smooth. When she's finished with that, he takes the bowl and with a plastic scraper he gets from a drawer he spreads the mixture over each noodle, like peanut butter on bread. He lines the bottom of the baking dish with them and then lays slices of zucchini on top, and after that spoons on some sauce, then another layer of noodles, then the spinach and mushrooms. When he's used up all the vegetables, he asks Helen if she wants to put on the finishing touch, the cheese, and hands her a bag of grated Italian mix, which she sprinkles on, tentatively at first. "Come on, don't be shy," he says. She sprinkles until she's used the whole bag. He covers the pan with tinfoil and raises his hand for a high five.

"Want to play Go Fish?" she asks.

"Hm, I think not."

"Gin?"

"We've still got salad and garlic bread to make. I hate to brag, but my garlic bread is world-renowned." He's standing in front of the oven, holding the lasagna. He opens the door and is reaching for the rack but stops short. "Shit. Where did that oven mitt get to?" It's sitting on the island, right in front of him. Helen picks it up. "Thanks, sous chef. Maybe I'll start calling you Susie for short, or maybe just Sue. How would you like that?" And then he starts to sing a song about a boy named Sue.

She doesn't like it at all—the name, the singing, the way he's acting in general. She wishes her mother would come home.

He takes a jar of chopped garlic out of the refrigerator door and sets it on the counter, then slices a loaf of bread lengthwise, butters each half, spoons some garlic on, adds salt, and wraps the whole thing in foil. After that he makes a salad, which he puts in the refrigerator, and after that he changes the radio station and starts to clean. "*Alison*," he sings, wiping down the counter, "*my aim is true*." He's so absorbed in the song, or maybe the cleaning, he seems to have forgotten about her.

She's about to ask if she can watch TV again when she hears the mudroom door open: her mother's home. "Mama!" she shouts, jumping down from the stool and dashing into the mudroom. Gina's cheeks are pink and her blue coat is unzipped. "Shh," she says, raising a finger to her lips and setting Cam's car seat down softly on the tiles. She sniffs the air and frowns. "What smells good?"

"We were cooking lasagna."

"We?"

"Me and Vance. It's to thank us for letting him stay here. He's staying tonight, and tomorrow too."

"You don't say."

Her mother seems a little strange, a little spacey, kind of like she acts when she first wakes up. Helen wants to hug her, to pitch herself into her arms, but for some reason she hesitates, standing on the strip that divides the mudroom from the kitchen. Her mother hangs her coat on a peg and tosses her hat onto the bench, then shakes out her hair. "What's the matter, peanut? Don't I get a kiss?"

Helen goes to her, burying her face in her mother's neck while Gina rocks her back and forth. "Hello, my angel," she says, and for no particular reason Helen wants to cry. She squeezes her arms tighter around her mom, who says, "Okay, now I can't breathe." When she lets go, Gina says, "When's dinner? I'm ravenous." She starts unwrapping the scarf from around her neck, and that's when Helen notices her ears.

"Where's the other birdie?" she asks.

Gina says, "Excuse me?"

"Grandma's birdie earrings," she says. "Aren't there supposed to be two?"

19

AGAIN VANCE IS RESTLESS. Curled on his side on the air mattress, head propped on his arm, he stares out the porthole window at the circle of night sky, watching for satellites or shooting stars. His head's fogged from the wine he and Gina drank (the expensive one meant for Dylan; he drank most of it himself), and he wishes he had some weed left to mellow his buzz. Usually he comes fully supplied, but he left DC in such a hurry, he didn't have time to replenish his stash. Maybe it's something he could raise with Dylan when—or rather, if —he sees her again. If she still smokes, that is. Lord knows she used to do that, too. They would take her brother's blue glass bong out to the camp and smoke themselves silly, listening to records, trying to pick out the chords on their guitars.

A noise—a voice—comes from the floor near his feet, from the vent. It's Gina, and he gathers she's on the phone. "Could you look again?" she says, and then, "Yes, but that's not why I'm upset. They're irreplaceable." She sounds so agitated, she must be talking to Craig. He takes off his sweater, folds it, and lays it over the vent. Then he turns onto his back and closes his eyes, though it feels unlikely that he'll fall asleep.

His thoughts go back to Dylan, to the afternoon. In his mind he can conjure the freckles scattered over her nose, the arch of her eyebrow, the unchanged and utterly familiar shape of her face.

And then he's thinking about all those years ago, the time after he first left the Cape. The countless hours he'd spent thinking about her. All those hours, and he never contacted her, not once. He wanted to, of course: to call, or write a letter, or even board a Greyhound bus, show up at her dorm room at Tulane, and explain. But how would he ever possibly explain? He had no idea why he behaved the way he did. Even now, when he tries to parse his actions, his behavior over those long-ago August weeks, it's like trying to plumb the motivations of some stranger on the street.

He's never going to fall asleep this way. He sits up, turns on the shepherdess lamp, and finds himself facing the row of labeled plastic boxes that contain Craig's and Gina's things. The one labeled *Craig H.S.* catches his eye. He pulls it out and snaps off the lid. It's filled with old school books—biology, chemistry, American history, algebra, trigonometry, calculus, *The Norton Anthology of American Literature*. He picks up the anthology and, when he pulls back the front cover, finds his name, not Craig's.

The pages feel thin and crisp, fragile. Carefully he flips through the first few sections: Hawthorne, Franklin, Melville, with his asterisks and handwritten annotations—*alliteration*, *foreshadowing*, *metaphor*—cluttering the margins. He comes to Poe: "The thousand injuries of Fortunato I had borne as I best could, but when he ventured upon insult I vowed revenge." He'd underlined the opening and starred it. *Direct address*, he'd written in the margin, and then, *Confession*, which he'd underlined twice.

He sets it down. Peeking out from under a book called *Great Political Thinkers* is *The Anchor*, their high school yearbook, the edition from their senior year. He lifts it out. He hasn't seen the thing in ages —probably since they graduated—and as he starts turning pages, he's assaulted by the smiling faces of people he hasn't thought of in decades, many of whose names, oddly, jump readily to mind.

It's strange to think that plenty of them are probably people Craig sees every day, living here. He pauses at the page devoted to the cross-country team: there he is, standing second from the right in the back row. He looks so skinny, almost scrawny, in his sleeveless top with his arms crossed over his chest, employing the trick the boys all used to make their biceps bulge, and his unkempt hair, which nearly reaches his shoulders, tucked behind his ears. He skims through his teammates' names underneath the picture. He hasn't kept up with more than a couple of them, or really anyone else from here.

He turns the page; it's the baseball team, and right smack in the middle, looking clean-cut and stalwart and virile, is Craig, the team captain. Looking at the photo, Vance can't help thinking of Amanda's team photo downstairs. As reluctant as he is to admit it, here's something the two of them share.

But something else is nagging him, the connection his mind won't quite make. He turns the page—photos of Field Day and Service Day, pep rallies and plays. The first image of Dylan he finds is of her onstage: she played Abigail Williams, he remembers, in *The Crucible* that year. The photo is of her, alone, kneeling in front of a fake willow tree. With her head covered, and in costume, she looks even younger than she was. He flips all the way to the back, to the quarter-page ad she took out for him. It's a Polaroid of the two of them taken at the holiday formal. He's wearing an (ironic) powder-blue tux with a ruffled shirt, and she's wearing a black dress and a Santa hat, and Christmas balls dangle from her ears. He has his arm around her shoulders, he's grinning, and she is too. He thinks of Amanda; she's the same age Dylan was then. He remembers that misty August morning, and Dylan's tears. Amanda's tears. But it can't be, *she* can't be—can she? He can hardly bring himself to finish the thought.

He doesn't have to; his phone is buzzing. *Celeste*, he thinks. *It's about time.* It takes a moment for him to locate his phone on the windowsill, and by the time he gets to it the ringing has stopped. When he picks it up he sees the number on the screen isn't Celeste's.

It's Amanda's.

His heart jumps. The clock on the screen tells him it's after midnight. He sits on the air mattress and calls her back. A girl answers, but she's not his niece.

"Is this Vance?" she says.

"Who's this?"

"It's Sybil," says the voice. When he doesn't say anything, she says, "Amanda's friend?"

His head swims. He says, "Sybil, yes."

"I'm," she says. "I'm with Amanda. We need you to come."

"Excuse me?"

"Please, it's—" He hears her draw a deep breath. "There was a party."

"After the plover thing?"

"No, today. Noah had a party. His parents are away. They—"

He rubs his face with his hand, trying to clear his head. "Sybil—from the Main Sail? Right? I'm sorry, I'm confused. The sleepover?"

"You have to come, please. She's really—she's"—she pauses, and he can hear her draw in breath—"she said not to call, but I didn't know what else to do."

In the morass of thoughts spinning through his head, one separates itself from the rest. "Why—why didn't she call?"

"She's, she's like—" She pauses.

"Can you please put her on?"

"She's in the bathroom. She won't open the door."

He begins to feel panicked. "Please just give her the phone."

"She's not—" Her voice trembles. "She had some drinks."

A pit opens in his stomach. He says, "I'm on my way." He snatches his pants from the floor, pulls them on, and scans the room for his shirt. "How many?"

"I don't know. Some beers, and maybe some shots?"

"I assume she's conscious?" She says yes. "Is she puking?"

"No, she's just—she's acting strange."

"Maybe you should call an ambulance."

"She said she's not sick."

He asks where they are, and she says she doesn't know the address and tells him to hold on, and he finds his socks and pulls his sweater on over his head while he waits. When she comes back, she says, "One forty-two Blueberry Point. It's in Southwich, right on the Sound." He grabs his wallet off the trunk.

"I'll be there in twenty minutes. You're sure she's okay?" he asks, starting down the stairs.

"Please," she says. "Just come."

In the mudroom, holding Craig's keys (it's not his fault the truck is more reliable than the Frog—it's Craig's), he spends a moment wondering whether he should wake Gina. But Sybil called him, not her, he reasons, and, saying a silent prayer that Gina's a sound sleeper, presses the white button that opens the garage. Instead of starting the ignition there, inside, he shifts into reverse and lets the truck coast backwards down the driveway, then starts the engine in the middle of the street.

The stereo comes on automatically—"Badlands," Philadelphia, 1995, according to the display. He can't remember how he got it to change stations before, so he lets it play.

According to Google, the address Sybil gave him is thirty-two miles away, and he drives fast, faster than he should. Even so, it feels like eons before he sees the exit for Southwich, a town he doesn't know at all, and then, just as he's approaching the village center, his reception goes out. Cursing AT&T, he pulls over and switches the power off and back on, but he seems to be in a black hole. He spends a few frustrating minutes trying to program the address into Craig's GPS, but he can't figure out how the damn thing works, so he gives up and wastes another endless fifteen minutes driving in circles on, or in close proximity to, Blueberry Point Road, until finally he locates 142.

The house is one of those modern atrocities someone at some point must have considered avant-garde: two huge, white-stucco silos connected by a glass and concrete hall. He pulls into a semicircular driveway, oyster shells crunching under the tires, and parks behind a black Porsche with New York plates. When he steps out of the truck, cold wind blasts his face; he doesn't know how far he is from the water, but from the briny tang of the air, he imagines not very.

Following a lit path to the glass corridor's midpoint, where there's a copper door, he rings the bell. Nobody answers, and he peers in through the glass. The corridor is brightly lit and empty, with a stone floor and a single sculpture at one end—a large, carved stone donut on an iron stand that looks like a Henry Moore knockoff, but judging from what he's seen of the place so far, it may well be the real thing. He tries the bell again. When no response comes, he bangs his fist against the metal. "Hello," he calls. "Amanda? Sybil? Is someone going to let me in?"

After a minute or two a tall, lanky kid with thick eyebrows and bushy brown hair appears. He's wearing baggy jeans, a rumpled oxford shirt, no shoes, and a cord of braided hemp or something around his neck. He opens the door six inches. "Can I help you?"

"Vance Lake. Where's Amanda?" he says, pushing the door open and stepping inside without waiting to be asked. In the middle of the corridor he looks right, then left. "Tell me where she is."

The kid says she's in the living room, and points. "She's fine. I know Sybil was wigging out, but you really didn't have to come."

Vance doesn't wait to hear more. He heads down the corridor, at the end of which is another copper door, which he pushes open, descends a flight of corkscrew stairs, rounds a corner, and finds himself in a sunken circular room almost completely encased in glass. In the center of the room, two C-shaped white leather sofas face each other; sitting cross-legged in the middle of one of these is his niece.

"Jesus, honey, thank God you're all right. You scared me," he says, going toward her.

She stiffens visibly, causing him to stop short. "You don't need to be here," she says icily. "I'm fine."

And strangely enough—at first glance, at least—she does appear to be. She looks tired, and maybe a little wan, but she's perfectly lucid, sitting upright, holding a black-and-red-printed pillow on her lap. He glances around the room. There are three more kids—Sybil, a girl, and a boy—sitting on a rough wooden bench at a marble-topped table covered with red plastic cups.

"She is not," Sybil says, addressing Vance. "Or she wasn't." She, on the other hand, looks wretched: her face is splotchy, her mascara's smeared, and her eyes, the whites of which are a pitiful pinkish red, fill with tears.

Sitting down on the couch across from Amanda, he says, "What happened, A?"

"I told you, I'm fine."

"She *wasn't,*" Sybil says, in a high, pleading voice. "She was, like—"

Amanda cuts her off. "Shut up, please."

Vance turns to Sybil again, raises his hand, and says quietly, "Could you give us a minute?" To Amanda, he says, "So you had too much to drink? Is that it?" She stares at the pillow in her lap. "Hey, it happens to the best of us." She won't look at him, so he addresses the side of her face: "Did you—were you sick?"

She shakes her head, and that's when he notices her hair is wet.

He feels a jolt of panic. Moving to the other couch, he sits beside her. "Can you please tell me what's going on?"

He may as well be speaking Russian, considering the response she gives him. He gets up and goes to Sybil, who's standing on the other side of the room, by one of the windows, holding a Kleenex to her nose.

"We were drinking," she tells him in a timid voice. "You know, beer, running boat races—that's a game." He nods, glancing over his shoulder at Amanda, who stares, stonily, straight ahead. "But then she started doing shots. And then at some point, it was like, dark out, and someone's like, where's Amanda? And everyone's like, shit. And I don't know why but I happened to look outside, and that's when I saw her, walking across the lawn." She nods in the direction of the windows. He looks, but all he can see is dark.

Sybil sniffles. "She was all wet—like, soaking, like she'd fallen in. And when I went out, she said stuff."

Vance shakes his head, trying to understand. "I'm sorry to be slow on the uptake here," he says, "but can we start at the beginning?" Sybil nods. "After the beach cleanup, you all came here."

Now Amanda speaks: "Jesus, Vance, how dense are you? There *was* no beach cleanup."

"You mean you've been here all day?"

She reaches for the gold A locket he gave her for her thirteenth birthday, which she always wears around her neck. And that's when he notices she's wearing someone else's clothes—jeans that swim on her and a sweatshirt that says *Property of Vanderbilt Athletic Dept.*

"Amanda?"

She shrugs, plucking a dark feather from the pillow in her lap and placing it in her palm. Squinting at it, she says, "I was fine. Sybil just freaked."

He looks around the room again, more slowly this time. The red cups are everywhere, and half-empty liquor bottles crowd a rolling cart.

The bushy-haired kid who let him in is sitting on the far side of the room, on the rough wooden bench. "I take it your parents are elsewhere," Vance says, feeling a surge of nausea that's eclipsed by one of rage when the kid says:

"They don't care if I drink."

"Amanda, honey," he says, struggling to keep his voice measured. "Did someone here hurt you?"

She glares at him. "Of course not."

"Are you sure?"

She doesn't deign to answer him, just rolls her eyes.

"Then come on, Cinderella. The ball's over."

She doesn't get up. She blows on the feather, which sails off her palm.

"You weren't okay," Sybil insists from the corner, her voice still unsteady. "I was scared."

"What are you, five?" Amanda says.

Now one of the boys at the table chimes in. "Don't blame Sybil. You freaked everyone out." To Vance, he says, "She did."

Vance puts his hand on Amanda's back. "Get your things. We're leaving." To Sybil he says, "You too." Sybil nods and exits the room, but Amanda doesn't move. He reaches down to take hold of her arm, which she jerks away.

She does stand up, though, and when Sybil appears with a bulging Rite-Aid bag and Amanda's coat, she accepts both.

Amanda sits in the back seat, Sybil up front. When Vance starts the engine, Springsteen comes on—"Glory Days" again.

"I hate Bruce Springsteen," Amanda says.

Vance asks Sybil if she can change the station for him. "It's ridiculously complex, this sound system," he says. She says sure, touches a few places on the display, and the music stops.

"Thank you," Amanda says. And that's all she says. The whole way back, more than thirty miles, the space inside the cab hums with strained silence.

When they approach town, Sybil directs him to a neighborhood near the elementary school. Behind the baseball field, in front of a shingled saltbox just off the main road, she says, "Here, the one with the carport," and thanks him politely for the ride.

He looks at the house. There are no lights on anywhere, not even on the stoop. He asks if her parents are home.

Her fingers are looped through the door handle. "It's just my mom. She works nights."

"Wait a second," Vance says. "We'll walk you up." He swivels around and looks at Amanda, who's staring out the window, her expression flat.

"It's really fine," Sybil says.

He glances at the dark house once more before removing the keys from the ignition and telling Amanda he'll be right back. She says nothing. He closes the door and follows Sybil up an uneven brick path to the house. It's a dark night—no moon to speak of, no hint yet of dawn—and cold. Halfway up the path he stops walking, removes his coat, and jogs back to the truck, where he opens the door and hands the coat to Amanda, who doesn't protest.

By the time he gets back to the house, Sybil's already inside, moving through rooms, turning on lights. He asks her when her mother will be home, and she says eight. "It's fine, I promise. It's always been this way," she says, seeing the concern on his face. He glances around the room: dingy pineapple-print wallpaper, mismatched furniture, windowsills crowded with plants. In the foyer, where he stands, a framed square of embroidery reads, *A Daughter Makes Life a Garden.*

Sybil leans against the arm of the sofa, arms crossed over her chest. She's looking down so he can't see her face. "She really was fucked up."

He clears his throat. "I believe you," he says.

She nods. He's reaching for the doorknob when she says, "She was saying stuff."

"What kind of stuff?"

She shrugs, reaching out and touching the waxy leaf of a rubber-tree plant.

He looks out the window at the truck. In the glow from the street-light he can make out the unmoving shape of Amanda in the cab, her head resting against the glass. "You did the right thing, calling," he says before he goes.

Outside, he opens the back door and asks Amanda whether she'd like to come up front. Wordlessly she concedes, floating around the front of the truck like some ethereal form and settling silently in the passenger seat, her hands hidden in the pockets of his coat. She doesn't look at him. When he starts the engine, she says, "There were just coyotes. You missed them. There were three."

"What were they doing?"

"Just, like, strolling down the street."

Vance starts driving, thinking she'll say more, but she doesn't. It's working on him, her silence. "You shouldn't blame Sybil," he finally says. "She was trying to help."

"I don't give a shit about Sybil. I hardly even know her."

Vance takes a moment to process this. "So what were you doing there? Besides shots, I mean." She doesn't answer. "Did you really fall in the water? You're lucky you're not in the hospital with hypothermia right now."

She's looking out the window, away from him. "I take back what I said last night. You're exactly like Craig."

Vance fixes his eyes on the road. He'll be damned if he's going to let her see how much her words sting.

Another few minutes pass before either speaks again. When they're a mile from the house, stopped at a red light at the intersection of Tonset and Main, Amanda shifts in her seat and faces him. "Please," she says when the light changes to green. "Don't."

A police cruiser, lights flashing, flies silently past. Then the intersection is empty except for them.

"Don't what?" Vance says.

She looks at him with wide eyes; her face looks just like it did when she was a kid. "Don't take me back there. Not yet."

20

"LADIES FIRST," Vance says, holding the door open and making a theatrical gesture with his arm.

Pushing mangy maroon curtains aside, she steps into the Lucky Panda's wood-paneled cocktail lounge, which is empty except for the bartender, a heavyset guy with tattooed arms, a bald head, and a scruffy red beard, who's resting his elbows on the bar and watching TV.

"Well, we haven't done this in a while," Vance says. He's followed her in, and he touches her shoulder, steering her gently toward the dining room.

At a fake-wood podium, he raises two fingers for the host, a pimpled, vaguely Asian-looking youth, who sets down his phone, gathers a couple of large red menus from a shelf, and says, "Follow me."

They do, to the back of the restaurant, to a booth by the windows, which in the summer, and in the daylight, offer a view of Town Cove. He leaves the menus on the table and says their server will be with them soon.

"This sure takes me back," Vance says. She can tell he's struggling to make conversation, and she wishes he would stop. "You know, back in the day, your dad and I used to—

"I know," she says.

"You know what?"

"You used to come here," she says. "They'd serve anyone. If you could see over the bar, they'd serve you a scorpion bowl. Between you and Dad, I've heard the story a zillion times."

"You have?" Vance says. He regards her with a concerned expression, and she wishes he would stop that, too. She looks away, slowly taking in the room. It's been a couple of years at least since she's been here, but as far as she can see nothing's changed: the same stained, deep red carpet, the same gaudy painting of a koi, the same gold bamboo wallpaper, the same plastic fish tied to the same fake coral reef in the same scummy tank. She wouldn't be surprised to learn the stains on the carpet are from drinks her dad and Vance spilled, back in the day.

There are only a few other customers: a rough-looking couple with a baby in a highchair, and a guy in a T-shirt that says *EMT*. The couple's table is crammed with dishes, more food than they could possibly eat, and she wonders if they're high. Probably. Tweakers, or maybe they pop pills. What else would they possibly be doing here, with a kid, in the middle of the night? The EMT, who has a handlebar mustache, stares into the middle distance, his hand resting on a beer.

A waiter appears, sets down two pebbled-plastic cups, and asks what they'd like to eat. Vance says they'll need a few minutes, and orders a pot of tea. Amanda glances up at the waiter. He has spiky hair, pitted skin, and a metal rod through his nose. His blue eyes are bloodshot, and he smells like he's just chain-smoked an entire pack of cigarettes. When he turns to go she notices an angry-looking scarlet rash on the back of his neck. She takes a sip of her water and, realizing how extraordinarily thirsty she is, drinks the whole cup.

"Getting drunk is hard work, isn't it? Here," Vance says, pushing his cup over.

She doesn't pick it up. "I wasn't drunk," she says.

"Really."

"I had one beer and a couple of shots the whole day."

"Sybil said—"

"Sybil doesn't know shit, okay?" She turns and stares out the window. Everything's black except for the lights from a couple of houses on the other side of the cove; second homes, she imagines, with lights programmed to go on and off. She picks up one of the menus and pretends to read. She can feel Vance watching her again. She sets the menu aside. "I'm not hungry," she says, "but you should go ahead."

"Nice try. Unless I'm mistaken, this was your idea. We go down together."

Soon the red-eyed waiter comes back with their tea, two paper placemats, and a bowl of fried noodle chips, which look saturated with grease and days old. Vance orders a few different dishes, definitely more than they need, but she doesn't protest. The waiter puts his pad in his shirt pocket and leaves. They both study the bowl of chips between them but neither partakes.

"May I?" Vance says, pouring her some tea.

The baby at the next table lets out a cry, and she turns her face away. By the window there's a bottle of soy sauce, a fake white carnation in a cheap glass vase, and a plastic cup filled with chopsticks in paper sleeves. She extracts a set, unwraps it, cracks the sticks apart, and starts rubbing them together, scraping them smooth.

"You trying to start a fire?" Vance says.

She stops abruptly and sets them down on her placemat, which is illustrated with the Chinese zodiac.

"So if you weren't drunk, how did you fall in the water?"

She can't bear to look at him. The back of her throat tingles. She stares at the placemat.

After what feels like a long time, he clears his throat. "What animal are you?" he asks, and when she looks up, confused, he nods at the zodiac. "Your sign."

"Oh, the pig," she says, and searches the chart until she finds 1970. "You're a dog."

"So I've been told."

She picks up her chopsticks again. "I'd like to go to China."

"You mean, like, right now?"

She smiles this time, she can't help it, and resumes scraping the sticks together. The baby is babbling loudly now, and the parents aren't doing anything about it. She says, "Who the hell takes a kid out at two A.M.?"

He glances over at the couple, then back at her.

"What? It's not my fault this place sucks."

"The Panda?"

"This town," she says. The baby yelps. "The whole Cape."

"Because of those people?"

She can feel his eyes on her, but she won't give him the satisfaction of looking up. "Because of all the people." She focuses her attention on the chopsticks. She must be using more force than she realizes, because one of them slips from her hand and she rakes the other, hard, across her palm. "Great," she says.

"What happened?"

She holds up her hand, showing Vance the inch-long shard of pale yellow wood that's lodged itself in her skin.

"You're on a self-destruct mission, aren't you," he says.

And then—she doesn't even feel them coming this time—tears spill down her cheeks.

"Oh, shit. Come on, now, it's only a splinter. Here, let me," he says, and before she knows what's happening, he's holding her hand. "It's okay. See? It's going to be fine." Very slowly, he draws the splinter out. "Impressive," he says, holding it up.

She swipes her eyes with the back of her hand and says, "I'm sorry."

"Don't be."

"I mean for being such a bitch. I can't—I don't—" She pauses and takes a breath, trying to collect herself. "Why are you so nice to me?"

Incredibly, the question seems to embarrass him. He sets the splinter on the windowsill, looks out at the dark cove, and says, "Beats me." But when he looks at her, he smiles.

She puts both hands around her teacup, which is still warm.

"Is all this about that boy?" he asks. "The one from the trip?"

She looks around—at the couple with the kid, then at the EMT, then into her tea. A few stray tea-leaf flakes—or she hopes they're tea-leaf flakes—have gathered at the bottom of the cup. Suddenly she feels so tired, she'd like to lie down, right here on the banquette, and close her eyes. She pushes the teacup away and weaves her fingers into a single fist.

"I don't really know how to explain," she begins.

"Try."

She takes a deep breath, buying some time, then says, "It sounds weird, I know, but I felt different there. Like—like a better version of me."

"And that was bad?" he says, as the waiter appears with a white ceramic soup tureen, which he sets on the table along with two bowls and two white flat-bottomed spoons.

Vance ladles out the steaming brown broth, which smells surprisingly good. She's hungry, she realizes, and picks up her spoon.

"How is it?"

"Hot," she says, but she doesn't stop eating. She's most of the way through the bowl before she sets down the spoon.

"So you felt good there," Vance says.

"Really good. Did you ever do something that just made you feel, like, *alive*? Like everything is in 3-D, or whatever's even more vivid than 3-D would be?"

"Do banned substances count?"

She knows he's joking, but she shakes her head. "It was so beautiful, like no place I've ever been. The air was so fresh, it smelled amazing, and it was so clear you could see for miles. The sky would get so blue, it was, like, vibrating. And at night, the stars, they were incredible." She pauses a moment, remembering. "Maybe it sounds weird, because I was being punished, but I was happier there than I've been in a really long time, maybe than I've ever been. Things just made sense, you know?"

Vance says, "Tell me."

"Like, I don't know, carrying everything you need on your back, being outside, in nature, all the time, depending on your own energy, your own body, and nothing else. We walked thirteen miles the first day, and carrying these gigantic packs. I never would have thought I could do that." She pauses to take a sip of her tea. "There was so much to learn, all these rules—like, when you're in the wilderness, you have to do everything a certain way. At first it seemed like a pain, but then you realize there are good reasons for them. Like packing: everything goes in plastic bags, sealed to keep out water, nothing extra, not even a nail file. There's a special procedure for putting up our tents, and for breaking camp—taking them down—and for drying our clothes, melting snow for water, going to the bathroom, cleaning the dishes, tying knots—oh my God, there were so many knots—and there was wilderness first aid, we were learning that, and dead reckoning, and plant identification, all this technical stuff. The point is, I felt like—I don't know, like I was *doing* stuff, and the stuff mattered. Even if it was just making rice, or securing a tarp the right way. It probably sounds crazy."

He doesn't agree or disagree. "Did you make any friends?"

She shrugs. "I liked this one girl, Kelsey, a lot. She was from Phoenix. The others were fine. Most of them were really rich, from fancy boarding schools, and they seemed kind of, I don't know, spoiled? There was one guy, Neil, from Canada, who was cool. A few were total freaks. This one girl, Gabrielle? It turned out she was afraid of heights and had to go home, back to New York City, after just a few days. It's like, hello, I know you're from the big city and everything, but have you never *heard* of a mountain? Because they're high."

She pauses again. She's not sure she's strung this many words together the whole time she's been home. She looks down at her soup, touching her spoon but then drawing her hand away, and looks up at Vance; he's waiting for the rest. The baby lets out another cry and Amanda looks over: his mother is struggling to wipe fluorescent-red sauce off his face and hands.

"So, there were two people in charge," she begins. "This guy, Lucas, and this girl—this woman—Nan. She went to Yale, I guess, and studied philosophy, and she was like super-pleased with herself. She was only a few years older than us, but you could tell she thought she was an adult and we were kids—or she acted that way. She had this annoying way of talking, like really slowly, as if otherwise we wouldn't understand."

Vance holds up his index finger; the waiter's back, this time delivering a scallion pancake and a sauté of what appears to be chicken in a clear, mucous-like sauce. Her stomach clenches, looking at it. She says, "You shouldn't have ordered all this. I'm full."

"Don't worry about it." He doesn't put any food on his plate either, and he's hardly touched his soup. "So, Nan?"

She takes a sip of her tea, which is tepid now, then dabs at her mouth with her napkin. Gathering all the courage she has, she says, "About a month in, my period didn't come."

She sees his face change — sort of go flat. She keeps talking, though, afraid to stop. She tells him how she attributed it to all the exercise, to the change of scenery, that kind of thing, but then the second time she started to worry. "I couldn't sleep," she says, "I couldn't think about anything else, and finally I told Nan because I didn't know what else to do." She nudges her fork, spins it around. "She was actually really nice, way nicer than I thought she'd be. She told the other kids I had an ear infection, and that she had to walk me out, so we walked out, just the two of us, for three whole days. She told me it happened to her sister in high school. God, she was really into it, going on about 'women's bodies' and 'women's rights,' the whole thing. Anyway, we finally made it to this random fishing village, I don't know what it was called, and they picked me up in a coast guard plane. Craig had to pay, I don't know how much."

"Craig."

She nods. She can feel a lump forming in her throat again and forces it down.

Vance says, "So he knows. They both do. Hence the house arrest."

She nods again. "It's not like I blame them for being mad. I've basically ruined their lives."

"That's a bit extreme, isn't it?"

She doesn't answer.

"I'm really sorry, honey, I am. But listen: I know this probably seems like the end of the world to you now, but I promise, it isn't. You're going to get past this, you'll move on, and you're going to have a wonderful life."

She shakes her head. He's not getting it. "You don't understand. I can't—" She pauses. "They won't."

"What, honey?"

"I need his permission. Dad's." And when he still looks nonplused, she adds, "To get an abortion. I'm not eighteen."

"But you will be soon."

"It'll be too late by then." Vance just blinks at her. She can't read his face at all, which makes her feel a little frantic inside. She keeps going. "I've told him how sorry I am, and that I know how badly I screwed up, but he doesn't care. He doesn't care what I say."

Vance frowns hard; a deep line bisects his forehead. "That doesn't sound like your dad."

"He says it's wrong—abortion. He says you don't fix one mistake with another. He says actions have consequences, and you have to take responsibility in life."

"I guess that does."

"Basically, I've wrecked his life, and now he's determined to wreck mine." She glances down at the food, and a powerful wave of nausea rolls through her. She covers her mouth, waiting for it to pass, but it doesn't. She stands up. "I'm sorry," she says, struggling to get out of the booth.

Hand still over her mouth, she half jogs across the dining room, making it to the ladies' room just in time. She's squatting in front of the toilet, waiting to see if there's more, when she hears someone banging on the door, then Vance's voice.

"Sweetie? Sweetheart? Can I come in?"

"No," she says, and he doesn't ask again.

She dry-heaves a few times but nothing else comes up. At the sink she splashes water into her mouth and spits it out, then washes her face and dries it with a rough brown paper towel. She washes her hands with soap whose chemical cherry scent is so strong she's almost sick again. To rinse it off, she runs the water as hot as it will go.

When she gets back to the booth, the food is gone and Vance has a strange, abashed look on his face. She slides back into her seat.

"You okay?" he says.

She shrugs.

He clears his throat. "It's not as if you're the first person—the first woman—ever to . . ." She plucks the fake carnation out of the vase and runs her thumb up the seam on the plastic stem. "What I'm trying to say," he says, "is that I want to help you."

She sits up. "Really?"

But when he says, "I'm going to talk to him," her heart sinks. "Don't look like that," he says. "He'll listen to me. He'll come around."

She doesn't respond.

"A?" he says. "Did you hear me?"

She glances around the room. The EMT is gone, so is the couple with the baby. They're alone. Doing her best to keep her voice steady, she says, "If you really want to help," she says, "take me yourself." She doesn't dare look up. Holding the flower like a pencil, she starts drawing an invisible spiral on the table and focuses her attention on that. When he doesn't answer, she says, "You could pretend you're him. All you'd have to do is sign a form. No one would know. I could tell him I had a—"

"I can't do that," he says quietly.

"Why?"

"It's against the law, for one."

Now she looks up. "So's pot."

He doesn't say anything. She hates the abject pity contorting his face; for the moment, she hates him.

"Then just give me the money," she says. "I'll go to a different state."

He's just looking at her. After another pause, he says, "I'm going to talk to him."

"There's no point," she says, unable keep the tremor from her voice. "You really think he gives two shits what you say?" He opens his mouth to protest, but she cuts him off. "He thinks you're an idiot, that you're immature, and selfish, and that your judgment's no better than it was when you were fourteen. He's been saying that forever."

He clears his throat. "Is that so," he says, looking a little stunned. She's cut him deeply, she can tell.

The waiter appears and asks if they're interested in coffee or dessert. Vance shakes his head. The waiter shrugs and reaches into the pocket of his apron, coming up with the bill and a couple of cellophane-wrapped fortune cookies, which he sets down in front of Vance.

Vance clears his throat. "And is that what you think, too?"

She glares at the cookies. "You really don't get it, do you? What I think doesn't count."

TUESDAY

21

WHEN GINA WAS PREGNANT with Helen, people, generally mothers, liked to tell her that once she had kids, she'd never sleep soundly again, but she didn't believe them. She'd always been an excellent sleeper (an ex used to joke that she could sleep through a stampede), and she'd filed the warning away with all the other unhelpful, and rather condescending, unsolicited advice veteran parents liked to dole out.

And they were wrong, as it turned out. The last satisfying night of sleep she had occurred well before she gave birth, probably a month and a half before Helen was born. She spent the better part of every night, those last precious weeks, wide awake, unable to get comfortable or to keep herself from worrying about terrifying, amorphous things: the restive creature shifting around inside her, whether she'd make a good mother, what the future would bring.

Now, a little after two A.M., she lies on her back, alone in their big bed, looking at the shadows the rafters cast on the ceiling and worrying—for a change, tonight—about something finite, something small: the earring. She thinks, miserably, about her sister. What will she possibly say?

She can't imagine. Telling Heather the truth is, of course, out of the question. She could never—she would never—confess; from her high mountaintop perch, Heather would judge her, she would disapprove —and Gina doesn't need that. She's already worn out and ragged from judging herself.

It *can't* be lost, she thinks, it just can't. Sitting up, she retrieves her phone from the nightstand and checks the screen: Dov promised he would go back to the inn today, and as soon as Kevin brought the Jeep home, he'd search every inch, but there's nothing from him yet. She looks at the clock radio: it's two-thirty A.M. He may not even be finished with work.

She lies back down. For the hundredth time, it seems, she tries to pinpoint when it happened. Was it when she took off her coat at the restaurant? When she freshened up in the ladies' room? Or was it later, in the Jeep?

A current of disgust moves through her, the current that's been moving through her since yesterday's lunch. She doesn't want Dov— she knows that now. She knew it then, the moment she walked into the restaurant and saw him at the table—something about the look on his face, conspiratorial, yes, but also smug. She felt sick to her stomach, was the truth, but she sat down—why? He ordered for both of them: the famous pheasant, foie gras, a bottle of wine. Why, oh, why? When they'd finished their desserts he asked if he should get them a room, and she felt herself blush deeply—not from flattery this time, but shame. She'd shown him exactly the sort of person she was; all he was doing was following her cues. She said no (thank God she'd found the word, finally), he asked if she was sure, and she said yes. But she got into his Jeep with him, and she let him tell her how beautiful she looked, once more, and she let him run his fingers through her hair.

Something draws her attention—the sound of footsteps on the stairs. Vance must be back. She has no idea what he was doing out —for all she knows he was at the Plum, drinking with Dov—and she doesn't care. His footsteps move down the hall, then ascend the attic stairs. She hears him cross the attic a few times, back and forth, and then the footsteps cease.

Sometime later—she doesn't know how long, she's just drifting off

—there's another sound. This time it's her door opening. She sits up, fully awake, alert. It's dark, but there's enough light to see Amanda standing in the threshold. She looks afraid.

"What's the matter?" Gina says, and that's all it takes. Amanda starts to cry.

Without thinking, Gina lifts Craig's side of the comforter, and to her surprise, Amanda slips underneath. She lies on her side, curling herself into a ball, and she seems so small somehow, smaller even than Helen.

"Hush, now, hush," Gina hears herself saying—her own mother's words, and ones she's sure she's never uttered before—and Amanda doesn't object. And when she reaches out and smooths her hair from her forehead—her mother's gesture—Amanda doesn't bat her hand away, or stiffen, or scowl.

"Everyone hates me. I'm a horrible person. I hate myself," she says, through quiet sobs.

"Shh," Gina says.

"I've ruined everything—my whole life, Craig's, yours."

Gina wants, more than anything, to tell her about her plan. But they're so close now—she needs to be patient, to wait just a little longer. All she says is "Hush, now, hush, honey. None of that is true."

It's a few minutes after nine, and Gina's three-quarters of the way through Hill Climb, the toughest workout on the treadmill. Usually she sets the difficulty level to four, occasionally five, but today she woke up wanting to punish herself, so set it at seven, and though she's sweating profusely, and panting so hard she feels dizzy, she refuses to dial it back.

She checks her phone: still nothing from Dov. On CNN, there's a story about a seven-year-old girl snatched from a campsite somewhere out west. In the photo they're displaying, the girl has her yellow-blond hair in pigtails with white ribbons on the ends. Periodically they show the parents; they look like death warmed over, the husband in an ill-fitting sport jacket, the wife in an ugly flowered dress, sitting shoulder to shoulder on a striped couch, begging whoever took their daughter, whose name is apparently Madison, to bring her back.

Jesus, Gina thinks. She picks up the remote to change the channel, flipping through until she lands on an *I Love Lucy* rerun.

The last stretch of the Hill Climb appears on the treadmill's screen, represented by red digital bars. She's starting the final ascent when in the mirror she sees the door to the room opening and Vance stepping in.

He looks surprised to see her. He seems disoriented, and unkempt, even for him, with his hair sticking up at all angles and sheet marks streaking his cheeks.

He says something she can't hear. "Wait a second," she says, plucking the earbuds from her ears.

"I said I'm sorry," he says. "I was looking for Craig's office. I guess I got turned around."

"No, this is it, or it used to be," she says. The treadmill's slope is getting steeper. She starts pumping her arms as she walks. "What do you need?"

He says he was hoping to talk to Craig, and when she reminds him he's in Boston, he looks dismayed. She suggests calling him, and Vance says Craig isn't answering his phone.

"Don't worry about it," he says. "Sorry for barging in."

He's reaching for the door handle when she says, "Wait." He freezes, hand still on the knob. She says, "Do you have a minute?" He nods. "Could you close the door?"

He does, and stands across the room from her, looking alarmed.

"Come closer? I'd rather not shout," she says. He takes a couple of tentative steps, stopping in the center of the carpet. He's such an odd guy, she thinks; simultaneously bold and timid, charming and coarse, presumptuous and polite. And, of course, so unlike Craig. "You can come closer. I won't bite," she says, smiling as warmly as she can.

He offers an uncertain smile in return and moves a few steps closer, standing a foot or so from the machine. He's wearing black jeans and a faded black T-shirt with a yellow smiley face on the chest, and his feet are bare. Nodding at an irregular-shaped mound in the far corner covered in plastic sheeting, he says, "Are those Craig's bikes?"

She nods. "Do you mind if I don't stop?" she says, elbows pumping, "If I do, I'll never start again." She lifts her hand towel from its hook on the side of the display screen and holds it against her brow, then the back of her neck, and finally her chest, aware of his gaze following along.

"Would you prefer to sit?" she says, nodding at the weight bench. He shakes his head; he looks half asleep and deeply ill at ease—which may work to her benefit, she thinks, watching him put his hands in the pockets of his jeans, then take them out. He's wearing some kind of tooth or claw on a leather thong around his neck, and he starts fiddling with that. "I heard you had quite a night last night," she says. He looks like he wants to flee but he stays put. "She told me everything."

His mouth falls open an inch or so but he doesn't speak.

"It's all right. I'd be surprised too, if I were you. Family crises make for strange bedfellows, so I'm discovering." The belt starts moving faster under her feet. "I'm really sorry you got dragged into this," she says between breaths. "I gather you're in the midst of something of a crisis yourself?"

He looks at her warily; she can practically see the synapses firing inside his head. "I'm glad she told me," he says in a cautious tone. "I just wish she hadn't waited so long."

"She was scared you'd think less of her. Or that you'd react like Craig."

"And yell at her, you mean?"

"Not just at her." She glances up at the TV. "I've pretty much quit trying to talk with him about it."

"Why is he angry at you?"

"He's decided the whole world's conspiring against him," she says. The earring flashes in her mind, then Dov's smug expression in the restaurant—assuming he already had her. Assuming she'd never walk away. She pushes him out of her thoughts and checks the treadmill display. She's almost there; a red digital heart flashes on the screen.

"I told her I'd try talking to him," Vance says.

"I know you mean well, but you're wasting your time."

"I know how his mind works. When does he get back?"

The machine makes a loud grinding sound, shifting gears; she's completed her ascent, summited the imaginary hill. As the belt flattens out, she lets go of the rails.

He waits for the noise to stop, then says, "I know he can be stubborn, but—"

"No, he's not being stubborn. He's being himself." She points at the bikes under the plastic. "Take those. Fifteen thousand dollars' worth of top-of-the-line bicycles he refuses to ride. Know why?" Vance shakes his head. "Because of Lance. He says the whole sport had been sullied, and he doesn't want any part."

"That's absurd," Vance says.

"It's beyond absurd, actually." Toweling herself off once more, she says, "And it's exactly the sort of logic—if you can call it that—that we're up against."

"We," he says.

She reaches for the water bottle. "Look, I'm going to be blunt. Amanda needs help."

He looks a little impatient. "I just said I'm going to talk to him."

She shakes her head and finishes what was left in her water bottle. She hasn't finished the cool-down yet, but she doesn't care. She presses the red Stop button, the belt halts, and the machine goes quiet. The whole room is quiet. She turns and faces Vance, resting her elbows on the rail. "Look, the time for changing Craig's mind has passed. She's ten weeks now, which means the window where they can take care of it medically has closed. The longer we screw around, the more complicated and unpleasant things get." He's looking at her uneasily, his face quickly going white. Is it possible he's this squeamish? She sweeps her tongue across her upper lip, tasting salt. "It's not a matter of *if* she'll get it taken care of."

"I'm sorry, but I don't think I—"

"A college friend of mine—she's a doctor—knows a clinic in New Haven where they don't require parental consent. They had a cancellation and can see her this week. Tomorrow."

"But she said—"

"She doesn't know. I haven't told her. I'm too afraid she'll tell Craig —to spite him, or whatever, I don't know."

He's frowning now, beginning to comprehend. The furrows across his forehead are pronounced.

"I'm planning to take her, but it would be much better—for her—if it were you."

He looks paler, even more disoriented, than he did when he first came in. His hands are in his pockets again. He takes one out and rakes his fingers through his hair. "I feel bad for her, for all of you. Really bad. But I don't see how I can—" He pauses. "Craig would—"

"This isn't about Craig. It's about Amanda, who's going through something really shitty, and it would be a whole lot less shitty if she had her family's support." She can feel her confidence beginning to fray. She shouldn't have told him; he's a far greater risk than Amanda, after all. But it's too late. "The consultation's at ten," she says, "and the surgery's scheduled for two."

"Tomorrow."

She nods. His eyes are clouded with distress. He shakes his head. "I'm sorry. I'd do anything to help Amanda, and all of you, you know I would, but I can't just—"

She feels something give inside her, a small eruption deep in her chest. "So you're Mister Morality now?" she says. "What an unexpected turn of events."

"Gina, wait. I didn't mean—"

But she cuts him off. "Does your drug dealer know? Or that coed you screwed? How about Celeste?"

He's looking down at the carpet. After a long moment, he says, "He's my brother."

"I don't know what that means."

He won't look up.

She gets down off the treadmill and stands in front of him. Like Craig, he's a good six inches taller than her, but she can tell that, unlike Craig, he's intimidated by her, that he's fighting the urge to step back.

"I know you think you're being principled," she says, "that Craig's the one you have an obligation to, that he's the one who needs protecting. I know you think you're doing the right thing." He opens his mouth to respond, but she cuts him off. "But let me ask you this: how do you think she ended up in the water last night? And please, for goodness' sake, don't tell me you're naïve enough to believe she fell in."

22

∾

KEVIN'S HOUSE — technically his mom's house now — is just over a mile away, and the termination point of a route she's walked so many times in the nine-plus years they've known each other she could do it in her sleep. Which is more or less what she's doing today, placing one foot in front of the other in a trance-like rhythm, cleaving to the white line, though in spots the shoulder is almost nonexistent, overtaken by old plowed snow that forces her into the road.

It's sunny but cold, colder than it's been, and she can feel her hair, loose and still wet from the shower, freezing into clumps. She should have worn a hat — or better, dried her hair — but she was rushing to get out of the house before someone made her stay. She forgot gloves, too, and inside her pockets her hands are balled into fists. Instinctively she picks up her pace, then forces herself to slow down. She still doesn't know what she's going to tell Kevin. She should use the time to think.

Making her way toward Champlain Road, she passes the Kanagas' and the Colliers' and the Koenigs' and the McPhees'. That everything looks the same as it always has — the chicken-wire fortress surrounding the Kanagas' garden, the Colliers' tacky gnomes and concrete-cherub birdbath, the Koenigs' barnacle-crusted Whaler on stacked cement blocks—seems wrong somehow. Maybe it's because she's a completely different person than she was before she left.

She goes back to thinking about what she'll tell Kevin. It's risky, not to mention deeply humiliating, going to him, but she can't think of any other way to get to the camp (forget trying to spirit a car away from the house today, and after last night's disappointing conversation, she's not about to ask Vance for help), and if she doesn't get to the camp, she's not going to get what she needs.

She spent much of the morning lying in bed, trying to come up with something, anything, to sell. First she considered her iPhone, then her computer, but they aren't worth nearly enough secondhand. Next she thought of Craig's tools; they're worth a lot, but he keeps them under lock and key—no way is she going to get her hands on those. Her best bet, she decided, was one of Craig's bikes: they're worth plenty, and he never rides them anymore. It would be weeks if not longer before he noticed one was gone. But the logistics: how would she get it out of the house without anyone seeing? And what would she actually do with it then? It's not as if the consignment shop in town is going to take it off her hands. The only other idea she had—the only thing no one would notice was gone—is out at the camp.

She still doesn't have a story for Kevin, and she's getting close. She takes a right onto Blue Meadow and then a left onto Lobster Lane, which is a cul-de-sac. Just before the circle, by the mailbox marked 3216, she stops. Kev's house is a split-level ranch with magenta shutters and a turquoise door, and she feels comforted seeing it, in spite of herself. A new sculpture (Lorna's—blue herons, she thinks) decorates the lawn, and, she's glad to see, Dov's classic Jeep is parked at the end of the driveway, by the barn, which must mean Kevin's here (since Dov isn't likely to be hanging around the place).

She feels a small quiver in her chest. She hasn't seen him since Christmas—Christmas Eve, actually, at the bowling alley, at a party thrown by one of his classmates.

She turns onto the rutted dirt driveway, reminding herself that she hates him—or at least that she doesn't love him anymore, that he has a girlfriend now—not the girl he kissed back in the fall, but someone new, someone "serious." She heard it through the grapevine, and then again that night at the bowling alley, from him. She did her best to look nonchalant when he told her. She even managed to say, "I'm glad."

The cranberry bog off to the right is still flooded, with patches of ice clinging to the shore. They used to skate there; kids from around the neighborhood would come, and Dov would build a bonfire in the side yard and they would skate until it got too dark to see the ice, then play flashlight tag in the woods while the grownups stood around the fire.

Kevin's room is in the basement, which has its own entrance in back, and instead of going to the front, she follows an improvised slate walkway around the house and down the hill, to a small patio with a fire pit, and peers through the sliding glass doors. Kevin is stretched out on the sofa under a striped wool blanket, holding his phone to his ear. Surely he's talking to *her*—the girlfriend. He doesn't see her, and for a moment she considers turning around. But she tells herself not to be such a coward. She needs this, she has no choice. Everything depends on it. Lifting a half-frozen fist, she knocks on the glass.

Startled, he sits up and, seeing it's her, waves her in. The slider is unlocked, and she steps inside.

"I'm not sure. Later," he's saying into the phone. There's a pause while he listens. "T minus three days," and then, "You too. Me too." Amanda stands awkwardly by the door, wishing she'd followed her instinct and bolted when she had the chance.

"This is a surprise," he says once he's hung up.

"I'm sorry. I would have called, but—"

"It's okay," he says. "Want to sit?"

She glances at the sofa, the achingly familiar plaid atrocity they always sat on together, on which he kissed her for the first time, on which he first put his hands under her shirt. She sits self-consciously on the floor.

"You look freezing," he says. "Did you walk?"

"Was that her?" she blurts out. When he looks confused, she says, "Your girlfriend."

He nods.

"What's her name again?"

"Nazneen."

Of course it is, she thinks, and imagines some sultry, raven-haired beauty—basically the exact opposite of her. "Is she premed too?"

He nods again, looking at her suspiciously. "Is that why you're here? To ask about Naz?"

She shakes her head. She feels like he's scrutinizing her. Unwilling to be intimidated, she scrutinizes him back. "You look tanned," she says.

"I was in Costa Rica with my dad."

She's not about to admit she already knows. "Oh, cool. Just the two of you?"

He nods.

"Was it weird?"

"A little," he says. "He's like revisiting his youth or something. He wanted to stay up late every night and drink and hit on girls. And he kept wanting to have all these heart-to-hearts."

"Yikes," she says.

"What about you?" he says. "I thought you said you'd be gone till June."

She wishes she could lie to him, just make something up, but she can't. She's made a mistake, she realizes, coming here. Standing up, she says, "I should go."

"You just got here."

"I'm not supposed to be out. I'm grounded."

"When did that ever stop you?" he says and smiles, but she doesn't smile back. "Hey, wait a second." She pauses by the door. "Why are you being such a weirdo?" She can feel her face contracting against her will, a lump forming in her throat. "What's the matter?" he asks. "A?"

He knows her way too well; this has always been true. It used to feel like a blessing, and now it's a curse. To hide her face, she looks out at the yard. The haphazard collection of chairs they've accumulated over the years, and which Lorna has painted crazy colors, are stacked against the shed for winter, and her famous flower garden is covered by a blue tarp. And someone—probably Lorna, too—has stuck an upside-down rake into the fire pit and hung an assortment of Mardi Gras beads from its tines. Seeing it all, being back here, feels like being punched.

She turns away from the yard. Reminding herself why she came, she says, "Actually, I have a favor to ask."

He looks a little wary, but he says, "Shoot."

"Could you give me a ride?"

"Where to?"

"The camp."

A curious look crosses his face, but he says, "Sure, I guess. Why not?" and starts scanning the room for his shoes. She spots them by the bedroom door, where he usually leaves them, and points.

He gets his coat, and she follows him outside and back around to the front, where he opens the passenger-side door of the Jeep. Dov isn't a neat person (in fact one of his mother's most frequent complaints about him, according to Kevin, was that he's a slob), but he cares a great deal about his cars, and the inside of the old Wagoneer is spotless: the chestnut-brown leather upholstery is rich and unsullied, the wooden dashboard gleams. Even the ancient, rust-colored carpeting looks pristine.

"Since when does he trust you with his baby?" she asks, immediately regretting her word choice and hoping he doesn't hear how rancid it sounds on her tongue. Quickly she adds, "Is it part of The Bribe?" She's referring to something he said all the time last summer—that after cheating on his mom, his father tried to worm his way back into his good graces by buying him things.

He turns the key and the engine growls to life. "Since Mabel died, I guess he doesn't have much choice. It's let me drive this, or chauffeur my ass around."

"Mabel?" she says. Mabel is—was—his 1992 Honda Civic; plastered with old beach stickers and spotted with rust, it was the car he drove all through high school. He'd wait for Amanda in the Civic every day after practice, idling on the service road by the field. She'd toss her backpack in the hatch and they'd drive to the Red Hen for Cheetos and Cokes and then on to the cove, where they'd park with the radio on and pass a joint back and forth, then climb into the cramped back seat and make out. And now it's gone, too. Why does it seem like everything she cares about gets taken away?

"I thought you knew."

She shakes her head. It's ridiculous—*ridiculous*—that her eyes are filling. She turns away.

"But it's not just that," he continues. "Everything's different now. He treats me completely differently, they both do."

"Since they split up?"

"No, since I left. You go to college and it's like suddenly you're a person. They actually listen to what you say. You'll see."

Swallowing hard, she looks out her window at the bog. "Remember skating?" she says.

"Sure."

"Remember when that kid—Donovan something? No, that was his last name."

"Willy Donovan?"

She nods. "Remember when he fell through?"

"Your dad pulled him out."

"No."

"Yes. I remember. He ran right in."

She looks out the window again. "*Wylie*," she says. "Wylie Donovan. What ever happened to him?"

"Didn't his family move to Egypt or something?"

The question is left unanswered, and they say little as he pulls onto the road and points the Jeep in the direction of the beach. In the public parking lot there are only a few other cars. He slows down and cruises past the clam shack, Dee's, where a laminated sign taped to one of the boarded-up windows says, THANKS FOR A TERRIFIC SEASON! SEE YOU IN THE SPRING!

They keep going, to the south end of the lot, where a semi-hidden dirt track takes them down a hill, around a couple of curves, and into a second, smaller lot. Here he stops, puts the Jeep in Park, and gets out to let air out of the tires. She asks if she can help but he says no, so she stays inside where it's warm, trying unsuccessfully to not think about all the times they've come here in the past. The very first time, she remembers, was the summer after her sophomore year. They'd been dating for a few months and it was her sixteenth birthday, and they caravaned out with a bunch of his friends. They spent the day playing bocce and cornhole and drinking beer, and when the sun started setting, the friends left and it was just them.

He gets back into the driver's seat and rubs his hands together. "Jeez," he says, "my fingers are numb."

"Did you just eat? If your stomach's full, all the blood goes there. It helps if you swing your arms in circles. The blood goes back into your hands."

He looks at her sideways. "Did you learn that in Chile?"

She doesn't answer. She wishes she hadn't said it.

The camp sits deep inside the National Seashore, a four-mile drive over the dunes, and they're on the sand now, bouncing along over a mostly intuited track. She sinks down in the seat a few inches and looks out. Everything's tan or brown today—the sand, the shrubs, the grass. Even the water in the marsh has a tawny cast.

He presses a few buttons and the radio comes on, a pop station playing an upbeat, pointless song she's heard a hundred times but can't name, and they ride like that, without speaking, all the way to the camp.

Surrounded by water on three sides, Land's End is the last man-made structure on a small rise before the sand disappears into the sea. When they get there, he slows down and Amanda jumps out before he comes to a complete stop, jogging over the sand and up the porch steps and looking around, performing a quick inventory. Despite a winter of storms, things appear to be intact: the boards are still on the windows, the grill and deck chairs are still lashed together with bungee cords, the twin blue cisterns that collect rain still flank the entrance, and the plank into which her grandfather carved the words LAND'S END still, somewhat miraculously, hangs over the door. Even the corrugated-steel sheets and sections of snow fencing that Vance piled around the perimeter to hold back the sand—the armor, he called it—haven't blown away. High on the flagpole, the pirate flag she picked out when she was little, now frayed and shredded, snaps in the wind.

Kevin joins her on the porch, where she removes the key from inside one of the downspouts and slips it into the lock.

Inside, it's dark—the boards on the windows keep out most of the daylight—so she finds a box of strike-anywhere matches in a kitchen drawer and lights three large propane lamps. Then she looks around. She hasn't been out here since September, when she brought some girls from the soccer team.

"Spooky," Kevin says, and she turns around.

"What is?"

"This place."

"You never used to think so." According to Lake family lore, Land's End was built on the ruins of one of the huts the Massachusetts Humane Society set up, two hundred years ago, as shelters for sailors whose ships wrecked off shore—Humane Houses, they were called. Kevin used to love trying to scare her, telling stories about drowned sailors' ghosts.

"Maybe it's just that I haven't been here for a while."

"Or maybe you're a giant pussy," she says and grins, and he grins back, and for a second it's like it used to be.

And then it's not. She stops smiling. "I'll be right back."

Before he can say anything, she leaves him, taking the stairs two at a time—there are only fifteen of them—and pausing briefly at the top. First she looks left, into the bedroom that her father and Vance once shared; their bunk beds are in there, along with a robin's-egg-blue dresser and a matching, child-sized desk and chair. She remembers sitting on that chair, on Kevin's lap, laughing because they were sure it would break, but it held, and they stayed there, kissing—for ages it felt like, they would kiss until their lips were sore—before he picked her up and carried her over to the bed.

She turns away and looks into the other room, the one that used to be her grandfather's. There's a double bed with an iron frame, a pine dresser, and over by the window, by an old wooden chest, the reason she came: the telescope. She crosses the room, bends down, and looks through it. It's pointed southwest, at the marsh. She adjusts the focus so the whitecaps on the water are sharply defined.

"See anything good?" Kevin asks from the doorway. He comes and stands beside her, close, so close she can feel the warmth coming off his skin, or she imagines she can.

"No," she says, straightening up and stepping to the side. "Water and sky."

He takes her place and looks into the eyepiece himself. "We'd need a wider lens, but you know you can see stars during the day? I'm taking astronomy, and . . ."

She's not listening. On the back of his neck there's a pale stripe of skin just below his hairline—he must have gotten a haircut since he got back—and she wants to touch it, the stripe. She wants to so badly, she has to shove her hand into her pocket to keep from reaching out. He's still talking about his astronomy class. She doesn't want to hear about it. She doesn't want to be around him, she realizes; it hurts.

She cuts him off. "Could you carry that downstairs?"

He straightens up and looks at her. "The telescope?"

She nods.

"No offense, but you're acting kind of nuts."

She'd like to punch him, then slap his face, kick him in the shins. Nuts? He dumps her on her ass, out of the blue, then acts like nothing's wrong, and *she's* nuts? She says, "Will you do it or not?"

He sits on the bed. There are no sheets on the mattress, which is ticking-striped and looks dingy and stained. "Only if you tell me why."

"Forget it. I don't need this," she says. Leaving him there, she flees into her dad's old room, pulls the door closed, and lies down on the bottom bunk, facing the wall.

It takes a minute or two for him to follow. He lets himself in and, without saying anything, lies down too.

"A," he says after a long moment, "what's going on?"

"I'm grounded, I told you," she says. "I can't drive. I needed a ride."

"You know what I mean," he says.

Her face is only a few inches from the wall. She covers an ancient protruding nail head with her thumb and presses down. "I need money. I'm going to sell the telescope. Nobody will care."

"Sorry to break it to you, but you won't get more than twenty bucks for that thing," he says. "The eyepiece is broken, there's condensation on the primary lens, and it's not very powerful to begin with."

She feels her throat constricting. She presses down harder on the nail.

"I'm sorry," he says. "I'm not trying to be harsh." After a long pause, he says, "What do you need money for?"

Without answering, she turns onto her back, reaches up, and traces their initials, AEL + KAA, which he carved years ago into one of the wooden slats holding up the top bunk, and thinks of the nights they spent here together. One of those nights, she lost her virginity to him, right here in this bed. She'd cried—not from unhappiness, but the opposite. He used to put his lips against her ear and tell her that he loved her, that he always would.

She clears her throat. "I dented Gina's van," she says.

"That's why you're grounded?" She nods. "Why didn't you just say?"

"I'm guessing you probably don't have five hundred dollars lying around."

He pauses a moment, then says, "You know I'd give it to you if I did." Another beat, then, "I could ask my dad."

Quickly—perhaps too quickly—she says no. She could never risk word getting back to Craig. She says, "Don't worry. I'll figure it out." They lie there for a few minutes, not talking. It takes everything she has not to turn over, put her body against his, and lay her head on his chest.

"I should probably get home," he says after a while.

Wordlessly they go downstairs and she closes up the camp. They get into the Jeep and make their way back over the dunes. The light has changed, some high clouds have gathered in a sky that's more purple, now, than blue. Back in the parking lot, he pulls up alongside the air pump, and while he reinflates the tires she looks out at the ocean, where banks of clouds line the horizon, light on top and darker on their undersides, like they've been bruised. A hopeless feeling comes over her.

When he gets back in, he says, "It's colder than a witch's tit out there."

Before she can think better of it, she says. "I miss you, Kev. A lot."

After one beat too many, he says, "I miss you too." He reaches over and amiably squeezes her hand.

In front of her house he parks behind Vance's motorcycle and asks if it's his, and she nods. "He keeps that thing in mint condition, doesn't he?"

"It's his baby," she says—again that word, like a foul taste in her mouth. She reaches down to unbuckle her seatbelt. As she's fiddling with the antiquated buckle, which tends to stick, her eye lands on something bright—something gold—in the narrow canyon between the center console and her seat.

Kevin is asking about Vance—what he's doing here, how long he'll stay—and she says, "I'm not sure," while covertly fitting her fingers into the small space and fishing the item out. It's an earring, a bird in a cage. She recognizes it right away.

Folding it into her palm, she transfers it to her coat pocket and looks up at Kevin, whose attention, she's relieved to see, is still on the bike. He's got one hand on the wheel, the other on the gearshift.

Eager to be alone, she thanks him for the ride.

"Take care of yourself, okay?" he says, reaching over her to open her door. She can see the twin moles on his shoulder, smell his peppermint shampoo. Sitting up, he says, "And remember, it's not the end of the world, okay? The van."

23

ACCORDING TO THE electronic message board at the wharf's entrance, Craig's ferry, the three o'clock high-speed from Boston, has been delayed. Vance parks the truck in the mostly empty lot and gazes out at the bay, which looks rough today, all whitecaps and chop. Off to the south, a few fishing boats bob wildly in their slips, their flag semaphores flapping in the wind.

It's a few minutes after five; the sun is just starting its descent, and the light coming off the bay is intense. He hardly slept and he hasn't eaten; ever since his phone rang last night, he's had a knot in his stomach, which his conversation with Gina only served to intensify. Again he wishes he had some weed to smoke, or a pill to take, anything that might settle him down.

He pulls down the visor and something tumbles into his lap: a stack of white business cards held together by a pink hair elastic. He flips the stack face-up and inspects the card on top. Half the space is taken up by a color photo of Craig's face, the other half by the words *Craig Lake, Owner, Lake Design Build, LLC,* then the motto and, of course, the blue wave. The photo can't be a very recent one, because the face smiling out at him is suntanned and lean; it looks a hell of a lot like his own, is what strikes him, and he feels a pang of anguish, recalling what Amanda said at the Lucky Panda. He shouldn't be so surprised, he supposes, to hear Craig's low opinion of him—he certainly doesn't act otherwise. But the news that he's said such things aloud, and to Amanda no less, feels like a betrayal, like he's breached some unspoken code. Worse still, Amanda gave no indication that she disagrees.

But he can't afford to dwell on his hurt feelings, not now. He made a promise to his niece, that's what matters. He takes a last look at Craig's face, then returns the stack of cards to its home behind the visor.

He looks out at the bay: still no sign of the boat. Directly across from the wharf there's a bar, the Wee Packet. He gets out of the truck and crosses the street.

Inside the bar it's dark, the air smells of stale booze and old wood, and the walls are decorated with Boston sports paraphernalia, banged-up buoys, and neon beer signs. Vance asks the bartender, a thick-necked kid with a silver lightning bolt in his ear, if they serve food, and he points to the rack behind the bar, underneath a flat-screen TV, where packages of beef jerky and bags of chips are displayed. Vance gets potato chips and a Heineken, the only import they serve, and he takes both over to a high table, where he chooses the stool facing the window, which is tinted glass and offers an unobstructed view of the water.

The beer goes down easily—and straight to his head, thanks to his empty stomach, his lack of sleep. All night, or what was left of it after he brought his niece home, he lay awake, tossing and turning on the air mattress, unable to steer his thoughts away from Amanda. How did it happen? To *her*? That's what kept circling through his mind. Maybe she's reckless, or impulsive, but she's such a good kid, a good person. She doesn't deserve even a fraction of the pain she's in.

And then—of course—he was thinking about Dylan. It's not like she deserved it either. And neither, for that matter, did he. They were just kids. What did they know? Before drifting off, he'd had the notion that history was repeating itself, but not randomly. He had the irra-tional, upsetting idea that this—Amanda—was punishment for how he'd treated Dylan all those years ago. Here, finally, was the price he had to pay.

He raises his beer to drink, but the bottle is empty. He'd like to order another, then another, but he knows better. He'll need all his wits about him, and then some, for his conversation with Craig.

He squints out through the glass. Beyond the wharf, close to the horizon, he sees something, a dark spot on the silver surface of the bay.

The air outside feels colder than before, biting, and the sun, lower now, is aggressively bright. Shading his eyes, he faces the mainland, scanning the horizon for the ferry, but the light coming off the water is like white fire. In the wharf's kiosk he buys a tin of strong mints, pops a couple into his mouth, and checks the board again: Craig's ferry, the *Mary Ellen*, is about to arrive. He considers standing outside on the dock, under the kitschy, oversized license plate that welcomes people to the Cape, but that seems far too blithe, and besides, it's freezing out. He gets back in the truck and waits. In a sedan to his right a woman is doing a crossword; to his left, a teenager alternates between frowning at the horizon and filing her nails.

Soon two extended horn blasts make the ferry's arrival official. It glides into a slip at the end of the long dock, and a couple of men in jumpsuits and boots appear and wrap two thick rope lines around two extra-large cleats.

No surprise, Craig is among the first to disembark. He's never had any patience; when confronted with the possibility of a line, he goes out of his way to ensure he's at the front. Vance watches his brother descend the narrow gangway. He's wearing pleated khakis, shiny loafers, a black *Lake Design Build* fleece, and mirrored sunglasses, and carrying a black-leather overnight bag. As he steps onto the dock, Vance has the unkind thought that Amanda was right, Craig has gotten fat: his face looks jowly and his pants bunch awkwardly around the crotch as he walks. Vance opens the truck's window to wave.

His brother's mood is foul, Vance can tell right off. "You shouldn't be driving this," he says as soon as he's in the passenger seat. "It's only insured for work."

"Gina gave me the keys," Vance says. "Yesterday. I picked Helen up." Craig doesn't seem to be listening. He has his phone out and he's frowning down at the screen.

Backing up, Vance asks how Boston was.

"Shitty," his brother says. Vance glances over at him, but Craig is still looking at his phone.

"Sorry to hear that," he says. They're approaching the exit gate, and Vance pauses a moment beside the machine, assuming Craig will pay. He doesn't, though, so Vance gets out his own wallet and feeds his credit card into the slot. Pulling onto the road, he says, "You were schmoozing some big client, Gina said?"

"The light's red, Christ," Craig says.

Vance steps on the brake just in time. He can feel the antipathy coming off his brother like a gas. "So what's new in Beantown?" he asks with forced cheer, and when Craig doesn't answer, he says, "Want to grab a bite?"

"I had a Danish on the boat," Craig says.

"A drink, then."

"I don't think so," he says, flipping his sunglasses up onto his head. He checks his watch, a stainless-steel Swiss behemoth, and shakes his head.

Vance thinks about Amanda, about his promise to her. He can't just cave. "Come on, one drink," he says. "It's against Lake code to turn down booze."

His brother doesn't smile, but he says, "Fine. One."

"Great. The Plum?"

Craig shakes his head and directs Vance to the Landing, the bar at the resort where he plays golf.

The place is all wrong, Vance knows it the moment they walk in: dark wood paneling, white tablecloths, plaid upholstery, framed pictures on the walls of ducks and guns and dogs. The bar is silent and devoid of patrons, and so are the tables, except for one in the far corner where a woman in a crisp shirt and green bow tie sits, using a funnel to fill shakers with salt.

Craig nods at the polished wood bar, at two brass-studded, leather stools under a TV that's showing basketball, a replay of a game he's already seen. The bartender, also in a green tie, sets down a bowl of nuts coated in something rust-colored. Vance orders a scotch, one from the top shelf, hoping Craig will follow suit—that he'll relax, in other words —but Craig only raises an eyebrow and says he'll take a Coors Light.

Craig shovels a handful of the nuts into his mouth. He's sitting with his body angled toward the TV screen, away from Vance, who has the strong urge to put his hands on his brother's shoulders and spin him around.

"I thought you said you ate," he says to the back of his brother's head.

Craig doesn't bother to look. "I did say that."

Their drinks arrive and Vance lifts his glass, holding it high over the bar and in Craig's line of vision. "Cheers," he says, and nods at the screen. "Here's to picking the winning team."

"I'll drink to that," says Craig.

Vance sips the scotch, which is pleasantly smoky and sweet, and wonders whether he should give Craig a few minutes or jump right in. He decides on the former, partly because he can see how wound up his brother is, and partly because, frankly, he's a little afraid.

"So this Boston client," he says. "What's his name?"

"It doesn't matter," Craig says.

"What's the project?"

"What are you, a reporter?" Craig says over his shoulder.

Vance sits back and regroups, taking a couple of deep breaths, sipping his scotch. He tells himself that Craig is under a lot of pressure and doesn't mean to be such a dick. More important, arguing with him isn't going to help Amanda.

Setting his glass down on a coaster, he says, "Whatever it is, I wouldn't sweat it. You're obviously doing great." He remembers what Carson Mulcahey said. "I can't drive two blocks in town without seeing one of your signs."

Craig's eyes are still fixed on the TV, which is showing a commercial for an allergy drug. He doesn't respond.

Vance looks into his glass; it's somehow empty. He catches the bartender's eye and orders them another round, though Craig is still nursing his beer. The bartender sets their new drinks down and refreshes the bowl of peanuts, and Craig digs in. Vance watches him chew, watches the muscles in his jaw move under his skin, watches him wash the mouthful down with beer.

To the screen, Craig says, "I really don't need to see this again."

Waving the bartender over, he asks him to change the channel to "literally anything else."

The new channel, ESPN Classic, is showing a long-ago boxing match. In grainy footage a crowd cheers while two lean fighters dance around the ring.

"You ready to get out of here?" Craig says. Though he hasn't touched his second beer, he looks for the bartender.

"Not quite," Vance says. Thinking of Amanda, he takes a final fortifying swallow, then pushes his glass away. "I was hoping we could talk."

"Isn't that what we've been doing?"

"About something specific. Amanda."

This gets Craig's attention. He looks at Vance for a long moment before turning back to the TV.

"She told me what's going on," Vance says. "Why she's home."

"Congratulations," Craig says.

Vance takes another deep breath. He glances at the TV screen, where a sedan careers across endless salt flats. "I told her I want to help."

Craig doesn't say anything. One of his hands rests on his beer bottle, and he flicks at a loose corner of the label with his thumbnail. "I already told you, you can't."

Vance nods as if he's agreeing. "She said you won't listen to her. I told her that doesn't sound like you—to just shut her out."

Craig says nothing.

"Don't you think you should at least *consider* what she wants?"

"Because her judgment's been so stellar up to this point?" Craig says. "It's almost funny when you think about it. You give a kid every single thing, you break your back to do it, and then they turn around and kick you in the balls."

Vance waits a moment for the echo of his brother's phrase to pass. "She's such a good kid—young woman—it's not as if she—"

Craig interrupts. "She's spoiled is what she is. She's never had to deal with the consequences of her actions. She just does what she wants, and someone's always there to clean up her mess."

Vance wonders how they can possibly be talking about the same person. In as measured a tone as he can manage, he says, "It's not like her life's been easy."

"And that's my fault?"

"Of course not. I wasn't—"

Craig's got a wild look in his eye; he doesn't seem to hear what Vance is saying. "You want to help? Stop telling me what a shitty job I'm doing raising my own kid." He turns away again.

Vance doesn't know what to say. The back of his brother's neck is flushed deep red. Vance reaches for his glass but doesn't drink. After what feels like a long time, he says, "She'll never forgive you, you know," to the back of Craig's head.

Without turning around, Craig says, "You really don't have a clue, do you? It's the opposite. What I'm doing is keeping her from making a mistake she'll always regret."

"Craig," he says, "what you're doing is wrong."

Craig spins around. "You want to talk about wrong? Okay, let's. Let's talk about her fucking her camp counselor. While she was spilling her guts to you, did she mention that the guy is twenty-three? That he's got a wife and a retarded stepkid back home?"

Vance struggles not to look shocked. Could it be true what Craig's saying? Why would Amanda lie to him? Did she really think he would judge her, like Gina said? Even more troubling, how could she have set him up like this, sent him into battle so unprepared?

"I figured," Craig says. "Now, can I please go home?" He draws a check mark in the air with his index finger and the bartender hurries over with the bill, and before Vance knows what's happening, Craig has put down his American Express card.

Vance says, "Wait, I wanted to pay," and reaches for his wallet, but Craig says, "Why start now?" And by the time Vance gets out his card, the check is gone.

Outside, night is falling. The sky is the color of coal ash, and a cold, raw-edged moon rises over the bay. At the truck, Craig holds out his hand. Wordlessly, Vance relinquishes the keys.

24

DINNER, apparently, is Vietnamese. The air in the house smells sweet and a little fishy, and cardboard containers from Saigon on Six clutter the kitchen counter, along with a pile of paper napkins and flimsy plastic forks. Craig sets his overnight bag down on the island and unzips his fleece.

"How'd it go?" Gina asks. She's standing in the front hall, in front of the mirror, putting on lip gloss. To his surprise, she stops, comes in, and kisses him hello. Nodding at the array of cartons, she says, "I didn't know when you two would turn up, so we went ahead. Where's Vance?"

"He just took off in the Frog."

"What happened?"

"You're going out?"

"Book club." She nods at the calendar over the desk. "Remember? Second Wednesday of the month. It's at Anne Stein's." Frowning, she says, "You look tired. I shouldn't be too late." She glances at the ceiling. "The baby's down, and Helen's in our bed."

"It's six o'clock."

"She's watching TV. She said she's not hungry. I hope she's not getting sick." She goes into the mudroom and comes back out, wrapping a scarf around her neck. He doesn't bother asking about Amanda, and she doesn't offer. "You sure you're all right?" she asks, buttoning her coat. Then she kisses him again.

Once she's gone, he fills a plate and carries it, along with a beer, into the living room, where he sits down and turns on the TV. He swallows a few forkfuls of food, but it's cold, the oils have congealed, and the gummy noodles stick in his throat. He considers heating it up, but for the first time in recent memory he has no appetite, and he carries the plate back into the kitchen and tilts it into the trash. Instead of returning to the living room, he proceeds through the laundry room, opens the door to the garage, and flips on the lights.

Since his office was commandeered for Gina's gym, this is the only place in the house that's officially and exclusively his. It's also the only place he can keep the way he likes it, which is neat. Very neat. Gina rolls her eyes and calls him anal-retentive, and the girls love to agree, but he refuses to be shamed. Unlike every single other space in the house, there is no clutter here—no stray baby socks, no earbuds, no dog toys, no doll parts, no chewed or abandoned books. Here, order reigns.

From the threshold, he makes a quick visual inventory. The back wall is for sports equipment—the two surfboards, boogie boards, various rackets, snowshoes, camping gear, skis and poles, each item in its designated and carefully labeled place. Along the north wall, on shelves he built himself, are the beach things: folding tables and chairs, coolers arranged by size, umbrellas, windscreens, the hibachi, the mini-Weber, spare propane tanks. And on the last wall, the west wall, is his workbench, plus the pea-green cabinets he salvaged when they renovated the kitchen, which contain his personal things.

These are items he can't bear to part with but that, for one reason or another, don't belong inside the house: sports memorabilia, his old hockey gear, his stamp collections, and, last but not least, the utterly undiscardable detritus from his life with Suzanne.

Tonight he goes directly to the workbench. Inside the top drawer, at the very back, are his cigarettes. Or that's where they're supposed to be, but when he opens the drawer this evening all he sees is his notepad and a straightedge and a laundry pen and his pencil sharpener and his yellow number 2 pencils, sharpened and held together by a green rubber band.

He opens the drawer all the way, even bends down to peer into the very back, but his cigarettes aren't there. *Fucking Vance*, he thinks, remembering the tantalizing stink that surrounded his brother the night before last. The idea of Vance out here, rifling through his things, irks him deeply. He opens a side drawer, the one for important documents, and checks all the way behind the hanging files, where he keeps his backup secret stash. These, also, are gone.

Without cigarettes, he has nothing to do in the garage, strictly speaking, but he'd rather be out here than inside, so he sits on the second-lowest rung of a steel stepladder and, because it feels heavy suddenly, lets his head rest in his hands. All he can think about is Amanda, and now, maddeningly, the things Vance said—things he wishes he could simply expunge from his brain. His brother has some nerve, that's for sure, waltzing into their lives practically without warning and, without knowing jack about what's going on—about anything—judging Craig. It's perfect Vance: so quick to opine, to act like he's on the moral high ground, and meanwhile his own life is in ruins.

And yet, something needles Craig. *What if Vance is right?* a voice inside his head asks. *What if she never forgives you? What if she never looks at you with anything but hatred again?*

But then again, Jesus, why is he even listening to this voice? This voice is Vance, and Vance doesn't know shit about kids, or about loss, or guilt, for that matter. He's like a child—or no, he's like an animal, a dog, existing outside of time, no future, no past. Somehow he's lived his life focused on what's directly in front of him, on gratifying his immediate needs, the consequences be damned.

What Vance doesn't understand, what Amanda doesn't understand —and maybe she can't now—is that her life isn't ending, it's the opposite. No, the circumstances aren't ideal—they're terrible. But the thought comes to Craig again: what if, seventeen years ago, he and Suzanne had "terminated" her?

There's a knock on the door, a tentative one. He sits up straight and opens his eyes.

"Daddy?"

It's Helen. He clears his throat and says, "Hey, peanut."

"Are you sick?" she asks from the top step.

"No." He sniffles. "I was just tidying up."

She's wearing blue pj's with yellow stars on them. She frowns. "Your eyes are all red."

"It must be the dust," he says, touching each eye with the back of his hand. "You ready for bed?"

She frowns, biting down on her lip. "I heard a noise in the closet and I got scared."

He stands up. "That's silly, sweetheart. You're home. There's nothing to be afraid of here."

He carries her upstairs and puts her in her bed, and after three and a half pages of the book they're reading she's fast asleep. He sets the book on the nightstand, turns off the lamp, and pulls her door closed. Instead of turning left, though, he turns right. At the end of the hall he stands by Amanda's door, which is also closed (and probably locked, its default state these days).

He listens for the sound of her voice but can't hear anything through the door, not even music. She's probably got her earphones on. He can almost see her, sitting cross-legged on her bed, typing on her computer (Gina wouldn't let him take it away). Or maybe she's reading. She used to stay up until all hours, enthralled by a book, her tattered old stuffed dog Sebastian perched on the headboard, keeping watch. He feels a rush of love for her, a warm feeling that starts in his solar plexus and radiates outward, like ripples in a pond. How can things be so complicated, so adversarial, when he loves her so much? He just needs to talk to her, to explain, to help her understand. He raises his hand and knocks.

"It's your dad," he says. "Can I come in?"

Shockingly, she says yes. He turns the knob and steps inside.

It's cold in the room—the window's wide open—and she's inside her purple sleeping bag, sitting up, computer open on her lap.

"Aren't you freezing?" he says.

She shrugs. "I like it this way."

He moves toward the bed, then reconsiders, and heads for the desk. "Okay if I sit?"

She shrugs again but doesn't say no, and he perches on the edge of her desk. He feels nervous, suddenly. It's ridiculous, he tells himself: what kind of man is intimidated by his own child?

A man exactly like him, he thinks: his heart feels like it might jump out of his chest. "I know I'm not your favorite person at the moment," he begins. He has no idea what he's going to say next. He pauses, hoping she'll say something, but she doesn't. "I was hoping maybe we could talk this through civilly. That you'd give me a chance to explain?"

"Gross," she says, looking at his hands, and he realizes he's cracking his knuckles, a habit she hates. Suzanne hated it too.

He has a vague notion of starting out by telling her how much she means to him, what a blessing she's been in his life. Instead, he says, "I was wondering, what do you remember about Mom?"

"Her hair," she says quickly, surprising him. "It was really long and thick, and she was always doing something with it—twisting it around her finger, fluffing it up, tying it in a knot. And it smelled good, like . . ."

"Vanilla," he says, and she nods.

They sit there looking at each other. He has no idea, from the expression on her face, what she's thinking. "She loved you so much," he says. "You know that, right?" She nods again.

"That's what I've been wanting to explain to you," he ventures. "You weren't exactly planned for, you know. But it didn't matter. You were her life, her universe—mine too, you still are. The love a parent has for a child, it's not like anything else. It's the best thing in the world." He stops a moment, weaving his fingers together and looking at his lap. "You don't know that now, you can't, but you will."

Head still down, he waits for her to respond, but there's only silence. After a long moment, he looks up.

"Get out," she says. Her face is ferocious.

"Pardon?"

"I shouldn't have let you come in. Get *out*."

"Baby, I'm just trying to—"

"Don't call me that. And don't pretend you care about me, because you don't. You're sick, do you know that, dragging Mom into this, using her to justify your fucked-up shit? She would never agree with you." Her voice is higher now, almost a shriek. "She would care about what I want. She would listen to me."

"Baby," he said, then corrects himself. "Amanda. Did you not hear anything I just said? Your mother—"

"Don't talk about her," she shouts. "And don't talk to me ever again." She lifts her hands and uses them to cover her ears. He opens his mouth to object, but she shouts, "I hate you. I wish *you* were the one who was dead."

Slowly he stands up. She's still shouting, "Get out, get out!" when he pulls the door closed.

Downstairs, he pours an outsized drink and carries it, somewhat unsteadily, to the garage, where he swallows half of it standing up. Then he sets the glass down on his workbench, opens the green cabinets, and removes a gilt-edged leather photo album from a plastic box labeled *Suzanne*.

It's their wedding album, and he sits on a metal footstool and opens the front cover. The first few pages are photos of Suzanne getting dressed, and she looks so beautiful and serene, looking at them usually has a calming effect.

Not so tonight. In one of the first photos, Suzanne stands in front of her sister, Ramona, who's buttoning Suzanne's dress. The dress was simple—white cotton with a chain of cotton daisies circling the waist —and he can't help thinking about what lay under those daisies. She was three months along, just a little past where Amanda is.

He turns a few pages, stopping at the ceremony. It took place in a neighbor's field, a rare undeveloped acre overlooking the harbor and the dunes. He and his father built a trellis that a friend of Suzanne's, who was a florist in town, covered with autumn leaves and white ribbons that rippled in the breeze. Everyone said how lucky they were: it was a perfect Indian-summer day, with endless sunshine and a sapphire-blue, cloudless sky. And he'd *felt* lucky. It was all so beautiful, and nothing was half as beautiful as Suzanne; that's what he'd thought, watching her walk toward him, the hem of her dress brushing the grass. "I'm the luckiest guy in the world," he whispered in her ear, and she grinned and whispered back, "And the sappiest." "Here's to my brother, the luckiest guy in the world," Vance said later—one of those funny twin coincidences—raising his glass, later, under the tent.

A loud mechanical sound brings him back to the garage. The door is opening, and Vance is pulling the Frog inside. Craig closes the photo album, stashes it in the drawer of his workbench, and stands up. He shakes his head at Vance, who rolls down his window, and Craig tells him he can't park there, it's Gina's space.

"Then how about we move your truck? It'll be fine in the rain."

"I'm not moving my truck," Craig says, still a little disoriented.

"Come on. You know as well as I do the hard top leaks."

"I said back it up."

But Vance doesn't. Instead, he cuts the motor, gets out, and closes the door. "A vintage piece of machinery like this doesn't belong outside. When was the last time you started it up?"

"Not this again," Craig says. His brother's eyes, he notices, look a little bleary. And he's leaning against the Frog in a telltale way. "Have you been drinking?"

"Are you the alcohol police?"

Craig shakes his head. "You're a fucking idiot. Are you trying to get another DUI?"

"I can take care of myself," he says.

"Despite all evidence to the contrary," Craig says under his breath.

"What was that?"

"Nothing. I'm tired. I'm going in."

"Sweet dreams," Vance says, pushing off the Frog and coming over to where Craig is. Before Craig can stop him, he's opened the workbench drawer and taken out the photo album. Craig lunges for it but Vance steps out of his way; he's quick, even in his compromised state.

"Give that back," Craig says.

Vance opens the album and his face changes, goes slack. "Jesus," he says. Craig doesn't say anything. Vance turns a couple of pages. His face looks sallow, unhealthy, under the garage's bright fluorescent lights. "She looks like an angel from fucking heaven, doesn't she?" he says. "Shit. She looks just like A."

"Please give it to me," Craig says. He's struggling to keep his voice under control.

To his surprise, Vance does as he asks, closing the album and handing it back. Silently Craig returns it to its plastic tomb and snap-locks the lid. Then he puts the box back into the cabinet and flips the latch.

"Listen," Vance says to his back, "I was thinking. I didn't like it earlier, the way our conversation went." He's swaying a little; he rests a hand on the hood of Craig's truck. "My only point was, I care about her a lot."

Craig has the urge to push him over. "And you think I don't?"

Vance starts to speak, but Craig can't hold back any longer. "It's none of your business, any of this. You're her uncle, her ludicrous, entertaining uncle. You're the sideshow — the guy who let her stay up late and watch movies her parents disapproved of and eat junk food behind their back." Vance's mouth hangs open; it makes Craig furious. "Would you look at yourself? You're pathetic. No, you're worse than that. You're selfish and reckless. And you're fucking deluded if you think you've ever truly given a damn about anyone but yourself."

For a long moment Vance doesn't say anything. Then his hand goes to his chest, as if he's been hit, and Craig feels the predictable — and infuriating — burst of remorse. "Don't be melodramatic," he says.

Vance's eyes look watery. He's leaning more of his weight against the truck. "I shouldn't have come here. I made a mistake."

"I'm not going to beg you to stay, if that's what you're waiting for."

At that moment, they hear the crunch of tires in the gravel driveway. Craig turns and sees headlights: Gina's home. She stops in front of the garage and gets out. "You two all right in there? I'll be in in a sec," she calls, leaning back into the van to gather her things.

"I'll be gone in the morning," Vance says, too quietly for her to hear.

"Right. And where do you plan to go?" Craig asks. "You told me yourself you're broke."

Vance doesn't answer.

Gina closes the van's door and steps into the garage, where she stands blinking under the bright lights. Her blue purse hangs from her shoulder, and she hugs a hardcover book to her chest. She looks at them suspiciously, her eyes moving from Craig to Vance and back to Craig. "It's so late, and freezing. What are you guys doing out here?"

25

⚜

CHASSÉ, CHASSÉ, *chassé, chassé,* arabesque. Under the covers, eyes squeezed shut, Helen does what Miss Genevieve, her ballet teacher, told her to do. It's called visualizing, and it means imagining herself doing each of the steps in her routine, over and over again. She pictures herself doing the high *relevé,* then the *plié,* the *grands jetés,* the small *glissade,* and the pirouette, but when she's in the middle of the second arabesque, they start up again.

"This isn't how mature people act," her mother says, and her father says, "So now I'm immature, too? Christ." She hears them through the wall. They've been doing it for hours, their voices starting out in loud whispers that gradually get louder, until finally Gina says, "You'll wake the kids, please," and they start all over, going back to whispering again.

Usually when she can't sleep (or she has a bad dream, or her throat hurts, or she hears a noise under her bed) she gathers her stuffed monkey, Maurice, and the blue, satin-backed blanket she's had since she was a baby and goes down the hall to her parents' room. Her father doesn't wake up, most times, or if he does, he just sort of grunts and turns over, but her mother always awakens; somehow, even if it's the middle of the night and she's been asleep for hours, she seems to know when Helen's standing in the doorway, like she has a special sense. Her eyes will snap open, she'll prop herself up on her elbow, and she'll say, "Come on, my angel," in a soft voice, holding up the corner of the covers so Helen can slip underneath. But tonight her parents are the problem, and though it's quiet now, she definitely doesn't feel like going in.

She pulls the covers up over her head and tries closing her eyes again, but she can't seem to concentrate on ballet. They've been doing it—arguing—so often lately, almost every night. It's been going on for a long while, probably since before Cameron was born, but it got worse when Amanda came home, much worse, which makes sense, because what they're fighting about now, mostly, is her. From all Helen's heard, she understands that her mother thinks her father should let Amanda get an abortion, but her father says no.

She doesn't know what an abortion is, but it's clear from the way they shout at each other that it's something big. She's thought of asking Mrs. Forrest at school, but for some reason she hesitates. Abortion, abortion: at first she thought it might be a kind of car, but that doesn't seem right. For one thing, Craig keeps saying it's not something you can just change your mind about later, it's permanent, it will stay with Amanda for the rest of her life, and that doesn't sound like a car. Also, he said, it will change Amanda—"She'll be scarred forever" were his exact words, so now she suspects it's something else, something to do with Amanda's body, like getting her ears pierced, or maybe it's a special kind of tattoo.

It's still quiet. She lies on her back with her eyes closed, counting backwards from one hundred like her mother said she should when she feels restless but sleep won't come. But she gets to zero and she's still awake—she doesn't even feel tired anymore—and she sits up and looks around. The room is dark except for her night-light, which is shaped like the moon. She wonders if she can see the real moon, so she sits up and swings her legs around, plants her feet on the woolly rosebush rug beside her bed, gets up, and crosses the cold wood floor. At the window she pushes the curtain aside. There's no moon, and the sky is a strange color, not black like she expected but a dirty dark gray tinged with pink.

She closes the curtain, but she doesn't feel like getting back into bed. She stands there, thinking about her parents next door. She's tired of them being mean to each other. She looks at her nightstand, at *Island of the Blue Dolphins*. She can read it herself—she's already read all the way to the end—but her father doesn't know that, neither of her parents do. She doesn't want them to, because then they'll stop reading to her, and she feels panicky inside thinking about that.

She picks up the book, which her father said was one of Amanda's favorites when she was younger, and which he took from her shelf. She thinks about the girl in it, Karana, who lives alone on the island for years and years. At first Helen thought that sounded scary, but now she doesn't. Sometimes she wishes she were like Karana, all alone with her dog, building fires and making dresses from feathers and spearing fish, on an island where no one would shout—or no, only *she* would shout. She would build a cave house, like Karana did, with an entrance so small only she and the dog could go in. And one day, when she got tired of the island, she'd look out at the horizon and see a ship.

Ships make her think of the attic, of Vance. Maybe he'll let her sleep up there, in his bed, or better yet, maybe he'll want to play cards. As quietly as she can, she leaves her room and tiptoes down the hallway to the very end, to the bottom of the attic stairs. The door is open, the staircase dark. She climbs with care, stepping lightly and keeping to the outer edges of the planks, which she knows from experience are less likely than the middle to creak.

When she gets to the top, though, Vance isn't there. His duffel bag is gone from the steamer trunk and so are the rest of his things. She feels confused, and the back of her throat aches. Why did he tell her he was going to stay?

The air mattress is still there, still inflated, and she lies down on top of the scratchy wool blanket and draws her knees to her chest, making herself into the smallest ball she can and rocking back and forth, pretending she's floating in the ocean, which sometimes makes her sleepy, but tonight does not. She wonders if Vance left because of all the shouting, and she wishes he'd taken her along. She stops rocking, opens her eyes, and listens. Now the house is silent, so silent she can hear her own heartbeat in her ears.

She sits up. Through the porthole she can see the sky changing; the sun must be coming up. She goes to the window and climbs onto the steamer trunk so she can see out — over the yard, over the Cavanaughs' house, over the treetops, all the way to the ocean. What she sees is very beautiful and a little scary: the sun is rising, and the clouds are red and orange and gold, glowing like embers, like the whole sky is burning. Her father would probably say it isn't, that it just looks that way, but she doesn't know if she would believe him; it seems impossible that what she's seeing isn't fire. From the steamer trunk, she watches until the last flames fade.

Back on the air mattress, she keeps thinking about fire. She checks the burn on her arm, the dark scar her mother covers with slimy, clear goo from a tube when she remembers, assuring her that the ash-colored mark the waffle iron made will fade over time. Helen didn't say so, but she hopes her mother is wrong, that it stays. She likes the scar. The day after it happened, when she went to school with gauze taped over it, Mrs. Forrest said, "Oh, dear, did you have an accident?" and she'd nodded yes, but that was a lie. It wasn't an accident. It was the Saturday morning just after Amanda got home, and her mother had plugged the waffle iron in and then forgotten about it. She was fighting with her father, they were yelling at each other in the laundry room where they thought Helen couldn't hear, but she could. She was in the kitchen waiting for her mother to come back and make her waffles, and it was impossible not to hear every word.

She knew the waffle iron would be hot. She didn't feel scared, brushing her wrist up against the metal and holding it there. And it did hurt; her eyes filled with tears, but she didn't scream; when her mother came in and Helen showed her what she'd done, Gina was the one who cried out. She put Cameron on the floor and filled a plastic bag with ice and made Helen hold it against her skin.

Now she thinks of her father talking about Amanda's abortion. *She'll be scarred forever*, her father said. Helen's tired of everyone paying so much attention to Amanda: her mother, her father, Vance — especially Vance. It's not fair. While Amanda was gone, from New Year's until three weeks ago, the house was quiet and her father was different. Now he doesn't tickle her before he tucks her in, he doesn't make smiley faces with her bacon and eggs. When she talks, it's like he doesn't hear her, and sometimes it's like he doesn't see her either, even when she's standing right there, and it's not much different with her mother or Vance. She looks again at her wrist. Why don't any of them care about her scar?

WEDNESDAY

26

AT FOUR-THIRTY A.M., Vance stands under the Main Sail's awning, hands dug deep in his pockets, wishing he had somewhere to go. The bars are all closed, the motels require money, and he can't drive out to the camp, which is the closest thing he's got to a plan, until it's light. He shifts his weight from one frigid foot to the other, peering periodically into the dining room, which is dark. He can make out the chairs stacked on top of the tables. He glances at his watch. Of all the places in town, the Main Sail opens the earliest, but that still isn't till five—so Vance is pleasantly surprised when a few minutes later, at twenty of, Irene, the hostess, emerges from somewhere deep in the bowels of the kitchen and unlocks the door.

"Early morning?" she says, and then, after a glance at his face, "Or late night?"

"Both, I guess," he says, following her inside and selecting the stool at the end of the counter, closest to the kitchen, which is filled with yellow light. Here at the counter, as in the dining room, nothing ever seems to change: the stool he sits on is upholstered in the same orange Naugahyde it's always been upholstered in, and the counter is the same white Formica with green and orange flecks. He finds it comforting.

Briefly he thinks of his brother: Craig would probably love to get his hands on this place, strip it down to the studs.

But he doesn't want to think about Craig. He turns his attention to the row of liquor bottles on a shelf beside the antique, stainless-steel milk dispenser and tells Irene he'd like a Bloody Mary and some coffee with cream.

"Sorry, no booze until eight," she says. If she has an opinion about his ordering a drink at this hour, she does a good job of keeping it to herself. She sets down a laminated menu and a heavy white mug, which she fills most of the way.

He upends two half-and-halfs into the mug and scans the menu. "What's the Fisherman's Special?"

"Two eggs, toast, and hash." Her voice is raspy, like a longtime smoker's.

"What's in the hash?"

"Depends," she says, and when Vance asks on what, she glances over her shoulder at the double doors separating them from the kitchen. "Mike."

"I'll give it a try."

"You're a brave man," she says, scribbling on a pad. She pushes through the double doors and disappears into the kitchen, leaving him thinking he can't remember the last time someone accused him of that.

She's gone a few minutes, and when she comes back she's carrying a plate for him, and though he didn't think he was hungry, he suddenly feels as if he hasn't eaten in days. While he shovels eggs and salty pink hash into his mouth, she fills pitchers with ice water and makes a pot of decaf. When he's eaten half the food on his plate he sets down his fork and sits up, watching her broad back strain against the purple cotton of her T-shirt while she wipes down her work surface with a rag, drinking every so often from a Styrofoam cup.

Without turning around, she says, "So, you're back for good?" which surprises him.

"No," he says automatically.

"Just visiting, then," she says, bringing the coffeepot over and topping off his mug.

"Something like that," he says, and adds, "Honestly? I have no idea."

She appears unfazed by his candor, returning the pot to its hotplate. "It's good to have a place to land," she says. "That's what home is. I should know. I've got my daughter sleeping in my basement and my son and his wife over the garage. All three grown people, bear in mind."

"You must be a very generous person," he says.

"It's not generous when it's family. Maybe it's a pain in the ass, a hardship, but it's just what you do."

"Someone should tell my brother that."

She raises an eyebrow. "The builder?"

Vance nods, stirring more cream into his coffee. He looks at his plate; there's still a lot of food on it. Pushing it aside, he says, "He thinks everyone should live a certain way, by a prescribed set of rules, which just happen to be his."

She asks him if he's finished, and he nods, and she picks up the plate but stands a moment in front of him, holding it. "My ex-husband was that way, always knew what was best for everyone else, couldn't keep a single opinion to himself."

"So what happened?"

"Like I said, he's my ex," she says, winking. She glances in the direction of the kitchen, then sets Vance's plate down by the water pitchers. In one swift motion she takes down a bottle of Canadian Club, uncaps it, tips some whiskey into his mug, then into hers, and sets it back on the shelf. She doesn't give him a chance to thank her, lifting a finger to her lips. Stirring her own drink with a straw, she says, "Cheers," and takes a sip. Then she squints at him. "I have a confession to make. I never could tell you and your brother apart."

This activates something primal inside him; instinctively, he wants to retract the things he said about Craig. "That's all right. Lots of people can't," he says, stirring his drink.

"I mean, for years, ever since you were kids and your dad would bring you in, I never knew. I was always too self-conscious to say hello."

"Really?"

"I was afraid I'd guess wrong and make a fool of myself. I was shy then."

He takes a drink. She wasn't shy with the whiskey.

"Is it strange," she asks, "having a person in the world who looks just like you?"

"I guess I don't think about it much."

"I always wanted a twin." As she speaks, her face changes and she looks younger; it's possible she's not much older than Vance. "I was an only child, and I used to put it in my prayers."

Before he can respond, a bell tinkles. He turns around. The front door opens and a couple of burly guys in work clothes and boots, maybe fishermen, enter with a burst of cold air. They hang their coats and hats on hooks and sit at the opposite end of the counter from Vance.

"Excuse me," Irene says, but before she goes, she leans forward and says, "I don't presume to know your situation, but I do know it's a lot easier to forgive other people for their shortcomings once we've forgiven ourselves."

He feels his face flush deeply, and is glad she turns her attention to the fishermen, whom she calls Ricky and Carl. He watches her fill their mugs, listens while she lists off the specials. His own mug is still half full, and he sips the now-tepid concoction slowly, feeling irritated. She meant well, sure, but it's true, she knows nothing about his situation, nothing about him. And certainly nothing about whom he does or doesn't need to forgive.

With some effort, he shifts his thoughts away from her and onto his own plans. He'll stay at the camp until he figures something else out, which means he'll need supplies—food, booze, batteries, extra propane. And what are the chances Craig's kept the place stocked with wood?

On her way back into the kitchen, Irene says, "You finished, hon?" and he shakes his head. "Take all the time you want," she says.

When his mug is empty, he leaves his coat on the stool and cuts through the dining room to the back, where he pushes open the saloon doors that lead to the restrooms. He pauses there, in the dark, narrow hall, regarding, in the half-light, the mural that's painted on paneling.

It's Amanda's. She won a contest, and she was so excited, he remembers, she called him on his office phone to tell him the news. He wonders now what he said to her in response. Did she have any idea how proud he was? That hearing her voice on the phone had the power to make even the most mundane day feel worthwhile?

Now, in the hallway, he can't help recalling Craig's words—*side-show, pathetic, reckless*—and, of course, that Vance doesn't care about anyone else. Craig is an asshole, he thinks, and moreover, he's wrong. Vance's problem isn't that he doesn't care enough, but that he cares too much. The membranes between him and other people are, somehow, too thin. This is what Janelle, another ex-girlfriend, once said, and he agrees. It even applies to Craig—especially to Craig. Like when they were kids: when they fought, Vance always held back, not because he wasn't angry, or because Craig didn't deserve a good pounding, but because he knew he had the power to cut Craig to the quick, with words or with his fists. But he wouldn't, he couldn't. It hurt too much to see Craig in pain.

And Amanda: he's been too timid, too afraid to open his eyes and see what's been staring him in the face all along. He should have guessed that very first morning—her pale, swollen face, the look of despair. He should've known that look.

After all, when what happened, happened, Dylan was the same age Amanda is now: seventeen. He wasn't much older, eighteen, legally an adult but in all other respects a child, and as much as he'd like to use that, his immaturity, as an excuse, a way to explain away what he did —what he didn't do—he can't. It's worse than that. There's a flaw deep inside him, a defect, a hole. There's no other explanation. This is something he's always known but only rarely, so very rarely, had the courage to admit.

They'd been together less than a year. All that summer he'd been sneaking into her mother's house, spending the small hours entwined with her in her single bed, sneaking back out before dawn. This particular weekend, the weekend she broke the news, was special: he was leaving for college in a week, and for once they had the camp to themselves. She told her mother she was spending the night at a friend's, and he picked her up outside the movie theater and they drove out to Land's End.

They'd spent plenty of time there before, of course, but usually it was with Craig, and almost always with their father, Frank. But that

August, Craig was already at Colgate for preseason soccer, and Frank was at a conference in California. Vance, if he tries, can still summon the feeling of giddy anticipation he'd had, of bliss, bouncing along the hot dunes in the Frog, her cool hand resting on his leg. He was thinking about the beers he'd put on ice in the cooler, and about the joint they passed back and forth, bouncing over the dunes, and mostly about Dylan's bikini, which was printed with tiny blue flowers he could see through the thin white cotton of her shirt.

At the camp he hauled the cooler up onto the porch and started unloading it while she sat in the sun. She had long, strawberry-blond hair then, which came down well past her shoulders, and he paused to watch her free it from its ponytail and shake it out. She looked so perfect, stretched out on the chaise longue, he had to stop what he was doing and go to her. He tugged on one of the strings at the back of her neck and slipped her T-shirt over her head, and they made love right there on the chaise.

Afterward, she'd seemed a little quieter than usual, but when he asked her if something was wrong, she shook her head, and he believed her. He carried the food from the cooler inside, started the generator, and transferred it to the fridge. Then, wrapped in towels, they hiked over the dunes to the beach, where they left the towels on the sand and swam, then lay on their stomachs letting the late-afternoon sun bake the salt into their backs.

At the camp, while the sun set, he cooked steaks and potatoes on the grill, and they drank beers and smoked and asked each other Trivial Pursuit questions, moving inside to escape the mosquitoes and helping themselves to his father's scotch. Before going to bed, they went back out to look at the stars. There were a zillion, so many more than you could see from town, and she sat between his legs on the chaise, both of them wrapped in a single blanket, her head resting on his chest.

Overnight, clouds gathered, and the next morning, when he arose, everything was blanketed in a thick layer of fog. He slipped out of bed as quietly as he could and went downstairs to boil water on the propane stove. She liked Darjeeling tea with milk and honey, and he fixed her a mug and brought it upstairs.

She was awake, perched on the window seat in one of his T-shirts with her knees drawn up, looking out the window, the fine sea mist pressing in through the screen. He can still remember standing in the doorway, struck, thinking he finally understood what all the fuss was about; he felt the impulse to get down on his knees, to bow, to somehow prostrate himself in the presence of whatever this unfamiliar and out-sized feeling was. But when she turned to face him, he saw her cheeks were wet. He set the tea on the desk and went to her, and he did kneel. He took both her hands in his, and she told him, through ragged sobs, that she'd taken a test from the drugstore and it came out positive, two of them had, and she was sorry, and she was scared, really scared.

He didn't get up; he didn't let go of her hands. He told her it was going to be all right, everything was. He promised her that.

"We'll handle this," he said, and when she said, "How? I don't have any money," he told her not to worry, he did, which was true. He'd been washing dishes at the Captain Crowley Inn all summer, and the next day, before his shift, he went to the Cape Cod Savings and Loan and emptied his checking account. That night, as he had done so many before, he snuck into the house through the unlocked back door, crept up the stairs, and, like always, she was there. But tonight was different. She wasn't under the covers, naked and warm and waiting for him. She was dressed in pajama pants and a too-big denim button-down shirt he'd never liked, and she looked pale and haggard, sitting on a painted wooden chest. He'd put the money in an envelope, which he handed to her, and then he kissed her, but that was different, too. He didn't reach for her, nor she for him, and he didn't stay over, and they didn't talk about why.

"Okay, nine-thirty" was the last thing she said. He kissed her again, this time on the forehead. She closed the door behind him; from half-way across the lawn, he heard her throw the latch.

He thought he wouldn't sleep at all, but he closed his eyes, and when he opened them it was light. It was Sunday, so the inn served brunch and his shift started at seven-thirty. He figured he'd report for work, put in an hour, then tell his boss he wasn't feeling right sometime after eight. The morning was a busy one; nevertheless, he couldn't pretend, even to himself, that he'd lost track of time when eight came and went, and then nine. And by two, when the flow of dishes from the dining room began to slow, something had happened in his head, something he never had the fortitude to question. He didn't go to her. He didn't call her that night, or the next day, or the next. And he didn't tell anyone what had happened, not even Craig. The days stacked up on one another; eleven passed, and then he left the Cape.

"Sir," a voice is saying now. "Sir?" He opens his eyes and stands up straight. It's one of the fishermen. "You waiting?"

"Just getting some air," he says. "You go ahead." The fisherman gives him a curious look, opens the men's room door, and steps in.

Vance presses the heels of his palms into his eyes until he sees bright spots. If only he'd had the guts, the strength of character, to show up that morning—to keep his promise. Or better yet, what if he'd persuaded her not to go through with it? He could have had a child now—they could have—they'd be a family. But he was too afraid. He was a coward, such a fucking coward. He tries to think of a single brave act, one valiant stance he's taken, a moment of boldness or distinction in the history of his existence, but he can't.

He opens his eyes. The toilet flushes and he can hear the tap open, then close. The fisherman steps out of the bathroom and he steps in. Standing before the mirror, he regards his reflection with disgust. How has he managed to look at himself, much less live with himself, all these years?

27

GINA IS WIDE AWAKE at five-ten, when Craig's alarm goes off, but she pretends she's asleep, and she goes on pretending, keeping her eyes closed and breathing slow, even breaths while he showers and gets dressed. Like always, he comes around to her side of the bed to kiss her cheek. (He does this without fail, no matter what unpleasantness may have transpired the previous night.) She feels his cool lips and smells his spearmint toothpaste and the lime tonic he splashes on his face after he shaves, and she wonders briefly if he'll kiss her tomorrow morning, or ever again.

Once he's gone, she lies there a while, watching the light change, fully awake but not yet ready to face the day ahead. When she hears Cam start his babbling in the next room, she heaves her body up and goes in to give him a change. He's smiling as usual, and it's impossible not to smile back. How, she wonders, did she and Craig possibly produce such a carefree child? She puts him in a fresh diaper and onesie and takes him back to their room, into their bed, where he dozes while she checks her phone and, finding nothing, taps out another text to Dov.

???, she types.

No luck, sorry, went over every inch.

Shit.

Maybe we should retrace our steps together this afternoon. I'll bring the wine ;-)

She cringes. *Can't, sorry,* she types. *Please text if it turns up.*

She lies on her back, looking at the ceiling and listening to Cam's breath, thinking about her mother. If Rosemarie were here, she'd surely be unhappy about the earring—she'd loved them—but, Gina can't help thinking, her mother wouldn't be surprised: not that Gina had lost it, or the pathetic manner by which she'd managed to do so. She always said Gina was too scattered, too easily distracted, too unsure.

Not Rosemarie. She was always sure about everything, or so it had seemed. She knew exactly what to serve, what to say, what drapes to buy, whom her daughters should and should not befriend. She dressed impeccably, never exceeding a size 4, never overcooked meat, never misspoke, never had lipstick on her teeth. She read the right books, belonged to the right clubs, and held strong, clear opinions but never stated them too loudly, at least not when company was around. (In private, though, she made sure her views—especially those regarding her daughters' choices—were heard.)

Gina turns onto her side and strokes Cam's cheek. He has Craig's profile—the famous Lake forehead, the gray-blue eyes, the nose: this would make her mother happy. She had adored Craig. The first time Gina brought him home to Fairfield, Rosemarie had pulled her aside in the kitchen, gripped her hands, and said, beaming, "Hang on to this one." The fact that he'd been widowed barely a year earlier, and that his seven-year-old daughter was part of the package, didn't seem to concern her nearly as much as whether or not Gina could reel him in. "Don't worry, you'll figure all that out" was all she'd said. She was right, as it turned out, but it was far from easy, and over the years, especially the early ones, Gina occasionally wondered whether, when deciding to marry Craig, the thrill she'd felt at finally gaining her mother's approval had overshadowed her innate good sense.

Whatever the answer, all of that feels like another lifetime now. She and Craig have been happy, on balance, and she and Amanda have reached a satisfactory, if not entirely affectionate, détente. What she finds herself brooding over most frequently lately is the deeply odd state of not having a mom. It's *strange*. She can do anything she wants, there's no one to disapprove, no one to judge—and no one whose judgments have the innate ability to cut to the quick. It's like being untethered, a balloon without a string.

Her phone buzzes, and she sits up. The screen tells her it's Dov, and she feels a burst of hope. "Good news?"

"No, sorry. I was just thinking."

She slumps back against the headboard.

"Don't you want know what I was thinking?" She doesn't answer, but he continues. "How much fun it is, having a secret. I feel like I'm walking around town with my pockets full of gold doubloons."

She doesn't respond right away. Then she takes a deep breath and says, "I've been thinking too."

"Tell me."

"I can't do this."

"Do what?"

"This. Us."

He's silent for a moment. Then he says, "Because of the earring?"

"No—or maybe. But only because it made me stop and think."

"And you feel guilty," he says.

"Of course. Don't you?"

"I don't believe in guilt. I never have," he says.

She laughs. "That's convenient."

"It's not about convenience. Guilt is a social construct, a byproduct of the idea that there is absolute right and wrong, good and bad. That universal truths exist."

"And I'm guessing you don't believe they do?"

"I don't think the universe gives a shit about us, no. And no, I don't think there's anything else. We're all just amalgamations of particles, of dust. We spend a few years milling around the planet and then the dust takes on a different shape. I think we need to do what makes us happy, now. How can happiness be bad?"

A few weeks ago, she would have thought what he's saying was profound, but this morning it just sounds juvenile, a pitiful attempt to get her into bed. She glances at the clock. It's after six. "The thing is, I'm happy. I have a family I love. And I love Craig. I do."

"Congratulations," he says. A hint of bitterness has crept into his voice. "Did you want a medal?"

"I'm sure you're disappointed," she says, "but there's no need to be an asshole."

He doesn't say anything.

"You still there?" she says after what feels like a long time.

He makes a grunting sound.

"I'm sorry. I shouldn't have called you that. And I shouldn't have let things go this far. I shouldn't have made you think—"

"I didn't think anything." Now he sounds more hurt than angry.

Because she doesn't know what else to say, she says, "I hope we can still be friends."

"We weren't before," he says matter-of-factly. After a pause, he says, "I'm not going to tell Craig, if that's what you're worried about."

"It's not," she says, though it's only half true. After another silence, she says, "Are you still going to give him the contract?"

He laughs, unkindly, at this. "Of course I am. Craig's got nothing to do with us. He never has."

She almost thanks him. Instead, she says, "Take care of yourself, okay?"

After they hang up, she lies there waiting for relief to come, but all she feels is fatigue—fatigue and shame. How could she have been taken in by his nonsense, even for a few minutes? She thinks again of the Millikens' garage, of his hands on her, only this time it's with disgust. What an idiot she's been, risking so much—risking everything—for so little. For *nothing*. She's only grateful things didn't go any further than they did.

She shifts onto her side again, resting her head on her elbow and watching Cameron sleep. His mouth is wide open and he's got both arms thrown up over his head, like he's declaring victory. And now, today, she can't help thinking, she'll place everything in jeopardy again. At least now it's for a cause greater than her own vanity. She glances at the clock: it's time. Gently she brushes Cam's cheek with her fingers. He doesn't stir. Unwilling to wake him, she leaves him there and heads down the hall to Amanda's room.

The blinds are all drawn, it's dark, but she can make out the shape of Amanda in her sleeping bag. She sits on the edge of the bed and touches the shape, a rounded ridge she guesses is Amanda's hip.

"Hey, there," she whispers. Amanda opens her eyes and blinks. "It's time to wake up."

"It's the middle of the night." Amanda groans, turning her face away.

"Hey," Gina says again, giving her shoulder a squeeze and turning on the bedside lamp.

Amanda winces, keeping her eyes closed, but Gina goes ahead and tells her about the appointment Rachel made. Then she stands up and steps to the window, which is wide open, and draws up the shade to let in what light there is. When she turns around again Amanda's sitting up, looking wide awake. "Seriously?"

"Rachel—she was my roommate in college, and she's a doctor now —knows the clinic. They had a two-week wait but she made some calls."

Amanda frowns. "The clinic. You mean, like—"

"Yes," Gina says.

"But Dad."

"He's on a site in Eastham all day."

"But what about when he—"

"That's not your main concern right now," Gina says, and nods in the direction of the clock radio. "If you want tea or any breakfast, you should have it now. That's why I woke you. After six, because of the anesthesia, you can't drink or eat."

Amanda still hasn't moved. She's just looking at Gina. "Are you going with me?"

"Of course."

"And you set it all up? Without Dad?"

Gina nods. She studies Amanda's face, which is expressionless. She goes back to the bed and sits. "Is this still what you want? It doesn't have to be."

"Are you kidding?" Amanda says. There's a slight tremor in her voice, though, and Gina wonders if she's scared. She rests a hand on Amanda's leg.

Through the open window, they hear the sound of a car pulling up outside, then a door closing, and she feels Amanda stiffen. "It's okay. It's just Meghan. She's going to take care of Helen and Cam." She applies gentle pressure to Amanda's leg. "I know it's all happening quickly, but I promise, you don't need to be scared. Rachel's got a hundred percent confidence in the place."

"Who says I'm scared?" Amanda says, scowling, and it's as if the previous night never happened—as if despite everything Gina's done, the enormous risk she's taking, nothing's changed.

Gina wonders if it ever will. "Nobody did. My mistake," she says, and withdraws her hand.

28

IN SOMETHING OF A HAZE, Amanda showers, dresses, and heads downstairs, where she encounters not Gina but Meghan, the girl from the store, standing in front of the stove, stirring something steaming with a wooden spoon.

"Oatmeal?" the girl says. "It's almost done." She's wearing skin-tight black pants, a long black sweater that clings to her body, and high-heeled boots; every time Amanda sees her, she's absurdly overdressed. She was four or five years ahead of Amanda in school, and now she's in design school or something, but apparently it's not going very well. Why else would she be back on the Cape?

"No thanks," Amanda says, and almost instantaneously, Gina's voice says, "You're going to eat something. It's not up for debate."

Gina's carrying the baby, and while she straps him into his chair, Amanda opens the refrigerator to look for some bread. Meghan just stands there, mute, in front of the stove, but when Amanda accidentally catches her eye, opening the toaster oven door, she offers a sort of sympathetic smile, and Amanda wonders what she knows. She doesn't smile back. When Helen appears in her pj's, with sleep creases striping her cheeks and crazy hair, and starts peppering Meghan with questions, Amanda's glad.

She starts the toaster and retreats to the breakfast nook, where she turns away from the chaos in the kitchen and looks out the window. It's a cloudy morning, ominous-looking, the sky several shades darker in the west. In the yard, the trees are still brown, their branches bare — but soon enough, she thinks, buds will come. And with that thought, she realizes it's been ages since she's imagined a time beyond right now. It's not exactly hope, but it's close.

When the timer dings she retrieves her toast, avoiding everyone's eyes while she squeezes a spiral of honey onto each slice.

"I'll have my cell," Gina is saying to Meghan. "Call me if there's anything."

Helen comes over to the table and instructs Amanda to watch her do an arabesque. "I can do one on the other side, too. Look! And last week we learned illusion turns. Can you do those?"

Amanda's gazing out the window again, and when she doesn't answer, Helen comes closer, thrusts her wrist into Amanda's face, and says, "Want to see my scar?"

Amanda angles herself away.

"Ready to go?" Gina says.

Helen says, "To where?" And before Amanda or Gina can answer, she says, "I want to come."

"That's impossible, love-bug," Gina says. "You have school. Amanda?"

"You said I have to eat."

"And now I'm saying we have to leave." She glances at her watch. "Besides, your time's up."

Amanda stands, leaving the toast on the plate. She watches Gina kiss Cameron on the cheek and Helen on the forehead, then takes her jacket down from its hook in the mudroom and follows her stepmother into the garage.

She brought her earbuds along, and before they've even backed into the street she has them on and selects the playlist she made for the flight down to Chile, which she named "Rad Travel Tunes," and which succeeded in keeping her relaxed on the twelve-hour flight. Contrary to what she told Gina, she's anxious, and the hope is that it will have the same sedative effect this morning. But as soon as the first song starts ("Radioactive"), she realizes she was wrong, it was a stupid idea;

not only did she listen to it on the airplane, she listened to it in the tent with Christian, and after just a couple of chords she's back there, as completely as if she's been teleported, the two of them lying on their stomachs, shoulders touching, each with an earbud in one ear. The rain on the tent, the cinnamon smell of his skin: how gently he kissed her that first time, how he apologized, then did it again. She stops the music. It's the opposite of relaxing, and she vows never to listen to any of those songs again.

She's not exactly in the mood to chat, though, so she keeps the earbuds in, which seems to do the trick. Half an hour passes in silence before Gina says, "Mind if I make a quick stop?"

Amanda shrugs. They're close to the Sagamore Bridge, but Gina pulls off the road anyway, parks outside a Dunkin' Donuts, and asks Amanda if she wants to come in.

Amanda says no, and once Gina's safely inside, reaches into her pocket, pulls out the birdcage earring, and holds it in her palm. Her plan, which she came up with last night, and which she already feels guilty about, was to find the other one, sneak out of the house, and try to sell them, maybe to an antique shop she knows about in Southwich, or one of the pawnshops in Provincetown. But now—she can't quite believe it—she won't need to. She brings it closer to her face. It's really gorgeous, such a finely crafted, delicate thing. How did they ever get the bird inside the cage? She imagines its creation: some artisan, somewhere, manipulating the minuscule wires, fashioning the tiny wings. She thinks of the ships-in-bottles her father used to collect, when she was small, and wonders what happened to them. They used to be at the camp, and after that on a shelf in his office, fifteen or twenty of them, but she hasn't seen them in years.

And then, without meaning to, she's thinking about her dad, the terrible things she's said to him. What a miserable person she's turned into, and how hurt and disappointed he must be. And surely he's not the only one. Gina. Vance. She told Craig she wished her mother were alive, but right now all she can think is that she's glad her mom can't see the wretch her daughter has become.

A lump has materialized in her throat, and she swallows, returning her focus to the earring. She wonders, not for the first time, what Gina was doing in Dov's Jeep, but part of her suspects she knows. Questions form in her mind: Are they in love? Will Gina and Craig get divorced? And what would happen to her and Craig if they do?

She looks up and sees Gina coming back, carrying a small white paper bag and a large white Styrofoam cup. She closes her fist.

"Sorry. I was getting the shakes. I guess I forgot to eat myself, in the rush," Gina says, settling into her seat.

Amanda slips her hand into her pocket but doesn't let go of the earring.

With the paper bag in her lap, Gina arranges the coffee in the drink holder between their seats, then apologizes for eating in front of Amanda. "I feel like I'm taunting you," she says. Amanda says it's fine, she's not hungry, watching Gina extract a wan-looking bagel sandwich from the bag. "I shouldn't be eating this," she says, "but some days just require carbs."

Amanda wants to put her earbuds back in, but maybe because Gina's clearly making an effort, it seems too rude, and she leaves them in her lap while they pull out onto the road, Gina navigating the rotary, then the bridge, holding the steering wheel with one hand, her sandwich with the other. Amanda has no doubt she would catch hell for driving so recklessly, but she doesn't point that out. In the middle of the bridge, she tries to look down at the canal—since she was a little girl, she's always counted boats—but they've installed new suicide barriers recently, wide wooden planks in addition to the nets, that block the view.

They ride in silence for what feels like a long time, Gina taking excruciatingly small bites of her bagel, chewing each bite extensively, then sipping coffee to wash it down. Amanda wonders whether she's eating particularly preposterously this morning, or whether she always eats this way and Amanda's just never noticed before. They pass the nuclear power plant, its twin hourglass towers of white concrete, then cross an expanse of flooded salt marsh. The sky is reflected on the water's surface, a mirror image; studying the thick clouds in the water, she imagines for a moment that they're not reflections but the actual clouds, and she's the thing that's upside down.

When Gina finally finishes eating, she balls up the paper bag and tosses it on the floor by Amanda's feet. "So," she says, "I don't want to scare you, but there are some things you should know."

The last thing she needs this morning is a lecture. She wishes she could put her earbuds back in. Crossing her arms, she slides down in her seat, keeping her face angled away. The sky's even darker now in the west, and the window shows sporadic streaks of rain.

Gina isn't deterred. "I just don't want you to be taken by surprise by anything," she says. "I'm not talking about the procedure," she says. "I'm talking about before." She clears her throat. "There may be protesters, Rachel said."

"Rachel," Amanda says.

"My friend. She said they may shout at you, and they'll be carrying signs. Ugly signs."

"Okay."

Gina glances over. "She said the best thing to do is keep walking. Don't engage them, don't even look at them. Just pretend they're not there." When Amanda doesn't say anything, Gina says, "Did you hear me?"

"Yes," Amanda says, sinking lower in her seat. She watches the scenery slide past—woods, more woods, old stone walls. For a while she closes her eyes. When she opens them, they're crossing into Connecticut (*Connecticut Welcomes You*). They pass the outlet mall. Reading the signs, she starts feeling a little lightheaded and closes her eyes again.

"You sure you're doing okay?" Gina asks. "Because it would be okay if you weren't."

Keeping her eyes closed, Amanda says, "I'm fine."

After a pause, Gina says, "Listen—I know I'm not your mom, you know I've never tried to be. I wouldn't want to replace her. I couldn't."

Amanda opens her eyes, shifts in her seat, and thinks, *No shit*, waiting for whatever's coming next.

Gina glances in the rearview mirror before switching lanes. "But I care about you, a lot," she says, "and I want you to be happy, to have a happy life. You deserve that."

Amanda turns and looks out the window again, at the shoulder now, letting her gaze ride the metal guardrail. She wishes Gina would stop talking, stop making her feel so bad. Her hand finds her pocket again, then the earring.

Another few minutes pass before Gina says, "You're awfully quiet."

"I don't get it," Amanda says finally. "I've been such a bitch to you. Why are you helping me?"

Gina takes her eyes off the road a moment to glance over, and she actually looks amused. "It's true," she says, "you have been pretty awful." She puts on the blinker and exits the highway, onto a ramp that curls around in a tight corkscrew and delivers them to a street light, which is red.

Amanda still feels wary, like somehow she's being tricked. "You really didn't tell Dad?" She watches the side of Gina's face.

"Are you kidding?"

"Does Vance know?"

"Yes," she says. "I asked him to come, but he couldn't make it." She doesn't say anything else—and she doesn't need to. It's not difficult to imagine what her uncle thinks.

The light turns green. They make a left onto a divided highway and follow it a few miles south to a large, single-story shopping center.

"It's in here?" Amanda says, reading the signs: Michael's, T.J.Maxx, an insurance company, a place called Fancy Nail, a Pier One, a state DMV. Gina chooses a space behind a blue-green van, the same model as theirs.

"*What would Jesus do*," Amanda says, reading one of the bumper stickers on the van's cluttered back door.

"I don't know, but I'm pretty sure it's not that," Gina says. She's looking off to the left. Amanda follows her gaze to a small cluster of people, men and women holding posters on sticks. Some of the posters display Bible verses, others gruesome images of what appear to be bloody baby mice. They're shouting something, but with the windows closed it's impossible to hear what.

Amanda says, "Don't they have jobs? Jeez."

"Remember, just keep walking. Where are your earbuds?" Amanda says they're in her pocket. "Good. Put them on."

When Amanda reaches into her pocket, her fingers find the earring first, and she lets her hand linger there a moment, turning the thing over, squeezing it in her palm. Then she takes her hand out of her pocket, rests it in her lap, and looks down at it.

"Ready?" Gina says.

"Not quite." Amanda's voice sounds less steady than she'd like when she says, "Are you leaving us?"

Gina's face flushes bright pink. "God, no. Of course not. What would make you ask something like that?"

"Because I'd understand if you were, I really would. Craig's such an asshole, and it's not like I'm—it's not like you—"

"Stop right there," she says. She reaches over and rests her hand on Amanda's closed fist. "It's no secret things haven't been easy lately. But I love your dad, and I love you. And I'm not going anywhere." She squeezes Amanda's hand and smiles. "You're not getting rid of me that easily. Okay?"

Amanda nods, then slowly turns her hand over, opening her palm.

"Oh, my gosh. Where did you ever . . . ?" She doesn't finish the question, and she doesn't meet Amanda's eyes.

"I was going to try to sell it. For this." She nods in the direction of the clinic, whose sign says *Eastern Connecticut Women's Health Center*.

"Thank God you didn't. May I?" Gina takes the earring and holds it up. "God, I've been so upset, you can't imagine. I thought it was gone for good. It was my mother's, and she . . ." She looks right at Amanda. "Hey, why don't you hang on to it? I mean for today. I happen to believe it's good luck."

Silently Amanda accepts, taking it back and closing her fingers around it once more, trying to imagine good luck flowing out of it and into her. They sit there a while longer, until Amanda says, "What's going to happen after? I mean with Craig."

Gina's watching the protesters. One of their signs says, *Babies Are Murdered Here*. Another says, *If Mary Was Pro-Choice There Would Be No Christmas*. She looks vexed. "Craig will be fine, and you will be fine. We're all going to be just fine," she says.

29

∾

THROUGH A THICK FOG of sleep, Vance hears a loud sound, someone knocking, knuckles against glass, and then a voice: "Hello? Vance? Are you sick? What are you doing here? Do I need to call 911?"

He opens his eyes and sees Dylan, looking bewildered, through the window glass. She's wearing a silky turquoise robe printed with pink, Hawaiian-looking flowers, and she steps back from the Frog and crosses her arms over her chest. He sits up, rubs his face, and combs his fingers through his hair before rolling down the window.

"What in the world?" she asks, hugging herself. "The dogs were barking, that's why I came out. Are you drunk?"

He shakes his head, which feels heavy. "I wanted to see you. I didn't want to wake you up. Do you still like maple-glazed donuts? I meant to pick some up."

Her expression shifts from confusion to consternation. "You've got quite the memory, don't you?" she says, looking up and down the street, which is desolate at this hour. "You've seen me. Are you satisfied? It's freezing. I'm going in." But she doesn't. She looks up the street again. Not particularly encouragingly, she says, "Did you want to come?"

He exits the Frog and follows her up the driveway and through the front door. The dog from the other day, Maisie, is waiting in the hall alongside a second one, some kind of mutt that growls at him when he enters.

"Amelia, please," Dylan says without conviction. Over her shoulder she says, "She's friendly, for the most part. She's just a little territorial."

"I can understand that," Vance says, and raises his hands in surrender. "I come in peace." The dog doesn't seem convinced. She emits another long growl and briefly bares her teeth before turning and trotting after Dylan.

He follows them down the hall, into the kitchen, which he is surprised to discover hasn't changed one bit in twenty-three years: the same honey pine cabinets, same yellow linoleum floor, same orange-and-yellow-plaid curtains, same white table, same molded white plastic chairs. On the wall hangs the same wooden shadow box displaying (presumably) the same dried beans, pasta, and wheat. Even the appliances—microwave, stove, fridge, dishwasher, trash compactor—don't appear to have been replaced.

"Wow," he says, "it's like stepping into a time warp."

"Tell me about it," Dylan says. She's fussing with a familiar-looking Mr. Coffee machine in the corner. "Try waking up here every morning."

He wonders whether she's missed him over the years—whether he's haunted her dreams, like she has his. He sits in one of the chairs.

"Coffee?" she asks, and he says, "Please." She fills a couple of mugs and hands one over. The mugs look handmade—blue with green flecks, and glazed. He remembers them well.

"Cheers," he says, but she doesn't join him in the toast. She's leaning back against the counter sort of squinting at him. "Are you sure you're okay?" she asks after a moment. "You look a little, I don't know, peaked?"

"I've been called worse," he says, hoping to lighten the mood. But her scrutiny continues, it's making him uncomfortable, and he gets up and goes to the refrigerator, whose door is, as it was in decades past, almost completely covered with photographs.

Maybe it's because everything else in the kitchen is old that he's surprised to discover the photos are new, and that only a few of the faces look familiar to him: Dylan's brother, Troy, her sister, Lily, and her mother, Carolyn. The others are unknown to him: a grinning bride and groom, a man and a boy on a sailboat, a little girl holding up a big silver fish. He's curious about all of them, but it's a snapshot of an infant that most powerfully draws his gaze. The photo is faded and curled up at the corners, suggesting age; the child looks very young, maybe six months, with a shock of blond hair and a dimple in the middle of its chin. He tries not to stare, but something about the photo sends an odd thrill through him. He studies the face: pointed chin, pink complexion, blue-gray eyes.

"He's not yours, if that's what you're wondering," Dylan says, as if hearing his thoughts—something she had an uncanny knack for back then, too.

"Of course not," he says, feeling heat rush into his face. He turns away, hoping she won't see.

"That's Gavin," she says. "He's fourteen, a freshman now. God, time flies. It feels like I sent Mom that picture last week." She joins him and points to a picture of a boy wearing white fencing garb and a mesh mask, wielding some kind of sword. "That one's more recent. Last year, I think. I guess it doesn't give you much of an idea. Here." She touches the sailboat picture. "That's from last summer. That's his dad."

"Good-looking kid," Vance says, trying to sound cool. The man in the photo is tall and muscular, with a square jaw and very short brown hair. "Your husband?"

"Ex," she says, "or soon to be." She raises her mug in a wordless toast.

"Is he in the military?"

She shakes her head. "He's a scientist. We live—oops, we lived—in Los Alamos. He works at the labs."

"Like, building bombs?"

"More or less." She sniffs. "Gavin, though? He's got the soul of an artist—you know, solitary, sensitive, utterly at the mercy of his moods. And God, can he brood. He's a little like you, as a matter of fact." She says this casually, as if it's the least inflammatory statement in the world. He makes an effort not to react.

"So he stayed behind? With—"

"Ned? God, no. I couldn't give Gavin up, not in a million years. He's just out there for the break."

Vance leaves the refrigerator and stands by the table, and she reclaims her spot by the coffeemaker. He asks her how long she's been back.

"It'll be a year in May," she says. "I first came because of Mom, you know, she needed help, and the visits got longer and longer, and then she died, and the house was here, and things had gotten more and more—complicated, I guess—with Ned, and I don't know, long story short, I stayed."

"You must like it here."

"Yes and no. I can't say it's not surreal sometimes, living here with all of this." She draws a circle in the air with her finger. "But at the same time it's so normal—maybe that's even weirder." She pauses, thinking. "You know, it's funny, I've lived lots of places—California, New Mexico, New York, we even spent six months in Dubai—but for better or worse, the truth is I've never really felt, I don't know, like *myself* anywhere else."

"I'm not sure I've ever felt like myself anywhere," he says. He's joking—again—but once the words have left his mouth, he wonders if there's some truth in them.

She smiles, looking down at her feet. The brown dog, Maisie, is curled in a C and rests her head on Dylan's feet, which are in suede moccasins decorated with beads. "That's my good girl," she says, lifting one foot and using it to stroke the dog's head.

He sips his coffee, trying to think of a way to say what he wants to say, what he needs to say, when she says, "And what about you?"

He clears his throat. "I'm also flying solo at the moment."

"Divorced?"

"Never married."

"I see." Is she surprised or unsurprised? Disappointed or pleased? He can glean nothing from her voice or her face.

"I've come close a couple of times," he tells her, though she hasn't asked, and when she nods, still opaquely, he feels compelled to say more. "This last time was the closest. Her name was—well, it still is—Celeste."

"That's a nice name."

"We were engaged," he says, aware of a strange, full feeling in his chest, like a bubble that's slowly and steadily expanding, making it hard to take a deep breath. "She was—she is—a great person, everything I thought I wanted, and she wanted to marry me, if you can believe that."

She says nothing.

"I couldn't, anyway—but she did, she wanted to marry *me*, and I fucked it up. Fucking things up, with women, I mean—relationships —that appears to be my special, God-given gift." Dylan still doesn't say anything, but she smiles, a little shyly this time, and maybe because he wants to fill the silence, or maybe because the bubble in his chest feels like it will burst if he doesn't, he begins telling her things: about Esme, the graduate student, and about Brent, and about getting fired, and about Celeste kicking him out. And then he tells her about coming here: the accident on the highway on the ride up, the attic, the air mattress, Helen, hearing Gina and Craig arguing through the vent. And about how unwell Craig looks, how unhappy he seems, and finally about the argument in the garage and the terrible, true things Craig said.

She's listening, eyes wide. When he pauses for breath, she says, "You don't look so terrific yourself. Do you want to sit down?"

He shakes his head. If he doesn't say it now, he never will. "I've done all these awful things is what I'm getting at. I've failed so many people, and the worst part is, none of it even compares to what I did to you."

She doesn't look surprised. She presses her lips together.

The bubble in his chest has moved into his throat. He takes a breath, then another. "Being back here, seeing you, it's opened up all these old doors, all these old rooms." When he says "I loved you so much," his voice cracks. "I don't think I've really loved anyone since. Not really, not like that. I'm pretty sure I can't."

She says, "Of course you can."

"No. Something in me is broken. Something's—"

"Don't say that," she says.

He takes a few steps so he's standing in front of her, and he gets down on his knees.

"You're not going to propose, are you?"

It's a joke—he thinks—but neither of them laughs. "I'm sorry," he says, "for abandoning you. I was a shit, a coward, and I've regretted it every single day since." ·

She's quiet for a moment. "Could you get up, please?" He stays where he is. "It's okay."

"What is?"

"Everything."

"You mean you accept my apology?"

"Twenty-three years later? Sure, why not? Now would you please stand up?" He does, and she says, "Look, I was devastated then. I hated you almost as much as I loved you." She makes a sound resembling a laugh. "Almost." Then her eyes sort of go out of focus. "I actually thought I wanted to have that baby with you. Can you believe that?"

The statement pierces him. When he says "Really?" it comes out like a croak.

"But afterwards, after you left—it took a while, I'll admit—I realized how stupid that would have been—how disastrous." Her expression is flat. "Your taking off helped me see that. In a way, you made it easier, or at least clearer. Being heartbroken alone was a lot easier than it would've been as a teenager with a kid."

She doesn't seem to expect a response—a relief, because he's not sure he can speak. She turns around to rinse her mug, and he fixes his gaze on a large purple bloom in the center of her back.

After what feels like a long time, he takes a deep breath, clears his throat. "Do you ever," he begins. "Do you have regrets?"

"You mean, do I wish I'd had it?"

"Yes."

She keeps her back to him. "You know, I was really, really sad afterwards. Not wishing I hadn't done it, exactly, more like wishing I hadn't had to. Wishing I'd been in a different place—wishing we had. Wondering, you know." She turns and looks out the window over the sink; she seems to be gathering herself. "That lasted a while, but it passed.

So do I regret not bringing a child I couldn't care for into the world? If that's what you're asking, the answer is, not a bit." She faces him. "What's wrong?" she asks. "You've been absolved. You're supposed to be relieved."

He feels neither; in fact his heart feels heavier than it did when he came. But it's not just the past that's weighing on him. "It's Amanda," he says. "She's pregnant."

Without missing a beat, Dylan says, "I know," and when he asks how, she says Gina. "She's here every week for Helen's lesson. We've gotten to be friends."

"So you know about—"

"I know everything, I'm afraid."

"And you think it's right? What Gina's doing?"

"Right for whom is the question. For Amanda? Yes. In terms of Craig? That's harder to say." After a moment, she says, "I know you see what happened between us, you and me, as this watershed event in your life, this fork in the road where you chose the wrong path, or your true nature was revealed. But it isn't—or it doesn't have to be. You were young and terrified and you came up short. You can't change that. You can't go back. But at some point you're just using the past as a crutch, an excuse to keep coming up short."

He stays quiet.

"Amanda's on her way to Connecticut now, right?"

He nods.

"And she doesn't have her dad with her."

He shakes his head.

"I don't care how tough she acts, I promise you, she's scared to death."

"I guess she probably is," Vance says.

"And you care about her."

He swallows hard. "More than anything in the world."

"Then shit, Vance, why are you here?"

30

✂

IN A WINDOWLESS WAITING AREA with flickering fluorescent lights and dingy, mauve-painted walls, Amanda and Gina sit in tweed office chairs underneath an oversized photograph of a palm-lined tropical beach. Opposite them, from behind a section of bulletproof glass, a receptionist summons patients by their first names. Amanda removes her earbuds, spools the cord around her fingers, and stows them in the pocket of her coat.

The receptionist says, "Alison?" and a heavyset blond woman wearing large black sunglasses who looks closer to Gina's age than Amanda's approaches the desk. The receptionist passes her a clipboard through a small cutout in the glass. The woman takes it, nodding at some instruction that Amanda can't hear.

"You okay?" Gina asks, slipping her arms out of her coat.

Amanda nods, keeping her eyes down.

"I don't understand those people. I just don't," Gina says.

Amanda doesn't say anything, but she thinks maybe she does. How nice it would be to feel that certain about something: how energizing, how electrifying, to be so utterly sure you're right—about anything.

There were thirty or so of them, clustered, and as if following care-

259

ful choreography, they parted as she approached, arranging themselves shoulder-to-shoulder in two rows so she and Gina had to walk between them, down the aisle they made, like a demented dance line. "Don't kill your baby!" they shouted, and "You'll never be the same!," shoving rosaries and pamphlets and Jesus trading cards into her hands. The most surprising part—what truly unnerved her—was that a handful of them were her age, a high school group, it seemed. One, a tall, broad-shouldered girl with copious red curls, grabbed Amanda's sleeve. "We've got funds to support your baby," she said, before Amanda had the wherewithal to pull away. And then, tearfully, "I'm going to pray."

The waiting room, thankfully, is quiet—almost too quiet. When Gina selects an outdated fashion magazine from a rack on the wall and begins leafing through it, it's like a thunderclap every time she turns a page. Covertly Amanda glances around. The place is indisputably depressing: scuff marks mar the walls, the mauve carpet is alternately faded and stained, and the room's décor consists of posters promoting handwashing and birth control, plus some withering potted plants.

As surreptitiously as she can, she surveys the clientele, eight or ten women and a couple of uneasy-looking men. Some look middle-aged and most much younger; some appear to have been accompanied by their mothers, some by a sister or friend, and others sit alone. One girl speaks into a cell phone, saying, "Fifteen more. They said right now. Come to the front." The blond woman with the sunglasses—Alison —is one of the few with a male companion, ostensibly her husband; he also wears sunglasses, and stares at the empty space between his spread knees. She has a clipboard balanced on the arm of her chair and Amanda notices she sniffles as she writes. Amanda has no way of knowing, but she imagines the woman's reasons for being here are vastly different from her own. She watches with morbid interest as the woman wipes her nose with a hankie and replaces it in her pocket. She wishes the man would put his arm around her, or something, but he just sits and stares.

After another ten minutes or so her name is called. She approaches the desk, where the receptionist, whose nametag says *Lavinia*, gives her a clipboard with a stack of papers to fill out, which she does, providing information about her medical and sexual history while Gina pretends not to watch over her shoulder, but she doesn't bother trying to hide what she writes. What difference does it make what Gina knows? Checking the boxes, she feels increasingly detached: nothing matters, not really. She signs her name robotically at the bottom of each form.

Lavinia tells her to sit back down, the PA will see her soon, and another thirty minutes pass before the mauve-painted door next to reception swings opens and a white-coated woman says her name. Gina asks whether she wants her to go with her, and Amanda says no and follows the nurse through the door, into a corridor where a piece of paper taped to the front of a vending machine proclaims, *No eating or drinking before surgery. This includes candy and soda, Ladies!!!*

Amanda follows the nurse, whose white clogs squeak on the white tiles as she weaves her way through a white-walled labyrinth to an exam room, where she instructs Amanda to undress and empty her bladder and hands her a Pepto Bismol–pink paper robe, which she says to leave open in the front. On the paper-covered examination table, Amanda waits some more, absently contemplating the wall decor: a detailed illustration of the female anatomy, a soft-focus photo of a kitten batting at a dandelion puff on a patch of grass.

The nurse returns and says the doctor's on his way. "You can go ahead and lie back," she says, and when Amanda does, her gaze meets a third poster, this one on the ceiling, a pod of dolphins leaping from a glittering wave. The doctor turns out to be an old man; he doesn't bother with small talk, or any talk for that matter, and Amanda is glad. The nurse arranges her feet in the stirrups, slathers gel on her belly, and asks her if she'd like to see the screen. When Amanda says no, she angles the monitor away.

After the doctor leaves, the nurse draws a couple of vials of blood, then presents her with two pills in a small plastic cup. "One for the body, one for the soul," she says. Then she instructs Amanda to go ahead and get dressed, the medication takes an hour or so to kick in, and to expect some cramps. Back in the waiting room, Gina is holding a can of Diet Coke, and a foil bag of Cheez-Its sits open on her lap. "Sorry to torture you again," she says. "Nerves."

Amanda doesn't know how the next hour and a half passes, but somehow it does, and when she's summoned the next time, it's not by a nurse. This woman looks just a few years older than Amanda, and instead of a white coat she wears rust-colored corduroys and a kelly-green blouse, her dirty-blond dreadlocks tamed into a fat bun. She says her name is Nicky and shakes Amanda's hand before leading her down a different tiled hall. She's a volunteer, she says, and asks Amanda how she's doing with "all of this."

"Fine," Amanda says.

"If there's anything you want to talk about, or if you just want me to hold your hand, that's why I'm here," she says.

Amanda can't tell whether the compassionate expression she wears is bullshit or sincere. "I just want to get it over with," she says.

Nicky says, "I understand," and guides Amanda to a bathroom that has two doors, hands her a fresh robe and treaded slipper-socks. She tells her to pee again and gives her a plastic bag for her clothes. "You sure you're okay?" she asks, and Amanda says, "Yes," then closes the door and undresses, stuffing her clothes into the bag.

While she's sitting on the toilet, though, her abdomen begins to cramp—gently at first and then more intensely, as if someone has taken hold of her insides and is squeezing as hard as they can. The pain passes, but she starts to feel strange, like it's hard to get enough air into her lungs. She tries to breathe deeply, but her heart feels as if it's beating too fast. Maybe it's the drugs, she tells herself. The edges of her vision seem to be darkening. She rests her head in her hands. A few minutes later she feels a little better, but when she stands up she's dizzy and has to lean on the sink for support. After what feels like a long time, there's a soft knock on the door and a voice.

"How's it going in there?" Nicky asks.

"I'm not sure," Amanda says, frightened by how frightened she sounds.

"Mind if I come in?"

The door opens and Nicky says, "It's a lot, I know," holding out her arm, and almost as if she's being compelled by some external force, Amanda grips her arm while Nicky opens the second door, leading her into an operating room and helping her onto a table, this one covered with clear plastic below Amanda's waist and with a kind of plastic bucket attached to the end, between her legs. A businesslike blond nurse takes her temperature and blood pressure, and then a small Asian woman who looks like someone's grandma puts a needle in her arm.

"It's going to be fine. Try to relax," Nicky says. At some point, Amanda's not sure when, she's taken Amanda's hand in hers, and Amanda is surprised to find herself holding on tight.

"You're doing great," Nicky says, and then, out of nowhere, hot tears are streaming down Amanda's temples, into her hair. She can't fight them this time; she doesn't even try.

Nicky squeezes her hand.

And then she starts to feel lighter, like she's floating a few inches above the table. A woman with dark, shiny skin lifts her legs one by one into stirrups and secures them with Velcro straps.

"You're doing great. You're very brave," a disembodied voice says.

"I'll never be the same," she hears herself saying, and then the voice is asking her what sports she plays, and she tries to answer but her own voice doesn't seem to work anymore. She feels extraordinarily light now, weightless, and then she's tumbling, plunging, something powerful is pulling her down. But she's not scared anymore, all she feels is relief. Closing her eyes, she lets herself fall.

31

CRAIG AND HIS FRAMER, Jason Bettis, are standing under the
tent they've set up in the yard at the Setter-Muldoon site, talking on
the phone with Hank Ludlow over at town hall, who's doing the first
round of inspections, when Jason knocks Craig's arm with his elbow
and says, "Who's that?"

Craig turns, following Jason's gaze, and sees Vance. He's wearing his
black motorcycle jacket and carrying his helmet, half walking, half jogging toward them across the wet lawn.

"Excuse me just a minute, Hank," Craig says into the phone, which
Jason's holding. "Explain the revised dead loads," he whispers, and
when Jason gives him an exasperated look, he says, "Just keep him on
the line," and ducks out of the tent.

He meets Vance in the middle of the lawn, beside a flagpole with no
flag. "Is someone hurt?"

Vance shakes his head. "I need to talk to you. It's important."

"It's not a good time," Craig says, gesturing in the direction of the
half-framed house. "I know it's a foreign concept to you, but I'm at
work."

Vance regards him a moment, then turns away and looks at the construction. "Christ," he says, "is this what passes for a beach cottage these days?"

It's no secret how little regard Vance has for what Craig does, but Craig doesn't have the time or the patience to indulge his brother's uninformed opinions right now. "What are you doing here?"

Vance faces the ocean—the place has a full, unobstructed view—and says, "Who's building this, anyway?"

"You don't know him," Craig says, and Vance nods as if his question's been answered. His face looks a little green, Craig notices, his hair more unruly than usual, plus there are dark, half-moon-shaped shadows under his eyes. He wonders if he's high, or hung over, or possibly both. "You look like dogshit," he says. "Where'd you sleep?"

"Do you care?"

Craig feels a stab of indignation followed by a wave of genuine remorse, and cringes a little, recalling the things he said. That there's truth in them doesn't make him feel any better. In fact he can hardly stand how pitiful Vance looks. Worse, it would seem he's come to make amends, which Craig didn't expect.

More kindly, he says, "Look, I'm on the clock. Do you think we could talk later?" He glances down at his feet. "For what it's worth, I was pretty worked up last night. Some of the things I said . . ."

Vance looks confused, then shakes his head, like he's trying to clear it. "I don't care about that," he says, frowning. "I need to tell you something, but you have to promise you won't get upset."

Craig crosses his arms, widens his stance on the wet grass, and says, "Tell me what?"

Vance squints out at the ocean for a couple of beats, then faces Craig. He takes a deep breath. "Amanda's in Connecticut."

Craig takes a moment to process this. Connecticut? He turns the word over in his head a few times. "Connecticut?" he repeats. "Shit. She's grounded and she knows it. She's *willful*, that kid."

Vance watches him with a worried expression. Then he says, "Let me try again. She's in Connecticut, at a clinic. A medical clinic." He pauses a moment. "Gina set it up."

It takes a several seconds for the words to sink in.

"Boss," shouts a voice—Jason's—from the tent. Craig turns. "Ludlow says he can't wait."

Craig waves dismissively and turns back to Vance. A queasy feeling has started in his gut. "A clinic?" he says. "You don't mean—" Vance nods somberly. "I don't believe it. Gina wouldn't—Amanda can't. I'm her father. She needs me to—"

"The thing is, she doesn't, there. That's why they went."

"They," Craig says. He feels lightheaded. "There must be some mistake. This isn't possible. Gina—" He doesn't finish the sentence.

Vance doesn't say anything, just watches him.

"Are you positive?"

Vance nods.

"God. How could she?" He's not even sure which one of them he means. He reaches into the holster on his belt for his phone, but it isn't there. He glances back at the tent, then holds his hand out to Vance. "Your phone."

Vance says, "There's nothing you can do."

Craig thinks he might be sick. He says, "Give me your goddamn phone."

"I know you must be shocked, and pissed off, but if you take a step back—"

If Craig hears one more word from his brother, he'll lose it. "I said, give me your phone." When Vance shakes his head, Craig says, "Fine. This is private property. If you don't get off it this minute, I'll call the police."

Vance puts his hands up. "Don't bother. I only came to tell you I'm going to New Haven. I'm leaving now so I can be there when she wakes up, and I think you should, too. I know you should."

"You can't be serious." He starts to walk away, but Vance grabs his arm.

"What happened to you?"

"Excuse me?"

"When did you turn into this—this person?"

"Get your hands off me," Craig says, shaking his arm free.

"If you don't come, you'll lose her, you know."

266

Craig says nothing. He means to walk away, but he finds his legs won't move.

"You've been so worried about her making a mistake, about her living with regret. What about you?"

"Please, just leave," he begs.

"Do you have any idea how it feels to be tormented, every day, by the past? To spend as much effort trying not to think about how badly you screwed up as you do wishing you could go back?"

Craig's heart pounds. His hands have curled themselves into fists.

Vance glances down. "You're going to hit me? If that's what you need to do, then go ahead." He thrusts his jaw forward and closes his eyes.

Craig only lets him hold the absurd pose for a moment. "I'm not going to hit you. We're grown men," he says, and forces his fists to release.

As he does, he begins to feel strange. The blood seems to rush from his head, and the ground undulates under his feet. He looks up at the sky; the clouds are behaving oddly, swirling, flashing, folding in on themselves. "I can't—I don't," he says, but loses the rest. Dizzy and disoriented, he sits down on the grass and rests his head between his knees.

Vance is saying his name, asking him something. But his voice is very far away, hard to hear over the crashing sound, which may or may not be the ocean, inside Craig's head. He lets his eyes fall closed, and on the backs of his eyelids, spectral forms appear. One is Suzanne, and it's like she's underwater, floating, her loose hair a liquid golden halo around her head. She's beckoning to him, and he swims toward her, swims as hard as he can. But when he gets closer, he sees it's not Suzanne, it's Amanda, and she turns and swims away.

Vance is saying his name again. Reluctantly he opens his eyes. Here's his brother, standing over him, offering his hand.

32

FROM SOMEWHERE OUT of sight, a voice is saying her name: "Okay, Miss Lake," it says, "we're all through."

"I was climbing the fence," she hears herself say. She's still half floating; everything feels like slow motion, a few steps removed from real. She allows the figures hovering over her to help her up and lead her, by the elbows, into an adjoining room. They guide her into one of several La-Z-Boy chairs, all empty, all fully reclined. Someone asks her how she's feeling, and she hears herself say, "It's done?"

A blue electric blanket is spread over her, and while the blond nurse from before takes her blood pressure and temperature again, she feels strangely euphoric, almost giddy. She hears herself saying how kind they've been. "You're wonderful, all of you," her voice says, as if disconnected from her head. The nurse smiles beneficently, removing the cuff from Amanda's arm, and asks whether she feels nauseated or dizzy, and Amanda says no. The nurse sets a can of apple juice and a package of peanut butter crackers on the tray beside Amanda and says she can rest there as long as she wants, at least until the anesthesia subsides, and again Amanda closes her eyes.

When she opens them next, what seems only a few seconds later, her first thought is that she must be even loopier than before, because she's begun to hallucinate: standing over her, asking her how she feels, is Craig. Or rather, two Craigs.

"Daddy?" she says to the first, who shakes his head. She blinks. It takes a second, and then she understands. She addresses her father. "Daddy. Are you mad?"

He doesn't answer. He's wearing his Red Sox cap, and with the fluorescent lights overhead it's hard to see his eyes under the bill.

Gina's there too, standing beside Vance. She says, "How do you feel?"

Amanda says. "Dad?"

Gina says, "You look pale. You must be starving. Did they give you any juice?"

"Hey, honey. You doing okay?" Vance asks.

Her father's just looking at her.

One of the nurses returns and suggests that everyone who's not Amanda go back to the waiting area, there's another patient on her way in.

"Take your time," Gina says.

Vance says, "We're right on the other side of that door."

Her father still doesn't say anything. His expression is stony, impossible to read.

They clear out, and the blond lady from earlier—Alison—is led in. She wears a pink gown, same as Amanda's, and her face is gray. Her eyes focus on nothing as a nurse guides her into one of the empty lounge chairs.

Turning to Amanda, the nurse says, "Well, it looks like you've rejoined the living." Pointing out the bathroom, she tells her there are pads on the back of the toilet, and whenever she feels ready, she's free to leave.

To no one in particular, Alison says, "This wasn't what I wanted."

The nurse covers her with a fleece blanket identical to Amanda's and tucks it around her hips. Patting her on the shoulder, she says, "There, there."

• • •

She sees them through the window in the door: Vance, Gina, and Craig. Gina sits in the middle, flanked by the brothers; improbably, she holds Craig's hand. Amanda takes a moment to touch the birdcage earring in the pocket of her jacket, saying a small, silent prayer of thanks before opening the door and stepping through. When she does, all three see her, and all three stand in unison.

It's Craig alone who steps forward. He says, "Sweetheart," and opens his arms, and she lets him fold her in his embrace, lets him press her head against his chest. He holds on tight and for what feels like ages, long enough for her to count twenty heartbeats, long enough for her to wonder what the other people in the waiting area think.

When he finally lets go, she steps back, looks up at him, and says, "You must be really mad."

He looks as if he's in pain. "Not at you," he says.

"Please don't be mad at Gina. She was—"

"It's all right, honey. You don't need to—"

Before he can say anything more, Vance steps forward and throws an arm, rather awkwardly, around her shoulders. "You just worry about yourself. Okay, kid?"

Amanda nods, dismissing him. "I'm really sorry, Daddy, I am. For everything, all this. And for what I said."

This time her father doesn't respond. She's not sure, but she thinks he has tears in his eyes. He looks down.

It feels like ages pass before Gina says, "We should probably get going if we want to beat the traffic on the bridge."

33

OUTSIDE, THE SUN IS SHINING, the clouds from earlier have been swept away, and a cold, bracing wind blows steadily from the west. Vance volunteers to drive Craig's truck back so Craig can ride with Gina and Amanda in the van.

Heading up 95, he drives fast, faster than he should, but he wants to get home before they do so he can drop off the truck and clear out without saying goodbye. Maybe it's lame, but he's trying to do them a favor, and besides, isn't lame about what they all expect from him by now? Craig certainly made that clear. Amanda too. The only one who'll be sad to hear he's gone, he guesses, is Helen—and that's only because she's too young to know better.

As he drives, he thinks about the three of them in the van—how right it seems that they're there, together, and he's alone, on the outside. It's his fate, apparently—and the thing is, it's nobody's fault but his. As the miles pass, he thinks of all the bad decisions he's made, the lies he's told, the people he's hurt—way more than a lifetime's worth of fucking up, and he's only forty-two. Watching the sun start to sink into the clouds off to his left, he remembers the old Hollies song his band, the Buccaneers, used to sing, "King Midas in Reverse." The chorus plays on a loop in his head: "Everything he touches turns to dust." Crossing the canal, he thinks that Craig was right; he may not have said it in so many words, but the message was clear: the best thing Vance can do for the people he loves is leave them alone.

At the house, he parks Craig's truck in the garage and leaves the keys on the seat. The Frog's out by the curb, his belongings still inside. He climbs in, turns the key in the ignition, and—go figure—the engine starts right up. From the driver's seat he looks up at Craig's house. The windows are all dark except for the attic's, he notices: the porthole glows dull gold. The shepherdess. He must have turned the lamp on last night when he was packing. He doesn't remember turning it on, but he wasn't particularly clearheaded at that point. Briefly he considers going in and turning it off, but it's too much of a risk.

In town he makes two stops: Shaw's, for foodstuffs, and the True Value for propane. The hardware store is just closing up when he arrives, a little after six, but the owner, a guy he remembers from high school called Mike McRae, lets him in.

"Craig," he says, holding out his hand. "Long time no see."

"It's Vance," he says.

"So it is."

"I'll be quick, I promise." He hurries down the center aisle, gathering what he needs.

Back in the Frog, he passes the laundromat and the car wash and ice cream shop where he worked when he was thirteen, the pharmacy and the Elks Lodge, the movie theater where he and Dylan used to make out. There's a burning feeling, like a tiny hot ball, in his chest. At the Hess station he stops and fuels up. It's turned into a cold evening, with no cloud cover, and he shifts the freezing pump from one bare hand to the other. It will be even colder at the camp. For a moment, he's tempted to go back to Craig's, and not just because of the weather. But Craig doesn't want him around, none of them do. And why should they? Everything he touches turns to shit.

He pays for the gas and gets back in the Frog. He's almost out of town, almost in the clear, when he approaches the Odd Fellows Hall. There are lights on in the windows, and instinctively he slows down. Through the tall windows he can see people—little girls—up on a stage. It hits him like the crack of a whip: Helen's recital. *Shit*, he thinks. Did they all really *forget*?

He should keep going. The later he gets to the camp, the darker and colder it will be and the harder it will be to get set up. And his brother's words echo like a chorus in his head: you only care about yourself.

But his foot, apparently unaware of what's happening in his head, engages the clutch, and his equally oblivious right hand downshifts.

The inside of the hall looks completely different from the last time he was here: skylights perforate a newly vaulted ceiling, the wide-plank floors have been refinished, the walls painted a pleasing yellow, and the audience faces a brand-new, lacquered wood stage. It's beautiful, he has to admit. He vaguely recalls Craig saying he was renovating the place at a cut rate.

Among the five or six rows of folding chairs there's a handful of empty seats, but he doesn't want to disturb the audience members, clearly proud parents, many of whom hold video cameras or cell phones aloft, so he stands at the back, watching the ten or twelve girls in black leotards, white tights, and buff-colored slippers move through their routines. It doesn't take long to spot Helen. She's third from the left, and a little out of step, keeping up but just barely. She has a look of intense concentration on her face, lifting one leg in the air.

"Mr. Lake, you're here. I'm so glad," whispers a woman to his left, and it takes him a moment to register that she's talking to him. Once he does, he turns to look at her. She's young—and attractive—with long brown hair, dark red lipstick, and a form-fitting black dress. Too young to be the mother of one of the dancers, is his guess, though that must be what she is. "I was worried you wouldn't make it," she continues. "I mean, with everything else." She nods in the direction of the stage. "Aren't they darling? Helen was so nervous all day. You should have seen her getting ready. She had me do her hair over five times."

So she's not a mom, she's the babysitter, and apparently she thinks he's Craig. He opens his mouth to set her straight, but something stops him.

"So how'd it go today? The surgery," she whispers, eyes on the stage.

He says, "Pardon?"

"I was telling Gina, my cousin had the exact same thing. She had some old blood coming out of her nose for a couple of weeks, but after that, no more sinus infections. It changed her life."

"She did great," he says, following her lead. "She's a soldier," and he's surprised that even now, after everything, he feels the same rush of pleasure he's always felt, talking about his niece. Quietly, he adds, "It may take a while, but she'll be okay."

Apparently it's not quietly enough, because a woman in the last row of seats turns around to shoot him a menacing look. He and the babysitter exchange chastised smiles, then turn back to the stage in silence, watching the girls pirouette on tiptoe with their arms up over their heads.

The music slows; they break into pairs. Helen crosses the stage, her arm linked with another girl's. Not quite in tandem, they lift their knees high in the air with each step, like horses in a show. She still has the intense look on her face, the tip of her tongue protruding from between her lips, and he feels himself concentrating with her, rooting for her; he even catches himself crossing his fingers inside his jacket pocket on her behalf. When all the girls have pranced in pairs, they form a circle, clasp hands, and start to move counterclockwise. The hot sensation in his chest from before has subsided, he notices, watching the circle turn.

When the music stops, the girls drop hands. Forming a single line, they curtsy one at a time as the crowd claps. Helen's in the middle of her curtsy, all her weight on one bent leg, when she spots him. Breaking form, she stands up straight, grins her gummy grin, and waves at him.

Tentatively he raises his hand. To his embarrassment, several of the parents have turned around in their seats and are watching him, as is the babysitter. His face burns.

"Uncle Vance," Helen calls, waving a little wildly now. "Uncle Vance."

Fuck it, he thinks. "That's me," he says to no one in particular, and waves back.

ACKNOWLEDGMENTS

Thanks, first, to Bruce Nichols and the many good people at HMH whose hard work brought this book into being: Liz Anderson, Siobhan Jones, Michaela Sullivan, Larry Cooper, and in particular my editor, Nicole Angeloro, whose wisdom, insight, kindness, and sense of humor not only made the editing process a delight but made the book much better. For time, space, and general, invaluable support, I'm enormously grateful to the Corporation of Yaddo, the MacDowell Colony, the Sewanee Writers' Conference, and Aspen Words, especially Adrienne Brodeur, Maurice LaMee, Jamie Kravitz, Caroline Tory, and Isa Catto Shaw and Dan Shaw, whose generosity provided me with a spectacular and highly productive October during which I wrote much of this book's first draft. I'd also like to thank my agent, Lisa Bankoff. Last but not least, thanks to the kind and, more important, astute souls who read and improved the book at various stages: Siobhan Fallon, Jim Gavin, Curtis Sittenfeld, Jenny Moore, and Andrew Stern, a whip-smart bunch I'm also very fortunate to call my friends.

And finally: the people and places herein are fictional, but I learned a lot about the history of the beach camps, and how life used to be on Cape Cod, from Frances Higgins's fascinating *Drifting Memories: The Nauset Beach Camps on Cape Cod*.

READING GROUP GUIDE

Vance Lake is broke, jobless, and recently dumped. When he takes refuge at his twin brother Craig's house on Cape Cod, he finds himself smack in the middle of a crisis that would test the bonds of even the most cohesive family, let alone the Lakes: seventeen-year-old Amanda is pregnant. Craig is heartbroken and full of rage, his exasperated wife, Gina, is on the brink of an affair, and Amanda is indignant, ashamed, and very, very scared.

Told in alternating points of view, *The News from the End of the World* follows one family into a crucible of pent-up resentments, old and new secrets, and memories long buried. Only by coming to terms with their pasts, both as individuals and together, do they stand a chance of emerging intact.

DISCUSSION QUESTIONS

1. *The News from the End of the World* unfolds over four days, across five different points of view, allowing each member of the Lake family to reveal what they know and their feelings about events. How did the rotating points of view affect your reading experience?

Did you sympathize more with certain characters when you saw things from their perspective?

2. Throughout the novel, Helen is caught up between the various adults, who seek to shield her from the dramatic events occurring around her. But by the end, we realize that she knows more than she lets on, and has in fact been so affected that she has harmed herself by holding her wrist to the hot waffle iron. At what point did you realize that Helen knows more than she lets on? How do her point-of-view chapters play into this and put her previous actions into perspective?

3. Secrets people keep, even from their families, are an integral part of the novel. Only at the end, when the truth comes out, does anyone begin to move toward catharsis. What do you think Miller is saying about families and the way they communicate—or don't?

4. Over the course of the novel, Craig and Vance are repeatedly mistaken for each other despite having very different personalities. Does this imply that perhaps they have more in common than they think? Or rather, that their similarity is only skin deep? In what ways are they alike, and in what ways are they different? What draws them together, and what drives them apart?

5. Over the course of the novel, Gina considers and tentatively embarks on an affair with Dov, her husband's best friend. By the end, however, she rethinks her decision and breaks things off. Why? What is Dov's significance in the story?

6. Much of the tension consuming the Lake family stems from Amanda's desire to terminate her pregnancy, and how each family member reacts to that desire. With whom do your sympathies lie? Is Craig within his rights, prohibiting Amanda from getting an abortion? Is Gina a hero or a traitor for helping her? Do you think that Miller portrays the different family members' viewpoints evenhandedly?

7. Music plays a key role in the novel, from Craig's obsession with Bruce Springsteen to the importance of Tom Waits to Amanda.

What do we learn about each character through the music they listen to?

8. The story takes place on Cape Cod in the off-season. How does this setting reflect, interact with, and shape events of the novel? How might the novel be different if it were set in a big city, or at the height of summer?

9. What is the significance of the book's title? Discuss the various things the phrase "the end of the world" refers to, both literally and on a thematic level.

10. In *The News from the End of the World*, decisions made years before shape the characters' behavior in the present. How, specifically, does each character's history influence his or her actions? What might this suggest about how people chose to live their lives?